Thanks for buying!

R. A. Smith

THE GRENSHALL MANOR CHRONICLES - BOOK 1

OBLIVION Storm

R.A. SMITH

Xchyler Publishing
www.xchylerpublishing.com

September 2013 Paperback Edition

Cover and Interior Design by D. Robert Pease, walkingstickbooks.com
Edited by Penny Freeman and McKenna Gardner

Published in the United States of America
Xchyler Publishing

For Mum.
A true heroine.

PROLOGUE

She shivered from the biting December cold but maintained her perch. The rooftop was hers—her place of refuge, where she heard horse hooves hammering rhythmically against the cobblestones as carriages passed below. Despite the stench, it was still her favourite spot in the whole of London. She had experienced far colder nights up there. The young noblewoman had no intention of leaving immediately.

Although she had moved on to greater things, parts of her old life brought her solace, comfort that no wealth or station could ever provide.

Tally Grenshall was sole heir to the Grenshall estate, a status hard-earned. She was just beginning to comprehend the weight of such responsibility. But, above the city, under the darkness of night, she was free—accountable to no one.

An hour before, she had made the most unladylike of shimmies up to the roof of the residence whilst nobody was watching, a skill honed over several years of her childhood. The vantage point had always been the same, the view itself different every time.

Tally watched an amusing snowball battle between several grubby, emaciated children, their hard day's toil complete. Some enterprising small-time crooks drew her attention as they extended their spree to richer targets.

The marks were too easy; even as a child, she would have had her pick of loot from the hapless lot. The mug-hunters were making a steady run of collections that night. In polite company, she might have raised the alarm, but if the swells couldn't look after themselves, they should not be out on the streets.

They would not miss the coin, either way.

She shuffled into a crouch once the icy, dirty slate numbed her backside. Another once-pretty dress ruined from her adventures. On the upside, she looked marginally less out of place in her dishevelment.

Clambering down to the ground, she headed towards the two thieves, ready to test herself—to see if she could still handle it out here. There were dangers to forgetting her previous life's skills.

One of them approached. The other crossed behind her to gain access to her bag. Which line were they likely to use this time?

"Excuse me, Miss . . ." The boy closed in on her, sobbing. She tilted her head, waiting. "Have you seen my little brother?" he asked. "I lost him, and he's really sick!"

"Actually, I have." It took real effort not to appear too self-assured. It would all go wrong if they identified her ruse; she was ill-equipped to deal with violence.

"He should be . . ." She caught the second boy's passing shadow in the corner of her eye and made her move. "Right behind me." Feigning a stretch and yawn, she tugged her bag just out of his reach.

She jolted forward, slipped her hands into the loose pocket of the first boy, and relieved him of the larger purse. "Get him home quickly and safely, do!"

The boy was angry. She was certain that had never happened to him before. He clawed at her bag; but, prepared, she leapt into a stack of ash bins, crashing loudly as she fell.

"HELP!" She timed her cry perfectly and smirked as the two boys scattered. She rapidly smuggled her acquisition into her own empty bag as the nearest crowd of adults ran to her aid.

"Goodness! What happened here?"

"Are you all right?"

Tally was aided to her feet and dusted herself off. Although bombarded with a series of questions and offered an escort home, she had no intention of going back. Not quite then.

After sending her champions on their way, she wandered toward the snowball fight. She crouched to prepare a globule of snow. The children were too preoccupied to notice her. With true aim, she sent a sizeable projectile against the back of the largest lad—one she had seen targeting a frail, red-headed girl who had not hit anyone all night.

He twitched with cold as it trickled down the back of his neck, his eyes watering as he fled for cover. The others laughed so hard that none even considered Tally a target.

She approached the frail girl and rubbed the back of her head as she looked up with a grin. Tally winked back. She emptied half the contents of her recently acquired purse into to the bare hands of her newest friend.

"Can I trust you to share this with the others?" The girl nodded hard as the others gathered round. Tally took a step back, ensuring the girl made good on her promise, before wandering away.

Eleven years earlier, she had *been* one of those children: plain old Iris Brown. She, too, had wandered the treacherous Bethnal Green streets with no real care in the world, other than her next meal.

She was a precocious child, to be sure, with a well-developed knack for self-preservation. She had made good use of her small, undernourished frame as a nine-year-old. She could pick pockets and slip out of sight before anyone was the wiser.

Food had been more use than money, then. Children with coin simply raised too many questions. Fleeing bakeries with tiny hands full of bread or cake helped her become light on her feet and shimmy up rooftops, then and in the future.

She had fed several friends for many days in that manner. She won favours and protection from the older children who stopped picking on her relatively early. She proved far too useful to them. Some of her old friends only ate due to her aid.

Even at that age, though, it was easy to grow tired of the lifestyle. The room where she sought shelter but never called 'home' provided space to sleep but nothing more. Mouldy and ramshackle, the reek of fumes rose up from the basement cesspit. There was barely enough room to turn, even for one her size. On warmer nights, a blanket and her favoured rooftop provided far better accommodation.

She shared the room with her mother and the constant smell of gin, learning nothing from the woman's constant slurred, intoxicated gibberish.

What she would give for someone to teach her something other than how to fend for herself!

The day came when tiny Iris Brown decided that particular part of her life could hang for all she cared. "I am going to find myself a home!" she boldly declared to her friends, and took a bite out of the carrot nose of their snowman. She strode away, setting off for a part of London she had never previously explored.

Iris stowed away on several carriages, travelling until she reached the streets of Belgravia. Once there, she hid, watched, and listened. It took additional effort to survive around there, her grubby rags betraying her true background. But it was worth it.

She watched the elegant glide of a mother and daughter as they crossed Belgrave Square, fondly conversing, wisdom being passed from eldest to youngest. The two were met by an expensively attired gentleman before the three of them left together.

Intrigued, Iris carefully shadowed them through a few streets. She listened to their conversation, specifically to the *way* they spoke, paying particular attention to the girl roughly her age.

She was sure she could sound like that—with some practice. Eventually, they stopped at a grand house, were greeted by a maid, and entered. That entire place was *theirs*, not shared with anyone else! It was a wonderful notion.

For a fortnight, she learned her way around the new place, observing how to survive there, too. Her eyes and ears were open to the way they walked and talked, quickly mastering the speech, but never quite grasping the movement.

But as wondrous as Belgravia proved, the name of one place, one family, came up in her eavesdropped conversations more than any other. The Grenshalls.

They were the talk of society, the cream of the crop, and invited only the most prominent names and faces to their exclusive soirees—but they did not live in Belgravia.

With careful investigation, Iris learned that Grenshall Manor was located in an uncommon place for wealthy residences, at the north end of London near Mill Hill. She travelled on foot when passing wagons were unavailable.

Grenshall Manor was every bit as illustrious—and outrageous in appearance—as the tales suggested. Each of the four corners of the mansion had a tower, each with arched stained glass windows near the top.

A clock tower dominated the entrance, with the walls standing like battlements. Small gargoyles with bat-like wings spread to full span were the only contrast to the beauty elsewhere. The intimidating sentries crouched, ready to pounce—or repel any unwelcome guests. Iris hoped she was not one of them.

She picked a spot in a tree and watched. Surely such a grand establishment would have room for one more small person? Perhaps this was it; the place she could truly call home. For several nights, she scouted the house, contriving a way in.

She learned that the movements of the mansion staff were regular as clockwork. Plotting a path through the servants' quarters one evening, she eluded the busy staff and found her way to a kitchen larger than any of the bakeries she had raided.

Unfortunately, the house cook caught her while she scavenged bread and cheese. About to be beaten soundly, Iris was saved by chance. The lord of the manor happened to be quite peckish and made a surreptitious run of his own to the kitchen.

Iris's cheeks stretched around her contraband as she shamelessly continued to chew in his presence. He examined her carefully before taking a seat near a table.

"I shall deal with this personally," he said calmly to the cook, dismissing her for the night.

If Iris had run then, she could have easily given them both the slip, but instead, she chose to stand firm.

"I should tell you," the solidly built aristocrat said, his voice authoritative yet somewhat jovial, "despite this being *my* residence, even *I* fear the wrath of my cook."

Slicing several portions of beef, he reached for two plates and split the meat between them. She received it humbly but showed no fear to the imposing, grey-haired man. Granted, being adorned in his night-clothes rendered him somewhat less intimidating than perhaps was usual. Still, she knew she was not going to escape lightly.

"Who might you be, girl?" he asked, his voice low and sonorous. "And why are you intruding upon my premises?"

"My name is Iris Brown," she answered without hesitation, looking him square in the eyes. She did not speak as a street urchin; rather, with boldness and eloquence, mimicking the way she had heard the mother and daughter speaking in Belgrave Square.

"I have come here because I am hungry, sir, and because I knew you would have food. I was certain I could enter without disturbing your residence, and quite sure I would be gone before anyone took notice."

"I see." His answer came with a turn of his mouth, which Iris could not decide was a smile or a frown. "Indeed, you seem somewhat cock-sure. Yet, here you are, caught. And taking a late supper with the lord of the manor. So tell me why I am not having you thrashed soundly or reporting you?"

She considered her answer. Even at her young age, she could sense sadness in his eyes, increasing as he stared at her. Smiling warmly, she responded. "Because if you wanted to, you would have done so by now, sir. But, instead, you offered to share with me." She took a bite of meat, carefully placed on a hunk of bread. It was heavenly.

She watched him go rather red at first, but he gathered his emotions and cut her another slice of fine beef.

Iris sat forward and looked him in the eyes, serious beyond her years. "I can help you, you know."

Lord Grenshall sighed heavily and placed his plate down on the table. "How could *you* possibly help *me*?" he asked, raising an eyebrow.

"Well, sir," she said, "I would very much like to stay here. I would be no trouble. Please?" She took a bigger bite and chewed loudly, stopping to offer a grin.

A raucous belly-laugh reverberated around the kitchen, ringing in her ears. "Bold," he said, catching his breath. "Audacious, to be sure. Impossible!"

"Why, sir?" she asked, genuinely puzzled. "'Tis a large place, and I am small. I should be in your debt."

"I am certain you would not." His laughter ceased; a stern look crossed his features. "Pray, what drives you to first invade my kitchen, and then demand to stay?"

"Please, sir—I ain't got a kitchen," Iris said. Her eloquence slipped with her nerves. "Not in my room, anyway. And it stinks in there—that room. Not like 'ere."

"And what would your mother and father say about that?"

"Nothin', sir. Mum's probably sleeping off the drink, and I never had a dad." She stepped forward and examined him, squinting an eye. "You look like a good dad. Make any child feel lucky."

He sat back in his seat.

He looked shaken, distant . . . sad. Iris made her way over and reached gently for his arm. "Something wrong, Mister?"

"It is not '*mister*'." A woman glided into the room, her voice sharp and haughty. Iris jumped.

Every inch the noble, the lady was of slender build with a striking presence. She carried herself beautifully. That was the part Iris could never quite master. The woman was pretty for her age, Iris thought, though what age that was, she did not know. Her dark hair still had most of its colour.

Probing blue eyes examined Iris thoroughly, and then the lady cuffed her with a firm hand which had never seen a day's work. "The correct form of address is '*my lord*.' Now, what is going on down here?"

Iris remembered her efforts to impress and gave a clumsy attempt at a curtsey.

"Goodness me," the lady said, shaking her head in disdain. "The curtsey of an urchin."

Lord Grenshall raised a hand. "Young Iris, here, is at least making an effort at civility."

"Indeed," his wife replied, "she trespasses with the greatest decorum."

"I didn't steal nothin'," Iris protested, "I was fed."

The lady turned to her husband. "Is this so?"

"She looked hungry," Lord Grenshall answered with a little shrug. "No harm in a slice of beef finding its way to her."

Lady Grenshall examined Iris again. "Hmm, she does seem somewhat malnourished. And most certainly in need of a bath. Where are your parents, girl? Where is your home?"

Lord Grenshall sighed. "She was just telling me she had none to speak of."

"How terrible!" the lady said. "Well, I suppose we can spare you some food, even at this hour. However, you ought to know, child, that we prefer our guests to enter through the front door—and they most certainly do not let themselves in. Now, it is rather late, young lady."

Lady Grenshall waited patiently for Iris to finish her food and then less patiently ushered her through the front door.

For several nights, Iris's routine remained the same. She watched the mansion, attempting to pluck up the courage to knock on the front door. Every time, panic gripped her and she decided against it.

But anytime no one was looking, she would try walking like Lady Grenshall. However, she tripped and stumbled where the lady appeared to walk upon water. Iris could never quite get it right. Lady Grenshall had already helped her once; perhaps she would be willing to do it again.

One night, fate presented an unusual opportunity. She had returned to her old streets, her old friends. Iris was joined by several older children she had never met before. She could smell trouble on them, though.

Because of her reputation—the prowess of young Iris now legend amongst her peers—she was made privy to some information. A daring robbery was planned. The target: Grenshall Manor. She was even offered the rarest of privileges: the opportunity to scout for the older gang committing the caper.

But no one was going to damage that place—or hurt the lord and lady.

Slipping out of her little gang's sight, she made her way stealthily back to the tree to watch. Soon, the sneaky band closed in; no mistaking their intentions. They did not take the path; they traversed the grass nearby, difficult to spot for those not looking.

Careful to stay out of sight, Iris reached the front door before them, knowing her way around as she did, and knocked hard. Amazingly, the staff had already been instructed to let her in.

"Young lady," said Lord Grenshall when she was escorted into his study, panting, "we have spoken, my wife and I, and we are prepared to help you find somewhere to—"

She stopped him and explained, somewhat frantically, about the incoming jeopardy. In short order, he mustered his staff, and within moments led a mob of his own to deal with the matter. The brigands were seen off and apprehended in short order.

"Well, now," Lady Grenshall said as she and Iris watched her husband return victorious, "It seems you have done us a rather good turn. Now we have one for you."

"I may stay here?" Iris asked, a touch of glee in her voice.

Lady Grenshall looked upon her quizzically. "Of course not, child. However, we have—"

"Please, *my lady*. They asked me to help them. But I said no. Never wanted to see you cry. Came to tell you first, I did."

"It is simply not possible." Lady Grenshall rose to greet her husband.

"Please, my lady. I want to be like you! You're beautiful and smart and you walk *so* - like - royalty."

Lady Grenshall smirked. "Well, you are certainly very intelligent," she said, smiling. "You have great potential. Perhaps it could be realised—with the correct guidance."

"We have already found this child a home," Lord Grenshall stated. "In her position, we have more than returned the favour."

"That mob was none to be sneezed at," his wife said. "If we had not interceded precisely when we did, we may have been in trouble. We most certainly cannot send her back out there—not after tonight. Why not *this* home, I wonder?"

The Grenshalls looked at each other for a moment, pensive. Eventually, Lord Grenshall sighed. "Sit down, young Iris," he said, pulling up three chairs. He and his wife took two of them before Iris joined them.

Lady Grenshall smirked. "I believe you have earned the kindness of a bath and clean clothing. Please endeavour to wear it the next time you arrive here. You cannot possibly continue to enter this house attired so."

"You want me *back?*" Iris asked, her eyes widening at the idea.

"Well," Lady Grenshall said, "you seem to find your way here with considerable persistence. As a reward for your assistance, you may stay here for tonight."

"Really? Oh, thank you!" Iris leapt from her seat and attempted to hug Lady Grenshall, but the lady raised a hand and halted her. "Bath!" she commanded. Iris obliged.

~ ＊ ~

The next day, Iris awoke to a knock at the door. She had slept in a soft, comfortable bed and a room she had all to herself. It felt like her very own palace. "Breakfast is served, miss." The maid could *never* have been addressing her, could she?

The girl helped Iris into the clothing laid out for her: fresh, clean, and with holes only where they belonged. She opened the door and was greeted by an older servant who guided her down to the dining hall, another new room in the wondrous palace. There, Lord and Lady Grenshall stood by their seats, waiting for her to take her seat at the lengthy table.

Lady Grenshall gave a proper curtsey before smiling warmly. "I hope you were watching carefully, Iris," she said. "As I said, if you are to be a visitor here, then you have much to learn." Lord Grenshall signalled for the two females to be seated. "Now," Lady Grenshall continued, "let us begin with dining etiquette."

Breakfast was a lengthy affair but a proper feast for it. Lady Grenshall instructed Iris in every step, from the correct way to hold cutlery to eliminating slurps. Iris did not stop smiling throughout.

"Now," Lord Grenshall said. "You asked me a question some nights ago. I wish to give you a decent answer." To Iris's great surprise, he explained their plight in great detail.

The Grenshalls had been unable to conceive despite several years of trying and had given up hope recently, particularly with Lord Grenshall getting no younger. "Grenshall Manor under control of any but a Grenshall is unthinkable," Lady Grenshall said in a very quiet voice. "We always wanted a large family."

"And now, I am the last of my line," Lord Grenshall added.

"Then I shall watch over you every night," Iris said, standing and giving her best attempt at a curtsey yet, "from my tree. You two need to stay alive for as long as you can."

"You shall do no such thing, young lady," Lady Grenshall told her. "That is not appropriate for—"

"But I'm not a lady, my lady," Iris said, looking at her as if she had said something ridiculous.

Lady Grenshall shook her head. "*Nor* does a lady interrupt her elders and betters whilst they are speaking. However, as I was saying: such behaviour is not appropriate for a young *heiress*."

"It is not," Lord Grenshall added.

"Evidently, I shall need to commence with you forthwith," Lady Grenshall said, her mouth curled into a thin smile, "if we are to have any hope of shaping you into the next Lady Grenshall."

Iris stared. "*Me?*"

Lord Grenshall beamed. "Well, we considered your words that first night we met. You require competent parents, and we would like a good child. Of course, if you have any more pressing offers . . ."

"No!" she squealed before throwing her hand to her mouth. "I mean, yes, please—I would *love* to stay here!" She stood up and ran to them. Lady Grenshall grabbed her with open arms and smothered her with a hug. Lord Grenshall soon followed suit. It was the happiest day of Iris's life.

~ ✲ ~

Thus, Iris Brown was duly taken into the Grenshall household. In the years which followed, Iris blossomed in the care of nobility. She rapidly caught up with the academic education she had previously missed, frequently impressing her governess with her insights.

Iris followed Lady Grenshall everywhere until she mastered that walk. She listened to Lord Grenshall, the only father she had ever known, lecture on what it was to be part of their prestigious family. When she came of age, she changed her name, officially becoming Iris Grenshall, although the lord had long since dubbed her 'Tally'.

By the time she entered society, she became the reason that the Grenshalls were the talk of the aristocracy, dazzling guests with her wit and effervescence. She held court over some of the eligible bachelors in London, each desperate to impress.

But it was not enough to simply make her name in society. A nagging feeling clung to her heart that if she settled down, she would be unprepared if anything befell her family—powerless against the vagaries of fate. To that end, she had to stay sharp; less salubrious surroundings called to her.

Hence, Tally perched on that rooftop, reconnecting with her past, and not for the first time. She had passed the first test of *that particular* evening: fleecing the two robbers and ensuring some children would eat.

She changed into more suitable attire kept on her rooftop, in order to spend the rest of her evening in different company. She preened herself, combing her glossy dark brown curls to hang just over her shoulders.

She knew of a gentlemen's club not too far away, one in which some of her alleyway rescuers were heading. She swiftly glided there.

"Excuse me, kind sir," she said to a gentleman about to enter. "Some rather helpful fellows got me out of a bit of a fix earlier. I would be most grateful if I could speak with them again." As he considered, she gave two descriptions and waited. Naturally, they did not leave her waiting long.

"I am *terribly* sorry to disturb you," she said to the gentlemen. She giggled as the two handsome men battled to be first out of the door. "It seems I find myself rather lost, my evening ruined. I could think of nowhere to turn other than to my rescuers . . ."

"Hmm," said the first out, a dapper, dark-haired chap with a twitchy smile. "It might be a touch tricky to get out of our—current commitments."

Tally smiled, turning away. "Well, on my wanders here, I have heard whispers of a somewhat exclusive card game. Now, if you would be so kind as to escort me there, I would ensure word reached of your *heroic* endeavours earlier this night. Who knows—that may well be sufficient to earn you both a seat at the table."

The gentlemen debated for a moment, then nodded as one. "We shall prepare to leave this minute," said the other, a bulky, lighter-haired fellow with bright green eyes.

She had known about the factory owner's card game days in advance. There was very little she could not find out between her high-life contacts and low-life espionage. It had always been her intention to go, but she required appropriate company.

Once there, she was true to her word; the house staff did not dare refuse Tally Grenshall at their doorstep. Nor, now that she was there, would the host dare refuse her a seat at the table. There were no other social activities planned at the house.

"You seem quite the natural card player, Miss Grenshall," the host declared after two hours of multiplying her freshly acquired coin. "Whether *chemin de fer* or *three-card loo,* you seem unbeatable."

"Beginner's luck," she said, counting her winnings.

"My dear lady," her escort murmured, "*beginner's luck* is only an acceptable statement for the first hour. You greatly defy the odds for a new player."

"Now where would one such as myself possibly find time to master illicit card games?" Tally smirked. "Mister Driscoll, might I prevail upon you for aid returning to Grenshall Manor? I have had a somewhat eventful day."

Mr. Driscoll went well out of his way to ensure Miss Grenshall got home safely. The night rolled into morning—the streets empty at this hour save for graveyard workers and other late-night adventurers. The sun hinted at an imminent rise. He paid the fare for a hansom and saw her to the front gates of Grenshall Manor. She thanked him before leaving the carriage and got as far as the front door before it opened.

There, as had been the case regularly, was a despairing Lord Grenshall, dressed in hunting attire. He pointed at her. "There she is!" he cried. "Tally-ho!"

He outstretched his arms. She ran into his embrace.

"Tally-*home!*" she said, grinning.

"One of these days, you will grow out of this madness."

Lady Grenshall joined them in the entrance hall. "One can only hope," she said. "This is most unbecoming of you. We have spent years preparing you to be the next Lady Grenshall, yet still you act as if we have deprived you of something. What is it, Tally? What do you need? What must we do to cure you of this?"

"As much of a game as we have made these jaunts of yours," Lord

Grenshall said, "it is deeply worrying to us that you frequently endanger yourself so. Please. Tell us."

Lord Grenshall released Tally to await her answer. There was none. The young noble shook her head repeatedly. "So sorry . . ." she said tearfully, before fleeing upstairs.

Nothing she could say or do would allow them to understand why. She knew they would never stop trying, however.

Neither could she hide from them her passion for riding trains. The penchant eased her soul like nothing else, although she knew it beyond their ability to approve. Even so, they never expressed the same depth of disappointment as they did with her nocturnal adventures, and she loved them all the more for the indulgence.

Each morning, she would rise early, gather a handful of fruit from the kitchen, and set off for Hammersmith. She loved to observe life around the wonderful *Metropolitan Railway*. Tally would ride purely for pleasure. She had come to know the regular passengers by face—and some even by name. It put a smile on her face just to be there.

By day and by night, Tally saw two sides of London in detail that the majority of residents never noticed. She considered spending the rest of her days that way, too. It was the strangest thing, but from her time as a hungry child to her days as a lady of leisure, she felt an instinctive need to watch over the people of London. But Tally was never certain how—or even why.

Perhaps she would understand when she finally became the next Lady Grenshall.

CHAPTER ONE

The woman had been out drinking for a few hours: a proper night on the town. Flashbacks of the night brought her joy. She sang a song stuck in her head from one of the bars earlier that evening.

It was a special occasion, which warranted a special dress: blue, expensive, classy. A master class in revelry: boisterous, full of out-of-tune song and wild dance, relentless hell-raising and kissing of strange men.

Her two friends propped her all the way to Bond Street Underground Station when it was time to go home. 'The Three Musketeers,' they called themselves.

But they each lived in a different part of town, so the trio dispersed. She waved frenetically at them, shrieking like a banshee, and then staggered down the steps. It had been a great night. One of the best.

Yet, they had gone. Everyone had gone. The station was empty—which made no sense, even for that time of night.

Through the ticket barrier. Still, no one around. She just sang louder.

Down the escalator. The advertisements blurred past.

One poster rolled into another. As she descended, she craned her neck back and smiled at one particularly athletic male model. *Wow. How much of that's real man, and how much is airbrush?*

"No way anyone real is that ripped!" she blurted loudly. Nothing but an echo answered.

Even the platform was without a hint of other travellers or trains.

"Are they even running?" she asked, shaking her head. "This is the middle of London! It's never this quiet! If the station was closed, I wouldn't have been able to get down here."

She checked the matrix sign:

STANMORE: 12 MINUTES.

A long wait, but not unusual for that time of night. She took a seat on the nearby bench and waited.

Twelve minutes passed. Then fifteen. Then twenty-five. Still no train. Just that same dark tunnel to stare down, that light, warm breeze particular to Underground platforms, and the distant, ghostly sound of trains somewhere on another line.

Her tired head slumped forward once . . . twice . . . three times . . . before she shook herself firmly.

"This is fucking silly." She huffed and flailed her arms. "Seriously, where's my fucking train? Someone's going to hear about this."

She grabbed the armrest, propping herself upright. She felt new-found determination to right the wrong of not getting home. "Sat here," she mumbled indignantly, "inhaling dead animal and tramp piss."

She hobbled back up to the main station area, catching an intensifying reek around her. It made a poor combination with the booze in her system, but puking would only add to the problem.

"Nobody wants to clean that up," she reminded herself. "Soldier on."

She ran straight into someone huge—and clearly the source of the stench.

"Sorry!" she said, hiccupping.

He shoved her off-balance and she stumbled back. Powerful hands clamped over her temples and cheeks, suffocating and inescapable. Her vision blurred.

The world spun around violently. A massive arm thwarted her desperate attempt to catch her breath and muffled her terrified scream. The spinning stopped, replaced by swaying: left, right. Cold, dirty white tiles filled her sight.

You're facing the floor. Stay on your feet. Don't let him get on top. Focus. Whatever he has planned, it'll be over my dead body—and not tonight.

She shifted clumsily into a crouch, writhing to keep him from further advantage. With his brute force, it felt futile but not pointless. Not while she still drew breath.

The monster's hold locked her head, but through fading vision, she scanned her surroundings. To her left, the track and a risky drop from the platform—the iconic red circle and blue-line logo of the London Underground standing firm on the wall at the other side. To her right, dark trousers on legs broad as tree trunks.

Escape seemed impossible. It would have been a job even had she been completely fresh, but tired and pissed, she had no chance of success. He dragged her back towards the platform. All she could do was gasp hard—and hope to God for some air.

She had to try *something.*

She reached desperately across the floor. A little fumbling produced her handbag. She wrestled it open. Her vision darkened around the edges.

Stay on your feet! Stay awake!

Stay awake! Stay alive!

She found a potential lifesaver: her mobile phone. She gripped the weighty, outdated model hard and swung it with every ounce of strength, straight between his legs. The strike connected and he howled in pain, instantly loosening his grip as he doubled over. She fell, knocked off-balance from the force of his movement. One breath, hard and desperate.

Get on your feet, stay alive.

The colossal brute began to recover as she clawed the ground and grabbed a nearby bench. She hauled herself back to her feet and made to run, eyeing the exit staircase.

As she took her first steps, he lunged forward with abnormally long arms and grabbed her right leg. He yanked, knocking the wind out of her as she landed heavily on her back. In an explosion of rage, she lashed out with her left leg and smashed him squarely under his jaw, breaking the heel of her shoe with the impact.

He held fast, however. She struck again with the same leg, drawing blood from his cheek. The heel snapped off completely, just missing his right eye.

It was enough to shake him. A third kick to the chest propelled her backwards. Shaking loose both shoes, she stood and took a single glance back to witness the giant dragging himself to his feet. He wiped a trickle of crimson from his eyebrow and grinned at her with filthy, yellow canines.

What the fuck is he?

She broke into a sprint and made it through the alcove signposted, '*Way Out.*' She ran twenty metres or so, constantly looking back for her pursuer, who was out of sight.

Can't have just vanished!

Exhausted, she paused briefly to regain her breath. She inhaled deeply, hoping to try and catch that distinctive stench—to try and find him before he found her.

Nothing.

One last push would see her up the lengthy escalator and away. She made it to the first step but then felt herself flung backward through the air, landing on her backside. The monstrous, looming silhouette emerged in front of her. She screamed, hoping that someone other than the brute was listening.

A response. A faint tune in the background. Her ring tone: 'Always Look on the Bright Side of Life.'

She had dropped everything whilst running. Now her phone was all the way back at the platform. That phone call—perhaps the key to her salvation. She turned and retraced her steps, but the recorded whistling grew fainter with each step. She paused, confused.

Her hesitation proved deadly.

"Gonna answer it?" he growled.

He held the ringing phone in plain view, a broken, alien grin spreading across his face. She got a proper look at him now: his huge boar-like head, shaved so low it was raw and dark. His soulless eyes stared with perverse pleasure. He wore torn and shabby clothes, a distinct air of rot and decay surrounding him.

She froze, overcome with fear, which compounded at the animalistic roar he released. He shattered the phone against the wall and charged after her. She tried to run, but with deceptive speed, he seized the back of her hair and yanked downward, forcing her eyes to the ceiling.

"You really shouldn't have done that, you know . . . hurt me like that . . ." He twisted her around slowly at arm's length.

The light breeze emanating from the tunnel heightened. A low drone grew louder. She squirmed and struggled uselessly against his incredible might. He pulled her backwards by the hair and pressed her face to the wall.

He wrenched her left arm behind her back until it snapped; a sickening scream tore from her throat with the biting pain. She collapsed to her knees, but reminded herself of the price of surrender.

Don't let the bastard beat you. Stay alive!

The beast released her limp arm, spun her around, grabbed her by the neck, and with just one hand lifted her off her feet. Face-to-face with him, she could barely keep her eyes from rolling back. She gasped.

There are no marks on his face—no blood, nothing! He's unstoppable!

His laughter, his raw brute strength—it was all too much. Her head became too heavy, flopping to the side as she prepared to die. She hoped it would all be over quickly.

"Looks like your train was on time, after all!" The monster took two steps back away from the platform, his right hand seizing the broken arm for additional leverage. She whimpered.

The distant drone of the train grew to a rumble and took on a high-pitched whine. She moaned in time with the rhythmic dirge. That familiar warm wind. Two white lights against the darkness of the tunnel grew brighter.

Her assailant gave a guttural laugh and launched her, face first, across the track. She rammed against the wall opposite the platform. Her nose and jaw shattered on impact. She bounced to the floor, landing just shy of the electric rail.

The grinding steel wheels screamed closer, the light blinding her squinted eyes. A blue tinge flashed across the light. Barely conscious, battered and bloodied, sheer will revived her mantra. "G-get on your feet, st-stay—"

The brakes of the oncoming train squealed hard, but it was too close. Nothing was going to stop it—least of all her.

~ ✻ ~

A valley of darkness surrounded her. The shrieks sounded miles away. The single, distant light faded to nothing, like the cacophony around her.

Where was she?

She reached out into the abyss of bleakness, searching for anything tangible. Nothing.

Yet she was stranded, immovable within an unseen cage of desolation. The industrial shriek of the train echoed around her once more.

Fight through this. Catch that train.

She moved forward with determination, having defeated the obstacle with the force of her will. But, unbound, forward remained an unknown.

She could not stay there.

I'll be here forever if I do.

With as much motion as she could muster, she made for the source of the sound, running for the train. A blast of frigid wind sent her spiralling backward.

She got up and continued her pursuit. Another gust floored her. Running brought it no closer. On hands and knees, tears streamed down her face. She heard the last shrill cry of the train.

Despite her struggle, she hadn't moved. The last train out of there, the last train anywhere—missed. The sound faded into a faint wail. The noise shook her to the core.

Not now. Not today. Not while I have breath left in me.

The chill wind mutated into a gale of excruciating cold. Exhausted, her heavy eyelids drooped, yet she fought for her life against the unrelenting force.

Everything blurred, clouded, as if she had fallen into a lake. A sudden feeling like being dragged through murky water at speed. Lungs starved. Drowning.

Breathe! Breathe!

A concerted effort to draw air; a moment of calm. Then, all too suddenly, again drawn under. She struggled against the incredibly powerful *other,* refusing to relinquish that one last chance. *Fight! Live. Do NOT give in!*

Her strength of will was all she had left. With it, she dug in and fought. She would not allow herself to die today. She resisted with everything she had, forcing the direction of the fight.

Forward . . . left . . . then right . . .

Closing in on the source of her despair. If she could catch it, maybe she could defeat it. *Gone. Can't keep up with that.*

Time passed but meant nothing. Reaching out, she felt nothing. The confused sensation of motion stilled. She listened . . . and heard nothing but a faint and regular bleeping. It sounded so distant, a lifetime away. It provided an odd solace. Something about the sound told her that as long as it stayed as was, everything would be just fine. She allowed herself to close her eyes and take in the brief, tranquil respite.

The bleeping rapidly increased in pace, growing shrill, scratching at her mind. Then . . .

~ ✶ ~

"Oh!" An aristocratic female voice muttered, sounding disappointed. "Argh—why does nothing *ever* work? Disaster! Why must you insist upon being so . . . difficult?" A deep sigh followed. "Ugh—disgusting! Goodness me!"

The Lone Musketeer opened her eyes. She was seated—comfortably—in a large leather armchair. In a study, perhaps.

"What's disgusting?" she groaned, blinking in an attempt to focus her vision. Fragments of multi-coloured brightness flickered from above and to either side of her. A silhouette moved a few feet in front of her.

"Well, *you*, my dear. But this is quite the mess. Quite some mess." She heard no malice in the voice.

"Nothing's wrong with me," she answered after a moment's consideration. "I'm fairly sure I'm no Rembrandt, but your assessment's a bit harsh."

"Indeed, my dear," the response came. "Believe as much, if it brings you comfort. But your judgement lacks one essential fact." She chuckled. "Come. Allow me to provide some illumination."

The Musketeer felt the sensation of being hauled out of the chair. The motion stopped as quickly as it started. The abrupt relocation brought her before two red velvet curtains, flanked by four vast stained-glass windows.

The warmly filtered daylight seeped from every window, conventional and stained glass alike, bathing the room in radiant orange. Row upon row of full wooden bookshelves, over twice her height, loomed on either side. A green leather couch and three matching armchairs complemented the style of the rest of the room. Two custom-made coffee tables had a letter 'G' engraved into the legs.

The young hostess wore a flowing, layered cream dress, laced with pearls. Like the room in which they stood, despite its opulence, it looked worn and faded.

From her neck shone a dazzling, silver necklace, clearly valuable even to the Musketeer's uninitiated eye. A blue crystal in the shape of a teardrop hung encased in the centre of a frilly cage worked in silver. It refracted light around the room with unmatched brilliance.

A vicious, silver fang protruding from the bottom belied the delicacy of the filigree. The Musketeer could not take her eyes off it. She had never before seen anything like it. The hostess twitched and glared at her with burning blue eyes.

She gracefully drew back the crimson draperies. They revealed another window, but no light came from it.

The Musketeer was persuaded to step in front of it.

"Oh my God."

As she stared, the dark window shimmered. At first, it exhibited—nothing—devoid of light. And yet, ill-defined forms seemed to mill around in the darkness, nothing but thin wisps of lighter grey with wills of their own, each one shambling toward the portal as if determined to escape . . . or perhaps invade. The Musketeer was filled with an unsettling sense of déjà vu, and she shuddered to consider why. Concentrating to sharpen her focus, the shadows faded. Colours poured into shapes until a clear image formed.

The view resembled a detailed oil painting depicting the Underground station, down by the tunnels, viewed from an overhead vantage: a train, stopped before entering the station completely; a poor soul lay mangled in front of it.

The hostess clapped her hands twice. The painting came to life.

The driver stooped over the body, shaking and sobbing as he looked on, powerless. The victim's entire left side had been crushed, with the arm attached to the body only by its tendons. A pool of blood coloured the ground, with matted crimson bathing the driver's hands from his futile efforts at resuscitation.

Anguished shouts came from the driver, imploring newcomers to get help. Shock. Screams.

"I know that spot . . ." Her words faded as she dropped to her knees, unable to move or look away. "It happened—*right there! That happened to me!*"

"Indeed." The elegant woman placed her hands on the Musketeer's shoulders, which shook with fear. "It *happened.* That *was* you."

She had no answer—only silence. She ran her hands through her hair and over her face, checking for wounds.

"It can't be me," she muttered. "I'm fine. I'm *watching.* I'm *right here.*"

How long have I—where the hell am I—how am I not—?

"Dead, my dear?"

Her host's flippant demeanour aggravated the Musketeer. Yet having her thoughts answered proved more disconcerting.

"Well, as I said, you look disgusting at present. And your immediate future also looks rather bleak, it has to be said. But all hope is not yet lost." She reached out a helping hand, and with considerable strength eased the Musketeer back to her feet. "Listen, Rose. Your aid is required."

Rose?

"Yes."

"Stop doing that!" The Musketeer slapped free of the woman's support, incredulous. "Why did you just call me Rose? That's *not* my name."

She felt unshakable conviction. *I don't know why, but I know it isn't.*

And the response was instant. "So what is your name, my dear?"

"I—" She shook her head and watched the smile on the young lady's face grow smug. "I don't know."

I can't remember!

"Rose it is, then."

"Why Rose?"

"Because you look like a 'Rose' to me." She winked. *Rose* still had no comeback to counter the strange yet charismatic woman.

"Whatever." She shook her head and sighed. "So who are *you*?"

"My name is Tally. And I own this mansion."

"If I'm 'dead,' what am I doing in a mansion? Not an afterlife I've ever heard of."

Tally chuckled, placing her hand on Rose's shoulder. "You are not exactly dead; however, your situation is a touch . . . *precarious* at the moment."

Rose was about to ask another question but was pre-empted.

"At the moment, you are dreaming—after a fashion. However, there is a little more to it than that. It would take far too long to explain, and whilst time is not the same here as it is . . ." She gestured once more to the window, a translucent obsidian. Rose noted the floating, animated shades on the other side, disturbing blobs of darkness with the merest hint of sentience.

"Out there.

"Time is on no one's side, as things stand." She looked back at the window and frowned. "It would be mutually advantageous to get you back to your world, quickly. I am grateful someone came along to help."

"With what?"

"Again, I have no time to fully explain," Tally responded. Rose bristled, chagrined at the dismissal. "Your continued existence depends upon our haste. Suffice it to say, I am certain that you have no desire to end your life in such a . . . *cheap* fashion." Once more, she pointed at the strange window, which had mysteriously reverted to the traumatic Underground image. "*I* had no desire for this to happen. But this is . . . well, it is as it is."

Tally seemed distracted by her thoughts. Rose watched a string of conflicting emotions war across her face. "It will not do," Tally said at last. "We must work with what we have." She again turned to Rose. "It's now out of my hands, but it may well be within yours. Would you help me? Whilst helping yourself, of course."

Although Rose could not see beyond the undulating Underground scene, the sense of nothingness, death—oblivion—heightened every time she directed her focus at the mysterious obsidian window.

And she could see something in those shining eyes of Tally's beyond the glamour. She sensed an undercurrent of fear, panic—fury. Frankly, given what Rose had just seen, that made them kindred spirits for the moment. She wasn't sure what any of it meant, but refusing Tally's request seemed unwise.

"Okay." Rose turned toward Tally. "What do you want me to do?"

Tally gave an assertive jerk of the chin and took the singular necklace into her hand. "Find this," she instructed. "Find it quickly. Less than benevolent hands now control it."

"Isn't that it, right there?"

Tally rolled her eyes. "I want you left in no doubt as to what to look for. *Obviously*, this is not the real thing."

"Would've been way too bloody easy, wouldn't it?"

Rose took time to examine the caged teardrop, careful to note each detail to ensure she could identify it on sight.

"Well, it's pretty distinct, at least," she said. "There shouldn't be too many around like it."

Tally nodded. "It is one of a kind—thank goodness."

Rose took in the whole of the apartment. Her attempt to better comprehend her surroundings failed. Her mind returned to one of Tally's earlier comments.

"So, I'm dreaming?" she asked.

"After a fashion," Tally replied cryptically. "At the moment, you're every bit as dead as you look down there. However, as you are willing to assist, we must have you alive and well forthwith."

"Dead? That's impossible, surely?"

"You are speaking to one of the dead, my dear. Consider broadening your horizons."

The condescension silenced Rose.

"Say, what is the date? In what year do you exist?" Tally questioned.

"2012. Why?"

"Good Lord! Has it really been that long?"

"That long?"

"Since I died, of course. It seems I have been dead for well over a century. I only catch glimpses of your living world, the occasional glance—the flash of an image. Thought I was going to end up the way of—"

Tally shuddered.

"The way of what?"

"I don't want to talk about it."

Rose considered pressing the issue but didn't think it would aid the situation.

"Okay," she conceded. "How does one go about saving the world?" She impersonated Tally's voice with over-nasal inflection, strictly tongue-in-cheek. Tally ignored the mockery.

"You will find a way. You are certainly a survivor, so you should adapt to your *life changes* with relative ease, I imagine."

"My *what*?"

Tally narrowed her eyes. "The rest you know already. See to finding that necklace. With all haste!"

Rose frowned. "'What aren't you telling me, Tally?"

Tally chuckled mischievously. "Rose, you really are as sharp as a fine needle! I think you actually may have been worth waiting for. Though certain *sacrifices* have been made to keep you alive. I dread to consider what would have come next had you not agreed to assist."

"I dread to consider what's coming next anyway," Rose said, shuddering at the deep shadows looming at the dark window. "So . . . what now?"

"Now you return."

Tally grabbed both of Rose's arms and winked, dragging her closer. "This will not be the last time you speak with a dead person. You are, after all, now something of a kindred spirit to us. We shall speak again soon. Goodbye for now, my dear."

She pulled Rose right up to her face and kissed her on the forehead. Rose felt a forceful shove away, back into the shadow. Suddenly, Rose's view of the room faded away as if she had fallen into a lake. She felt herself dragged under . . .

CHAPTER TWO

Rose shot upright with a start, instantly back in a world of light and colour. Too quickly. Her spinning vision recovered, but the contents of her stomach were projected over the side of a bed. She wiped her mouth with the back of her sleeve and looked around.

The light was sterile, clear, and monochromatic. Different from just moments before. The weird floating sensation, the ghost named Tally, the necklace—it had all been a strange dream.

A rhythmic beeping comforted her. She must have heard it even in her sleep. She took a gasp of breath, feeling as if she'd been underwater all this time. But that made no sense.

She noticed IV tubes in her arms, which was understandable, all things considered. She could have been out for days, weeks—longer.

Less expected were her black and pronounced veins against deathly pale skin.

"What the hell?" she muttered, pulling at her lank strands of silver hair. That was wrong.

"Bloody hell," said a voice at the door. A male nurse stood staring at her as if he had seen a ghost. "You're awake! I should get a doctor."

Tall and dashing, with spiky brown hair, he was probably just a little older than her. Instinct told her as much, but for the moment, she couldn't quite remember her exact age.

"How long have I been in here?" she asked, playing with the dangling tubes.

The nurse stared at her, stuck for words.

"Mate, how long have I been lying here?"

"What? . . . er . . ." He shook his head; clearly something about her unnerved him. Perhaps some dramatic change in her appearance during her unconsciousness?

"Um . . . right," he struggled with a reply. "We had the call for you more than three days ago. But you're . . . you've . . ."

"What is *up* with you, man?" She threw her arms high into the air and swung around the bed until barely perched on it. "Okay, I get it. I probably look like a fucking zombie, but you know, I reckon not bad, considering. So spit it out!" Rose caught herself. That rant had flown involuntarily out her mouth, a sudden burst of rage. From where? He seemed nice enough; he didn't deserve that.

The nurse looked apologetic as he forced himself back to his senses and, from across the room, examined Rose with narrowed eyes. With greater confidence, he explained himself.

"Listen, this probably sounds weird, but when you first came in here, with the state you were in, I am amazed you are alive at all."

Alive. Her mind flooded with images. A strange black window. Red drapes. A scene of bloody carnage. Had he seen her as she appeared in that window? "Let me guess," she groaned, "got hit by a Tube train? Looking damn good for it right now, huh?"

"Yes," he responded, "The driver thought he had—" He stopped abruptly with a puzzled stare. "Seriously, I've no *idea* how you've cleaned up so well, so quickly. I've never seen anything like it! They're going to think I'm bloody *mad*."

Rose grinned. "If I told you half of what *I've* seen, I'd end up transferred straight to the nuthouse."

"Don't rule that out," the nurse retorted. "But how are you even sitting up, let alone talking to me?"

"Err . . . same as I ever did, I think?" Her stomach cramped again. She looked around for a bowl.

He anticipated her needs and handed her a basin. "Maybe, but with most people I've seen coming in here the way you did, we just wait for the doctor to call the time of death. Yet, here you are. How there was even enough of you to save in the first place, I'll never know.

"I've watched you fighting as hard as anyone I've seen come through Intensive Care. You clung on, and I thought to myself, 'Fair enough. Hope she is able to have something of a life in a few years' time.' Then I turn up today and you're looking ready for discharge—apart from running some scans and seeing what's up with your veins.

"Who are you, anyway? Nobody's so much as recognised you; nobody's come to visit, called about you. Sorry. How are you feeling, by the way?"

Rose tapped the bowl, but a few seconds of heaving interrupted her chuckling. She paused as her nausea settled. "Fine," she answered at last. "Better than you, by the looks of things. They overwork you nurses, you know. You should clock out and get some sleep before you harass any more of your patients."

"Oh, I didn't mean to," he said. "It's just that . . . well . . . I . . ."

"I know. It's okay." Rose smiled. "I might not look it, but I'm feeling perfectly fine."

He picked up the tablet from his workstation and frowned as he attempted to update her chart notes.

"Listen," he said. "Even taking into account the miracle healing, that doesn't explain the hair or eye change from when you first came in here. If I didn't know better, I'd say you were a completely different person."

"I'm flattered you've been paying me that much attention." She winked and grinned mischievously before leaning forward toward him. He froze, unsure of what was coming next. Her hand slowly reached for his name badge. "*Jack*?"

"Well, there seems to be nothing wrong with your vision." He gulped, backing away. "So who are you exactly?"

"Ah, yeah," she replied. She rolled her eyes, defeated by her sketchy recall. "Call me Rose for now, but that's the best I can do."

He directed a strength test: a shuffle left and right, a shake of each leg, arms lifted outward, and circular head rolls.

"Everything seems to be in perfect working order."

She stretched, cracking her knuckles. "About that," she said, "I feel far from full strength—but more importantly, I can't remember a damn thing except how I got here in the first place."

"Not that surprising, given you sustained a head injury," he told her. "I'm surprised to see you up and talking so soon. These things can take weeks—months. Any doctor will tell you that." He looked bemused as he made his way to the door, peering down the corridor. "Speaking of which, one should have been here by now."

Jack disappeared briefly to grab a mop and bucket before returning, gently closing the door.

"No idea where the doctor is," he said, attacking the mess on the floor beside her bed.

"That's fine," Rose sighed. "I need to go home anyway. I'm sure I'll be okay."

"You'll need at least another overnight here and probably a bunch of tests before they'll even think about letting you go, miracle or not."

"It's not like I can remember where home is, anyway."

"That could be a problem. You didn't have any ID on you or anything. Were you running away from something? Do you know?"

She looked up at him sharply, wide-eyed. She drew her legs back into the bed, curling herself tight into a ball. Her heart pounded as she relived the shrieking of brakes and blinding light rushing towards her, the face of the beast-like man, grinning at her with yellow fangs.

A light breeze gathered in the hospital room with no obvious source. Perhaps it was just someone walking on her grave, but everything seemed so vivid. So intense. So frightening. So real.

Blink. Deep breaths.

Calm.

She concentrated on the non-threatening, concerned caregiver in front of her. "Yeah," she forced from her constricted throat. "You could say that."

Jack gently stepped toward her, placing a comforting hand on her arm. "Okay. We'll get you back on your feet as soon as we can." He frowned. "Where is the bloody doctor? *Someone* must have heard me."

Rose scrunched her face as she forced herself to think about her lack of memory. "How in the hell don't I even remember where I fucking *live*?" she demanded. She thumped the bed with more force than she was capable of. Every object in the room shook.

Jack didn't answer. He eyed the rattling surroundings and backed away. But someone else had arrived. The whistling told her whom.

She knew the tune all too well.

Always Look on the Bright Side of Life.

A massive shadow against the drawn curtain drew her eye to the observation window. The source moved ponderously towards the door. A fit of shivering struck her with a vengeance, and the breeze in the room burst to a gust. The medical equipment in the room vibrated in perfect time with her shudders, the room itself at one with her terror.

Every light in the room flickered and then blinked out. The door burst open, the monstrous frame a silhouette against the hallway lighting.

She screamed with mindless terror. The more she screamed, the more equipment flew violently around the room.

The brute had failed in an attempt at disguise with a shredded medical coat—the previous owner's fresh blood still oozing through the threads. He threw a disembodied arm at Jack's feet.

Half the size of the bestial mound of muscle, Jack flinched but still moved to intercept. "Y-you need to leave before I call the police."

"Jack," Rose wheezed, "run for help! Go now!"

The giant gave a loud laugh, stooping to examine his obstruction.

Jack stood firm. "Listen, I don't know who you are, but you need to get out. Now."

"Move, insect!" the monster growled. Jack recoiled.

"I can't do that. I—"

The bestial man drove his fist down onto Jack's head. Rose gasped in horror and fumbled for anything she could use as a weapon while the giant bludgeoned her friend. With one final crack, Jack crumpled to the ground.

She scrambled to the head of the bed, but a mammoth hand wrapped around her right ankle and dragged her back into a supine position. He pinned her down by the throat and leaned over her, grinning widely.

She grappled for the saline drip pole and drew it down onto his head, but her attack proved ineffectual. He seemed insensible to her flailing limbs.

He drew back his free arm and grinned. "Time to finish the job." He stroked her hair with a finger from his restraining hand. Rose closed her eyes against the terror.

A screech filled the room, but not from Rose. She opened her eyes, watched the giant roar with agony and fall to his knees. A long, white lab coat flumped onto the bed beside her.

Behind the wounded beast stood a tall, blonde young woman with razor-like talons dripping fresh gore. "Time to go," she commanded Rose. Rose grabbed the coat and donned it as she darted out of the room.

As the pair ran down a hallway, Rose stared at the woman's bloodied talons and gasped as the sharp appendages suddenly reverted to a regularly shaped hand. The blonde paused to assess the attacker's persistence. The giant poked his head out from Rose's room, recovering rapidly from an injury that would have finished anyone else. He located the pair and glared.

"Interesting," the woman mused. "A fair fight. Rare."

She pulled Rose toward her with far more strength than expected. Her eyes darted around, searching for an escape route. "That way," she said, pointing to a corridor on their right. "I'll catch you up."

"But what if there—"

"Go!" She grabbed Rose by the hand, about to sling her down the way, but recoiled from the touch as if burned. They looked at each other, completely baffled. The assailant crashed towards them, swatting aside everything in his path.

His low, guttural laugh chilled Rose to the bone. Fear, pain, and helplessness all took hold, rooting her firmly to the spot on which she stood.

"Hey!" her protector called to her, breathless. "*Move.*"

Rose took one last look back as she dashed down the hallway. Either her eyes played tricks on her or the woman's appearance had altered. Blonde hair, once long, had shortened to dull and brambly. Her features looked sharp, pointed, and feral. She gave an animalistic snarl as she leapt at her opponent.

A few paces down the corridor, a nearby fire extinguisher caught Rose's attention: another option. She pulled up short and placed a hand on it while she considered. Looking to the escape route, then back to her new friend, she turned on her heel, grabbed the weapon, and headed back.

The woman had sent the attacker skidding down the corridor on his back. Bystanders fled for their safety. The blonde propped herself against a wall, winded.

As quickly as before, he returned to his feet and advanced. He cut short a security guard's radioed plea with one brutal swing of an arm. His blood and teeth spraying with a loud crack, the guard smashed through the drywall and into the next room. Chortling, the giant pressed on.

The feral woman snarled in her combative stance.

Rose watched in horror as the enemy charged, gaining an advantage. He lifted her friend by the throat and started to squeeze. It looked all too familiar.

Sadistic pleasure played across his face as he starved her of breath with one hand, crushing the very life from her. Cocking his head sideways, he turned his full attention to Rose with a perverse smile. She could feel her helter-skelter pulse dance with terror.

Her friend had turned blue. A popping sound from her throat echoed off the linoleum.

Rose advanced on the pair, anger fuelling her fatigued muscles.

His victim's struggling hands went limp. But the woman drew her knees up to her chest with considerable elasticity and lashed out—hard—high enough for the heels on her boots to slam into his throat, all but spearing him.

He gurgled, unable to howl, and instantly released his grip.

As her friend dropped into a balanced crouch, she inhaled once, deeply poised as if the last few seconds had not happened. She glared fiercely at Rose. "Didn't I tell you to get out of here?" she hissed, frothing at the mouth.

"Well, there's fucking gratitude for you," Rose spat back. Seething, she readied the extinguisher like a golf club.

The monster coughed up blood and returned slowly to his feet. She swung the extinguisher at her would-be killer with every bit of force she could muster. He caught it in one of his massive hands.

The merest twitch of his wrist sent Rose careering across the floor, well away from the fight. He wielded the extinguisher himself, swinging wildly in an attempt to crush the interloper.

The feral warrior proved far too elusive. She made him look clumsy with every swing. He appeared a drunkard trying to swat a fly as she dodged and weaved. Every time she rolled forward or backward, he lunged, half a second too late.

Within the space of a few failed attacks, he had swung himself completely off-balance, exposing his back to his opponent. A precisely measured thrust-kick connected, knocking him clean off his feet and smashing him into a nearby wall. The extinguisher rolled down the corridor, unmanned.

"Seriously," said Rose, gaping with awe. "Who *are* you?"

"Name's Jennifer," her new friend barked. "Let's go."

The hospital staff began to react to the chaos around them. A significant number of medical and security personnel sought to intercede, while other people with cameras edged closer to the action.

"Why the hell would anyone want pictures?" Rose snapped, suddenly reminded of the fact she was wearing only a hospital gown and lab coat as they rounded a corner.

"Take your pick!" Jennifer panted breathlessly, finally smiling. Somehow sarcasm bled through the animalistic face. "A couple of freaks fighting? Or the unknown miracle lady?"

"Fair point."

"Take the next left!"

After taking an elaborate, winding route down through the maze of corridors, the pair gained some breathing space. They reached the atrium, leading to the main exit below. They looked down, scoping the situation. The entrance was surrounded, panicked citizens boxed in as police officers and security guards allowed no one in or out.

"Be ready," Jennifer said, placing an arm across her. "I'm getting you out of here if it kills me."

"Don't say that." Rose was amazed by the selfless aid. She looked nervously behind her. "A few pains in the arse are still better than a potential murderer, right?"

"We don't know there's not another one like him in that crowd," Jennifer said. "I'm not chancing it, and neither are you."

"Fine. So now what?"

"That isn't the only way out of here. Come on!"

Jennifer flung her head forward once to cover her face with hair and waited a couple of seconds before pulling it back. It had again grown longer and assumed a silky golden colour. The animalistic angles disappeared, replaced once more by a warmer, more wholesome face. The cat-like eyes widened and became more pearlescent green than yellow. Her skin softened to a smooth olive tone.

If Rose had not seen the transformation for herself, she would have been hard-pushed to tell it was the same person. She buttoned up the coat to hide her hospital gown a little better.

They retreated from the bottleneck and took a different path through the hospital. More visitors were being shepherded by security from the direction they headed. Jennifer shoved some of them clear before the guards intervened. With one swift movement, she seized the arm of the closest guard and kicked him into his colleague. Rose and Jennifer bustled through the freshly created gap.

Doors to the fire-exit stairs were dead ahead.

Down the corridor stormed the gore-splattered giant, enraged and holding his chin with one hand and the fire extinguisher with the other. He hurled anyone in his way through doors and walls as they cowered in fear. Once he spotted the pair, he ignored his injury, roared savagely, and broke into a charge.

"This time, just go for the exit, okay?"

Rose nodded, trusting Jennifer to carry on with what she had started. Jennifer received the charge, and despite being almost at a standstill, managed to stop her huge opponent dead in his tracks. The two locked grips, and Rose watched in amazement as her friend dictated the direction of the grapple—away from the escape route, which bought Rose vital time and space. Rose ran as fast as she could.

Rose emerged from the door and picked up the pace. She almost leapt down the first flight of stairs. Despite her fatigue, she stopped for nothing. Through the fire-exit doors, then the basement car park up ahead. Perfect. Rose made a spirited charge toward the car park, freedom within reach. She took a stumble, still not quite back to full strength. In the dim flickering light, she glanced back once, scanning for friend or foe. She flung herself at the double doors, bursting through.

Blissful silence. She had managed to evade everyone. But it was *too* quiet. Something was wrong.

The ceiling lights, once uncomfortably flickering, began to blur into bright white lines. However, they provided the only light down there; shadow and darkness pervaded the scene. Soon even that light faded, and the pall consumed all around her.

The buzzing she had first heard sounded a great distance away. Billowing black smoke belched out and obscured everything it touched, despite the surprising absence of cars. The vapours engulfed every-thing—sight, smell—even sound. When it at last dissipated, it left noth-ing but shadow upon shadow.

Echoing, pounding footsteps faded into the sound of her own heartbeat, of her exhausted breathlessness. Soon this was all she could hear, and even though she needed to stop, to catch breath, it felt unsafe even with no one in sight or hearing range. If anything, her change of environment had made things worse. She didn't know whether she had been running for seconds or minutes and could barely see her own hands in front of her.

She stopped dead, assessing the situation.

The uncontrolled floating sensation—that void—that dream-like darkness. Rose had been there before. She quickly remembered to grasp her thoughts, focus, steer herself around this murk. Tally. That ghost. They had met somewhere in this place. *Not* the hospital.

Wherever it was, the only clear landmarks were cloudy wisps of a lighter grey and more static, jagged lines at the edge of her vision. Shades of darkness, indeterminate shapes, floated around her at un-certain distance. Others with a wretched, slimy chill about them flitted past like bats. A light breeze in the air bore a sharp chill unlike any she had ever felt.

Deeper concentration—or perhaps more desperate thoughts—stopped the listless drifting.

The shadow flickered. Even through limited visibility, there were definitely shapes there . . .

. . . or were they faces?

More blurry images stood behind her, taking shape; animated shadows formed heads, shoulders, bodies, all trapped in the shade. Beyond her own noisy panting, whispers, a cacophony of incomprehensible mutterings. No single voice was clear.

The sea of shadows edged closer to her, the front of them within touching distance and showing no signs of stopping. Tentatively, she reached out into the shapes, trembling. She imagined touching a cloud would be thus: cold, slightly damp—but viscous. Her hand sliced through each face with a little less resistance than a hand in water—water as cold as ice.

With her touch, the noise gathered, the whispers hissed, the darkness encroached upon her. She wanted to run again, but each step felt like sludging through tar. It required every ounce of her strength to keep moving at all. Her movement became more akin to swimming than running, but she would not stop . . .

. . . *not while I have breath in my—*

Do *I have breath in my lungs?*

Shit, shit, shit . . .

"Let me out of here!" Her screams tore at her throat.

A loud screech. Something knocked her into the air. She flung her arms out, just catching herself before she smacked face-first into metal.

Car?

She cowered, overwhelmed by an onslaught of light and sounds. Other vehicles took evasive action, swerving and blaring their horns; some mounted pavements. As she looked up, a horrified face stared back at her. Still boggled, she pushed herself upright. The driver rushed to her and grabbed her arms.

"I'm sorry," the middle-aged man said, panic-stricken. "I didn't see you! You just weren't *there*—"

She slapped him away, shrieking, and retreated. "Get off me!"

Screeching tyres. She jumped as another car swerved past and obscenities spewed from the driver's mouth. The desperate honking and abuse continued, London at its worst.

"You're lucky I braked in time," the man said. "If I hadn't seen you when I did, you'd have been—"

"But I wasn't even outside!" She took a breath to calm herself, then met the driver's eye and offered a feeble smile. "I . . . sorry. Where's the nearest hospital, please?"

~ ✱ ~

Rose reached the hospital easily enough by following the regular trail of emergency services vehicles in the vicinity. The entrance was swamped with a rubbernecking crowd.

She scanned the building, looking for another way in. A figure suddenly blasted through a window several floors up; shards of glass rained through the air. Rose watched as Jennifer twisted in the air, shifting like a cat, and landed gracefully on her feet. The terrified crowd screamed.

Several police officers surrounded Jennifer, looking to question her. Rose knew neither of them could afford the delay. She ran towards her friend. "Hey!" she called, attracting the attention of two constables, who immediately cut her off.

"OUT OF MY WAY!" she ordered. Her voice carried a chilling echo, otherworldly and implacable, an aura of unquestionable command. It didn't feel like her; she never knew she had that in her. "NOW."

The two backed away a step or two, then turned and ran.

On Rose's approach, the police detaining Jennifer released her and fled in terror. Jennifer edged away a few paces but did not run. Rose took her by the arm, careful not to directly contact skin, and gave a smile. The winds dissipated as she did so. "As you said—time to go."

As they walked, the cuts on Jennifer's bottom lip, cheeks, forehead, and arms closed more with every step taken. The woman muttered as they moved, "Lucky punch . . . should've had him."

"How the hell are you not a smear on the pavement?" Rose demanded, staring through narrowed eyes.

Jennifer shrugged and pointed at an unoccupied black cab in the distance, just about to wriggle clear of the traffic jam and drive off. They both broke into a run. Jennifer quickly outran Rose, pulled the rear door open, and spoke to the driver. Rose caught up and they both entered the vehicle. Jennifer's lips shifted subtly into a smile, soon followed by a small chuckle, quickly escalating to a roar of laughter.

"What?"

"Nothing." The guffawing continued. "I was just thinking—how am I alive? That's *seriously* rich coming from you of all people!"

Rose closed the door before breaking into laughter at the thought.

CHAPTER THREE

His wounds had healed. He'd lick them for a while, though.

The new person had caused him to bungle what should have been a simple task. How could she have fallen from such a deadly height— *and not died?!* She matched him for strength, bested him for speed, and *what* was with those claws? Thanks to her, *the* designated target got away. And that meant his mistress would be very, very displeased.

"And that little bitch doesn't answer to anyone," he muttered to himself. He smacked a straggling civilian aside as he strode out of the deliveries exit. His explanation would not go well for him.

His mistress had waited for him to come out of the hospital for more than an hour, expecting him to have done his job. She already knew he had failed; he felt her rage from that distance—probably could from anywhere in the world. He sensed her emotions, and if especially unfortunate, heard her thoughts. *Come here,* she summoned. He knew exactly where to find her when he escaped the hospital, leaving a trail of destruction behind him.

She waited for him in the backseat of an unfamiliar car, driven by an equally unfamiliar young woman of average looks. His mistress's own appearance posed a terrible reminder of what might have been.

At one time he had been a regular man—a regular *human being*—by the name of Thomas Barber. He had lived a relatively normal life working in the city. Nobody knew him back then—which was how the entire mess started.

He had always kept himself in the best working order possible. He knew he was considered handsome. His golden hair grew down to his neck. He kept it groomed, his face clean-shaven, and his physique nicely toned. Since his schooldays, people commented upon the warmth of his grey eyes—or at least he recollected overhearing as much. Nobody actually had ever said such a thing directly to him.

Each morning when he reached his office on the fourth floor of a nondescript office block just off Bishopsgate, he would stand by his window and watch the thousands of commuters scurrying to their jobs, much as he did. His daily cup of coffee wafted satisfaction with such evidence that he was not alone in the world.

The people in his office barely acknowledged him, unless their computer or printer was not working. He was fine with that—it paid the bills—but occasionally it pleased him to remember that he was not the only person staring out of a window, contemplating his existence. Even looking into the sky was a humanising reminder that he was alive; the mildest paranoia about a repeat of 9/11 provided just enough adrenaline to push him through his dullest days.

Not that *any* of the days were exciting. He was in entirely the wrong occupation for that. Financial stability? Yes. Relatively sensible hours? Yes. Something he was competent at? Definitely. But excitement? No; not so.

'Excitement' was generated by keeping his brain sharp with crosswords and Sudoku. It was by taking pride in his appearance, with painstaking attention to detail. The casual observer would have thought him middle management at the very least, with his constant supply of new and expensive suits, shirts, shoes, and ties, and the visible results of the hour and a half he would devote daily to immaculately grooming himself and polishing his shoes.

He spent two-hour stints at the gym at least three times a week, with a meticulously researched programme to ensure that his fitness regime kept his physique well above average, but not a steroid-inhaling monster. A glass of wine every evening—maybe two—were neither disruptions to his routine nor, by any standard, extreme behaviour.

It started that way two years ago. However, over the previous year, his deteriorating sleep patterns altered everything. He had no obvious explanation for it, but he felt disinclined to mention it to anyone. Consulting his doctor smacked of weakness, and there were none amongst his work colleagues he would approach with such a thing. Most would not offer him a cup of tea in the mornings.

With limited options, he chose a slight change in lifestyle instead. He added another day to the gym schedule, and before too long, the nightly glass of wine increased to half a bottle and, on occasion, the whole thing.

A couple of weeks into his new regime, he also increased the time devoted to his voyeurism of the city below him, which meant that he observed a little more carefully than normal. Using the camera on his mobile phone, he could zoom in on the crowd below—the best function it could serve for him, as it turned out. He received hardly any personal calls.

On this closer examination, he realised he had been missing something all along: the human interactions taking place. Not all of the people were solitary while making their way in that hub of world commerce—not by any means. He saw groups of commuters, male, female, mixed and matched, laughing, joking, and chatting, despite the majority of those he spotted parting for different workplaces. He even spied couples sharing various intimacies.

Not long after, Thomas took to booking another timeslot at his window to watch them further: at 5:30pm. He noticed that many of these groups and couples reunited with one another at the end of their workday. In this, he realised precisely the cause of his unhappiness.

He was *totally* alone in the world.

When he returned to his flat, he took one last glass of his favourite claret. He poured the rest down the sink and sat down to think about how he was going to rectify his problem, starting with the very next day.

That evening, he rooted through his wardrobe to locate his very finest suit: nothing from a Savile Row tailor, to be sure, but fine clothing nonetheless. He worked on his shoes, black brogues, ensuring that before he had headed for bed, he could see his face in them.

The next morning, he got up, took an additional half hour with his shave, gelled his blonde hair into trendy spikes, and replaced his standard glasses with a set of bright blue contacts. He looked into the mirror and liked what he saw.

Singing to himself, he made his way into work. That day, he decided to break out of his safety zone. Though he was well-hidden behind smoked glass, he felt he knew the glamorous couple from the banking head office whom he observed daily better than anybody he had bumped into at his own firm. His extra grooming efforts made him brave. He had a tentative look around his own office and actually made an effort to be *seen*.

But then he found her. A rare beauty: tall to a striking degree, slender and sleek of movement, long, flowing, silky blonde hair, and eyes of sapphire. Her smile had melted the hearts of hardier men. She had clearly spent time preparing her appearance for the day, much as he had—or was possessed of a natural grace like he had never seen before.

She wore a grey suit featuring a knee-length skirt, which wrapped itself around her perfectly. He wondered if that day was her first. He was certain he would have remembered seeing her previously. He felt compelled to reveal the new and improved Thomas Barber first to her, and so approached, levelling a warm but nervous smile at her.

As self-conscious as he was, relief washed over him as she returned the gesture with equal warmth. She brushed back her hair as he drew near. He thrust out his hand and uttered the first words of his new life. "Hi! My name's Thomas."

"Sarah Bliss." An incredibly soft, perfectly manicured hand took his and shook firmly, business-like. Her smile and unabashed gaze smacked of far more than professionalism.

"I've never seen you before." He failed to let go of her hand following the end of the handshake. She looked down at their hands, but looked back up at him, amused.

"That's probably because I'm new here."

"Really?" His voice squeaked way too much for him not to squirm. "Er . . . like . . . how new?"

"Like, this is my first day."

"Oh."

He had finally gathered the presence of mind to release his grip, but they had not broken their gaze in the interim. Suddenly, others arrived and Sarah became the centre of attention. Another woman pushed her way between them. "You're going to be late," she said to Sarah. "This way."

Sarah had turned back to smile and gave a very small wave as she was carted off. "Goodbye, Thomas." He was almost certain he had heard the other woman muttering the word, "Creepy." But he could never be sure.

The helpful co-worker had literally shunted Sarah Bliss out of his life.

Sarah barely noticed him after that, but he saw her. A lot. His daytime schedule had altered greatly, to the point where he stopped monitoring the banking couple on the street, although they had once dominated his thoughts. There was a new pairing in town. It was just a pity she did not know it yet.

If he could just talk to her . . .

He spent some considerable time pondering how to engineer a meeting. He had found the floor she worked on—the seventh—and would, when not busy elsewhere, visit her area to do a 'routine check-up' on a computer nearby. He went at least twice a week, and occasionally sabotaged the odd machine just so he could be near her for half an hour or so. But he never caught a moment alone with her. Her friend hovered like a guard dog.

The longer this went on, the more their relationship deteriorated. First she stopped saying 'hello' every time he visited, always busy with work. Then the brief smile she would occasionally offer him ceased. Finally, she started to look at him with much the same contempt as her friend, as if he was some sort of freak. It ate him up inside.

He hoped a series of evening conferences would present some opportunity to clear the air and get things between himself and Sarah back on track. They would all have had a few glasses of wine and be a little more relaxed, a few more guards down. It was the perfect time.

He planned his attendance from the day of the announcement. He had spent a fortune to make absolutely sure she could not ignore him.

On the day of the event, Thomas sat attentively through the business meetings at his assigned corner table. He politely endured the day's questions from his colleagues. The object of his desires was elsewhere, laughing and joking with her peers—in particular, a handsome, dark-haired man he had never seen before. They seemed to be getting on extremely well.

At the end of the day, he disappeared back to his hotel room and started his ritualistic preening. And after two and a half hours of compulsive preparation, he headed down to the bar with the shiniest shoes, his tailored dark grey suit and blue silk shirt, meticulously gelled hair, recently trimmed, and a fat wallet. She was not there when he arrived, but her friend was. They exchanged stares before heading to their assigned dinner tables.

At last, he was noticed as he wanted to be—but not by whom he wanted. A couple of young starters smiled over, and the company director stuck on his table commended him on his attire. The director even offered him a drink, but it was too late. Sarah Bliss had ghosted over to her allotted table, and dinner was about to be served. Still her new gentleman friend entertained her. Time was fast running out for Thomas to act.

He picked away at his three-course meal, preoccupied. Those sitting nearby attempting to converse with him ran into monosyllabic responses and evident dispassion. Thanks to the director, though, Thomas's glass was full for the duration of the meal.

The music grew louder. The lights dimmed. A horde of waiting staff descended upon the room to clear up. After little time, most of the guests took to the bar or the dance floor. Thomas moved quickly to intercept Sarah.

And still he was not quick enough.

That other man, his slick rival, got to her first, taking her hand to dance to a quick-tempo number. Thomas was stunned by her looks, her slender figure perfectly poured into a tight-fitting blue silk dress with a slit up the right thigh, and not a golden lock out of place. She looked for all intents and purposes like a movie star. Nobody could touch her that night.

Thomas watched them gaze at each other as each danced with impressive skill. He froze, unsure whether to carry on or to retreat to his seat. The area was packing out fast.

A short, curvaceous woman with a fiendishly strong grip seized his hand and yanked him back to the centre of the floor. In his confusion, he did not resist but remained focused upon Sarah and the mystery man. The pair were the king and queen of the dance floor. Cheered on by all comers, they milked the crowd for everything it was worth. Thomas's dance partner twirled him away from them.

After a brief moment of shock, he realised who had captured him. He had never met her, but he had seen her face on the Intranet before: a company director. He stared, attempting to put a name to the face.

She was at least ten years older than him, he was sure, and the very image of glamour. She wore a tangibly expensive, low-cut pearlescent dress and had professionally styled curly, shoulder-length auburn hair. Large hazel eyes examined him carefully. This was Beatrice Fox, a high-flying woman with a reputation for getting exactly what she wanted. Which at that time, for unknown reasons, was him.

"Erm, you do know I just work in IT, don't you?" he asked. Just for the briefest moment, he lost track of Sarah and her friend.

"Well, that answers one of my questions, anyway!" she purred in a deep voice, barely audible over the blaring music. Full, bright red lips formed a cheeky smile as she moved one of his hands to the small of her back and the other to her shoulder. "Guess you know who I am then?"

"Yes." In a matter of seconds, she had obliterated the courage he had spent the day building. Her smile dropped. "Pain in the arse being famous sometimes, you know. A girl can't get a dance without the whole bloody room watching."

It wasn't the entire room. Even as she spoke, Thomas still looked elsewhere. But Sarah Bliss and her 'friend' only had eyes for each other. Jealous as he was, he left them to it. His dance partner turned to look around.

She was correct. There were whispers and unsubtle pointing. He even spotted his recent nemesis, Sarah's colleague, chatting to one of her line managers, looking over. His grip firmed on Beatrice, and he leaned forward to speak in her ear. "They're all watching you because you can do whatever the hell you like." She turned back to face him. "And in that respect, a great majority of people in here just want to be you."

She smirked at him, then pushed him gently back. "Very nice of you to say. But I find that rather difficult to believe, all things considered."

"Why? I don't know who people in my own building are, and I still know who you are. You must have made a big impression for me to know that much."

"Yes." She sighed and shook her head despondently. "Big impression, all right. The bloody laughing stock of the division!"

"What do you mean?"

She looked at him for a minute. Their dancing slowed. The song faded. She released him and scratched her cheek, never once taking her eyes off him. "You really don't know, do you?"

"Know what?"

The next song started, a faster one. "Anything about me."

"I told you, I'm just the IT guy."

Beatrice flicked a curl of hair by the cheek she had been scratching and jiggled her hips in time with the song. She sharply exhaled and grinned with incredibly white teeth before grabbing him. "I love this song! Come on!"

In the moment, he had completely forgotten about Sarah Bliss as this vibrant, charming woman he had no business being with put everyone to shame with her practised dance moves. She even managed to coordinate his movement to look anything but cumbersome. For that moment, he felt truly happy.

The couple smiled at each other; Beatrice giggled hard and nudged him playfully.

How quickly his joy was taken away from him. The two people who had not been paying attention to him, one of whom being the reason he had even turned up, managed to miss his finest hour. And worse, he could see Sarah gripping that slick-looking fool tightly around the neck, pulling him slowly in . . . kissing him!

"No!"

The DJ quickly selected the next song, but Sarah broke the embrace to glare furiously back.

"How could you?" He shook his head at her. Trembling with a rage, he confronted the couple.

"How could I what?" Sarah's red face contorted the mask of beauty. "What do you think you're doing, you—you weirdo! Stop stalking me!"

"But I-I'm not—"

"Don't think I haven't seen you, hovering around, saying you're fixing things that have sod-all wrong with them, just so you can look up my skirt!"

Thomas gasped in protest. "I'd *never* do that!"

Sarah proceeded without a hint of mercy. "You make my skin crawl. Just piss off, okay?"

He had become rooted to the spot, utterly defeated by her words. "Since when did I—?"

"Since always," she snarled venomously. "I only talked to you because I thought you were someone important."

"Like this chap?" He didn't know whether to break down in tears or to slap her for publically destroying him.

"*This*—this is Robert Grayson. You might know his father?"

He did. Michael Grayson. One of the 'Big Three' company bosses.

She held up her left hand and brandished an engagement ring.

Robert spoke, "You should probably shuffle off back where you came from, little man, while you still have a basement to hide in."

Thomas took a step back. Robert strode closer, arrogant. "Actually, I think it's best that you clear your desk and don't show up again. It won't be too comfortable for you around here from now on." From Thomas, he shot a disdainful look at Beatrice, who met him glare for glare. He retrained his gaze at Thomas.

Beatrice barged forward. She glared daggers at the pair offending Thomas. "And if you want to continue making yourselves look like prize idiots, I would suggest *you* shuffle off somewhere nobody will accidentally find you. Because if it's *me* you come across after tonight's performance, I'll have *you* replaced by the morning. Don't bang your worthless backsides on the door on the way out."

Thomas grinned.

Robert sheepishly retreated back to Sarah, and the pair of them exited hastily. Thomas looked back over at Beatrice in awe. He smiled gratefully. She smiled back with more warmth than he had received from anyone before. She tapped the top of his hand and spoke again. "I would like to go somewhere else now. I can't take much more of this circus. Come on."

Though a straightforward request, he could have said no. But he had no reason to. They took their leave, their captive audience dissecting their every move. He felt relieved to climb into her car, an expensive Mercedes two-seater.

~ ⭑ ~

"This isn't a hotel," he said. He looked up in awe as they stopped outside a massive house illuminated with spot-lit areas of green neon and a front garden containing a lavish kidney-shaped pond. The dry, warm night lent well toward showcasing the place. A pebbled pathway led them right to the front entry.

Beatrice grinned at him playfully and lifted the keys from her designer leather handbag. The door swung back to reveal more lavish accoutrements in a marble-floored corridor. An array of shoes lay underneath a side table in a small rack, and he removed his own out of courtesy and placed them with the others. A maid took his jacket as he followed Beatrice into the vast lounge, strewn with fur rugs, in which various portraits hung, including of one of the lady herself.

"I suppose coffee would be customary at this stage." She flicked herself free of her own shoes and threw her coat at her waiting staff. "Don't much care for the stuff myself, but I have several varieties, if you so wish?"

"No, thank you." A brisk, nervous response. "I don't mean to be rude, but what are we doing here?"

"Would you rather have gone on to a club?" Not a hint of being ruffled. "You were about the only person in there I've had a proper conversation with all day. I wanted to continue it."

Thomas found it very much the right answer. "Well, okay then!"

She met his enthusiastic response with a mischievous grin, and within a short time, they had worked their way through a bottle of fine red wine. Her station did not matter to either of them. They were simply two ordinary people wanting to connect, and just now, to each other would do.

Hours passed; stories and jokes were exchanged—mostly from Beatrice. Thomas found himself more at ease than usual, but he lacked decent anecdotes about his life. By the end of the second bottle of wine, she had fallen on his lap in raucous laughter over, of all things, the tale of her marriage.

He had finally plucked up the Dutch courage to ask her whether she was married, and she answered him after a slight pause. "Yes—yes, I'm on my second now. The first husband—that didn't work out so well. Mostly, I'm married to the job!"

"And how's that going for you?"

"Well, up until the last few weeks, very well, indeed. But it's been a little on the rocks lately. Say, you really *haven't* heard, have you?"

"Heard what?"

"You need to step out of the basement sometimes, Thomas. I'm disappointed—yet heartened—that you haven't heard. They want me *out*. I mean, *really* want me to go."

"Who's *they*?"

"Most of the directorate, actually. It's not just the fact my ex-husband is on it; the rest of the politics are turning sour, too. Basically, I've had it there."

"That's terrible." He paused, considering whether his next words would be well-received or hasten his request for a taxi. "So just like me after tonight's performance, eh?"

She guffawed as she toppled into his lap in an uncontrollable fit. He joined her jocularity, and when they ran out of breath some time later, they stared at each other through water-filled eyes.

"Got something to show you!" she announced. Beatrice propelled herself upright and grabbed his hand. "Come on!"

They staggered up the stairs. As they arrived at a door, he almost fell through it.

Thomas found himself in a vast, immaculately white bedroom, contrasted by the polished wooden floor. Two sets of drawers flanked each side of a king-sized bed draped in silk. The minimalistic design left him wondering what she wanted to show him. Beatrice dragged him around to the right-hand side of the bed, pointing to the top drawer. "Open it! Go on!"

Nothing could have prepared him for what he saw.

"It's . . . it's absolutely . . ."

"I know! Isn't it fabulous? I treated myself to it at an auction." She jumped up and down like a teenager, but the sight before him would have had that effect upon many people. The drawer contained a magnificent piece of jewellery, the like of which he had never seen—at least, not in person.

Slowly and carefully, he picked up its flat tray to gaze upon the full glory up close. The main body drew his eye: a giant, lovingly cut sapphire in the shape of a teardrop, glowing within a cage of silver gauze with a fang-like bottom.

Beautiful as it was, it resonated with an eerie . . . *something*—perhaps the cold, blue glow that seemed to emanate from it, or the way it almost seemed to suck the light out of its little blue corner. Yet this unique effect made it more alluring, and he understood why Beatrice would think he might want to see it.

He could see that the fang was extremely sharp. When he removed the necklace from its housing and held it up, the fang looked potentially painful to wear around the neck. The design made little sense, but the jewel was far too wondrous to question.

Thomas considered how special it must have felt to wear it. However, what honoured him most was the trust Beatrice expressed in showing him such a valuable treasure. It better suited an A-list celebrity than a troubled company director.

Then he felt smooth, delicate hands slip around his waist from behind and slowly wrap themselves around him. Beatrice pushed herself against him, leaning against his ear to whisper, "So . . . do you think it'll suit me?"

He turned to answer her, and her hands shifted up to his neck and pulled his head down to hers. She pressed her lips softly to his. She thrust her tongue into his mouth and ran fingernails lightly through his hair.

He had never experienced such a pleasurable sensation before. His wildest dreams scarcely touched it when he envisioned what he might one day do with Sarah Bliss. During that moment, he let Sarah go and allowed Beatrice to carry him beyond his fantasies. And for that moment, on that night, he had everything he could ever wish for.

And was about to get much, much more.

~ * ~

Thomas leaned over and smiled. It was going to be different now, better. He could forget all about that horrid woman and get on with his new life. It was almost as if he could hear her agreeing with him—only she was not.

"You're so much better off with *me*, you know."

"Yes, I—"

That voice! He shook himself from his semi-conscious state to see with his own eyes.

"*Sarah*! How did you—"

The willowy blonde slid over and rubbed his shoulders like some form of heavenly massage. Her eyes glowed as sapphire as the gem she wore—the very same one that had been left by Beatrice's bedside. Larger than life wearing the jewel, it seemed that the tall, gorgeous lady and the necklace were made for one another.

Glorious in her long, flowing white dress, she dazzled but engulfed him. Small gold threads caught the light. Her facial features seemed more angular than usual, though. The look she gave him, though alluring and determined, carried an authority which he had not previously seen in her.

She eased her face into the slightest of smiles and moved her hands up from his shoulders, slowly to his neck, and eventually, the backs of her fingers stroked his cheeks. The lightest of nudges directed his gaze to her eyes.

Beatrice was nowhere to be seen. The space upon which she once lay was smothered in white, but he couldn't tell whether the duvet or the dress concealed her. He scrambled across the bed to check, but found himself simply shifting about masses of silk. Sarah's soft but firm hands grasped his own and pulled him to her.

"Hey, it was *always* me you wanted, remember?"

"Where is she?"

"What do you care?" She smiled. "I can save you, you know. I'm the only one who can."

"From what?" He scanned the room, searching for Beatrice, but again felt Sarah's strong grip drawing his attention back to her.

"From *yourself*. From . . . *repercussions*. It is too late for her now."

"What do you mean?"

Sarah's smile mutated into a predatory grin.

"She's dead. When you wake up beside her, you'll see. And everyone will think you did it."

"I'm dreaming."

"Yes, you are. But when you wake up, she'll still be dead."

"No, no, no! I'm going to wake up now. This is wrong."

"You'll see. And you'll *know*. Nobody will be able to help you but *me*. And if you want to get through this, bring me the necklace. You'll need me to survive." She gave a playful giggle. "And it looks so very much better on me, don't you think?"

"Stop this! It's not funny!" He tore at the bed, desperate to uncover Beatrice. However, the more he floundered, the more flowing white silk surrounded him, until it wrapped around and pinned him still. Sarah brushed a hand against his face and comforted him until he calmed a little.

"You know what to do if you want to save yourself." She leaned forward to kiss him on the forehead, and with that, the very silk that he battled swirled all around him until all he could see was brilliant white.

He never should have stayed the night.

~ ✱ ~

The dream had been disturbing enough to wake him. But, in looking to his left, he found only Beatrice. He rolled over to kiss her on the cheek. She was cold to the touch. Thomas shot upright and stared at her. She didn't move—didn't breathe. She was *so very pale*.

Just as he had been told by Sarah in his dream. Beatrice was dead.

He recoiled from the bed, sheer shock catapulting him into motion.

The door to the room was closed. Nothing was out of place, nothing stolen, nothing moved, nothing added. What had happened to her? Nothing he could see made any sense.

It had been just as Sarah had told him in his dream. The singing of the birds sounded amplified that day; it was all he could hear against the silent screams from the body next to him. The expression on her face belied any peace. Even in death he could see her pain, her anguish, her misery—and it was everything he *thought* he had dreamed.

Dream Sarah was right. He had nowhere to go. After the performance at the party, who would believe him now? Everyone thought he was going to do something like this, and now, by all appearances, he had.

Bring me the necklace.

You'll need me to survive.

The words from the dream echoed loud and clear above the tumult of fear in his head. Sarah could help him. She was the only one who could. He needed to find her again. The sound of police sirens in the distance reminded him of the urgency of the situation. The first order of business became escape, concealment, and delivering the necklace where it insisted it belonged.

He located Sarah's flat easily enough. She and that fool, Robert, were far too busy with each other to notice him behind them as they made their way back from work. Thomas realised Grayson posed a serious threat. But he could handle that corporate scumbag. He would have to . . . he could not run forever.

He chose that evening to return to Sarah's flat. He banged on the door. She was waiting for him, after all—or, at least so she said when she swung the door wide. However, the look of terror on her face at the sight of the hooded man on her threshold suggested that she was not expecting *him*.

"Thomas! What—what are you doing here?" She tried uselessly to shut her door. She backed away as he advanced.

"I've got a present for you. Here." He thrust out the case and opened it to display the necklace.

"Where did you get that?" Awe mixed with dread in her eyes.

"Well, you *asked* for it."

"Oh my God," Sarah almost squeaked. "What is *wrong* with you? I'm calling the police!"

"But . . . you . . ."

Thomas despaired as she edged toward the phone. He had to get to it before she dialled. A short sprint and brute force accomplished it. She mattered only in respect to his own peril. Blind to her panic, he forced her back into the lounge area, settled her by the coffee table, and lifted the necklace out of the box.

"Here. It's for you, just like you said in the dream!"

"*What* dream?" she squealed, her eyes wide with fright. "You . . . you're insane! Just like they said!"

She clawed at his wrist to pull herself free, but he maintained his grip, insensible of the pain.

"No! You don't understand. I didn't kill her—I—"

He attempted to place the necklace on her, but she fought as if for her life. But he *had* to see it through; there was no other way. He wouldn't have a chance in hell of surviving prison.

Sarah writhed and struggled against his attempts to restrain her. Her bite on his arm spurred a yelp of pain and a rush of anger. A back-hand to her face sent her toppling over the coffee table.

That wasn't him. He wasn't that kind of man. She just didn't understand what was at stake.

"Please! Stop fighting me! This is *yours*!"

He scrambled to where she fell and opened the necklace, distracted from the woman herself. Sarah swung a heavy onyx cat ornament hard into his stomach. Her dead-on strike to his groin brought him to his knees.

The attack almost incapacitated him. He bled from his mouth. However, he reached down to the floor once more for the necklace and held it loosely in his right hand, staring at the sapphire.

As Sarah struggled to her feet, he snagged the top of her ankle and sent her sprawling. She hauled herself upright by the table and made for the front door, but he pushed it into her path and knocked her knee so hard she collapsed.

She attempted to crawl away, but Thomas had caught enough breath to rise to his feet. "Look," he insisted. "I'm trying to *help* you, for pity's sake!"

Limping over to her, he got the necklace around her neck and tried to secure it. She still fought him, teeth and nails sinking into his bleeding hands. However, he was resolved, and around it went.

Thomas trapped his fingers between the chain and her neck as he latched the clasp and could not extricate them. The delicate chain tightened suddenly into an iron grip. He pulled, attempting to free his fingers, but it only tightened more. Sarah gurgled, thrashed, and pulled at his trapped hands, but both their efforts were useless. After several seconds, she relaxed, freeing him. He could feel the fury within him subside. All that remained was dull throbbing from the injuries he had sustained. She slumped to the floor.

"Sarah?"

He leaned forward to lift her from the head up. There was no life to the body; the heavy head flopped about unless manipulated by his hands.

"Oh God, no. Not again!"

In desperation, he shook her shoulders, but to no avail. Finally, he lifted her halfway to her feet. The body exploded back into movement. A tremendous force catapulted him through an unopened door.

He landed awkwardly, barely conscious, on the bathroom floor. Blood and wood surrounded him. His left leg was bent in an unnatural way, bone protruding from the knee. A sudden sense of his own mortality hit him.

He couldn't tell whether the injuries or the regret he carried caused him the greater pain. He stared up at the ceiling through blurry eyes as heavy-heeled feet approached slowly. Sarah stopped as she reached him. The necklace nestled with elegance against her heavenly body. She loomed over him with the same contemptuous glare she had given him at the party.

Yet she looked different from that angle. Clothing damage and chaotic hair aside, she showed no wounds, no other signs of the altercation—perhaps she appeared a touch pale.

Resigned to his fate, he slumped against the wall, exhausted. He closed his eyes and waited for the inevitable to happen.

It never did.

"Pathetic. Utterly pathetic."

He tried to respond, and all he could manage was a bloody cough.

"But," Sarah added—and it was only now that he realised that there was something distorted about her voice—"as you have been good, I will let you stay with me." He could not quite put his finger on it, but she sounded younger.

"*H-how* . . . ?" he mouthed without breath to voice the words.

She had no interest in conversation. Rather, she held his injured leg and shoved the bone back into his knee. He howled in pain, which her touch only augmented. A crippling cold from her hands accompanied the popping sound. But the bone held, reconnected. His broken skin regenerated.

She pulled hard at both of his arms, which felt as if she was ripping them off, then repeated the process with his legs. Despite the excruciating pain, none of it compared to the torment he felt when she somehow forced one of her hands down his throat. His insides burned from whatever she did. It seemed to go on for hours—like it would never end.

And from that day it did not.

But he grew in size, stature, power, and resilience. Nobody would humiliate him or make him feel small ever again.

From the moment she released him, he had an instinctive understanding of what he needed to do to ease the perpetual torture.

She dragged him, still debilitated from the pain, to a mirror. "I told you I would help you," she hissed. "See? No one will find you. No one will know you. Just me. Just *us*."

She was right about that. She forced him to gaze upon the horrid distortion of what he had once been: his hair greasy, patchy, and falling out in clumps; his face deformed by muscle, jutted jawbone, and animalistic teeth.

He stretched almost a foot taller than he had been, yet rippling with impossible new muscle. Within his eyes, he could see the faintest spark of Thomas Barber trapped inside this new body—this instrument of violence and torture.

Nobody else would see that spark again.

He let out a deafening bellow and destroyed whatever remained of the bathroom in a flood of tears. She stood and watched him do so until he exhausted himself. Then she went to him, took him into her arms like a lost child, and stroked the back of his head.

He had nothing left in his life but to ease his own suffering. To do that, he would serve her.

Thus, Thomas Barber died.

~ ✲ ~

Sarah Bliss. She . . . it . . . *they* . . . continued to wear her soulless body without the slightest regard for him. He would *never* be allowed to forget. They cared nothing for Sarah's appearance either. They never truly knew her, after all—only what she was to him. So every day, for six months now and counting, he watched her gradually deteriorate into a shambolic mockery of a beautiful woman. And every time he believed he had met all of the many personalities that came with her, he met another.

Of all the beings possessing Sarah's flesh, he heard the youngest voice the loudest, the most often, and he had become aware that it intentionally chose Sarah's body as a vessel. Whatever that voice's original form, the living Sarah best resembled its image of itself after all that time. How much time that was remained unclear—who or what these presences were defied his understanding.

He *knew* two things: the childlike voice called herself Violet. To gain respite from the constant agony he endured, he must inflict it upon others.

Beyond that, he no longer cared.

He followed as she hunted. He cleaned up after her each and every time, disposing of bodies as she killed with reckless abandon. But she was after someone specific. He did not know who, nor dared he ask. Then he discovered his target was called Rose—young, guilty of nothing, her entire life in front of her. He thought he had completed his task.

But he had failed. Twice.

They sat in the back of a random victim's car under circumstances neither he nor Sarah Bliss could have ever imagined. The driver certainly hadn't seen it coming.

"Why is she not dead?" Violet demanded.

The protesting driver shut her mouth and turned toward them with wide eyes. She blinked. Then, without a word, she turned back and reached forward for her door handle. From her place in the back, Violet seized the driver before she could escape, pulled her back, gagged her with one hand, and pinned her to the headrest.

Unruffled, she turned her demanding gaze to Thomas.

Thomas bowed his head. "Don't know," he mumbled. "Someone new came along. Really tough."

"She *was*," Violet said. "I saw her. I should have waited for *her* instead." She ignored the driver's resistance but looked distracted nonetheless. "Something special about her . . . I've never seen—" She addressed neither occupant. "I shall go after her and feed! No! Tally's friend first!" After a moment, she turned to Thomas. "Get Rose."

She then focused on the driver, leaning forward to peer at her closely. She attempted to smile sweetly. Both the driver and Thomas cringed.

"What is your name?" she asked delicately, moving her hand from her mouth to her shoulder.

"What? Get out of the car or I'm calling the police!"

Violet turned to Thomas, shrieking hysterically. "She's not listening! Why won't she listen?"

"Right. That's it! I'm—"

With lightning speed and crushing force, Violet choked her. "What is your name?" The driver struggled uselessly.

"She can't answer if she can't breathe," Thomas interjected.

Violet's empty eyes looked at him quizzically before easing her grip on the woman.

"What is your name?"

"Natalie," the driver gurgled.

"*Natalie . . .*" Violet repeated dreamily. She released her grasp and beamed at the driver with a childlike grin. "*You* won't leave me, will you?"

Thomas gulped, wondering if his tenure was about to be terminated. Natalie again lunged for the door handle but to no avail.

Violet snarled and tapped the necklace she wore. The jewel glistened and within seconds, a heavy shadow bore down on the car. Violet gave an excited squeal. "Stay there, Natalie. You're my friend! Not like *him*. Funny, horrible man!"

She shoved a knee-high boot into his chest. His mouth opened briefly, but no sound came from it, and it closed just as fast.

Natalie wriggled hard, but Violet's spare hand smacked a fist-sized dent into the roof. "Stay still!" she commanded. Natalie cowered and whimpered, staring at the fresh dent. Violet then lashed a swift kick straight into Thomas's face. She pinned him once more with her heel.

"I made you *really* strong!" Violet wailed at him. "How did she beat you??"

"She was really strong, as well!" he protested. He rubbed the blood off his face. "And quick, too! I couldn't catch her half the time. It was like—"

A stiletto heel hoofed into his ribs three times. He started sobbing. "I don't care, I don't care, *I don't care!*" she screamed. "You failed! *Twice* now!!"

"I didn't mean to!" he protested. "I'm sorry! I'm sorry!!"

"I should get rid of you!" she said, ripping at her hair. "I bet *Natalie* would get her!"

The giant shook his head frantically. "Don't! Please!"

She gave a girlish giggle, and then suddenly stopped. "Silly little man! You shall have to get them *both* for me now!"

"But how?" He ducked away from her, expecting further punishment, but instead she gave another excited squeal. She jerked Natalie backwards with one hand and retracted her leg from Thomas. "With help, of course."

Thomas watched as Violet moved both hands onto the driver's shoulders, closed her eyes, and whispered into Natalie's ear. The young woman jumped suddenly and attempted to cry out, but Thomas knew she was in serious trouble: inescapable hands colder than freezing metal. Natalie was going nowhere.

The poor woman managed a partial twitch but beyond that was completely paralysed, more so as the fingers on the creature's hands extended, needle-like, boring deep into her victim's flesh.

Next followed the endless, searing agony—that contorted face of the silent scream. Natalie's eyes rolled downward, where she could see the rest for herself: the veins on her arms darkened, protruded, and looked ready to burst out; the colour drained from her skin by the second. She tensed; the muscle spasms and tearing began. But Violet went further. One small trickle of almost black blood fell from Natalie's lip before she stopped twitching altogether.

Violet retracted her bony appendages from Natalie's shoulders, and the body slumped forward. She reclined back into the seat with a satisfied grin. "Mmm . . ." she said, dabbing her tongue against icy blue lips. "Yummy."

Thomas had curled himself into a ball in the opposite corner of the car. He trembled as the tall blonde stretched like a yawning cat. She refocused her attention on him. She chuckled, then sprang into the front seat and looked down at the corpse. She snapped her fingers impatiently. "*Rise.*"

On her command, the body reanimated. It lifted itself upright with no less mobility than it had in life. It wore a blank, glazed expression as it turned and faced its new mistress, who pointed her back to the steering wheel.

"Yay!"

His mistress applauded, pleased with herself, before suddenly dropping her excited smile and lunging at Thomas. She seized his nearest arm. His skin began to burn, and his eyes forced themselves shut through the excruciating pain she inflicted. As his strength gave out entirely, she released him and let him sink into the seat.

He whimpered. She slapped him in the face and pulled him right up to her. "Now," she said, waiting until he opened his eyes again. "Last chance. Okay?"

He nodded quickly, but she turned away from him. "Natalie?"

The corpse in front of her animated its head forward and back in acknowledgement.

"Help him. And if he fails again, do tell me." With that, she exited the car and shut the door, striding purposefully towards a crowd of bystanders and police staff.

"She's still hungry, isn't she?" Thomas said to his new companion, who stared straight at him. "God help them."

CHAPTER FOUR

Their escape from the hospital mayhem provided Rose and Jennifer a much-needed break. Conversation was limited; both took time to recuperate.

Rose sweated profusely in the summer heat, the vehicle's air conditioner broken. Jennifer, somehow, looked as cool as an autumn breeze.

"How do you do that?" Rose asked.

"Deep breaths and a calm environment," Jennifer replied. "You've some pretty impressive party tricks, yourself; though you still freak me out."

"Join the club. Right now, I freak me out, too."

It didn't take long to reach Jennifer's place. With the windows opened, it felt much cooler inside, the majority of sunlight hitting the other side of the house. A tall glass of fruit smoothie was thrust into Rose's hands as she sat in the front room. She brought Jennifer up-to-date on everything she knew about her ordeal—the Underground station attack, the dream, Tally.

"Any time before that," Rose said, looking lost, "there are gaps. Big ones." She took a shaky sip of her drink.

"Take your time." Jennifer sat back and relaxed.

Rose frowned. "I don't think it would matter if I thought about it all day," she said. "It just— it doesn't feel like it's *there*. None of it. Jeez, I don't even know where this 'Rose' name came from, but it isn't right."

"So what do you want to do about it?"

"Well, what *can* I do? The best lead I've got is this necklace I don't think I've seen before in my life."

Jennifer nodded. "Sounds like our best shot, then. But first, we get you fed and cleaned up. What do you say?"

"Best plan I've heard all day."

The midday bath provided an hour of bliss after what had seemed like a lifetime of hell. The pronounced veins had receded, no longer black. Although her skin was still looking pale, it was no longer deathly so. This seemed to be her natural complexion. The troubles of the day mostly washed away with the dirt on her feet and lower legs.

Relieved of that awful hospital gown, she threw on the clothes laid out on the bed for her: a neutral set of black jeans and a plain white T-shirt that looked too small to have been Jennifer's. But, given her recent appearance alterations, Rose assumed nothing. Thoughts of more elegant, old-fashioned clothing looped over and over in her mind and, try as she might, she could not shake them. That didn't feel like *her* style, though.

"The spare room's free for as long as you need it," Jennifer told her reassuringly. "The clothes are Kara's, but I'm sure she'll understand. Reckon you might be here a while."

"We'll see," she said.

Jennifer snorted. "This is her house. She's—what does she call it? A parapsychologist at University College London. I'll let her tell you all about it when she turns up, but we're . . . kind of her field."

Jennifer showed her to more of a closet than a bedroom, cramped, but warm of ambience. Scented candles on a mirrored dressing table produced deeply soothing floral fragrances. Soft white fairy lights contrasted beautifully against the dark blue wallpaper.

A small bedside desk left little room for anything else.

She left the miniature sanctuary and headed downstairs. Jennifer's combative poise and forceful presence had disappeared entirely, replaced by elegant deportment and a kindly, almost maternal temperament.

Jennifer's flowery summer dress complemented her smile, as warm as the season itself. Jennifer waved an offering hand toward an array of fruits, cakes, and liquid refreshment on a small table.

Rose flopped onto a soft seat, piling a small plate high with cakes before Jennifer joined her. Cup of fruit tea in hand, she focused unequivocally on her guest. "Now that you're comfortable, I have some proper questions for you."

Rose sniggered. "Thought you might."

Jennifer smiled. "I'll start with the big ones, shall I?" She took a sip of her fruit infusion. "Who was I fighting, and why are people trying to kill you?"

Rose gave a shrug. "Wish I knew," she said, mouth crammed full of chocolate brownie. "Truly."

She paused to finish eating, the relatively large cake not standing a chance against a seriously worked-up appetite. "What's *your* story, Supergirl?"

"I run a stall."

"You run a stall," Rose repeated.

"I run a stall. In addition to being Kara's lab rat—I mean, *research assistant*."

"Yeah, okay, smartarse." She shoved the next cake into her mouth.

"I meant regarding your ability to wrestle bears one-handed whilst taking on Bruce Lee in a fist fight."

Jennifer gave a dismissive roll of her eyes. "I know what you meant."

She pondered for a moment and answered. "You know, I went to the hospital today to check out your story. Kara got fixated on some high-profile suspicious death several months back that remains unsolved. It was a long shot, but the second I heard the words, 'exceptionally pale' I thought I'd get down here and look into it. If there was nothing to report, then great. But it turns out there's plenty. I've never met anyone like you, or that monster guy. Ever. I'd love to know more about this 'Tally,' and I'll bet my life Kara would, too."

"You were saying something about us being 'Kara's field'?"

"She took me in a couple of years back when I was going through a bit of a rough time. I'm like a continuous thesis project for her, and she's the only good friend I really have."

The prospect of becoming a guinea pig for anyone unsettled Rose, although it was still a step up from murder attempts. "Yeah, about that," she started nervously, "I may have mentioned that I can't remember much. That includes where I live." She shook her head to snap out of self-pity and looked up at Jennifer, the patience of angels on her new friend's face. She took another sip of the smoothie. "So tell me more about Kara, then."

Jennifer grinned, finished her tea, and sat up. "She helped me understand and control my—gift."

"Really?" Rose perked up, optimistic. "You mean to say, she might know something about what's happening with me?"

"I'm not sure, but she did with me. I discovered some of this *unusual talent* when I was quite young. Not out of choice." Jennifer's face darkened. She gulped to steel herself enough to continue. "Stepmother—tried to kill me."

"*Shit!*" Rose said, raising hands to her open mouth. "What happened?"

Her question was heard but not answered. Rose decided not to press.

"So . . . you can just wish things into happening?" she asked, changing the subject.

"I wondered that myself, first of all," Jennifer replied. "But no, not really."

"Do you suppose we come from the same kind of thing, you and I?"

Jennifer considered her response very carefully. "Not the same," she said, tapping her fingers against the plate. "No."

"Why do you say that?" She took another swig.

Jennifer frowned. "Whatever it is you have is . . . different. Completely different." She took a small pause. Rose could see she carefully chose her words. "I'll be honest, it's pretty creepy."

"Well, *thanks!*" The sudden bitterness and contempt in Rose's voice took her by surprise. As she uttered the words, Jennifer shuffled backward in her seat nervously.

"See?" Jennifer said, straightening herself in the chair. "This is *exactly* what I'm talking about!"

Rose slammed her glass down on the desk, stood up, and marched towards the door. "Tell you what: I'll just take my creepy self and piss off, shall I?"

As she stood to leave, Jennifer rapidly closed the gap between them and with a deceptively strong grip, took Rose's arm. "Wait, I didn't mean any offence. It's just—"

Rose spun around. "It's just *what?*" she snarled. Jennifer released her grip and took a step back. They faced off in an uncomfortable silence.

"Look, I know better than most what you must be going through," Jennifer ventured. "What if I told you that just by looking at them, I can also tell when people are healthy, sick, or even dying, sometimes before even *they* know?"

Startled by her sudden surge of anger, Rose met her friend's gaze and relaxed her shoulders a little. "Before today, I'd have said you were bloody mad. But given that I've seen you leap out of a high-rise, I believe you." She tapped her foot on the floor awkwardly, looking sheepish. "That must be bloody hard to deal with."

Jennifer rolled her eyes. "You either learn to cope or end up mad."

Rose returned to her chair and sat back down. "Yeah, I suppose." Still hungry, she attacked another muffin. "So what do you see when you look at me? Seems whatever it is freaks you out."

Her host frowned. "This is the thing," she said. "You actually appear perfectly healthy, but at the same time, your—" She returned to her seat, hovered over it, and bit her lip, pensive. "I want a better word, but I haven't got one. I've never seen an *aura* like yours before. I don't know how to tell you more, other than it's kind of unnerving."

"Yeah, I *get* that part," Rose said impatiently. "Give it your best shot. You're all I have right now."

Jennifer sighed and took a deep breath. "Well, it's like you're positively glowing with health, but not in a *real* way. Like, you're one of the healthiest people I've ever seen, but I'm just seeing a mask. The real *you* is really well-hidden, somehow."

Rose looked at the nearest wall and said nothing for almost a minute. She looked back at Jennifer contritely. "Sorry for giving you such a hard time. But, well, to say this whole business has put the shits up me is a colossal understatement."

"No harm done," Jennifer reassured her. "Anyway, Kara will be able to tell you a whole lot more about it, I'm sure." She perched herself on the edge of the seat.

"So," Rose reached for her glass once more, tilted her head back, and finished the contents. "She *sees* things, as well?"

"Not the way I do, no." Jennifer slurped down the rest of her drink and placed the cup on a nearby coffee table. "But she talks about things that I can't even pretend to understand. It helped a lot."

They sat in silence for a time; both reflected on their day, and their unusual lives to that point. Jennifer broke the silence. "The man chasing you," she said, "he certainly wasn't normal, but surely if he *could* have killed us both like that, he would have, right?"

"How do we know he didn't try?" Rose tapped at the now normal-looking veins on the bottom of her right arm. "Something was done to me, and he's Suspect Number One at the moment."

"Suspect Number Only, really."

"Yeah."

"So do you know anything more on the news story? What are they saying about those two?"

"They passed it off as some sort of mystery disease. Might have been why press buzzed the place. Seems a bit stupid to me, but being stopped by the police would still have been a bad idea. Of course, now they have the murder of a doctor and a nurse to deal with, too. Some madman's on a rampage."

~ ✱ ~

Rose looked in the bathroom mirror, the first real opportunity she had that day to take a good, long, hard look at herself. To see if anything triggered her memory.

She stood a little over five feet, six inches from guesswork, and considered herself a touch scrawny, but attributed that to recent exploits. Her skin tone provided an alluring contrast against her facial features; her lips, a stand-out shade of plum, worked a treat alongside her new hair.

Now that she had washed it, it looked healthier—a silky raven black that complemented her pallor. She shrugged; the silver must have been a symptom of her strange wounds, just like the veins. Brushing it brought order back to the previously chaotic strands.

As she stroked it, she noticed that the deep tones of her irises were something of an anomaly to the faded tones elsewhere. Furthermore, they were incongruent unto themselves.

They were bright blue when she had first looked, but whether by a trick of the light or simply an initial misjudgement, they had faded, darkened. As she stared, the room descended into shadow, unsettling her. She wanted to look away, but did not dare. Besides, it was only her reflection.

Jitters grew into cold despair.

Miserable thoughts entered her mind. Nobody was coming to rescue her; death was coming for her again, this time more slowly, more painfully.

"Why am I even thinking this?" she asked, blinking once, twice—enough to break her staring duel against the reflection and her sudden fit of despondency. However, she realized why the police—why Jennifer—had reacted as they had.

She could see it for herself. Whether it was beautiful or terrifying, she was unsure. Yet she stared again, entranced by the duality of sensations, which intensified. She gave a wide-mouthed smile—a triumphant leer, a sense of raw power.

Nothing will stop me.

I am master of all of this darkness.

The door slammed shut, taken by a sudden gust of wind. The lighting in the windowless room shuddered with the familiar, chilling breeze, negating all the progress she had made brushing her hair.

She sensed an additional presence in the room and spun around. Nobody. She shrugged and picked up the brush to finish the job.

Finished, she made for the door, but felt a repeated light pressure on her right shoulder, like someone had tapped her. She leapt back with a start.

The room grew shadowed—some parts pitch black, others resembling moonlight shining in. Impossible, given the lack of windows. She touched what had once been solid objects, the bathroom sink being the nearest. It felt no more solid than the featureless faces she had passed her hands through earlier that day. A whiff of lavender rushed up her nose.

Another gust, strong enough to make her stagger. She reached out to grasp the sink—curiously, this time, solid enough to break her fall.

"Jennifer?" she called out. "Jen?"

Her cries echoed and faded, consumed by the fierce, howling storm within the confines of the bathroom. A high-pitched screech descended into a low, heavy drone, followed by distant rumbling.

A dense mist gathered, obscuring her vision. The remaining shades of light in the room faded out until she could see nothing besides the mirror beyond her hands.

Within the mirror, she saw a small pinprick of brightness grow with each second. Two parallel lights merged, the sudden light blinding.

She turned away—just in time to feel another tap on the shoulder. The light dissipated.

"Jennifer?"

"No, dear." Another voice, at last, and the familiar face from her comatose dream.

The woman stood in front of Rose, dark, curly hair and billowing black dress all oddly visible, even in shade. Sapphire-blue eyes stood out most prominent.

The visitor looked surprised. A civil but less-than-warm smile crept onto her lips.

"How did you get back here so soon? You—"

"Tally?" Rose asked, bewildered.

"With that level of observation, your quest will be a rather short one," Tally responded icily. "How did you summon me, exactly?"

Rose scratched her head and blinked several times. "I wish I knew. I'm sure I haven't dozed off again, and as far as I can tell, I haven't taken any strange pills, eaten anything labelled, 'Eat Me,' or inhaled anything that wasn't air freshener. *And* I've had some chill time. So why am I seeing this shit?"

The light level increased, and with it the colour; the obscuring fog faded to nothing. Tally remained elegant and aloof. Rose sniffed hard, identifying that the lavender emanated from Tally. She pinched at the flowing dress, feeling its smooth velvet until the wearer slapped her hand away.

"What *are* you doing?" Tally asked her, miffed. She brushed the fresh creases on her dress and then stopped, looking down at Rose. "Oh. Oh, I see. Hmm, you seem to be growing in strength, certainly. The trouble is—so is *she.*"

"Who's '*she*'?" Rose asked. "Are you talking about Jennifer?"

"Jennifer?" Tally looked lost. "Who are you—? No, no, no. I have no idea to whom or what you are referring. It is quite right that she considers you such a grave threat."

"*Who?*" Rose asked, but before she had the chance to react further, the bathroom light flashed back to full strength, leaving her dazzled. Tally had vanished. The bathroom reverted to its original state.

"That was theatrical," Rose said to herself. "Time for more tea, I think."

CHAPTER FIVE

Tally watched a multitude of carriages pull up outside the gates of Grenshall Manor. Footmen hopped down and aided the descent of their passengers. It was an unusual number of guests, even for a Grenshall function.

Ordinarily, as heiress to the family estate, Tally was required to formally attend any such event. To have been overlooked greatly surprised her. Whilst under normal circumstances, it would have provided an unexpected opportunity to leave the house unnoticed, the snub piqued her curiosity.

None of the guests were any she had encountered at previous gatherings. The first few were clearly peers of Lord Grenshall—gentlemen's club pals and of no real interest.

She almost left, thinking they were simply reconvening. But as she turned to go, someone—most definitely not gentlemen's club material—caught her eye.

This was Lady Aurelia Raine—and her reputation preceded her. Many of Tally's peers spoke of the reclusive woman with the bearing of Queen Victoria herself—if Her Majesty wished to inspire terror in her subjects. They spoke of a chilling stare that, once seen, was never forgotten. Rumours circulated that she had cowed her now-husband into courting, and eventually into marrying her, although none would dare accuse her of it to her face.

She appeared perhaps in her thirties, with glossy raven locks, much like Tally's own, and impeccable taste with her eye-catching silver dress. She might have been considered comely, but had a dangerous look in her eyes.

She leaned forward, looking down her nose at the herd of men fawning over her, on the arm of her husband, Lord Lucas Raine. A slight man—timid, despite his station—he wore attire decades out of fashion, which lent some bulk to his otherwise diminutive frame.

A curved silver knife glistened from her open velvet reticule, ostentatious but vicious of appearance. A bright blue necklace shone in the light against her velvety skin, every bit as extravagant as the blade. They seemed of a piece, although Tally could not say why. She instantly fell in love with the sapphire.

A third figure accompanied the Raines to the soiree; most of the attendees gave him a wide berth. Towering over all the others, the thin male veiled himself within a grey cloak. A hood obscured his face with shadow. The serving staff displayed an unusual dent in their composure, polite and nervous attendance shifting to terror-riddled subservience.

Lord Grenshall seemed immune to their strange disquiet, in keeping with his nature. "And what is your name?" he asked, staring straight into the hood.

Lady Raine answered on behalf of the stranger, meeting the host with her famous burning gaze. "He chooses not to give a name," she answered, her voice low and powerful. "But, as one held in great esteem in matters of the black arts, he is here per your request. One simply pays for his presence at a séance and is guaranteed success."

"I simply wished for conversation with my grandfather." Lord Grenshall sighed. "But if he is, as you said, *the best . . .*"

"Trust me when I say, there are none more accomplished at creating the suitable ambience we require."

So it was that Tally's usual plans were forgone this night, as Grenshall Manor promised far more entertainment. Her stealth and guile proved invaluable, for staff guarded the door, allowing none but the listed guests anywhere near the dining hall.

Despite the fuss she had made, even Lady Grenshall was forbidden from entering. Tally, watching carefully from a concealed location, observed the lesson. She retreated to her quarters, and climbed out of her window via an alternate route.

It took no effort to pry the dining hall windows open from the outside, given her considerable practice, and she slipped in without the slightest ruffle of draperies.

From her concealment, Tally saw Lady Raine standing in the centre of the arranged guests seated around her.

The hooded figure sat perfectly still as the woman demanded the attention of her audience. Lady Raine outstretched her arms and the room fell silent. Even from her distance, Tally felt an instant chill take the room—take her. Whatever else was true of her, Lady Raine possessed an unforgettable presence.

"And now, do you all give your will freely to witness one of the most powerful visitations man can behold?"

Never! Tally said to herself, grinning defiantly, but a triumphant smile appeared on Lady Raine's face as she closed her thin outstretched fingers into fists. The room fell dark, and the briefest of winds drew gasps from the guests. Through the darkness, a faint blue light radiated from the jewel at her throat.

The lighting returned to normal, and Lady Raine had the undivided attention of her crowd. In her hiding place, Tally split her attention between the display, the necklace, and the hooded figure's lack of reaction to any of it. Even *she* flinched at the impressive theatrics.

"Now, to summon our mighty guest here, you must first each look into your soul. Then, you must offer part of it as a gift for our arrival. Should there be any unprepared to do this, then they should leave this manor, and *never* speak of this to any as long as they draw breath. Are there any such faint hearts amongst you? None will speak poorly of you if you choose to depart now."

Murmurs of consideration rumbled throughout the room. However, Lord Grenshall sat firm, a show of courage amidst doubting minds. All remained in the room.

"Good." She took in a deep, slow breath, and a bitter chill washed across the room. Her next words whispered along the breeze. "Close your eyes. Keep them closed, lest you risk more than you know." The crowd did as ordered.

Tally, of course, was far too fascinated to even consider doing so. The necklace glowed a baleful blue as the conductor outstretched her fingers, from which crackling, shadowy strands of electricity slowly arced, snaking towards the other audience participants—all apart from the cloaked man.

An arc reached out to the chest of each gentleman in the room, jolting them on contact. They winced, their backs arched as far back as possible without breaking. Their chairs creaked back on rear legs, which splintered under the spasms.

Not one of them dared call out despite the evidently painful process. The electrical strand caused a pale blue glow in each victim on contact. The wisps of light travelled toward Lady Raine, swirling once around her before being absorbed into the glowing sapphire centre of the necklace. It was brief, but impossible to miss—for those looking.

The hooded figure slowly turned his head in Tally's direction and the dense, dark curtains concealing her. Her heart raced against her will. She prayed he would not get up. She remained still, holding her breath before reasoning she would have to exhale eventually.

After a moment, Lady Raine's victims exhaled loudly as they slumped back into their seats. The movement drew the attention of the hooded man, providing Tally an opportunity to escape. Another gust of wind blasted through the space. She felt a presence—perhaps more than one—affect the room, although she could see nothing.

Stage magic or not, the sensation prompted Tally to be on her way. Undetected, she escaped the way she came and for once stayed in her quarters all night.

The following day, ensuring everyone was out or otherwise occupied, Tally returned to the dining hall and examined every corner of it. Nothing was out of place. She knew where her wanderings would take her that night.

At roughly nine in the evening, just as she had so regularly before, she made her way unnoticed out of her quarters and across to Mayfair, to the primary Raine residence.

Getting inside would present an entirely different challenge. She blended in with passing crowds, watching, but her efforts did not provide any useful information. Further consideration was required away from the scene. She never returned to her favoured rooftop again; the allure of that necklace, and attempting to understand the mystique surrounding Lady Raine, became an obsession.

She could have simply requested an invitation to their residence, but what reason would she offer for such an appeal? She had never been introduced in or out of society. And she could hardly broach the subject. She didn't want it to get back to her father.

Then it hit her: perhaps the simplest way would be to gain invitation to a similar gathering?

Changing her strategy, she set about trying to find where and when her new infatuation would next appear. She went back to the streets, far away from the social circles she kept—again, discretion was paramount.

It surprised her that no one had heard of the Raines partaking in any activities within occult circles. Even though such interests had fallen out of fashion in recent years to spiritualism, the Raines kept their activities even quieter than Tally first suspected.

On the fourth night, Tally managed to acquire, through a watchful eye and quick fingers, an invitation to a less exclusive gathering near Fleet Street the following night. She purchased a black, veiled hat and dull, nondescript attire. That evening, she adopted her subtle disguise and attended.

Unfortunately, neither Lord nor Lady Raine did.

A 'Mister Blake' was the host of this gathering—one by no means exclusive to nobility, but exclusive to those with enough money to pay the considerable fee. Yet despite the elaborate trappings around the room in the hired establishment, Tally found her endeavours an extreme disappointment.

For over one-and-a-half hours, Mister Blake entertained his audience with an interesting performance, but a performance nonetheless.

It did not compare to Lady Raine's offering. The only presences in the room were those with paper invitations. Feeling robbed, she successfully located the inn at which Blake was staying, sneaked into his room, and stole back her entrance fee.

Over the course of a week, her initial objective became somewhat lost to finding another who could genuinely replicate Lady Raine's effect. Upon each occasion, she found herself continually disappointed with what she saw.

She relented and headed, in disguise, to the front entrance of the Raine residence. Some distance short of the gates, she stopped, surprised to see her father entering the front door.

Although taken aback, it was still the opportunity she had been waiting for. But, what then? Would she confront Lady Raine in front of her father? Preposterous! Would she attempt a closer look at the necklace? Tally doubted that Lady Raine would let it out of her sight. If the roles were reversed, she certainly would not.

As she pondered her next move, the tall, cloaked figure from the original séance arrived at the entrance. He wore a silver and patterned cloak, but his face remained as obscured as ever. He stopped dead just before pressing the doorbell, his head once more slowly rotating in Tally's direction.

Try as she might to avoid notice, she felt as if he knew right where to look for her. His stare continued for what seemed an age, but eventually he looked away and pressed the doorbell. He was soon ushered in.

She had to act or miss the rare opportunity presented to her. Just before the door closed, she moved quickly, taking care to lift the veil only when she reached the front of the house. She smiled before speaking. "I am here to see my father. I understand he should already be here?"

The butler looked perplexed at first, but soon nodded. "Miss Grenshall? Ah, yes. The lady is expecting you. Let me show you to the room, my lady."

"My thanks," Tally replied, wriggling ahead of him, "but that shall not be necessary." It would be better if they were not alerted to her presence just yet. "I am already late, so I believe the less fuss, the better."

"Very good, my lady." He pointed up the stairs. "They are upstairs." She replaced the veil and made her way upstairs.

She heard familiar voices coming from a salon. The conversation was heated. Curious, she pressed her ear against one half of the double doors. It leaned forward with a tiny creak.

She backed away, but, having remained unnoticed, returned to take advantage of the gap and spy on proceedings. Lady Raine glared coldly at Tally's father, who looked uncharacteristically shaken.

"Payment is no longer sufficient," the woman said with a predatory look. Her long fingers curled as if to draw him in and devour him whole. "Leave her or I shall ruin you."

"And what then?" he demanded, red-faced. "Are you going to divorce Lord Raine? Surely, that would also ruin *you*."

"Oh, *him!*" She gave a contemptuous smile. She reached to stroke his cheek, but he blocked her gesture, repulsing her several steps. She retained her smile. "I can assure you, you have no need to concern yourself about that old fool."

"You have no interest in me, and well you know it, nor I in you. It is money alone you seek, so take it as you have done!"

Lady Raine let out a cruel chuckle and closed her outstretched hand into a fist, pulling it back a few inches. Tally suddenly shivered as a blast of cold gripped the room. She clasped a hand against her mouth as she gasped for breath. Lord Grenshall clutched at his chest. His face reddened. It took every ounce of Tally's will to refrain from dashing in to help her father, but it seemed unwise at best.

Lady Raine unclenched her hand and used it to brush back her glossy hair. She stared as Lord Grenshall fell to one knee, spluttering and wheezing. She stood over him as he fought for breath.

"I have no further interest in your money," she spat, "it has financed everything I require. However, Grenshall Manor is of great interest to me, and I shall not rest until I am resident there—one way or another."

"You *know* I cannot give you that!" He struggled to his feet with the support of a nearby chair and glared at her. "My wife would never agree to it—not on her life!"

"Your wife is little more than an impediment, both to you and to the future of the Grenshall legacy. Mine is a simple enough request. *I* should be at your side, your Lady Grenshall—not here bickering with you."

"You're mad if you think I would—"

"I *think* a great many things, Lord Grenshall." She touched his cheek and he tensed, frozen. "I *know* the consequences will be considerably worse for you should you persist with your obstinacy."

Lord Grenshall wheezed. "Do not presume to threaten my life. If I was to die this night, Iris would be Lady Grenshall by the morrow."

She released her touch. "Rest assured, if I wished to simply kill you, I have been presented multiple opportunities. And besides this, you have a more *legitimate* claim to your title. One of your own blood."

"Iris is my legitimate heir. She is my family in every way."

"Save one. *Violet* is of your own seed. Her claim is stronger."

She stroked his face once more, without resistance. "I would make an excellent Lady Grenshall, you know." She kissed him slowly on the cheek and then slapped him hard. "Comply with my wishes. Your happiness and wellbeing depend upon it."

"I will have but one Lady Grenshall: *Arianna*." He touched his raw cheek, glaring. "And whatever your actions, *you* will suffer the most." He retreated towards the door. Tally drew away.

She needed an escape route. The front door was not an immediate option, as her father headed in that direction.

She took flight down the corridor, bolting towards another room with a solid and well-crafted—but most importantly, ajar—door a few yards further. She silently entered.

"You should have taken my proposal, Augustine!" echoed the threatening tones of Lady Raine in the distance. "This will end badly for you and yours!"

Tally heard the front door slam.

Something stirred behind her. She whirled around to see a small four-poster bed occupied by a sleeping young girl, disturbed by the noise. Peering from the door to check if her exit was clear, a seething Lady Raine looked down from the top of the staircase.

Tally grimaced, muttering under her breath, "Move away, you deranged—"

"Hullo?"

Perhaps it had not been under her breath after all. Behind her, a high-pitched but strong voice piped up. "Who are you? And I am not *deranged*, thank you very much!"

She turned to the girl, who sat upright and stared at her through indignant dark brown eyes as wide as saucers. Tally raised a finger to her lips and rushed to the edge of the bed, sitting down next to her. "I am sorry for waking you," she whispered, "but I was not calling *you* that."

"I heard you!" The girl's voice was no lower than last time. "You clearly said—"

"I was speaking about your servant!"

The anger was disrupted by a giggle. "Very well," the girl replied in a whisper, too, "but I still have no idea who you are. Are you a friend of Mama's?"

Tally thought quickly before answering, knowing a wrong answer could cause her any number of problems. "Yes—of a sort."

"Ah!" The girl lunged forward faster than Tally could recoil and grabbed her wrist, squeezing tightly for a short while. She looked confused at first, before suddenly letting go and sitting back, batting straggly blonde hair away from her face. "Hmm," she said, frowning. "How odd."

"What do you mean?" Tally asked, puzzled.

"If there is *anyone* up there who should not be," boomed Lady Raine's voice, "come down *this instant*! I promise things will be considerably easier upon you this way."

She looked over at the girl, grabbed her wrists, and drew her close. "Where can I hide?" she asked frantically. "I beg of you, please do not give me away!"

"Why should I help you? Are you a thief?"

"Goodness, no! I just came to look for my father. But I was not invited here."

"Who is your father?"

Tally hesitated, but forced herself to answer. "Lord Grenshall. But *please*—do not inform your mother of my presence!"

"*Lord Grenshall*?" She grinned. "I've heard of him. He has been here a lot. Mama thinks I'm asleep when he comes around, and I am sometimes, but not always." The girl leaned forward and whispered directly in Tally's ear. "He visits quite often. But they never seem happy about it."

Tally looked frantically for somewhere to hide, even as she heard the approach of Lady Raine's contingent. "Another reason not to tell on me," she said, moving away. "*Please*?"

The girl considered for a second, then nodded and smiled. "Very well, on two conditions."

"Name them!"

"Well, first of all, I get to keep your hat!"

"Fine—*here!*" She removed the hat and handed it to the girl, who placed it in the bed with her, tucking it neatly under her sheets. "The second?"

"The second is that you are now my friend, not Mama's. Deal?"

"Undoubtedly. Now, where can I hide?"

The girl leaned and pulled her bed sheets upward. She created a gap for Tally and winked as she crawled under the bed. There was a dull thud as the girl flopped back on the bed, pretending to be asleep again.

The door burst open. The floor creaked. A steady tread. The bed lowered with the weight of someone sitting on the edge. It shook as Lady Raine attempted to wake her daughter, but it seemed unnecessarily vigorous—almost violent. It would have woken the dead.

"*Mmm*, Mama, what is it?" she whined.

"Has anyone been in here?" Lady Raine asked.

A nervous pause.

"Answer me girl—I am sure you have no want of me arranging more . . . *visitors* for you now, do you?"

"N-no, Mama," the girl whimpered.

"Then I shall ask you once more—has anyone been in here to see you?"

A long silence was followed by an angry growl from Lady Raine as she lifted herself from the bed. "Have it your way," she barked. "But woe betide you if I discover you have lied to me." Lady Raine loudly exited the room.

"Good girl!" Tally whispered. She waited a few seconds before scrambling out of her hiding place. The girl stared at the door, terrified, but Tally gave her a grateful and reassuring hug.

The girl whipped the hidden hat from under her sheets and placed it on, smiling. She lowered the veil and poked Tally in the ribs.

"I hope you will keep your promises," she demanded.

"Oh, have no fear," Tally replied. "I most *certainly* keep my promises—especially regarding new friends." She pulled the girl's veil back up to see her smiling, but a little frightened. "May I use your window?"

The girl pointed just beyond Tally to a set of thick black-velvet curtains drawn closed. Tally gave a nod and then smiled. "Thank you!" she whispered. She kissed the girl on the cheek and found the gap in the draperies.

"Wait!" Tally cringed at the shout and turned back to the girl. "Do you have a name?"

"Iris," she said, relieved that this was all the girl wanted. The girl's eyes widened. "Though Papa and my friends call me Tally."

"*Iris*," the girl repeated. "That's a flower, isn't it? Like mine."

"Oh?"

"My name is Violet!" the girl said proudly. Tally, in turn, gave her an admiring smile and slipped through the curtains to commence her escape. "Well then, *Violet*—friends it is. I shall be seeing *you* again very soon."

CHAPTER SIX

I t had been a restless night.

The sun blazed through the window of the lounge and dazzled an already bleary-eyed Rose, adding to her state of irritability. She moved from her dining-table slouch over to a smaller and more inviting rear window. She took with her a glass and a bottle of strong whisky from the night before.

Pulling the window open with one hand, she filled half the glass and quaffed the contents. She tried, in vain, to make some sense of the numerous sleep-disrupting dreams which had driven her out of bed in the first place. Half a bottle later, she seemed no worse for wear.

"So then," she said to an audience of none and poured another, "I'm seeing stuff, hearing things, thankfully not dead, and can't get pissed for trying. One way or other, I'm going mad. Oh—and now I'm talking to myself." She slapped her forehead with the palm of her hand. "Yep."

"First sign, right there," Jennifer chirped.

Rose jumped at the sound. She turned slowly to face Jennifer, so perky it was sickening—a sharp contrast to the dishevelled, tired figure faintly reflecting from the window.

"So, ready to get to the bottom of your little mystery today?" Jennifer asked energetically, but with a hint of annoyance. "Or would you rather I just left you to get to the bottom of that bottle?"

Though she had seen her own reflection, it was only through Jennifer's words that she truly saw herself. Amnesia or not, whisky for breakfast was just *wrong*.

She placed the glass down on the table, well out of reach. She attempted to rub her unkempt strands of hair. Not once had Jennifer broken eye contact with her.

"Look, I know I sound a little hard on you, considering what you've been through," Jennifer said with a gentle tone, "but I'm pretty sure sitting around here, drinking yourself unconscious, isn't going to help."

Rose cleared enough space in her mind to reply sensibly. "It was only meant to be a swift shot. I was trying to knock myself out. Couldn't sleep."

"Understood," Jennifer replied with a nod. "You've hardly had the most relaxing time lately." Her eyes narrowed. "Although, if we don't get you sorted soon, I suspect sleep's going to be the least of your worries."

"That, or I'll have all the time in the world for it." Rose grimaced even as she thought the worst—a gruesome demise without ever truly knowing why. Even if she hadn't been drunk, this was a truly sobering thought. "Wonder who I've pissed off badly enough to want me dead?"

"Look, Rose," Jennifer said, scowling, "maybe we should stop worrying about the things we don't know and focus on what we do?" She looked around the room as if checking for other occupants. "All this other stuff you keep seeing—experiencing? This Tally person you were telling me about over tea?"

A worse-for-wear Rose blinked a few times and then stood up, getting into Jennifer's face. "Tally?" she snorted, "Something, or someone,

I *know*? She just turns up in my dreams—or maybe hallucinations—all prim and snotty, and tells me to go and find some necklace or *watch the world explode!*" She backed down, suddenly saddened. "I need to get back to my life, whatever it was."

"Take it from me," Jennifer said sternly, "if your changes end up like mine, there are some things you will *never* get back to."

The thought was enough to turn Rose's stomach. She fled backward a step or two and lapsed into high-pitched, shallow breathing. Jennifer caught up and placed a calming arm around her. "Okay," she said, shaking her head, "maybe that wasn't the best choice of breakfasts."

Jennifer raised an eyebrow. "Do me a favour," she said, "if you have trouble sleeping tomorrow night, let me know?"

"Why, what are you going to do?" Rose sniggered. "Tuck me in and read me a bedtime story?"

Jennifer smirked. "Actually, I have a special bedtime hot chocolate." Rose couldn't work out her level of sincerity. "Though one thing that'll help you sleep is to straighten out your life. First of all, I think we have to soak that whisky. Get you ready for the busy day ahead."

"Your high levels of bounce sicken me, you know," Rose said with a grin.

"I get that a lot," Jennifer said, returning the smirk. "Now come on, get changed. A good breakfast will be waiting for you when you come back down."

Rose nodded as her newest friend went to the kitchen. As Jennifer exited, a shadow appeared at the front door. Rose shrieked and darted behind the small table. Had he found her again, already?

She gathered some resolve and seized the whisky bottle, gripping it by the neck in case of the worst. She settled, though, when a key turned in the door.

The door clattered open.

Rose screamed. The bottle slipped from her hand and shattered against the floor.

The figure in the doorway echoed her scream. A slim woman in a business suit dropped a suitcase, startled. She stooped for the bunch of keys she had fumbled on the way in. Her hair comically appeared as if caught in a hurricane, though still had the hint of a tailored cut about it.

She rescued the suitcase, slammed the door behind her, and swept her hair back to reveal a warm, pretty face under the mussed black mop. Rose thought she had beautiful skin—a rich, dusky tone.

Through the muss, a slender pair of designer glasses covered dark eyes, and long but wide bright red lips smiled in reaction to recent embarrassment. Any discomfort Rose had felt eased.

Jennifer almost knocked down the kitchen door, bounded towards the woman at great speed, and latched on with a crushing hug. The woman hugged back and grinned. She freed herself and ran hastily over to Rose. "Ah, the lady of the moment!" she said and offered a hand.

Rose duly obliged, receiving a firm handshake and dazzling grin. The woman's accent rang with a slightly northern twang: Manchester at a guess. "Doctor Kara Mellencourt, Occult Studies, UCL, at your service! You sound *fascinating*!"

"What have you heard?" A small frown shaded Rose's face.

"Well, several things actually," Kara said, sidestepping the remains of the broken bottle. "There's this story going 'round about a train accident on the London Underground. Statistically rather dull; to be honest, you won't be the first or last person hit by a train. Not even newsworthy."

Rose's mouth fell open, summoning a cheesier grin from Kara. "You know, you really should hear me out before you judge. Seems all sorts of madness broke out yesterday at the hospital. They can't work out whether it's a disease, a chemical attack, or what. But Patient Zero stands right in front of me. You've practically regenerated since the incident. I mean, *look* at you!" She pulled Rose's cheeks hard and lightly slapped them.

"Hey!" Rose protested.

"Nothing a little sun couldn't help, but other than that, no proof at all you were near death."

Kara brushed back Rose's hair to check for scars, rolled up her sleeves, and repeated the process with her arms.

"Seriously?"

"Bloody hell!" Kara blurted. "This is *fantastic*!"

"What is?"

"I am the most privileged human being in the world right now. *Two* living miracles! Standing in *my* house!"

"Wouldn't exactly call myself a miracle," Rose mumbled, feeling anything but.

"How can you even say that?"

Rose reconsidered, reminding herself that despite everything, she was not yet dead. She nodded, and the smile on her face grew broader. "Yeah," she said, staring at Kara. "I'm a genuine miracle."

Kara looked at her as warmly as if she had just found a long-lost sibling.

"And here is another force of nature!" Kara said, turning towards Jennifer, who blushed and shook her head. Rose shot an amused look at them, found a seat, and watched them idly chatter. A few moments later, Jennifer returned to the kitchen.

"Sooo . . ." Kara bounced into a seat, yawning and stretching, cat-like. "In the night's sleep you've had, without being comatose or having your head bashed in, have any more useful memories come back to you?"

"Depends what you mean by useful," Rose answered, suspicion in her voice.

"Old home address? Place of employment, perhaps? Boyfriend?"

"Not you, too," she sighed.

"No, you're right," Kara said, shrugging. "I reckon he'd be in for a bit of a surprise anyway."

"So if I do have a man out there somewhere," Rose said, "maybe he would've let someone know I was missing or something? Police appeal by now, perchance?"

Kara looked serious. "Yeah, two problems with that, love. First thing, we don't know what name to look under for you, do we? I'm guessing the name Rose won't be much use for searching, especially as we don't have a surname."

Rose looked deflated but nodded. "Pictures?"

"Maybe worth a shot, though it'll be a long trawl. I don't suppose you've got a spare week, have you?"

"Got all the bloody time in the world."

"We should start soon, then." Kara raised a hand. "Wait a minute— this brings up your second problem. What if your bloke was the bugger who arranged for you to be done over in the first place?"

"Not that likely, surely?"

Kara frowned, spreading her arms on each of the chair's rests. "Unlikely doesn't mean impossible, sadly. And we're already dealing with impossible in your new life, aren't we?

"Now, let's have a bit of a think about this. First off, does anyone know anything about the twenty-six who died at the hospital?"

"*Twenty-six*?" asked Rose. "I can confirm two. Jack and another poor bastard doctor."

"Take that as a 'no', then." Kara collected a laptop computer and a nearby pile of books. She opened the computer and keyed in the relevant link.

Rose's eyes immediately gravitated toward the lead image, a number of people sprawled on the pavement outside a familiar hospital. Even an image of the hole in the window eight floors up underscored the connection. It provided a distraction from the real story, the images of bizarre death below it. "How did we miss *that*?"

"Don't know, but *they* didn't."

Military personnel dressed for chemical warfare combed the area, apparently searching for an unidentified substance they assumed had done the damage. However, the proximity of unprotected, panicked civilians in the graphics confused her. They ran around screaming and crying, even holding some of the victims.

As Kara scanned those and played some video footage, she realised none of them showed signs of violence, merely anguish for the dead. Later shots showed the containment unit unmasked, unable to fathom the cause of the sudden deaths but certain enough that whatever had been the cause was long gone.

Some still cautiously covered their hands and mouths as they examined the fallen, but the same frowns of uncertainty could be found on each of their faces.

One final image revealed a significant clue: a close-up of one particular victim—a well-dressed young man sprawled unnaturally on the ground with darkened veins raised above the surface of his skin. It looked surreal, as if enhanced by computer graphics.

"Now, Rose, am I right that these victims match up with the way you looked when Jen first caught up with you?"

Rose examined the victim carefully. "Not exactly, but close." She trembled. "That wasn't me." She wasn't entirely certain of the truth.

"Well, someone after you was definitely responsible for two of those deaths. If you can kill two people, you can kill twenty-four more. Jen?" Her friend burst out of the kitchen, bearing drinks and snacks. "Were you able to dig up anything after our phone call last night?"

"I was." Jennifer opened up several books to marked pages.

"Okay, then." Kara deftly divided her attention between the laptop screen and the books. "No info anywhere here, here, or here on famous Victorian women named Tally, although I'm wondering more about this jewel. Sapphires aren't that rare, really, though the cage design you mentioned can't be common. Can you provide me with a quick sketch?"

Rose nodded and illustrated a detailed image of the design from memory. Her work temporarily distracted Kara from her academic trance.

"Wow, that's *really* amazing," she said, peering around the screen.

Rose stared proudly at her achievement, but the accurate image suddenly triggered deeply buried memories. She cleared her throat and pressed forward. "This is the chain, this is the cage,"—she pointed at each aspect with her pencil—"and this inside here is the jewel."

Jennifer whipped the computer from Kara's hands and pulled up a matching image. "Yep. You can't miss that." Rose leaned in around her, Kara following suit. "You remember this, Kara? From the *Sotheby's* auction site?"

On the screen in front of them flickered the image of a necklace resting on black velvet, with a silver-wrought cage and a sapphire teardrop identical to Rose's sketch.

"It was auctioned under the name *the Grenshall Teardrop*," Jennifer said. She made a couple more clicks. "That's the one from the Beatrice Fox case. Seems there *is* a link between you after all."

Jennifer clicked to open another news story.

BUSINESSWOMAN IN BIZARRE DEATH MYSTERY

"Ooh, yes," Kara said. "I'll *never* forget this one. They concluded natural causes—I wasn't so sure, but couldn't quite put my finger on why."

"*That's* what rang a bell when I first heard about her," Jennifer chirped. "I knew there was something."

"Good spot." Kara gave a thumbs-up.

Rose read the related segment of the report aloud. "*Police want to question IT technician, Thomas Barber, the last person seen with Beatrice whilst still alive.*"

The piece showed a photograph of Thomas Barber. "This your man?" she asked Rose.

"Can't be," Rose said. "The guy was, like, seven feet tall and about as wide. *He* looks like he could've been one of my attacker's toothpicks."

"All the same," Kara said, "I wonder what happened to him."

"Disappeared the same week Beatrice died," Jennifer said, tapping the screen. "One of the other employees, the son of a director there, was found brutally murdered in his apartment, and his fiancée vanished off the face of the earth. As for Barber, they never found him."

"How much did the necklace go for, Jennifer?" Rose asked.

"Two and a half mil according to this," Jennifer answered. "A fair chunk, but considering what some of these go for, it's a steal."

"Yeah," Rose said, nodding. "It's the 'steal' part I was thinking about. You don't suppose he fled abroad or something, do you?"

"That's what the police believe," Kara said. "They reckoned Barber was in league with the fiancée to nab the necklace. Sarah Bliss, her name was. Wouldn't forget that name in a hurry. Anyway, the reports said something about a company party getting out of hand."

"Don't they always?" Rose asked.

"Wasn't an arse-on-photocopier incident. The broadsheets reported a staged argument between Barber and Bliss, whereas the tabloids went down the road of a full-on brawl. Either way, both left the party separately."

"And neither have been seen since," Jennifer added.

"It gets better. Turns out there were signs of a serious struggle at Sarah's place, too. Forensics determined *between* Barber and Bliss. But they haven't found a body—his *or* hers."

"Curiouser and curiouser," Kara said pensively. "Still, bit of a red herring, seeing as that picture wasn't your man, Rose. Back to you."

~ ✳ ~

Within an hour, Rose had explained her recent history, leaving nothing out. Both Kara and Jennifer interjected with questions and additional information respectively.

"So you're telling me that you fled several streets across an underground car park without anybody noticing, and just appeared in a street?" Kara asked, her laptop packed with notes.

Rose nodded. "Meanwhile, you saw—you say—*faces* while this was happening, and don't remember *any* of them?" Rose considered and then nodded. "Hmm. You were conscious the whole time?"

Rose pondered Kara's last question with a grimace. "Well, I *must* have been, or surely I'd have woken up somewhere weird."

"Yes, good point. Any history of blackouts or—oh—you wouldn't know, would you? Bugger. Okay, do you have any recollection of your exact emotions at the time?"

"Yeah," Rose said, her temper fraying. "Something along the lines of, 'Shit, I'm going to die!' How do you *think* I felt?"

114

Kara simply muttered and continued to scrawl notes onto her pad. "So you felt the natural instinct to take flight. That makes perfect sense. Unlike most people, though, it seems you managed it *literally*, in a manner of speaking."

Rose grinned, on reflection.

"I know that hospital very well," Kara said quietly, "and the street you described to me—that's a good half a mile away. To get that distance in that time? Even Jennifer can't do that."

Kara looked at Rose, rather impressed. "You told me you never went through that door at any stage. Am I right?"

"Uh-huh."

"So it's fair to say you are capable of moving at immeasurable speed and are uninhibited by walls?"

"Seems so," Rose said with a grin. "One thing, though; something else happened back at the hospital that freaked us both the fuck out." Jennifer gave a single nod and sat back. Turning back to face Kara, Rose continued, "Look, you know about Jen's ultra-keen people sense. I know you helped her to hone it."

"Okay," Kara said. "And you were wondering whether I know what that was about?"

"Well, *do* you?"

"Can't say I do, no. You don't seem someone who naturally inspires terror. Believe me, love, I've seen scary before, and you're not it. Putting aside one or two previous dates and looking in the mirror after the Christmas bash; I've just come back from something that tops my scary charts. Speaking to a friend who lectures at Harvard."

"What's so scary—your friend or Harvard?"

Kara shot a tame glare at Rose. "That's *not* quite what I meant. Doctor Sankram invited me over there and told me about odd goings-on in one of the rooms in the Liberty Hotel in Boston. Haunted, he reckoned. Turned out, he was right. If it wasn't for him catching me, I'd have flown off the balcony and fallen to my mushy doom. *That* was lively."

Rose sat up and took notice. "You saw a ghost?"

"Nah," Kara answered, actually looking disappointed, "more *felt* something, really. The worst thing about all of this is that there's actually been a dramatic increase in these phenomena recently. In the last month alone, I've picked up around thirty-two cases I'd consider worth looking at, whereas in the previous year, I had maybe two.

"Most have been in Western Europe, but when Dr. Sankram asked for me, I got on the first flight over the pond, entirely justifying the expense. I've actually pulled a few all-nighters looking into these properly, but they don't seem related. So I'll give that a break for now and look into something a little more concrete. Get yourself ready and we'll head out."

"In case you've forgotten," Rose said, folding her arms like a sulky little girl, "somebody's out there trying to kill me."

Kara pulled her glasses down her nose—an old school teacher look. "I *know,* love, and I don't especially want any unwanted folk around my house wrecking the place, either. But it seems to me we'd have just as good a chance on the road of not being found, especially if we're somewhere he isn't likely to look."

"How would you *know* where he's likely to look?"

Kara pulled a sour face. "That's just it—I don't. And neither do you or I think you'd have said so by now. Which makes it more important we get things sorted, rather than just sit here and wait for them to go away, agreed?"

Rose was silent.

"Good enough."

"I'll get myself ready, yeah?" Jennifer asked, heading up the stairs, before being halted by Kara snapping her fingers at her.

"Sorry, Jenny," Kara corrected. "I want you to keep an eye on what's been happening at the hospital. Check news reports; see if we can get any more on our 'friend'... CCTV ... PhotoFit impressions—anything. My phone will be on."

Jennifer looked bemused but nodded in acknowledgement. Rose stood, neatly stacking her plate onto the table. "What happened to safety in numbers?" she asked. "Jen's the only reason I'm still here to have this conversation with you, and you're leaving her *at home*?"

Kara nodded, accepting a valid point. But she was not to be swayed. "I still need Jenny, but she can't be in two places at once. Whoever he is, your mystery stalker, I want us ready for him. That's not going to happen if he just turns up on our doorstep.

"A bunch of hacks banging on the door would be just as bad, because they'll lead anybody looking right back to us. If she's on her own, Jenny has a number of tricks she can employ and may do better not having to look after the more breakable likes of me and thee."

Rose returned a nod, trusting in Kara's assessment. "So, where are we going?"

"Down the pub," Kara said with a joke East End dialect. "Place called the *Half Moon* in Croydon. Several guests over the years claim they've seen and heard things in the guest room. Nobody plays pool there anymore."

"So? What's this got to do with me?"

"I want to test a theory. The kind of activity I've got documented at the Half Moon—you can read up on it in the car—sounds like classic haunted house stuff to me. I've got someone with me reckons she can see dead people, and the case studies are all non-malicious, so it strikes me as a relatively safe environment to have a proper look at you.

"I would have left this to the TV shows normally, but reports from the last seventy years seemed far too consistent to just be ignored. If I'm wrong, nothing happens and we get back to keeping an axe out of your head. If I'm right, we've got something solid—if you'll pardon the pun—to work with. Okay with that?"

"Well, the idea sounds fine," Rose replied, finding it impossible to get annoyed with her infectious enthusiasm and impeccable logic. "But I still don't understand why we're not trying to figure out stuff about me, who I really am."

"You don't get it, do you?" Kara bowed her head, looking disappointed. "That's *exactly* what we're trying to do!" She put a hand on Rose's shoulder and smiled reassuringly. "Listen, for all the study and travel I've done over the last few years, I've met two people in my entire lifetime who I am genuinely aware have something beyond what I'd term 'normal human capability,' and both are in the same house as me right now.

"I have two interests in this of any worth; one: obviously, it is work-related—though hardly a burden; and two: you both needed help when I met you. Jen's fine now, but your case is totally different."

Rose's eyes widened. "Jennifer needed help? I find that hard to believe."

Kara frowned. "I've probably said more than I should have. All I'll say is don't be fooled by the way she appears to the outside world. It's not been easy for her, none of it." There was a solemn, awkward silence, broken by an animated Kara ushering Rose toward the stairs.

"Come on; I'm leaving in ten minutes. Mush!"

CHAPTER SEVEN

It wasn't long before Rose again feared for her life. However, it was entirely down to Kara's driving this time.

Kara cut through the London traffic with the expertise of a rally driver, and much of the daring. Her black Mini Cooper S was pushed to its limits, the driver reacting as fast as a fighter pilot, though Rose suspected she enjoyed herself a little too much.

The alcohol in Rose's system gave way to adrenaline as she clung for dear life, the vehicle weaving and thrusting through traffic gaps, much to the chagrin of several bus drivers en route. She felt compelled to say something after the fourth bus driver gave a lengthy honk.

"I thought we were trying *not* to attract attention? You know, to blend in? Maybe not get stopped by the police?"

"Yeah, you're right." Kara assaulted Rose's nerves by looking over to her as she replied. "But remember, we're up against the clock. Have you read the file?" Her concentration back on the road, Kara passed a gesture at a teenage driver determined to race her.

"No spare hands," Rose said. "Too busy hanging on!"

"There's always an excuse with students, isn't there?" Kara sighed, accelerating. "All right, here goes. Pay attention!"

"I'm all ears."

"Good. Now, you'll remember that I mentioned people would go into the guest room, claim to hear voices, and experience 'unusual occurrences'?" Rose nodded. "Well, one of the first recorded instances of this was back in 1947. The pub had just re-opened following post-war refurbishment, ownership changes, and the like.

"The very first night of it, in fact, young barmaid Greta Sampson locks up after a very busy evening and tidies the guest room. She gathers her belongings to go home. But she hears noises, inspects the room, and directly informs the landlord that every single glass she had collected and left on the table has systematically smashed on the floor.

"He, of course, puts it down to her overbalancing things or carrying too much and says nothing, other than that the difference will be docked from her pay.

"The following night, the same thing happens, and this time, he straight out accuses her of being clumsy. The two have a massive row and she ends up walking out on him. The very next time they open, he sends one of his other barmaids up there.

"To his great surprise, the same thing happens again. She explains that she left them dead centre in the table—the room was solid as anything, so no vibrations or suchlike—and she took particular care to stack them properly and not too high.

"So the next time, he says he'll do it himself. He does just that, and as he turns away from it all, he catches in the corner of his eye the front row sliding off at speed and watches, shocked, as they shatter. The rest all follow and before he knows it, he's left with a pile of broken glass and heads downstairs with a face like thunder. For no good reason, other than he's annoyed, he asks the barmaid from the previous night not to come back and locks the room up for about a month."

"That doesn't sound too bad." Rose's nerves had calmed a little, and she let go of the door handle, lightly skimming the file for photographs. It was only a few pages thick, most of it transcripts from interviews or local news articles. The photographs came from bomb damage during the course of the war and various stages of renovation, including the newly completed 1947 guest room.

"Isn't this just some old tale the pub owners use to sell more peanuts while people listen?" she asked.

The vehicle had reached a red traffic light that even Kara's sense of haste had to respect. As she slowed to a stop, she considered Rose's question.

"There's more to it than that," Kara answered. "I'm sure of it. Anyway, the room wasn't used again for a few years after that, following a couple of changes in ownership in that time. However, in 1959—ten years later—Greta Sampson, now Greta Miller, comes back as the landlady along with her husband, Peter. It's not long before her last visit here nags at her again.

"She gives the whole room a good tidying, ready to open it again, and leaves a glass or two lying on a table. Sure enough, it's not long before they hit the floor. So she decides to spend a couple of hours deliberately putting out glasses and watches as, one by one, they slide from the table. Then our Greta catches one of her staff sleepwalking."

"So?"

"Well, the sleepwalker sets up a chessboard."

"Again, so?"

"Thing is, it happens repeatedly over a series of nights. Greta finds it pretty funny at first, but one night, she decides to stay up and see if she can catch her at it. Greta follows behind her very slowly one night and watches the whole thing. Get this—it's that *same* table. But nothing happens to the board."

"Okay?"

"And the best part of it? Greta watches as she plays everybody's favourite opener—King's Pawn. Don't know how well you know your chess, but it turns out that the opposing move is Queen's Pawn—"

"What's this got to do with *anything*?"

"Had you not interrupted just then, I would have got to the important bit. The black pawn is moved all right, but not by her staffer! There's no one else in the room, so—"

"You're saying the piece moved itself?"

"There you go again with the interruptions! But yes. Well, yes and no. I'm saying that someone, or something, moved that piece, and it wasn't anyone Greta could actually see."

"Clearly someone who likes chess but doesn't like clutter, such as pint glasses, on their board."

"Exactly! It's got to be irritating, hasn't it?"

"Sure. But I still don't see how this helps."

They found their way onto a clearer road, the drive hurried, but safe.

"Not one of the many incidents reported has done any harm to anybody since Greta first kept a journal on her experiences," Kara said.

"For that reason, I would deem this a reasonably safe place for us to go gather our thoughts and see what exactly is going on with you. I prefer to have at least an element of control if we are dealing with something as potentially dangerous as . . . you. Sorry to be blunt, love, but looking at the facts, this is where we are."

Kara continued in a soft voice, "To be honest with you, Rose, there's another reason I didn't want Jennifer along for this."

"Oh?"

"I wasn't entirely truthful back at the house. There's *plenty* about you that scares me."

"What's brought this on?"

"It's not in the way you probably think. Listen, I can't see what Jen sees in terms of life forces, poisonous stuff, and just—just her extra grasp of the world around us. But with what I know, I'm speaking to someone who didn't so much cheat Death, but utterly fleeced the miserable old goat! And also, you have no idea of all that you're capable of—the same problem Jen has."

"She looked more than capable from where I stood." Strangely, it felt to Rose like an affront to a close relative.

"Oh, she is," Kara replied. "I've no doubt of that. I just feel there's still a *lot* more to come from both of you."

"And you've never brought this up with her?"

"I meant to, but there's never a good time." Kara slowed her driving, looking deflated. "You know, when I first met her, she was a real wreck—not a hint of what you see now."

The vehicle veered left into a parking space and came to a sharp stop. "We're here."

The Half Moon had just opened its doors for the day, and only one member of staff was present. The scruffy, greying man smiled courteously, pleased at the prospect of two more customers.

But whether it was something Kara had mentioned to her in the car, the dossier itself, or just her own anticipation, Rose felt far from alone. She could feel it the instant she walked through the door. She stopped halfway to the bar and looked around with narrowed eyes.

She pictured the room at the height of its activity—a Friday evening at its most raucous. There were many faces from as many walks of life, laughing, joking, singing, revelling, partying.

Panicking. Running. Cowering. Crying. Screaming.

Clattering their glasses together in a toast, one and all, to their triumphs, however great or small.

Toasting absent friends before drinking as if it was to be their last.

Or perhaps it was just the barman putting away glasses after all.

"What you having, love?"

The voice sounded distant, as if coming from another room entirely. She blinked twice before looking back at the bar, with full view of it obscured due to the many bodies in the way.

That wasn't there before.

Each and every one of them were total strangers to her. She shook her head, remembering that somebody had asked her a question.

"Huh?"

The barman looked to be miles away as he waited for lemonade to fill the tall glass placed under the tap. Kara, however, looked impatiently at her, snapping her fingers close to Rose's face.

"To drink. I asked what you're having? Where *are* you, girl?"

"Uh, whisky, please." She barely heard herself say the words.

"Bloody hell; coming off the wagon, are we?" Kara shook her head. Rose had genuine difficulty telling whether she was pouring scorn or simply teasing. "Try and remember we're on duty here, eh?" She turned back to the bar. "And one of them."

A somewhat muffled rendition of the Steve Miller Band's "Abracadabra" played from Kara's pocket. After the first bars of the chorus played, the phone was retrieved and answered.

"What's up?"

Pause.

"Sorry, the signal's awful in here. Hang on a sec."

She threw a ten pound note at the barman, shooing him into keeping the change. She mouthed the words, "The dean—back in a minute," to Rose as she ran outside.

"Great." Rose glared toward the door and then headed to the bar to retrieve her beverage. She heard a male voice shouting in French.

She looked over at the barman, who dried pint glasses fresh from the washer. His mouth had not moved at all.

Listening harder this time, she realized the voice did not come from the first floor and did not match his. "What the—?"

"You say summin', love?" the barman asked.

"Who's upstairs?"

"No one. Why?"

"Nothing."

It was definitely coming from upstairs.

"Where's the Ladies', please?"

"Gents' is all that's open. Upstairs on the right."

"Okay, thanks." She took a large swig from her glass and strode over to the staircase. There was the brief sound behind her of a television being switched on, and she just managed to catch the words, ". . . *BBC News* . . ." uttered before going out of range.

Rose heard a faint whistling as she ascended the staircase. A slight chill ran across her face and down her neck. As she drew breath, she was surprised as to how dry the air was. She choked lightly at the lack of decent oxygen.

A vicious shiver forced Rose to stop as she reached the top of the stairs. She took stock of the three doorways in front of her. The ladies' toilet could clearly be seen on the left-hand side, its male counterpart directly opposite. A few feet down the corridor was the third room with a dull turquoise door and a small window, filthy to the point of opacity.

She peered through both toilet windows. Nothing out of the ordinary there, so her interest returned to the central door. Blackened as the window was, there were no visible shadows through it.

"Hello?"

A voice, male and drawling, middle-aged if she had to guess, sounded miles away. First a couple of words, and then . . . babble. Or at the least, it was to Rose. Speaking French was not something she excelled at.

"Oh, for God's sake, speak English will you?"

She glared at the door in frustration for several seconds before turning back to the stairs. She caught a faint rattling from the direction of the shouting. Spinning around, she heard a click and watched in surprise as the central room doorknob twisted.

But he said it was all locked up apart from the Gents'!

Unless—

Rose sprinted to the turquoise door.

She reached for the handle. It was ice cold, not at all in keeping with the temperature of the rest of the place.

She slowly pushed the door open and took small steps forward, not loosening her grip on the handle. Though her nose was blocked from the dust, there was an unmistakable mustiness dominating the area.

She could see tables stacked upon one another and chairs all neatly along a row to her left. Another couple of steps and she could see there was a small bar, with various old, unfinished bottles of spirits. Many glasses had been stacked on and behind the bar, gathering dust like everything else in the room.

She heard a faint cough roughly towards the rear and made her way a little further inside to investigate. The wooden floorboards shifted heavily under her weight. She stopped.

"Anybody in here?"

No response. She looked all around and saw at the top of the bar some neatly arranged photographs.

She stepped over to find a light switch—to the left of the doorway on the inside. As she did, a sudden gust of icy wind slammed the door shut. The door was locked when she tried it.

She found the switch with her outstretched left hand but fumbled before she could flick. Her eye caught a small object moving slowly in the room. Her eyes fixed in that direction. More movements were accompanied by the faintest sounds—light scraping, followed by a *clack, clack, clack*. The sound was not too dissimilar to glasses clashing.

She released her hand with a sudden, adrenaline-fuelled stoop to her right as something whizzed past her head and shattered against the wall. Two more headed her way, which she only narrowly avoided.

She moved, rapid and twitchy, keeping her clear from a further barrage, but a projectile made her stagger backwards to the floor. Catching herself, she winced as a small piece of glass jabbed into the top of her palm but refused to let it distract her from further danger.

Too far from the light switch now, her concentration fixed upon the source of her attack. She squinted hard to track movement. A shape became clear in the background.

It darted behind the bar, crouching. The amount of glass now on the floor made any kind of stealth impossible. But the short lull in the onslaught provided an opening.

She sprang back to her feet and ran just as two more glasses became airborne. They rose to the ceiling, hung in the air briefly, and descended at a tremendous pace, homing in on her. Already leaning forward, she propelled herself with all of the strength she could muster into a dive, just as both whistled past her ear and disintegrated upon impact with the wall.

Her landing barely took her past the rest of the glass on the floor, but the sheer velocity of the last two sent several shards into her left calf. Rose cried out in a vicious cocktail of rage and pain.

From her new position, she could see a short but widely built male hiding behind the bar. Despite the lack of light, she could tell that the expression on his middle-aged face took the shape of fear; he trembled as he reached back to replenish his missile supply.

Determined, she pressed on, oblivious to splinters from the wooden floor and glass fragment digging further into her bloodied hands. She charged over to him before he could throw the next lot. Nobody was more surprised at the action than her.

"Stop it!" she snarled, stern and full of authority. "Put 'em down!"

He hesitated, but drew back his loaded arm.

"Now."

That voice again. Her single word echoed with a power that caught her off guard. So guttural did it sound, a shiver trickled down her spine.

If the man had looked fearful before, he was now paralysed by terror—confirmed by the ease with which she plucked his weapons from his hands and returned them from whence they came. She did not once break her gaze with him. He slowly took two steps back and began to whine.

"Please. Don't hurt me, not like those others."

"*Hurt* you?" she asked, thrown. "Wait a minute, you *can* speak English, then?"

"Yes, a little—but my English is very poor!" The man was clearly terrified.

"It sounds fine to me," she mumbled, still looking quizzically at him. She caught a quiet dripping noise. She looked down and could see it was coming from her hand as blood fell drop by drop to the wood floors.

The discovery of a fresh wound raised her anger. "Give me one good reason why I shouldn't glass the crap out of *you* now." She grabbed his neck, squeezing with considerable force. It already felt cold, lifeless; he wouldn't feel a thing, after all. A sensation of power flooded her brain as she started to squeeze whatever life remained from this man, to put him out of his misery forever.

She released her grip and stared, horrified with herself as he fell to the ground sobbing. She took a step back, grasping her temples between middle finger and thumb and sighing.

"Please! I'm begging you! Don't! Don't make me next!" His pathetic pleas returned her focus, but the room had changed—that cold, echoing state of shadow, which had been prevalent when she last saw Tally.

She shivered. "What are you on about?"

"Those poor people. I heard them. All twenty-four. I counted each and every one of their dying screams, even as you ripped their lives from them and sucked them dry."

She took a breath to calm her growing frustration. "I have no idea what you are saying. Who are you, and why did you attack me? And think *very* carefully before you answer, because I have a feeling that I could probably cause an awful lot of harm. You don't want that. I don't want that, either. Really."

He propped himself back up to his feet, never taking his eyes off Rose. A look of surprise took him as he wiped the top of his mouth. "You don't?"

"I don't." Her voice was quiet, gentle.

CHAPTER EIGHT

y-my name is Serge," the terrified apparition panted. "I-I honestly thought you had come here to destroy me, like the others."

"What *others*, Serge?" The effort at stern assertiveness remained, but so did her confusion.

"I-I'm not sure. I couldn't see from here. Just hear. I couldn't miss the screams, the suffering. I think it was a long way from here, but new faces, greatly tormented, innocent."

"When?"

"Just once. There was light. There's hardly ever light. Not this side."

"You're not making any sense." Once again, she could feel her temper shorten, but was sufficiently aware to rein it in before anything came of it. A distant howling rushed past her ears, and dust blasted off the bar surface directly at Serge.

"I have seen many things change in your world," he responded without hesitation. "And yet, I cannot leave this room. Day after day I have tried, but to no avail. When this room is locked, very little light comes to it—only that small sliver just there." He pointed to the gap underneath the door. The daylight looked considerably brighter than normal, almost blinding, and yet contained within its small area.

"My world?" she asked, turning back to face him. "How long have you been up here, Serge?"

"I am not entirely sure. Some time passed before I lost my sense of day and night, and only then did I start to count the light under the door. Several thousand have passed now, but in that time, some have opened and closed that door. But not for a good couple of hundred changes in light now."

Rose scratched her head. "Do you remember what year it was when you last left this room?"

"*Year*?" He had calmed himself a little, the weak defensive stance becoming more of a relaxed slump. "Ah yes—I think nineteen forty, forty-one . . . you know, this is the first time in a long while that I have had a 'conversation'; that has been more than—"

"1941!" she gasped. "You were around during the war?"

"War, yes!" he replied after a brief hesitation, almost in a daze. "Has it finished since I have been in here? Is it over?"

"Yeah." She nodded. "A long time ago now."

Serge fell silent, and Rose could tell that he was in deep thought, trying to rationalise something. Although she wanted to ask him more—much more—it was clear that his reasoning had descended into sorrow. His shaking head slowly sank to face the dusty, wooden floorboards, and a glaze crossed his eyes.

When he finally spoke, his words were little more than a mumble. "*Decades*? But that means . . ."

Once more his words trailed into nothing.

"Yep; reckon you've probably been dead for some time now."

It was Serge's turn for a flash of temper. He looked up at Rose and raised a fist to shake at her. "Of course I'm dead, foolish woman! The bomb would have done that! Like the others downstairs."

She indulged him his brief defiance, too busy thinking about *what* he had said to worry about *how* he had said it to her.

"Bomb?" She snapped her fingers as she remembered the information from the file. "Okay, the pub was bombed; that's right. Not totally demolished, but fire and wreckage did the damage downstairs—and the upstairs rooms, including this one, were flattened, rebuilt after the war. So," she pointed to Serge, "what are you doing here?"

"Waiting, of course."

"For *what*?" Frustrated, Rose clutched strands of her hair into both hands, squeezing them into fists.

"Not, what—*who*. For Stephanie!" He collapsed back into loud sobbing. She found herself oddly moved at the thought of nothing to show for several decades of patience beyond his natural life.

She moved slowly forward and grabbed his hand, helping him up. As she did, she could sense a cool energy all about him—and the ability to tear that from him.

She looked him straight in the eye, never releasing the grip she had on his hand. He quivered a little as she examined him before smiling warmly and turning away. "You want peace." She headed to a stool at the other end of the bar and sat down.

"Who's this Stephanie, then?" Rose asked as she eyed one of the old whisky bottles, opening it and giving it a sniff. It seemed perfectly fine.

Sufficiently at ease, Serge backed slowly into a chair and reached into a pocket, preparing a pipe and lighting it. The room quickly filled with the smell of tobacco as he took some time to recompose himself. "My daughter. I came to look for her as soon as I knew of her."

"You didn't know you had a daughter?"

"No." His answer was firm, but tinged with sadness. "Only when I received the letter from her mother. We met in 1921, you know,

Elizabeth and I. I had come to visit an old friend of mine whom I had not managed to see since just after the war. The letter he sent me arrived late, and our plans to meet went a little wrong. We never did manage to meet after that, and my time had come to head home.

"As I waited for my train back to the coast, a woman walked past me, crying. I stopped her to find out what the matter was. She told me that she had visited someone there, a man who had courted her for a couple of years. It seemed he had failed to mention he was married and, unfortunately, she discovered this the hard way.

"She had left his house and got to the station as fast as she could, but when she went to get on her train, she found she had lost her tickets."

"And let me guess—she asked for money to get home?" Rose asked. "Sounds like a bit of a scam to me."

"No." he answered with bluntness. "No trick. She had money; she was just in such a state that she could not find her purse straight away. She got off the train and was going to phone—now let me see, who did she say? Oh, I'm not certain, sorry."

"That's fine," Rose was now becoming surrounded by static smoke and distracted by a glow reflecting from her. At first she had noticed only her hands, but also to a lesser extent her right ankle as she sat cross-legged on the chair. Areas her clothing didn't cover.

As she looked more carefully around the room in this strange monochromatic view, she observed Serge did not glow nearly as bright; nonetheless, a faint, pale light seemed to emanate from his person. No other object in the room provided any source of illumination, at which point she remembered she had never gotten around to switching the light on.

Serge's glow was complete; his ghostly clothing made no difference.

He continued, "In her panic, she had not looked properly in her bag for her purse. Thinking she had left it at his house, she assumed the worst. We found it within the bag after we had a moment to talk, for her to calm down, and for us both to laugh about the day's events. We laughed a lot, actually, and stayed far later than either of us had intended, for which the tea shop was very happy. Ah."

"You were saying something about a daughter?"

He nodded. "We insisted upon meeting again after getting on so well. After an exchange of letters, we did so.

"Sometimes she would come to visit me in Marseille, other times I would come to London for her. And after two years of this, I felt the time was right to ask for her hand in marriage, and I knew, just knew, that the most difficult part of her decision was going to be whether we lived in France or here.

"There was no wedding." He muttered, but no other sound was present to prevent her hearing him. He spoke the words with the discomfort of a painful memory.

"The day before I was due to travel, I received a letter from her, telling me not to visit her again, and not to bother looking for her because she would be gone. There was no explanation as to why. Nothing."

"So that was it, then?"

"Almost. Of course I went over anyway, just to see if it was true, and sure enough, her house was empty." He turned away after he had finished speaking and covered his face with his hands.

"I stayed for a full year, searched London looking for her, and found not a trace. So I went back home and tried my very best to forget about everything. It took a few years, but finally I was able to get on with a quiet life, out of the way of things. So by 1938, I had forgotten because there was too much else to distract me."

"And half of Europe, I should imagine!"

"Quite." Finally, a smile. "Of course, just as I got my life back, another letter arrived, this time with handwriting that I did not recognise. It was from England but written in perfect French. I was asked to confirm my identity and whether I knew an Elizabeth Palmer in the early 1920s. It was signed: *Stephanie Palmer*."

"Your daughter?"

"As it turned out, yes, but I did not know that at the time from what she sent me. Whilst a small part of me considered the possibility, I had long since told myself that she had left me for a man closer to her home."

"Understandable that you would think that."

Serge nodded. "I immediately wrote back and told Stephanie Palmer that I did know Elizabeth, of course, and I wrote about everything that I have just told you now. She was actually the very first person I mentioned any of this to."

"No family back home?"

"None. And my friends simply thought I had taken a liking to London. I felt no need to bother them with further details."

"Wow."

There was a long silence as Serge gathered his thoughts. Rose briefly wondered if she, too, had been making a conscious effort to suppress memories—wondered if this was the reason for her current condition. She had certainly gained some familiarity with her abilities in a very short time.

"What happened next?"

"Stephanie wrote back rather quickly. She explained she was indeed Elizabeth's daughter, and that she wrote to me after finding letters from myself to her mother.

"I wanted to know, of course, where she had been all this time, though I assumed from the address on the letter that they had all moved to Edinburgh with her husband. Another month later, I received a reply to tell me that whatever her mother's reasons for leaving, there had been no other man, and that unfortunately we would never get an answer as Elizabeth died in early 1924 from childbirth complications with Stephanie."

He stopped himself, choking back tears. Even Rose could feel the lump in her throat from his words.

"I'm sorry," she said. As she looked at him, though, she felt a sense of calm that battled the tension she had dealt with since waking in the hospital bed. A small smile flashed across Serge's face as he reached out to touch her hand warmly. She could feel that warmth, every bit of it, and instinctively smiled back.

"It's okay," he replied, his own smile broadening. "I don't understand how, but knowing that I can tell you about this, I feel everything will be okay." In the instant he told her so, she also knew.

"So now that you knew Stephanie was your daughter, you arranged to meet as soon as you could, right?"

"Exactly, yes. I had no idea of her monetary status, but I did not recall Elizabeth being particularly wealthy, so I said I would come over myself. It was by now 1939, and naturally even this did not go as smoothly as we might have hoped. I was, however, extremely fortunate to have gone when I did, because as you are no doubt aware, had I left it another few days, leaving France would have been . . . difficult."

"Uh-huh."

"In my rush to get here, I left my letters back at home and could not remember the address. After a few months of searching, I found the house in which she had been staying, which was her aunt's. I met with the aunt's husband, who eventually explained to me that Stephanie had not received my last letter, and nor had I received hers! She was to come and visit me at my home!"

Rose was now sitting forward on her chair, eager to know the rest of the story.

"My first thought was to figure out some way back, but realised it would be extremely difficult. The uncle, Ted, told me I could stay there for a while, if I wanted. He was not able to tell me much more of Elizabeth, as his wife was her sister and they had hardly met.

"But he was a good man and treated me very well. Some months passed and both Ted and I worried greatly, but saved each other from despair with good whisky and daily games of chess."

"That explains something." She grinned at the thought of a chess board. "Why did you feel the need to take over the odd staff member? And *what* is your thing with breaking glasses?"

"Take over? Wha—? No!" He appeared genuinely bewildered when he answered, but seemed to know what she was talking about. "It was an accident, a most unpleasant accident. You know, I cannot keep track of time in any sensible way and usually end up trapped doing the same old things again and again. But that one night, the stupid idiot got drunk and fell asleep in this room! Nobody ever sleeps in here!"

"And you just thought you'd nip in and teach him a lesson?" Rose barely allowed him to finish his sentence before asking.

"I didn't 'think' anything. I never do." He let out a resigned sigh and continued. "This time with you—it has been wonderful. For the first time since I've been here—proper conversation, proper thoughts!"

"Proper thoughts?"

"Yes, instead of the usual few I cannot get beyond. Something about you being here and listening, I feel almost . . . normal."

"So you've waited all this time, hoping your daughter would walk in one day for a game of chess?" Rose asked to distract herself from choking up after everything she'd heard.

Serge scratched his head, mumbling as he considered Rose's words. Eventually he nodded. "I remember hearing one of the explosions. This was not the first part of the pub to be destroyed. I wished I had stayed in Scotland with Ted. I knew I would never have a chance to meet my daughter or see Elizabeth again.

"I was angry more than anything, you know? I think I threw a glass at the wall in tears when everyone else panicked. They all fled, hid under tables. That was the last thing; the last—" He stopped, breaking down in tears.

Rose gave him a moment to grieve. "It's okay. But we have to talk about this. You can't just sit around here and attack people any time you feel like it. Someone is going to get badly hurt."

"I can't help it. It's not *me*."

"What do you mean?"

"I told you, those four or so thoughts I have, they were the only ones I *ever* had. If they were at least partly the kind of thoughts to keep a man going, I should imagine they would have driven me quite mad by now!"

"How come you can think straight now?"

"I'm not sure. It feels strange, as if—because you told me to, I can. True power, indeed."

Rose took time to digest what she had just heard. "What happens now?" she asked.

He threw his arms wide. "What do you mean?"

"I mean, once I leave here, what are you going to do? Go back to that thought loop and continue to harass people who can't even see you, let alone help you?"

"I don't want to, but what else is there?"

"I can help you."

"Oh, no. I've seen what you mean by 'help.' You'd destroy me; you almost did before."

Rose was pensive as Serge paced the room, terrified. She could hear him muttering, "At least if I stay here, I'll just go insane over time. Better than *that*. Fate worse than death. Worse than death."

The inspiration was as vivid as a recent memory, and yet was nothing of the sort.

"There *is* another way!" She leapt into the air excitedly. Although the nervous Serge tried to dodge out of her grasp, she was far too quick for him. Gripping his wrist, she grinned at him. "It's all right," she declared, though still without truly knowing how or why. "Everything's going to be all right!"

Serge felt perfectly real to Rose. But as she held him, it was more than that. Within seconds, she knew his fear; the absolute knowledge that he must not leave this place until he had fulfilled the reason he came here; and the despair that, in knowing so much time had passed, he could never achieve this goal.

The terror when that first bomb ripped the pub in two and killed people who had been singing so defiantly just moments before—she understood it all, even the brief sting of pain when the second bomb came for him, and the frustration of never being able to leave this room again—to never be able to settle his affairs in person.

And then it all started again; there was no leaving until the reason he came here was dealt with . . .

In that borrowed thought, Rose, too, felt there was much purpose to her visit, beyond even that which Kara had mooted.

"One more thing I want to know," she asked, gently drawing him towards her into a motherly hug. He made no attempt at resistance. "You say you can't leave this room. Why?"

"I don't know." He shook his head slowly against her shoulder. "I just can't."

"I know someone like you who I've seen in at least two places, so there must be a way."

"Not for me. I have ties here!"

"You *had* ties here. Why would you stay?"

A light shrug. "As I told you, I cannot leave the room."

"What if you could?"

"Well, that's hardly important seeing as I—"

"It's *extremely* important. What would you do?"

"I'd look for her. See how she's getting on."

"Of course you would. It's only natural. And then you'd find that she couldn't see or hear you properly. It wouldn't stop you trying. You'd eventually get even more frustrated, and it *would* show. Perhaps you'd even cause her and her friends and family harm."

"I wouldn't want to."

"I know you wouldn't. But do you see where I'm going with this?"

His response was muffled and hesitant. "Yes. But you understand why I just *can't* go?"

"Completely—more's the pity."

She lightly held him away, just enough to regain eye contact, and with a hand on each side of the face, retained it. "How about I cut you a deal? I can't offer much, but I'm in a much better position than you are to look for anyone still about. So how about I do, and if I have any luck, I'll let them know everything you told me. *Everything.*"

"But what if you don't find them?"

"Then I don't find them. But what if *you* find them? More smashed glass and misery? Better you take the chance than go on as you have been forever."

Serge's face contorted as he gave serious thought to her offer. Rose again made no attempt to push him. A shiver ran down her back as she considered the possibility, however remote, that she was only clinging onto life for one last task, too.

After what seemed like an age, he finally raised his head and looked at her once more with a nervous smile. "Fine," he said. "I can see no reason that you would lie to me. And I have no wish to do as I have been for all this time, or to torment any family and friends I may still have. So, I must go. Though I warn you this—if you make me suffer as I heard those . . . others, then you will be the first I come for. Do you understand me?"

"That's only fair," she said. "I'd say exactly the same in your position. But what happens here will be no more painful than you being able to speak with me like a human being again."

He gave a wry smile. "Strangely, you have no idea how painful that has proven in some ways." He moved back and held out his wrists as would a criminal preparing to be cuffed. "Okay. Do what you have to do. Just make it quick."

"Actually, I don't have to do that much at all," Rose replied with an authority and confidence that she could not find a reason for. She knew exactly what she was going to do, but had no clue how. "To be honest, it's you who needs to do the hard work!"

"Me? How so?"

"All that's keeping you here in this bar are those thoughts you've been clinging to. Raw emotion, nothing else. You're not *really* here, in my world. Not many people can actually see or communicate properly with you, so I don't think anyone wants *you* around that badly that you need to stay for them.

"You just have to let go of those thoughts. I know it must be seriously difficult to break the habit of a virtual lifetime, but that's how it works . . ." She trailed off into silence as she considered her words. How did she know that?

"And then what?" Rose's fading speech and the look on her face caused doubt to rear its head with Serge again. It was fleeting, though; Serge's own reaction proved sufficient to break her concentration. She placed her hands on his shoulders and gave a small but warm smile.

"And then," she closed her eyes, making a concerted effort to relax, dispel any tension she may have felt, and replace it with calm. With meditative focus, she cleared her thoughts entirely of her last several, turbulent days. "Then you may finally feel some peace."

She idealised her own inner peace, taking the mangled image she saw of herself at the train station and making it whole again. She visualised a happy young woman, just returning from a night out.

She imagined a full head of glossy black hair down to her shoulders, and the adrenaline belonging not to someone running in terror but from someone buzzing with excitement.

As she did so, she could feel a warm tingle run from her head down to her toes, not the vicious chill as she had when she first entered that room. She opened her eyes once more to see Serge fade into the shadow, his eyes closed with a blissful look on his face.

His thoughts became hers—the prospect of finally meeting his daughter, and likely now also his grandchildren, of one last game of chess with his good friend, and of the day at the train station, the hours that melted into nothing as he and Elizabeth talked. There was nothing else he wanted to remember.

He waved at her, serene, simply mouthing the words, "Thank you," as his features merged entirely into the darkness. Now all that remained in the room was carnage: shards of broken glass everywhere, minor cuts and scratches on her hands, legs, and face, musty old cardboard beer mats, and on the floor propped vertically on a tilted table, a chessboard with many of the pieces lying on their sides surrounding it.

She took a deep, dust-filled breath and blinked as the lighting in the room shifted from moonlit to the tiny sliver of light edging from behind her. As she made to turn around, she could hear an echoing whisper which sounded like it was coming directly from her head.

"Just one more thing—*congratulations*!"

"*Congratulations*?"

Her mind raced on to all manner of possibilities. *Driving test*? As she considered it, she did know she was able to drive, legally or not.

Wedding? She checked her fingers, not just for rings she hadn't considered she was wearing, but also for marks where one might have been. Nothing.

Pregnant? Quickly ruled out.

"Congratulations on *what*?"

The door rattled behind her. As she turned to it, three words whispered in her ear.

"On your graduation!"

"Of course!"

The reason she was out that night in the first place was to celebrate an honours degree in Art. If she could at least remember her name and where she lived, then her true identity would be around there somewhere.

CHAPTER NINE

Tally was sure to keep her promise to the young Violet. She had left the house that night with a nagging doubt that it was a healthy environment for the girl. Simply knocking on the door and offering to chaperone Violet was out of the question, unless she ascertained some way of befriending Lady Raine. Given what little she had seen of the woman, she was rather unconvinced the two of them would get on.

To this end, she managed to effectively shadow the girl whilst accompanying on her walks, striking a deal with the servant assigned to the duty so that she would get a few hours' access.

Through her observations, Tally identified that she did not have a regular nanny. The walks were allocated time to ensure Violet was out of the house—undoubtedly for unsavoury reasons, and to maintain the nominal appearances of a normal family life. To the casual observer. Tally's scrutiny was considerably greater.

An accord was not difficult. The Raines did not pay nearly as well as might have been expected from one of the most powerful families in London, certainly not sufficient that any working person could ignore a purse of even half of Tally's illicit winnings.

Violet, of course, had no objections. Tally, remaining incognito in a new veiled hat, was one of very few people who paid the girl the time of day. Lord Raine was increasingly distant; Lady Raine only communicated with orders and threats.

The prospect of confectionery treats and a ride on the Serpentine was, of course, considerably more appealing. Over the fortnight, Tally noticed Violet developing a taste for it. She grew increasingly eager to escape the house. For very little cost, Tally gained herself a valuable source of information regarding the strange goings-on at the Raine household.

"I shall be in real bother if I blab any more, miss," the unusually scruffy young servant said after Violet had stepped inside the bakery one day. She handed him extra coin. He shook his head, handing it back. "Coin's not going to save me if the lady gets wind of this."

"Quite," Tally replied. She thrust the bag into his lap. "And yet here you are, speaking with me, already enjoying the benefit of my purse. Little point having an attack of conscience now."

Trembling, his head darted from left to right. He slipped the purse into his pocket. "Not a matter of conscience, miss. You have no idea what she's capable of."

"Which is why the purse is twice the weight. *Tell* me."

A bead of sweat ran down his brow. "'Tis a horrid thing having to collect her of a morning from the top of the stairwell, miss. Sounds foolish, as there is nothing there to see, other than a scared young 'un. But that hallway gives me the chills. Not just cold, mind. Something ain't right. You can see it in the girl's eyes. Now don't think me addled, but there's something in that room with her. I never seen it, but I just *know*.

"Seeing as you've obliged me as you have, miss, the lady talks about a 'display' she puts on, that she needs practice. Just the other night, she caught one of our maids stealing. I know when someone loses their job, but this weren't it. We know she went to meet her and talk about it, but there was some bright flash or other behind the door. Never seen anything like it. Never seen the maid since, neither."

Tally shuddered. "What is she doing to Violet?"

"Not sure, miss. What I do know is after Elsie puts the girl to bed of an evening, the lady often follows her up. Soon as she leaves, I often pass by, check Elsie's not too shaken up. She knows something's not right, too, but gets on with it, like me.

"Most nights, I hear the lady tell Violet she's done wrong, even when she's done nothing. The door blows shut, like a gust has flown through the house. I do my duties upstairs and I can see that odd light, under the door. I see it every night.

"The lady will leave and shut the door, but then it'll start rattling in there. Then voices. Like there are several folk in there. And it feels icy as January, even from outside the door. Just comes on from nothing. I walk down the other end of the corridor so I'm not just gawping at it, but you can't miss any of it."

Tally was about to ask another question, but Violet returned, laden with cakes.

It was no simple matter of reporting the Raines to the authorities; they would not have any idea how to deal with it. It was fortunate that Violet had even spoken to her. The girl could easily have betrayed Tally the very second she entered her room that night, fearing for her own safety or to protect herself from any further transgressions in her mother's eyes. The issue would take considerably more than a few bribed visits to resolve.

Sneaking into the Raine mansion was out of the question. If an evil such as described by the servant roamed the house, Tally would have nowhere to run. But she needed to see for herself. It was time to take to the rooftops once more.

That night, she made her way back to Mayfair, dressed in loose-fitting clothing for ease of movement. Having scouted the area around their estate, she entered through a hedge near the rear boundary and climbed onto the roof of the caretaker's house.

Equipped with a telescope borrowed (without his knowledge) from her father, she positioned herself on the roof with a clear line of sight to Violet's bedroom. The moonlight gave her a viewing advantage, but also created a greater challenge in avoiding detection.

For a good hour, nothing happened, and she prepared to leave. But suddenly, a ferocious gust of wind shook a tree near the window. Peering through the telescope, she watched as the bedroom window blasted open.

A vast shadow poured out of it, the wind dissipating rapidly. A shriek came from that direction, and the shadow grew wings and a head, like a giant bird. Behind it trailed tendrils, one of which held a small person. *Violet.*

It accelerated out of the window, flying around with the girl, who had stopped screaming and gone limp. Inside the house, from a lower floor, came a blue flash, like lightning within the mansion. Tally put her head down and lay totally still as the shadowy creature circled around the Raine estate, right above her, before flying back inside.

Tally had seen enough. Though tempted to run in and rescue Violet, she had no idea how to deal with such a creature. She withdrew the way she came, certain to cover her tracks as best she could.

How could any mother treat her daughter so? A fleeting memory of Tally's natural mother haunted her. But that drunkard was nothing compared to one who would employ a terror worse than any she had known against a child.

Tally might be Violet's only chance at a normal life. Lady Raine's list of atrocities grew long indeed. She had to be stopped.

Tally considered how she would maintain access to Violet. She had the measure of Violet's mother enough to know that if she kept coming home happy without due cause, it would raise suspicion and make everything much, much worse. But at least she had developed mutual trust between herself and Violet—one less potential pitfall. If she could stay well away from Raine House for two weeks, it should reduce any chance of scrutiny.

The welfare of her hard-won family came to mind. Mama and Papa had come to her rescue, of course, taking her off the streets and into safer surroundings. However, she found herself in an entirely different situation.

Violet could not be hidden away in Grenshall Manor. Nor could one deal with Lady Raine as one would with a street robber. She held formidable sway around London—and likely beyond. She would not simply leave; no bargain could be struck with her beyond Lord Grenshall relinquishing their family home.

Tally briefly entertained the possibility of asking her parents to concede the drain on their fortune that was Grenshall Manor and just let everyone get on with their lives. But it was their *home* and had been for generations. The Grenshalls would not idly give up their ancestral manse, and she was a Grenshall now in every way.

Lacking options, she thought that perhaps it was worth having a conversation with one of her parents after all.

One afternoon, she said goodbye to Violet after their usual lunch in Hyde Park and returned immediately to Grenshall Manor in an effort to catch her father. She found him pacing up and down in his bedchamber. Without knocking, Tally let herself in and caught him off his guard.

"Papa, how do you propose to deal with Lady Raine?"

She watched him first shake, then splutter, before finally giving a response. "I beg your pardon?"

"*Father*," she said mockingly, "I am unaware as to how long you have been allowing this woman to bring such *evil* into our lives." The mockery quickly shifted to feigned anger. "Yet something I *do* know is that I will not stand idly by and watch her destroy the Grenshall household stone by stone." She took a breath, just long enough for him to interrupt.

"Iris Grenshall! You forget your place."

"I will *have* no place if she persists!" She took a deep breath. "I cannot bear to see harm come to you, to Mama, nor to little Violet."

Lord Grenshall looked stunned at her outburst. "Wh—what do you know of—?"

"I know that she is a wonderful little girl living an abominable life under the care of that—that *vile* woman! And if you saw fit to pluck me from the streets out of charity, then I would implore you to remove her from the insufferable existence she is forced to endure! Surely we have fortune enough to answer that blackmailing creature's demands and get her out of our lives!"

His initial shock gone, he considered her words, clearing his throat and adjusting his dressing gown to compose himself. "Close the door, Iris." She did as she was asked and also followed his gesture to sit on the bed beside him.

"I have no idea how you know all of this, but you will no doubt understand that the situation is not a simple monetary request."

"Of course," Tally responded, sitting up tall. "We are talking about you making a decision which would possibly be our ruin. And you are the very *last* person I would expect to do that."

Her father nodded, reservation etched on his face. "You know me well. But if you know anything of Lady Raine, you know exactly why I am even entertaining the notion. She is dangerous in ways you cannot even begin to imagine."

"Oh, I think I can." Fury clouded her thoughts, her focus on the suffering their adversary had caused. "You need to get that woman out of your life, and quickly. Have you spoken to Lord Raine? Tried to reason with him at all?"

He sighed, slumping in an infuriating manner of defeat she was not accustomed to seeing from him. "Do you know, I only ever see him in the occasional public appearance? I have not encountered him alone in some years, not since his marriage to Aurelia. He rarely speaks with anyone, as it happens. I am just going to have to be patient and see if a solution comes to mind."

"Patience is for people with too much time on their hands." Tally had to restrain herself from physically shaking the defeat out of her father. "You—*we*, do not. I will *not* watch the spirit be sucked from you daily or sit and wait whilst we are ousted from the seat of House Grenshall, even if you *will*!" She got up and headed to the door. Her father grabbed her, but she shook herself free and glared at him.

"Iris Grenshall, I will not allow you to—"

"To *what*? Concede defeat to, well, to whatever it is this parasite is trying to do? I am *not* going back out on to those streets for any reason other than those of my choosing! If you want to stop me, you stop *her*, do you understand?"

Lord Grenshall attempted to answer, now himself full of rage, but he stopped, merely bowing his head with a feeble nod. "Yes. Yes, I understand."

"What has happened to you, Papa?" She turned away from him,

slowly making her way back through the large wooden doorway. "There was a time you would let nobody get the better of you."

"That time ended the day I met you."

Tally wiped her eyes dry and broke into a sudden laugh. "Now *that's* the spirit, Lord Grenshall! Perhaps you *will* come up with something by the time I return."

"Where are you going?"

"I told you, something must be done about all of this!"

"But you just said—"

"And I stick by it, but the fact remains I have sat idle quite long enough. It is time Lady Raine and I had a small parlay. I shall see you when I return!"

"I shall not allow it! That woman is dangerous!"

"So I keep hearing." She slammed the door behind her.

~ ✴ ~

Tally made her way to Hyde Park. Rather than heading straight to the Raine residence, with no guaranteed access, she planned to perform her usual bribery to arrange some time with the girl.

This time would be different, however. Tally was going back home with her. The purchased time was to prime Violet with the correct information; it was of paramount importance that they were not at cross-purposes.

But when they met up again, the girl looked wide-eyed, terrified. The servant with her held her hand in an iron grip, alerting Tally that something was amiss.

"Violet!" she shouted, ensuring everyone on the street could hear her. The one person for whom it was intended stopped walking and turned to face her friend. Tally sprinted over, unable to hide her joy at seeing the girl again.

Her happiness was short-lived. The servant seized Violet and with one swift movement, placed himself between the two. Normally, the man was approachable, with a hungry look as he waited for his customary bag of money (which Tally did have on her). Today, there was just a vacant stare.

Once she closed on them, she made a more detailed examination. The servant looked gaunt, his skin grey and clay-like. He should not even have been out in public, let alone in charge of a young girl. He looked upon Tally with unexpected hostility.

"Tally, please—go away. It's not safe," Violet pleaded.

"Not safe from what, dear?" Tally asked casually, not breaking eye contact with the servant even as his vacant stare endured. Violet's words increased her resolve.

"*What* is not safe, Violet?" Sidestepping suddenly to her left, the motion was met by the servant. Agile as she was, it was going to be difficult to reach Violet without causing a scene. She produced slower movements, an attempt to circle around again countered by equal reaction. She stopped, re-evaluating her situation. "Violet?"

"Go away, Tally! He'll hurt you!"

"No dear, he really will *not* hurt me. Not *here*, in any regard." Whatever had become of this man, she would not walk away without her friend.

"Hand her over," she spat with venomous authority. Even curious passers-by granted her a wider berth. However, the servant refused—although the force of her demand captured his attention.

She allowed a few seconds—enough time for the obstructive man to do the unlikely thing and comply. To no surprise, he did not. She feinted a strike to his face. The servant released the girl and attempted to parry. He lashed out with savage brutality. She moved to evade, but the attack glanced her face, enough to knock her to the ground.

Tally's instincts remained sharp. She rolled to avoid a follow-up blow and then struggled halfway back to her feet. "Have you any *idea* who I am?" she cried, ensuring everyone around could hear her. "Someone arrest this man."

Nearby police ran to the aid of the stricken woman, attempting to seize her assailant. She had achieved her main objective, which had been to free Violet, but it fascinated her to see how easily the servant fended off the two constables attempting to arrest him.

With tremendous strength, in one punch, he shattered the first constable's face. The second struggled for a moment before the servant effortlessly threw him across the road, sending him crashing into a wall. Tally scooped Violet up and sped to the nearest alleyway as the servant turned his attention to her.

Tally checked on Violet, quickly confirming she was unharmed, but did not once consider stopping. As she looked back, the clay-like man maimed everyone in his path. He remained in hot pursuit. Tally's knowledge of the streets proved invaluable.

She knocked over everything she could to slow down the relentless assailant. She and Violet weaved around halted carriages, tipped hand barrows, lobbed fruit aimlessly, and burst through shops in an effort to shake him.

Still he came.

Quick as Tally was, even with Violet over her shoulders, he was gaining. She had run out of useful ideas to shake such a pursuer. Except for one—the Hammersmith and City Railway entrance of Paddington Station.

She put Violet down and, not letting go of her hand, merged the two of them into a large crowd, not making any attempt to dampen their distress.

Grabbing one large gentleman on her way past, she whispered into his ear whilst pointing behind her. "That man is trying to kill me!" She grasped his left hand with both of hers, a despairing plea in her eyes, and slipped a wedding ring from his finger with the greatest of dexterity.

Forgive me.

The two breathlessly dashed through the entrance to the station, agilely weaving through crowds. An engine at the nearest platform wailed and belched steam the second Tally's feet hit the bottom step.

She sprinted across the platform and threw several coins at the conductor as they dashed aboard. There were screams in the distance as the servant forced his way through the obstructing throng, crushing bones and battering heads against stair rails. His terrifying blood-soaked charge ended as the train left the platform. He stopped, looking left and right several times.

"He can't see us!" whispered Violet. She ducked beneath the window. Tally checked for herself before following suit. The other occupants of the carriage looked on at the kerfuffle outside, some echoing the screams in shock, others muttering disdainfully at the disruption.

The pair needed a few minutes to catch their breath. Finally, both took a stealthy look from the window to make certain they were well on their way.

"That was amazing, Tally!"

"Well, I did promise, remember?" Tally breathed a sigh of relief and gave Violet a strong hug, kissing her on the forehead. Then she shook her head. "What happened to him, Vi?" she asked, remembering that the man had looked a lot better—more . . . *human*—on the last occasion they had met.

"*Mother* did it."

Any remaining playfulness between the two went away. Tally felt a sense of dread. Every possibility sounded as horrid as the next in her mind as she remembered what she had witnessed that night in the dining room, at Lady Raine's hands.

"What *exactly* did she do, Violet?"

The girl trembled. Her mouth opened to answer, but no sound came forth. Again, Tally came through, offering compassion and kindness—the one real source the girl had. As Violet could see they were getting gradually further away from the initial danger, she felt sufficiently safe to mumble at her friend.

"—killed him."

"What was that?" She heard her the first time. She just wanted to be sure.

"She *killed* him, Tally."

The noise of the train and an otherwise empty carriage prevented anyone else from hearing the girl's words. But there was one question that Tally needed to ask. She needed to know precisely what she was up against. There was no way Lady Raine would stand for such opposition. Consequences were inevitable.

"How did she do it, Violet?"

"It was horrid."

Violet trembled. She clearly wanted to say no more, and Tally recognised this. Just one poorly timed sentence could, in seconds, undo weeks of productivity. "Yes, Vi," she said, patting her on the shoulder, "I should imagine it was."

They sat, staring at each other for a time, before a calmer Violet spoke again. "Where are we going, Tally?"

For the briefest time, Violet appeared to have hope for her future. Tally wanted to do nothing to dispel it.

"Somewhere pleasant, I hope," Tally responded, "Somewhere quiet, far from all this madness."

They rode the train along to the Addison Road stop, Kensington, before disembarking. Although both were familiar with affluence, the place still impressed, looking suitably different to their more regular surroundings.

Violet was, of course, particularly interested, having had relatively few opportunities away from home. And to have travelled here in such style! Tally's passion for riding the Underground shone as she told tales of her many solo excursions, the experiences she had, the people she had met, and the routes she had taken.

Tally explained that she thought travelling the lines from start to finish was quite the adventure. Violet voiced her opinion that riding without actually wanting to go somewhere was a little silly.

Tally had actually been to Kensington once or twice before to make a little money, but this did not provide an opportunity to look around during the day. They both agreed this was a good place to stay, at least for a while.

A good, solid meal and a comfortable bed for the night was the first order of the day, and the Baileys Hotel in particular appeared to fit the bill perfectly on all counts. She took the opportunity to slip the looted ring onto her own finger—it was a loose fit, but enough to keep up appearances. They wandered in, bedraggled as they both were, and booked in under the name of Elizabeth and Victoria Turnham.

"Fine English queens, past and present!" Tally explained once they got to their rooms. "Just like us!"

"Who is Queen Turn'em?" Violet asked, puzzled.

Tally answered, giggling. "Turnham is from *Turnham Green*—another Underground station. Sadly, I could think of nothing else!"

Violet shared her amusement and for some time, the two enter-tained themselves by making up nonsensical names from stations. 'Ealing-on-the-Hill', 'Willesden Cottage' and 'Brompton Blackfriars' were all mooted, and 'Kensington' was most certainly going to be the name of Violet's pet cat—once she had one.

They left the hotel once again in order to purchase suitable clothing and other essentials. After cleaning up and having a delicious supper, they eventually made their way back up to the hotel room and threw themselves on their beds.

Tally considered it the perfect opportunity to speak with Violet before the adventure ended. She was not foolish enough to think they could go on the run forever, but if it was long enough to save them both from Violet's mother, that was good enough. It had to start there.

Tally pulled Violet onto her lap, ensuring she had a firm hold of the girl. "Vi, I'm very sorry; I know you are comfortable there, but I have to ask you again. What *exactly* did your mother do to that poor servant? How could she have possibly killed him when he was taking you around town?"

There was an expected moment of silence, but whilst still looking rather frightened, Violet steeled herself quite well to speak. Tally had clearly gained her trust

"She asked about you," Violet explained. "Mother, I mean. She asked Master Hayes whether you had been around that night you hid in my room. He said you had gone away after looking for your father and she let him go. She said she thought he lied, though. Then, she . . . she . . ."

"Go on."

"Well, I think that pretty necklace did it. It got very bright, and he started screaming. He never screams. I heard something crack and he fell back. She walked out and wind blew the door closed. She just left him there. I had a look, but he was on the floor, not moving.

Then another wind blew. My windows opened and something . . . horrid came out of the shadows. There was howling and shrieking, and I screamed, but nobody could hear me. It kept me awake, Tally. Every time I tried to sleep the wind whispered. It said, 'This is what happens to lying little girls.' I heard it! I wish you could have helped me, Tally."

Tally was uncertain whether terror or blind rage prevailed. She bit her lip, attempting to remain calm. "What happened next?"

Further trembling and a fit of tears ensued. Tally gave all she felt she could—a firm hug and soothing strokes through her great plume of blonde hair.

"That *thing* in the shadow came back. It grew like a great bird and made the whole room even darker! Then the wind stopped, and the room grew brighter, and I got up to look around. But then a snake wrapped around my leg. I tried to get it off, but it was too strong.

"I was pulled off the bed. It was the shadow bird. It was outside the window, but it was pulling me with the snakes. They were part of it. I screamed, but nobody heard me, and it pulled really fast until I was out the window. I banged my head on the ledge on the way out."

Tally moved away from her a little, rooting through the child's hair to search for injury. Sure enough, there was a nasty-looking bruise on the left side of Violet's forehead, well covered by the hair and past its worst stages, but there nonetheless. Tally nodded once for Violet to continue.

"I grabbed the ledge as hard as I could. It was far too strong and pulled me away. And then the shadow got longer, let me drop on my head. I thought I was going to, but it pulled me up just before I did. I looked up and begged it to stop. It just gave a terrible cry. Nobody else could see it or hear it; two of the maids just carried on with their work. They looked sick, too, like Peter."

Tally released her grip and dropped backwards on the bed. Whatever had befallen the Raine household was well beyond anything even her guile and cunning could match. It was hopeless; she was up against an opponent who would wilfully allow her own daughter to suffer at the hands of her minions.

Her mind raced. Attempting to calculate a way out of the horrendous ordeal, she could do little other than to continue stroking Violet's hair, and to tell the girl what she knew to be an awful untruth. "Try not to fret so, Vi. You and I are going to be just fine now, no matter what. I promise I shall never allow those creatures to come for you again."

CHAPTER TEN

Thomas Barber knew what he had to do. Even if *he* contemplated defying his mistress, Natalie would not. Twisted as his form now was, at least he was still a living being. Natalie, on the other hand, was a walking corpse—a pitiful parody of what was once a human being.

Iron bar in hand and grinning, the thing still managed to move *too* gracefully, even more so than it had in life. The look on Natalie's face was distant, alien. Breathing was no longer a necessity, but the fact that she continued to pull air in and out of her lungs through sheer habit just rubbed his face in it all the more. The more he thought about it, the more it sickened him.

He knocked hard on the door, already pitying anyone unfortunate enough to be inside. It was answered by a dishevelled-looking young woman paying very little attention to her guests. Instead, her focus remained firmly on a boy and a girl behind her, running at high speed around the lounge.

"Stop jumping on the sofa!"

That lack of attention allowed Natalie the opportunity to drop the iron bar, gag the mother with one hand, and lift her by the throat with the other. There was the briefest muffle of protest from the woman before Barber barged in, closing the door quietly behind them.

He scanned the room and saw the children had done as their mother had asked, though not due to her command. They stood, awestruck at Natalie's effortless feat of strength, and no doubt his unsettling appearance. That suited his purposes just fine.

He gestured to Natalie, who held the woman firm, but left her able to talk.

She manipulated the woman's head to face him directly, and he drew closer, exposing his bestial teeth, slavering. "Where is the driver?" he asked.

Another gesture towards Natalie. She dumped the mother on the ground and wandered over to the children. Their brief attempt to flee was short-lived. In truth, Thomas knew that none of them would leave the place again. He crouched down and lifted her chin, smiling in a twisted pretence at civility. "Answer me."

"He-he's not here!"

He pulled her by her hair back up to her feet. Before she could scream, he placed his hand to her throat. "Then *where* is he?"

"I don't know!"

"Yes, you *do*." He looked at her left hand, spotted the single gold ring on it, and gently stroked until he had a firm grip on the ring finger. "Surely you know where your husband is at this time of day?" The hand around her throat was forced into her mouth, before he snapped her finger backwards.

"He went to work—AAAAGH!!"

The brief moment of clarity he tried to gain eluded him once again, his instinct returned to ensure the suffering of the wretched being in his grasp. Sheer sadism was not the only reason. The fact was, the longer he could sustain his victim's pain, the longer he could dull the agony which constantly wracked his stretched, oversized body. It was the only thing that worked.

He gagged her again and snapped another finger. She bit into his hand. He didn't care. He couldn't feel it. In fact, for the first time in a few days, he felt no pain at all. "If he was at work . . ." he said, dragging her to the front window. He tapped at it with his free hand and pointed at the driveway. "Surely he would have taken the car?" He looked down at her freshly injured hand. "Next time, it'll be one of theirs."

He turned his head towards Natalie and the children she held securely. She eyed both of them hungrily. He returned his attention to the mother, still howling even as her teeth remained firmly entrenched in his hand. He watched, distantly, as a tar-like blood oozed from the freshly created wound, yanking his hand away.

"He's gone to the shops . . . he'll be back any minute now!"

She was not lying this time.

"Then we wait. I'm in no hurry."

Barber knocked her to the floor with his injured hand before rubbing his wounds against his chin. The bite marks sealed. He turned his attention back to Natalie, nodding once. Grinning maniacally, she hurled the girl to the floor and retrieved the iron bar.

As soon as he saw Natalie raise her weapon arm, Barber sat on the couch, turning his back, blanking out everything he could hear behind him. He sighed, rubbing his temples as he waited on the one person he actually needed.

"Why?" he mumbled. Natalie would not have stopped even if she had heard him. "Why did I allow all this to happen?" Had he not, he would not be sitting here, in a stranger's lounge, about to add to his ever-increasing kill count.

For there, in that rare moment of clarity, he was able to personally recall every one of his victims. Even poor Beatrice, whom he did not intentionally lay harmful hands on, would have survived had she not run into him. He remembered every detail of that fateful dream perfectly.

The monster that was once Thomas Barber got back to his feet, peering through the window as a man walked up the path, cheerily prepared to greet his wife and children. His stomach knotted with every step the man took—another step to his doom, but he remembered the consequences of failure.

"Him or me . . ."

Only through the suffering of another could his own be eased.

She—his mistress—whatever she was, had grown tremendously in strength since her emergence. He was under no illusion that he had done anything other than kill Sarah that night. 'Violet' was as a goddess in stature, even to him. Although she grew in power, she was getting more difficult to fathom—growing increasingly unstable. He daren't defy her now.

And what of his prey? Although at their last meeting, he was undoubtedly capable of killing Rose, Violet placed some real urgency on the task—as if she had something to fear from this young woman. But if she did . . .

"Enough!"

With one blow from his fists, he disintegrated the mantelpiece. It silenced the whimpering in the room and even gave pause to his otherwise distracted assistant. He bolted towards the door as he heard a key turn.

The moment the door opened, Barber seized the shocked man by his shirt with both hands and plucked him inside, shutting the door behind them. As the man looked to cry out, Thomas punched him, smashing his nose.

"Taxi driver, right?" Barber said, getting into the man's face. "Worked yesterday afternoon? Hospital passengers?" He struck him hard in the stomach. "Well?" His captive nodded feebly, at which he was allowed to fall to the floor.

"I need to know where you dropped some passengers."

Thomas took his time with the driver. He felt almost sorry for those he had left at Natalie's mercy, but that was as much room as he had for remorse. Their collective suffering would feed him, give him strength for everything to come.

But, even though he had not thought it possible—inside, another part of him died.

CHAPTER ELEVEN

Rose leaned her head against the cool glass of the door window, exhausted from her exploits at the *Half Moon*. Helping Serge had drained her. Even Kara's driving—or her incessant demands for information—could not keep her eyes open. There was time to sleep on the way back.

'Everyone is staring. Why?'

'Don't know. Don't care. Hungry. Again.'

Where the hell am I?

Cinema queue.

Confused, disturbed thoughts raced through her head. She stood amongst a loitering crowd, in a hurry and yet moved forward slowly, if at all. Where were they going? Why couldn't she make it make sense?

'Follow. This queue is fastest.'

Am I dreaming again? Can't be. We didn't go out to the cinema. This isn't me. So who?

"What film would you like to see?"

That voice was clear. Booth staff. But the others, hundreds of them shouted all at once. Voices as much a part of herself—and as inescapable—as her own.

Too *many* voices. Too much chaos. She couldn't hear him.

How can anyone live like this?

'What does he want? Why is he talking at me? Oh. Money. Here, somewhere. Give him money and I can pass.' She reached in to her bag and flung him several notes.

More staring. He looks confused. Why is he stopping me again?

The vendor handed her back most of the money and also a ticket, then waved her past. He spoke again.

'Rude. Talking about me. Silly man.'

'Follow the crowd.'

Another staff member. He ushered her to the seats.

She's really confused. Whoever this is. Whoever I am.

The noise wasn't so bad in there. A few voices. Some noisy eaters. One horrid teenage boy near the front.

'Staring at me. Talking about me.'

Bile rose in her throat as she felt the eyes all directed at her. She wanted to tear their eyes out. The teenager pointed at her.

'So rude! And why is he waving?'

'Oh, I know. It's who I chose—this form. This *Sarah*. She's beautiful. That must be why they keep staring.'

Sarah? Sarah Bliss? Oh, no.

'But the way they look at me. I am NOT a monster!'

The loud voices descended into low whispers as the lighting dimmed.

'Dark. Much better. But why is nobody on stage yet? Why are there flashing lights? That noise?'

The film is starting. Why's she freaking out?

'Too noisy in here—can't bear it. Be quiet, all of you!'

That boy was shouting at her again. "Freak!" he called. "Sort your hair out!"

'What does he mean? Getting cross now.'

"Shhh!" they all said. But the boy did not obey.

'Shhh!' She covered her face with her hands. 'Go away!'

He did not. He just got louder.

Everyone fell silent, apart from the boy, who stood up and gave a mocking laugh. Her own voices remained.

Two of his friends next to him joined in.

'I said SHHH!'

They really should. This won't end well for them.

"Whatever," he said. He glared at her before sitting back down. "Crazy-haired bitch."

'What did you call me? Rude again! Should tear your head off!'

Explosions flashed on the screen. Heavy rumbles rang out, as well as shouting, loud bangs and rapid gunfire.

Dozens of voices—and memories, all babbled and howled at once.

We remember these noises. Fire! Gas! INCOMING! Not again! Spare us! So horrible! She covered her face with her hands again and placed her feet on the chair, drawing her knees under her chin. She rapidly rocked forwards and backwards.

'Stop it, stop it, stop it!'

Please, you idiots—do as she says! She's not messing around.

"Excuse me." A nearby gentleman stood up and smiled nervously at her, tentatively placing a hand upon her shoulder. "It's not really for me to say, but maybe you should take a few minutes out until you feel a little better?

She stopped rocking and turned suddenly to face him. "Nothing to worry about," she muttered, "nothing at all . . ."

"I beg to differ. You don't look well."

"Why do you say that?" she growled. "Nothing wrong with me."

The gentleman gave her a little space but did not retreat. "You just look . . . well, sick. Can I help at all?"

"NOTHING WRONG WITH ME!" Everyone covered their ears.

Ow! That hurt like hell! They all yelled at once. Who are all these voices with this—Sarah, is it?

"Told you she was a freak!" That boy again. This time, some heads nodded with him.

"You think that, too?" She glared at the helpful gentleman, who trembled. "You *do!*"

"No!" He shook his head vigorously. "But you *do* look unwell and I think you should be at home or something."

Come on, Sarah. He's trying to help. Accept his help. You're not well.

"Stop staring at me!" She leapt to her feet and gripped his neck before he could react.

'I can feel the life in him.' She smiled. 'Hunger. Ravenous hunger. Sate us. Starving. Eat. Feed.'

A blue tint overcame his natural colour, and the veins rose to the surface of his skin. Each visibly blackened as she consumed all that *life*. She dropped his empty body to the floor without blinking and looked around at the others. They were screaming now. This was better.

For pity's sake, Sarah, stop this!

A flash of blue burst from the jewel around her neck. She spread her arms out wide and closed her eyes. The voices all chattered, delirious, frantic with anticipation.

'Free!'

'Feast!'

'Break them all! Just like at the hospital!'

From the tips of her fingers flew crackles of pure darkness, raw power. Shards of black lightning sucked the light from every last corner of the already dim auditorium. Out of control, undiluted rage and destruction surged through her in weaponised form.

'Die, die, die!'

It felt so good—such a relief to let it all out.

A deadly, bitter wind grew around her, rapidly accelerating from a breeze to a gale so freezing as to petrify any it touched. The dark lightning flicked and lashed like whips before seeking out every other living individual in the vicinity, bar one.

'That boy laughed at me. Squeeze his head off myself, yes . . .'

Shit! This is horrible! Got to get out of here.

'DIE!'

She watched them run, to try and escape. In their panic, they fell over chairs and each other.

'So afraid.' Frenetic laughter laced with malevolence.

Rose battled to escape from the nightmare. But although she told herself to writhe free, the body ignored her. She knew it beyond her control. It was not hers.

Let them go! For God's sake, stop it!

Rose tried to focus her mind, to force motion. Still the assault pressed on. The crowd couldn't run far, any of them. Each became extraordinarily heavy-legged and slow, as if trying to run through tar. Rose felt trapped, helpless and motionless, as she watched them attempt to run.

'Hopeless for you.'

If she could not move, then she would at least try and fight. *Enough! They've done nothing to you!* But her voice got drowned out—just as did the others.

'Teach them to laugh at me. Foolish people.'

The baleful blue glow from the jewel around her neck provided the only light in the room. It soon became unbearable. Rose averted her eyes and tried again to summon her will. She remained trapped, but the voices, the *others*, grew quieter. More focused.

In that moment of concentration, Rose could see the true malevolence of the light burning from the jewel. She could triangulate the hungry voices there, too. She knew it to be a vessel of concentrated anger, with an all-consuming desire for destruction. Just like the man who had offered his aid just moments ago, each of the others succumbed to the unstoppable force.

'Tear . . . their . . . lives . . . from . . . them.'

Rose could see the excruciation on their faces. They both could. She—Sarah?—cackled with every snapping bone and tearing vein. The power channelled through her like a wave. But Rose could feel it, too: the exhilarating power of life and death flowing through her. She was as a goddess, ecstasy flooding her every glorious act of violence.

The voices of the victims grew deafening as they joined the many others she heard screaming. The jewel glowed brighter with each additional tormented voice.

Done.

Her arms lowered. The light in the theatre returned to normal. She slapped at her head in a futile attempt to straighten the strands of chaotic blonde hair.

Can't have anyone laughing at me now.

Bodies fell to the floor.

What have you done? Jesus, Sarah, what have you done?! No! No, no, no—leave him be! He only laughed at you.

The look of horror on the boy's face tasted delicious. He would be, too. She took her time ambling over to him, watching him tremble and knowing he would not attempt to run. What he was about to experience was no laughing matter.

Don't do it, I'm begging you!

No!

CHAPTER TWELVE

She's been asleep the entire drive back," Kara told Jennifer upon their return. Her friend had been sitting near the front window of her house, waiting for them. She dashed out before Kara had finished parking and, before one word was uttered, carried Rose back inside. Jennifer laid her on their couch, standing over her, watching her disturbed sleep pattern.

"What's she mumbling?" Jennifer asked.

"Don't know," Kara answered. "I didn't want to wake her. She just completely crashed out. Although, whatever she did at the pub must have caused it."

"Not a great surprise, really." Jennifer lightly stroked Rose's hair back, pausing to look carefully at it before placing her palm on the clammy, sweaty forehead. "With what she's been through, it's *going* to take it out of you."

Kara nodded. "I'd genuinely love to know what went on in the bar," she said, drumming her fingers against her sofa. "I missed most of it taking a call." Both of them stared at Rose, breathing shallowly and sweating profusely. Oddly, in some ways, she looked the height of health.

"Say," Kara said, "she still giving you creepy vibes?"

Jennifer gave a lengthy blink, inhaling slowly and deeply before fixing her gaze on Rose. Kara squinted as she observed a subtle but definite brightening of the green in Jennifer's eyes. She always seemed to do that when she *really* examined someone. However, Jennifer looking surprised after such an inspection was rare. Jennifer then reached to check her pulse, which was extremely odd.

"No," Jennifer said, startled, "Actually, it's an awful lot *better*." After a few seconds, the surprise became relief. "That's a drastic change from what I was picking up before."

Kara gave a devilish grin. "Come on; let's wake her up." No sooner than she had said it, she reached forward and started shaking Rose from the shoulders. "Oi!"

"Hey!" Jennifer called, weakly pulling Kara away from Rose. "Take it easy, will you? Remember what she's been through."

Before Kara could respond, Rose suddenly opened her entirely pitch-black eyes. She sprang to her feet, and her icy cold hand clamped around Kara's neck.

"*Not so funny now, is it, boy?*" She spoke with a voice that echoed low and chilling.

As Kara's vision began to blur, she felt the temperature in the room plummet as a sudden gale whipped paper through the air.

Kara struggled uselessly against the stranglehold as she felt her breath torn out of her. Sheer agony seared every muscle.

"*You should never have made fun of me!*"

In less than a heartbeat, silenced, helpless, Kara sensed her inevitable death; her arms slumped to her side. The eyes looking into hers widened, a satisfied smile breaking out on the face of this *other* dominating Rose. The darkness took over. Kara felt herself being drawn into a deathly oblivion . . .

"Get off her!"

A sledgehammer of a punch broke Rose's grip, and Kara slumped to the floor. Drained of all strength, she watched as Jennifer launched herself over the couch to where Rose had landed on the other side of the room. Despite Jennifer's advantage, Rose blocked each attack with embarrassing ease. However, Kara saw she appeared uninvolved, detached, like she was—elsewhere. Kara attempted to halt the melee with an ailed wheeze.

That instant, Rose appeared aware of her surroundings—right before being knocked out cold by a clean punch she did not even try to defend.

~*~

The rage. The anger. The hatred. The despair. It all flooded Rose again, hard and heavy. For a fleeting moment she thought she had escaped, but she was dragged back in, try as she might.

Again, the screen showed a noisy and elaborate car chase, despite the carnage amongst the audience. She was face-to-face with the only survivor of the attack—the teenage boy. She held him a couple of feet off the ground by his throat. Rose knew what was coming next—she had said the words to Kara. But they weren't her words. That wasn't her.

She had no control over what was happening, but with a mighty force of will, she managed to look down.

The shades of light in her vision rapidly changed and drew her focus to the caged jewel and its eerie glow hanging around her neck.

Her sight snapped forward again. The despair was deafening.

177

The boy. Too late.

The teenager thudded to the floor. He fought for air and tried to stand. The hand that clutched him turned palm upwards, her other hand following suit, and black strings tore out of its fingers.

I said leave him be!

'He must suffer. Then die.'

The strings coiled around his limbs, snapping him into an unnatural contortion.

He's suffered enough! I've suffered enough.

As the fingers were drawn in, the boy arched unnaturally far backwards, his mouth wide open.

He's not screaming. But I can hear him. Let him go. That's enough.

The monster yanked the strings like a puppet master. Rose could feel the strings and attempted to stop their movement. But it was hopeless. Sickening pops and crunches followed as he broke his own back trying to escape.

Leave him! Get off him! The monster was relentless. She crouched at the prone teenager and thrust sharp fingernails into him.

'Feel the power.'

Yes. I do. It's wrong. Stop it now!

'Don't want to stop. Feed. Feel the power.'

Rose felt an unbelievable rush of energy wash over her. It felt hideous, *wrong*.

'But nobody can stop me. Nobody can hurt me *ever again*. Now they do what *I* say. Yummy!'

No! This is an innocent life being murdered. I'm not here. I'm somewhere else. Wake up. Wake up!

~ ☆ ~

"Don't, Jen!" Kara called feebly. Jennifer straddled Rose, her fist raised, her intent deadly. The command stayed her hand, and she turned to Kara.

"She almost *killed* you, Kara!" Jennifer snarled, a murderous glare in her eyes.

"She didn't mean to." With every last ounce of strength, she raised her voice to normal volume. "Who do you know who refers to me as, 'boy'? There's more to this."

"What??" Jennifer rolled off Rose, but stood over her, glaring her animosity. At last, Kara's best friend turned to face her. Kara knew she inspected the damage inflicted by the attack. Jennifer turned back to Rose, and then once more to Kara. "If you're sure."

Kara attempted and failed to return to her feet. "I'm sure." She gave a feeble cough and sat upright against the wall. "That was unpleasant. Worst experience of my life."

"Then why did you call me off?" Jennifer snarled.

"Because it wasn't Rose." Kara forced the weakness from her voice. "Did it sound like her to you?"

Jennifer looked suspiciously back at Rose, who began to stir. "I don't know. She's done a creepy voice before."

"That exact one?" Kara snapped back.

Jennifer considered a moment before answering. "Well, no, but—"

"So let's not make assumptions, eh?"

Jennifer looked as if she wanted to press her argument but stopped herself, trust winning out over protectiveness.

"But you look like *she* did—like *them*."

"Who's *them*?"

"The people at the hospital—the ones in the news images."

Rose gave a low, weak moan.

"Get her over to the couch, will you?" Kara whispered.

"But she—and you're injured—"

"Please, just *do* it, Jen." Kara coughed again, barely remaining upright.

Jennifer wandered back to the collapsed Rose and stared assertively at her. "All right," she said, unconvinced. "But if she so much as looks at you funny, I'm putting her down."

Jennifer picked Rose up by the collar and dumped her unceremoniously on the couch. She never took her eyes from the interloper, poised in case of another assault. Within seconds, Jennifer leapt on her again, glaring fiercely.

"The eyes," she accused, ready for violence, "they're changing again!" Both Jennifer and Kara then watched as Rose's eyes shifted from inky black to a more normal, piercing blue. They darted in numerous unfocused directions. The bruise under her chin rapidly disappeared, and Jennifer seemed unable to turn away. Rose blinked several times.

"What was that about?" Jennifer asked, retaining an aggressive undertone. "Are you done trying to kill Kara now?"

Rose nodded but leaned around Jennifer. Kara was still worse for wear.

"She's still sick," Rose advised, a pleading look in her eye. "I can fix her."

Jennifer gave an incredulous, horrified look. "Do you think I'm going to let you *near* her after what you just did?"

"If I do nothing, she may die." Rose's tone was low and controlled, though she looked tearful. "Just let me try and put it right. Please."

Jennifer pulled back and stood up once more, turning to her sick friend in a questioning way. Kara gave a single nod before being wracked by a hacking cough. Jennifer turned back, pulling Rose back to her feet, and almost threw her at Kara.

"Get on with it, then!"

~ ✶ ~

Rose, still dazed, tentatively took Kara's arms and placed a thumb on a vein at the crook of her elbows.

She reminded herself of what had happened at the Underground station, trying desperately to think of what had kept her alive that night, and whether any of it related to this. It had not.

Concentrating even as she did, there was nothing forthcoming about having saved a life. She remembered her work with Serge, but that was more saving a soul.

"Hurry it up if you're doing something!" Jennifer snapped.

"I don't—I don't know what to say. It wasn't my—"

And then Rose gave a gleeful squeal. "That's it!" she cried. "What I got from Kara wasn't mine to take! It was hers! All I have to do . . ." She closed her eyes and focused upon remembering the peace she brought to Serge, gathering herself into a state of calm and serenity. ". . . is put it back!"

The darkness in Kara's veins started to fade away slowly. She raised both hands closer to her face and stared at her wrists. She grinned with approval. Suddenly Rose withdrew her hands and recoiled in sudden fear.

"What's the problem?" asked Kara, sounding very much her normal self. She waved away Jennifer, who was still on high alert.

"I'm sorry," replied nervous Rose. "It's just that last time I did this, the guy vanished on me. I'm sure it was all perfectly peaceful and all, but I don't want to send you on or anything."

"On?" Kara asked, intrigued.

At Kara's demand for information, Rose quickly explained everything that she had experienced in *The Half Moon*. "That . . . is *amazing*!" Kara asked for her laptop and commenced typing.

"There is absolutely no recorded data on what you just said any-where. Believe me, I am very thorough, and no one has *seen* what you have. Actually, that's amazing. I'm a pioneer of the paranormal!" She punched the air.

"Now, are you finished fixing me, or are you still flapping about it?"

Rose shrugged. "How do you know nothing else will happen to you?" she asked. Jennifer nodded, giving a concerned frown. "You've already told me you've never seen anything like this—like *me* before. How do you *know*?"

"Because I'm damned confident that if you wanted to kill me, you'd have done it already. God knows you've had enough chances. And let's face it, if you can stop purely out of self-doubt and to tell me a story, you can certainly stop when you've fixed *me*." She gave her familiar reassuring look and then placed her computer on the table. She held out her arms, beckoning Rose.

"Come on; I'm in the middle of the greatest experiment in occult history and I want to see it through."

"Be *very* careful what you wish for."

Rose knelt in front of Kara again and took her by her arms.

"Do it," Kara commanded. Rose cleared her mind and once more fo-cused, imposing her will. She watched, determined, as the greyed veins still at the surface of Kara's skin faded, and her regular complexion returned in full—all recent blemishes eradicated, a blissful smile on her face and her eyes closed—as did Rose's.

Rose released her hold as a multitude of images flooded her mind. She bowed repeatedly to a standing ovation and threw a wand into the crowd. Then, somewhere else, a middle-aged couple, a dapper, shaven-headed black man, and a tall, attractive raven-haired woman lectured her, reminding her to concentrate on her studies.

And then, the first meeting with Jennifer. Rose knew it was her, but she looked so mouse-like, dishevelled. And yet, something extraordinary was present about her, warranting further investigation. She could help her. They could help *each other*.

As she opened her eyes, Kara looked bemused. But she could not help herself blurting out. "Kara? You did stage magic?"

"I haven't done that in—wait a minute; I never told you anything about—how do you *know* about that, Mary?"

"Because I just saw—" She stopped. "Wait—did you just call me 'Mary'?"

"Why wouldn't I? It's your *name*."

"Yes . . ." she mumbled, thinking about it even as she spoke. "Oh, Jesus, it *is* my name." She knew it, and somehow, had known all along. "Mary . . . Mary Hall."

"Amazing." Kara's presence had seemingly returned with an enthusiastic vengeance. "Sit down—I'll tell you a bit about what I got. But you breathe a bloody word about—"

"Fine—your secret's safe with me. Well, us." Mary looked to Jennifer, who shrugged. "But I need your help, both of you, and I need it now."

"With the memory loss and Mister Muscles, you mean?" Kara asked, a bullish look about her. "Sure. We could do with getting to the bottom of both of those things."

"No." Mary shook her head dismissively. "I think I know who was behind all the killings outside the hospital. Sarah Bliss. She's got the necklace I was talking about."

"How do you know that, love?"

"I *was* asleep, but that wasn't just a dream. I was *there*, Kara. I saw everything. It was very bad."

"One way to know for sure," Kara said. "Let's find a news report. Jen—big screen, please."

Jennifer duly obliged.

The scenes were shocking and somewhat strange. The reporter was speaking outside the cinema, a recent evacuation evidently having taken place, but for whatever reason, ambulance and police crews were not actually carrying any wounded, or indeed doing much at all. They could see emergency services staff involved in heated discussions outside the cinema, the entire area cordoned off. The ticker tape headline stream simply read:

SECOND TERROR ATTACK KILLS
DOZENS IN LONDON CINEMA

After a couple of minutes of everyone just staring at the screen in silence, Kara spoke. "This was what you were talking about, I presume?"

Mary nodded. "Yes, and I'm pretty sure I know what happened in there. *She* did this."

"I don't get it," Jennifer said quietly, her gaze remaining fixed to the screen. "They've not actually shown any footage from anywhere other than outside the cinema, and there's a whole load of *trained* professionals standing around doing *nothing*! They handle crises for a living—they shouldn't be looking anywhere near as terrified as they do."

"Does seem a little unusual," Kara said, looking up briefly, but keeping the bulk of her focus on Mary.

"A *little?*" Jennifer scowled. "I've seen them deal with earthquakes, volunteering to head halfway around the world, and never a hint of hesitation. And it's not just one of them—it's *all* of them. Like they've had the fright of their lives."

"They *have*." Mary looked pale, but not unnaturally so this time. "Shhh!"

"The latest received from this extraordinary situation is that, despite direct orders from the top of their chain of command, every single member of the Metropolitan Police or London Ambulance Service despatched to the scene has refused to enter Screen Three of the cinema. Everyone who has attempted to enter has stopped near the front door. None of them are able to provide a suitable explanation as to why."

"I've got a bloody good idea." Mary glared at the screen for a moment before moving to the front door with purpose. "And now we know where to go. Come on!"

"Wait!" Kara said forcefully. "Before we rush off, we should know what we're up against."

"I'll tell you on the way," Mary spoke, but with a subtle menace in her quiet voice, and the deathly breeze returned.

Both Jennifer and Kara took a step back from her. But after a second or two, Kara beamed widely. "Aha!" she cried. "Just as I thought!"

"What?" Mary and Jennifer called out in perfect unison.

"There go your eyes again—entirely dark. You've only ever done that when you've been pissed off about something. And those cold winds— good God! That's all *you*."

"Sorry," Mary muttered, backing away from the two, "I didn't mean to."

"It's fine," Kara said, closing on Mary calmly, like a trained negotiator, "no harm done this time. I think we're working you out, lady—and you're quite the little goddess. We now know some of what you do;

you channel through anger, but not everything. Bringing Serge peace and fixing me were both the opposite. I might have been out of it, but I could tell just by looking at you.

"On top of all that, we know you managed to travel very, very quickly, and walls don't bother you. Just like with ghosts. It still almost defies belief—*almost*, but I get the impression you can get around in a different way from most of us, if you put your mind to it."

Jennifer reeled forward, gagging.

"Jen? You all right?" Kara rushed to her aid but was shoved away.

"I . . . I'm fine." Still spluttering, she brought herself to her feet. "I'm just feeling a little off. Like I'm surrounded by the dead or something."

"Why now?" Kara asked.

"Trying to do too much, I think. I was trying to keep my senses up so I could know quickly if you were about to get worse." Jennifer cast a look at Mary, clearing her throat. "And I won't lie—I had to be certain it wasn't going to come from *her*."

"And *are* you?" Mary stared back coldly.

"That's the problem," Jennifer answered, "I don't know *what* you are. And it freaks me out more than anything. See, a bit like you, Mary, I can see things. I can tell if people are sick when they don't know it themselves.

"I can spot a spiked drink at a club or a bit of cooked meat that'd poison someone. Enough about what's in a syringe to tell you whether it'll kill or cure the person it's meant for. But you—I've got *nothing*. I can feel death around you; you're surrounded by it. But there's more to you than that, and I can't decide whether that's for better or worse."

"Hold up," Mary said. "Surrounded?"

Jennifer gave a nasty cough, lurching forward and clutching her stomach. She looked up, sweat dotted across her brow. "Yeah—*others* . . . really close . . ."

"*Others?*"

Jennifer wiped the sweat away with the back of her hand and forced herself back to her feet. Once upright, she appeared in better shape.

"Right." Kara leapt to her feet. "Odeon. Now."

With her words, a mighty impact slammed into the front door, bulging the centre, though it remained on its hinges.

"Kitchen!" Jennifer yelled. "Back door!" As they turned, both entrances were breached, felled by the intruders.

"Get down!" Jennifer cried. The others dropped as the door shattered. A familiar hulking brute stood in the doorway. Entering from the rear was an accomplice, bestial hunger on her sickly pale face.

Jennifer and Kara looked on in terror as the two closed in on them slowly. A realisation suddenly hit them.

"*Mary!*" Jennifer said frantically. "Where's Mary?"

The monster spoke in a chilling voice, baring sharp yellow teeth in an aggravated semblance of a smile.

"That's what I was hoping you two could tell me."

CHAPTER THIRTEEN

Rose—*Mary,* in fact—felt an overwhelming urge to flee.

Just as when she had faced the assassin both times before.

Try as she might to face him . . . to fight this . . . to fight *him*—no sooner had the door buckled than her instincts took her as far away from this monster as possible. And proved Kara's theory. Her surroundings suddenly darkened; a lash of icy wind whipped at her face. She had got as far away as possible, to this increasingly familiar other world. However, as fast as came the thought, a blinding white light overwhelmed her.

Recoiling the instant she came to a stop—strange, as she had taken no actual steps—the ferocious light was nothing like the greying shadow, the never-ending darkness of before. The only time she'd seen anything even close was when she had encountered Serge—and that was from . . .

". . . Me."

With her hands cupped over her eyes, she found that she could clearly identify the shapes of her fingers, which provided a bright light source. Something, or someone, was a *lot* brighter. She had to choose: return and face the evil she knew (and the new companion she knew nothing of), or stay and figure out another way of getting them all out safely.

She quickly became aware that, although she had physically vacated the area she had occupied, she was, to all intents and purposes, still *there* in the house. It was like another world all right, but one parallel to her own. And that meant she was still with her friends and her enemies.

Intuitively, she understood. In this other world, she shone brightly when beside the dead. This time, Kara and Jennifer factored in.

Jennifer. She remembered her words from earlier. *"I can see things. But unlike you, not ghosts. Kind of the opposite."*

Then in this shadow world, life equated to light. *That* was why she shone next to Serge, why he, the ghost, was a faint echo in comparison, and why Jennifer shone so brightly as to blind her. She was a special case—a 'force of nature' as Kara had called her.

She felt new power the more she learned, but she needed something to temper the light.

Something like sunglasses?

She closed her eyes, and reached out with thought, with memory, to discern where she had been standing, where the stairs were, and where the bedroom was located. Instinctively in her mind, a short trail became clear. Her feet did not need to move. The rules were different there. She only needed the thought.

~ ⋆ ~

Kara had leapt for cover behind a sofa as Jennifer faced off against the massive intruder. She peered over the top. From the kitchen, she caught a silhouette of his accomplice flailing wildly and smashing a path.

"Kara," Jennifer called, loud but calm. "Find a way out of here. Do it now." She took a deep breath, which mutated into a bestial growl.

The giant poised himself for battle, sizing up his opponent. "Sort the other one out, Natalie," he ordered. "This one's mine."

Kara continued to observe. From where she was, the front door was the closer exit, but her way out relied on Jennifer. The kitchen was not an option. The giant—now that she could get a proper look, there was something familiar about him. Vestiges of a handsome man she had seen in a computer screen image in that research. It would have involved some hideous mutations, though.

Everything else Kara had seen made that very possible.

"Barber?" She did not even realise she had uttered the word aloud until the beast gave a pained roar and lurched toward the sofa. She scuttled backwards, but behind him, Jennifer took the opening and tripped him.

"Get out of here!" she barked at Kara, who turned to her and just shook her head.

"I'm not going *anywhere* without you and Mary," Kara asserted. But Natalie closed in on her, crowbar raised.

In a flowing move, Jennifer shoved Natalie hard in the stomach with both of her razor-sharp hands, sending her sprawling back into the kitchen. She hurled a coffee table at Barber. Despite its velocity, Barber found the projectile a mere distraction.

"I'll find her and catch you up," Jennifer cried. "Go!"

Kara crouched, hesitant, as Barber rose once more. Jennifer leapt onto his back, but Barber plucked her off and launched her clear of him as if throwing a cat. Jennifer winced as she crashed into the mantelpiece, destroying a shelf.

She immediately dug her razor-like fingers into the carpet and roared whilst leaping at him again, raking his face hard. Barber howled in pain. He swung fists at Jennifer with all his might—but too slow. Kara sidled around the sofa as her friend rhythmically weaved and dodged each of the brute's blows, drawing him away from the door.

"*Now!*" Jennifer screamed. Barber looked in Kara's direction, and Jennifer unleashed a flurry of lightning-fast punches on him. Kara took the opportunity to make a dash for the door, only to be tripped by a strong, cold hand, which wrapped around her ankle. She was yanked backwards hard and fast. Kara rotated to face her attacker, Natalie. The undead raised a crowbar-wielding arm high into the air, ready to deliver a mighty blow to Kara's head.

"Wait!"

Barber raised a hand. Natalie obeyed. In his other hand, he held Jennifer above the ground by her throat. Turning back to Jennifer, he continued, "Last chance. Tell me where the bitch is and I *might let you live.*"

As Barber talked, Kara fumbled for the computer power lead on the table as Natalie loomed over her, fascinated and yet somehow mindless. Finding it within reach of her left hand, she gently and discreetly began to pull it so that the computer edged across the table. She started wailing profusely, ensuring the creature was looking at her face, not her hands.

"No takers?" Barber squeezed harder on Jennifer's air-starved throat. "AAAARGH!"

He suddenly released his grip and dropped Jennifer, her razor-sharp fingers dripping thick, dark blood. He retaliated with a back fist, but above his fallen opponent, who stood and slashed across his throat.

She took a step back before launching a fierce kick between his legs and held his bowing head. She then retracted her razor fingers and made a fist, before raining a series of punishing blows on the back of the head. She let go. Barber fell, motionless, to the ground.

Natalie turned to aid Barber. Once she was distracted, Kara seized the computer with both hands and stood, smashing it on Natalie's head. Kara seized any mugs she could find in the room and hurled them, more to distract than to damage, and bolted for the door.

Natalie gave chase but was floored by a mighty tackle from Jennifer, who ripped away the crowbar and battered her head until it wedged there. Kara grabbed a bunch of keys and ran to the car with Jennifer close behind. As the engine revved, Kara turned to look back to the house. "We're still missing someone," she said.

~ * ~

Once the strange lifting sensation went away, Mary tentatively opened her eyes. Nothing blinded her. There was still one source of light nearby, but that was her; that was fine. It wasn't as bright as before, though.

As in the *Half Moon*, within her line of sight, only her hands were exposed through her clothing. There must have been a difference this time.

Sure enough, she found a set of dark glasses right at the bottom of the rack in Kara's room. The second her hand was on the rims, she found herself returned to regular surroundings, of light and life. Something was wrong, though. The cold of the dead place remained around her. And there was someone *else* in the room, standing right beside her.

"Hmm. Well, you seem to have had the good sense to identify the problem—*almost*, anyway."

Tally had returned. "Go ahead and put them on. They probably *will* help you, but not for the reasons you think."

Mary turned on her heels to face the sneering ghost. "Keep this brief and useful," she said coldly.

"Good Lord—bolder by the minute, I tell you!" It was impossible to tell whether the tone was congratulatory or contemptuous. "But perhaps such bravado should be saved for dealing with your more immediate issues."

"That's right, I have *immediate* issues." Mary put the glasses on and determinedly walked straight through Tally, attempting to gather focus to return to the dark place. However, her concentration was broken, and she stopped, turning to respond through clenched teeth. "I'm going down there, okay? *Right now.*"

The room fell darker, but there had been no shift back to the dead place. She heard violent crashing sounds coming from downstairs, but she was frozen into place by Tally's next words. "I wasn't talking about those two."

Mary turned to face the ghost, who now wore as wide a smile as was possible without opening her mouth. "So what *do* you mean?"

Tally shook her head, clicking her tongue. "Look around. Properly. Stretch your sight beyond merely what is nearby and where you want to go."

"I haven't got time for this." The words were aggravated, low and stern.

"You really need to *make* time for this. What you saw at the theatre was just the start. When you last lost consciousness, I attempted to establish contact. To see how you were getting on. But you were instead drawn towards the force *Death's Teardrop* unleashed—it almost drew you in entirely, in fact."

"That's right; I found the bitch killing people with that necklace at the theatre."

Tally hissed unexpectedly in a way that set Mary on edge. "*Do not* speak with such derision about Violet." The ghost's eyes darkened and her features became jagged, dangerous, suddenly terrifying.

"*Violet*?" Mary said, cautiously. "Her name's Sarah. We checked it out. We are talking about the same crazed killer, right?"

Tally looked at her for a moment with some confusion, calming, taking her more conventional appearance. "Violet is the loudest of the voices in that abominable prison of souls. And when she screams, people die and end up joining her torment. I suspect this 'Sarah' you have mentioned is in there somewhere."

"It's her body."

"Oh." Tally looked thoughtful. "Violet must have liked that one; imagined how she would have—"

"You call the necklace *Death's Teardrop*?" Mary asked, noting sadness on Tally's face now. "It might have been useful to have known that earlier."

"She cannot help herself, you know," Tally said very quietly.

"What?"

"Try to imagine you have been trapped in the most confined space you know, with hundreds of people screaming at you constantly. Then add to that each person reliving their own deaths over and over again— deaths in all likelihood violent. Finally, imagine being able to hear and feel every one of those deaths as if it was your own. It would dement the very strongest of minds. Hence, a child would not stand a chance."

Tears glimmered in the ghost's eye. "And yet, we do what we must, do we not?" Tally faded almost to nothing in the time it took Mary to blink. She returned, a determined glint in her eyes.

"When *she* accessed the necklace's power back at the Alhambra, she also tore another hole between the two worlds in which you walk.

The consequences will be dire, and I need you to see for yourself, so concentrate—and look."

"*Another* hole?" Mary said, trembling.

"Look for yourself," Tally commanded.

Mary did as she was asked. Channelling a will to live above everything, her sight altered back to shadow and light. And for a fleeting moment, she was back in the auditorium in which Violet had stood. There was darkness within the darkness, a void around three metres in height, spitting jagged forks of shadowy lightning. The little light around drained into it, the death winds picking up and circling in a black vortex.

She could sense the trail of screaming souls Violet carried with her. The torment, the anguish was unmistakable—and meant she could sense Violet's presence in a way, as well. It was out there, somewhere, but impossible to track precisely. It was as if she was in hundreds of places at once.

Mary wondered if Violet was having the same problem with her.

As she concentrated, she identified the presence of more holes elsewhere around London, sensing the danger Tally spoke of. It was all building to something much larger.

As her sight stretched further, she heard nothing but childlike whispers. Painful as it was, she pressed on, attempting to drown out the rest of the noise. Then a piercing shriek expelled her from her search, back into the bedroom and the world of the living. Dazed, she covered her ears in pain and reached out to balance herself with the dressing cabinet. "How—?"

Tally interrupted, looking concerned. "You haven't found them all yet, dear. Keep looking."

"I can't!" she spat, trying to regain her orientation. She headed once more for the door. Her attempt was hampered by a sudden bout of dizziness, the entire room seeming to spin around her.

"You need to," Tally calmly replied. "The next could be the most important one for you to see."

"I can't now. I just *can't*! I have to help Kara and Jen."

"I told you; focus upon the priorities. Those two can look after themselves! What could you do to aid them, anyway?"

Though the answer bred uncertainty, Mary knew she had to at least try. "Actually, I've got my priorities straight this time. Follow me if you want—you obviously do most of the time anyway." With that, she donned the glasses and made a run down the stairs.

She had not shifted back to the shadow London before she ran—the cold, lifeless place where, ironically, she was safer than she had been anywhere else. She stopped running as soon as she came off the last step and watched in horror as the two attackers rose from the ground, listening as bones popped and warped back into place and the female pulled a metal bar out of her forehead.

The wound started to close up seconds after she had done so. She quickly scanned the wreck of what once had been a quaint house and a source of sanctuary. Her friends being nowhere in sight sent relief rushing through her.

The two intruders became aware they were no longer alone and turned to face her, grinning. To her great surprise, she found herself smiling back the minute she saw the massive monster's bloody mouth, missing a number of those hideous teeth of his.

"There you are, you little bitch!" he said, spitting out blood and a broken tooth. "Not sure why you're laughing, though. You won't be when we're done with you."

She donned the sunglasses. "You reckon?" she taunted, stubbornly maintaining a smirk, though hiding a slight tremble. "You were expecting me to be crapping myself, didn't you?"

"I would in your place," Barber said, slight doubt in his voice evident.

Why hasn't he gone for me yet?

She smelt blood. "'Course you would," she said. "I can see you for what you *really* are."

As she gave her last jibe, Barber's companion gave a nasty hiss and lunged at her—too late. With a controlled effort, she slid herself back into the shadow world with relative ease. This time she was not instantly blinded by light. In fact it was down to *darkness* this time. She could hardly see at all.

She lifted the glasses to rest on her forehead . . .

. . . and her vision was exactly as was before she removed them.

"Damn!"

After a few seconds, her sight eventually adjusted to the new environment. She caught a dim but solid area of light, *red*, unlike the bright white light she understood to be generated by the living. The source was tall and thick like a tree trunk, with snake-like wisps at its top, each coiling as if swimming underwater.

Between the wisps, there were two small, black circles, staring widely, blinking, and (it was hard to tell in this light) swirling. Just below it, Mary could make out a gap like a wide mouth, with a row of shadowy, sharp teeth.

It was scrambling closer to her, letting out what sounded like a loud scream, but many miles away, as if from a hilltop. One of the branches lashed out at her. Although Mary found her fear had returned to her twice as hard, she stayed rooted to the spot, knowing she had no chance of evading the thing in time.

To her great surprise, the entire creature simply passed straight through her. As she turned a half circle to face it, off-balance from her own momentum, she blinked and took a closer look. A reddened, shadowy version of Barber's monstrous partner was there—if anything, looking *more* human.

She bore an excruciated expression on her face, with deep, powerful roots binding her legs to the ground. A number of the roots appeared to be coming up from the floor and had burrowed into the young woman's stomach. It looked excruciating.

Behind her, the only other source of light, the monstrous man, moved closer. However, his connection to the ground appeared considerably different to that of his companion. His legs, free of roots and clearly visible, appeared bound in *chains*, as did his arms. They wrapped around his entire body, squeezing him hard, crushing him.

There was a face under the tethers—a face which she recognised much more readily as the one on the computer photographs—Thomas Barber. The expression on it somehow managed to convey even more torment than that of the girl's. His mouth was open so wide, it looked as if he was about to rip his own face apart.

Mary focused herself, reaching back into the living world. She snatched books and ornaments from the shelves and flung them hard at the two invaders, watching from the shadow world as slavering jaws roared in fury, darkness and tethered limbs reaching out to protect the hideous faces. There was no real force behind the attacks; she wouldn't have known how—the exercise was intended as a distraction.

As they defended themselves from the missile assault, they countered by completely destroying the offending areas. But this bought valuable few seconds for her to take her leave completely undetected.

CHAPTER FOURTEEN

W e've *got* to go back for her!" Jennifer cried. They looked back at the house, breached and broken.

"And do *what*, exactly?" snapped Kara. "We barely survived back there!"

"Wasn't the whole purpose of this to keep her *alive*?"

"I *know* that, but we can't bloody well save her if we're dead ourselves, can we?"

They hesitated a moment, assessing the best course of action. Kara took deep breaths, imposing reason over panic. They looked at each other, nodded in unison, and reached for their relative door handles.

"We see this through—" said Kara.

"One way or the other," Jennifer finished.

"Personally, I think we should just drive."

The pair nearly jumped out of their skins at the comment from a disembodied voice behind them. Mary, translucent as wax paper, materialised from nowhere on the rear seat behind Kara.

She grinned at their reactions. "Odeon, Leicester Square, please. And I'd step on it—those two you laid out in there are up and running."

Within a second or two, she became fully corporeal, tapping the back of Kara's seat.

"Really?" Jennifer sighed. "Thought I'd done enough to put them down."

"You did. But *keeping* them down is the trick."

"Odeon it is," Kara said. The tyres squealed as she slammed her foot on the accelerator.

"By the way, I ran into Tally just then. She had a lot to say."

"Cool. Has she given you a plan of action?"

"Kind of, though I'm going to need to have a crack at a different problem once I reach the cinema."

"Ah. You mean the emergency services circus in the way?"

"Not what I was talking about, but that won't be a problem." Mary felt a quiet confidence, determination.

Kara grinned and calmed her driving to coolly negotiate the traffic, parking as close as the surrounding chaos allowed. "Mary, can you ghost us inside the building?"

"Not sure," Mary answered after a few seconds' consideration, "but, at a guess, it would be pretty dangerous for you."

"In what way?" Kara asked, raising an eyebrow. "More dangerous than those two we just fought?"

"Look, where I go is a place for the *dead*, not the living—and even then, only some of them. There's a bloody good reason people don't generally visit there."

"In the name of Science," Kara said jovially, "I'm coming with, when you do."

"I'm *not* taking you, Kara. I won't risk your life like that."

"I'm with Mary on this," Jennifer said sternly. "As *you* said, dying saves no one and proves nothing."

"I really should go with you, you know," Kara responded like a child begging for sweets. "You might have the practical knowledge, but in here"—she tapped her head—"I have more theories about this than you've had time to read half of. Do you know anything about extra-dimensional portals?" She gave little time for an answer. "Didn't think so. You *know* you could use my help on this."

Mary changed the subject. "So, about that history lesson, Tally called the necklace: *Death's Teardrop.*"

Kara scrunched her face for a moment. "That makes no sense. I've come across that name before, but it was in reference to a knife. I distinctly remember that much."

"It's what she called it."

"Did you ask her if she'd heard of the *Grenshall Teardrop*?"

"Didn't have time." Kara snapped her fingers. "*Of course!* Everything makes sense now!"

"It does?" asked Jennifer. She peered over her left shoulder, watching out for trouble.

"Yeah, totally. Bloody hell—I didn't even think to make the link! The very thing that got me into this game in the first place, too. An old document I had. It never ever meant anything to anyone other than me.

"It was a leather-bound journal, written in several languages, though predominantly German. It contained my first complete translation from Arabic. One of my tutors gave it to me. He couldn't tell me a thing about it, but he thought I'd find it interesting—and he was right!

"I made a point of studying every word of the collection. Some of the entries were as recent as last century, but one part—the one I'm thinking of—was a copy of something far older. Let's see:

"*'As far as I can discern, she was the first. She was believed to be an assassin operating during the First Crusade, but her exis-*

tence has descended into myth. She was known as 'The One Who Speaks In Whispers,' and the few who presumed to see her said she always dressed in loose, black garments and obscured her face with a mask.

"'It was said to look into her eyes was like staring into the darkest corners of Hell. Just to see her was an omen of your final days. To see her with her blade unsheathed would likely be the last thing you ever saw. The few who lived to tell the tale reported that the blade, no more than a dagger, bore a sapphire the shape of a teardrop.'"

Kara smacked the dashboard, making the others jump. "Damn it! How could I be so stupid?"

"Stupid?" Mary said. "Well, I wouldn't have made the leap unless I'd known—"

"This is what I *do*, though," Kara said, disgusted.

Mary gave her a tap on the shoulder. "So, tell us the rest," she said. "There may be something else useful in there."

Kara nodded. "Within the entry, a tale from a lone Saracen who claimed to have witnessed her in action. He said he'd seen her surrounded by nine fully armoured Knights Templar, each ready to run her through with their blades.

"She drew her weapon, and the source quotes, *I then witnessed a thing both beautiful and terrible, much as I imagined her to be.*' He claimed she vanished into thin air. Three of the nine knights held their throats, fountains of blood gushed from them, and the circle was broken. She would appear, kill, and disappear again, until just one remained—their greatest champion.

"In single combat, he couldn't catch her, *'for she moved so fast as to be untouchable, so light as to be invisible.*' Each time he lunged for her, she would cut him and vanish once more, toying with the brute until he had a hundred cuts. Eventually, she tired of her game and plunged the knife through the heart of the gravely wounded man.

"She watched him sink to his knees before she removed the weapon. The witness said, *'The jewel in the blade shone as bright as the sun, though in the dead of night.'* Nobody had ever defeated her."

"Well, there are *some* similarities," Jennifer observed, "though that's not much to go on."

"Gives us half an idea of how bloody old the thing is, at least," Mary said.

Kara shook her head. "Not really," she said, "it could be much older. So, what else? That's right. It next showed up two centuries later in France—a widow who demanded vengeance on her husband's killer.

"From what I remember, it said she slew her way through dozens of soldiers to get to the murderer, and when she did, rather than just stabbing him, the account said the two of them vanished in plain sight, never to be seen again.

"The blade turned up again some generations later, oddly enough as a wedding gift to a lady who took a bit of a liking of it. She ended up burnt at the stake for witchcraft, but on their last night together, the husband swore vengeance, so says the account from his own diary.

"That didn't end well for anyone. He butchered every last one of the inquisitors and their assistants before taking his own life with the same knife. And so it was, one bard at a time, the tale of *Death's Teardrop* was born."

Mary remembered everything Tally had told her about Violet's suffering and winced. "Okay," she said quietly, "this *does* explain a lot. Yet, not the part about how it becomes a necklace."

"I know," Kara answered. "The last thing mentioned in the journal was something about stolen research notes from around—oh, *of course* it was the 19ᵗʰ century. The weapon resurfaced around then and was thoroughly examined by a member of a metaphysical society.

"Whoever studied the notes realised that the uniquely lethal blade could do far more than simply kill in the hands of those who understood its true purpose."

"Like, you know, trap souls or rip open holes to a world of *even more* death and destruction." Mary grimaced. "Well that's just great. Was there any more to it than that?"

"Sadly, no. The last thing I read was that the rest of the notes were lost in a fire. Coincidence? Not from what I've read."

"Yeah," Jennifer said. "Bang goes our chance of an action plan."

~ ✝ ~

Outside the cinema, Mary turned to her friends and smiled. "Right. Time I got on with it." Her face went blank with concentration; her eyes darkened once more. Kara stared at her intently for the duration of her mini-ritual. All too late, Mary realised she was not doing this purely out of curiosity. It was only when she heard the whispered words, "Sorry about this," in Jennifer's ear that her intent became clear.

"What are you—?" Jennifer began, but was too late. "Kara, *no!*"

At the last possible moment, Kara seized Mary's hand and shared her step between the two worlds.

"Oh, shit. Kara, you stupid—"

Mary attempted to swat her stowaway clear, but the bitter, forceful winds surrounded her, whipping up to a furious crescendo. Darkness fell upon her.

When the storm calmed, she stood alone, a path to the Odeon's shadow clear to her spectral sight.

"Kara?" she called out. Nothing but an echo stretched for miles.

"*Kara?*"

There was no answer, no sign of her. With no idea where to even start looking, she pressed on, the speed of the wind itself carrying her to her destination.

~*~

"What were you *thinking*?"

Once recovered from Mary's exit, Jennifer pushed Kara lightly. "For the smartest person I know, you can be *incredibly* thick sometimes!"

Kara retorted angrily, "I'm telling you, she needs my help! I've got to get in there somehow!"

"Then you're going to need *mine*." Jennifer shook her head, but pointed at the staircase and headed down. "Come on, then. Let's go."

It did not take them long to reach the police cordons surrounding the cinema. From there, they had a good view and could quantify the manpower dedicated to the endeavour. As expected, the police presence was very high, and with it, a huge crowd outside gathered around the area, their emotions a strange mix of curiosity and fear.

A chemical warfare team, no more able to access the area than anyone else, still debated the situation, unaware of the true factors hampering their entry. The police closest to the building looked unnerved, twitching at every loud noise or distraction.

Kara and Jennifer took into account the odds of the police firing upon anything that moved. The two looked at each other as if comparing notes, and took in the rest of their surroundings.

Tensions were high between the numerous parties. Senior police officers held heated debates with their medical and fire counterparts. The Army's representatives had withdrawn and were debriefing, just as the civilian services had done earlier.

It was a powder keg of frayed nerves, uncertainty, and concern at the front of their minds for those trapped inside the building. Almost from a clear sky, rain lashed down hard on the standing masses but did nothing to dissipate them. The terror was there, but morbid curiosity won out.

"Got an idea," Kara said to Jennifer, a smirk on her face. "Go with me on this, okay?"

Lacking better ideas, Jennifer nodded. "Sure."

Kara strode towards the cordons, herding the crowd out of the way. Jennifer followed. As they reached the front, they lifted the barrier and moved under it, making it most of the way before an armed constable intercepted.

"Get back!" he bellowed. "Nobody's allowed past here!" His weapon hand twitched, but he held firm.

"I need to speak to the inspector immediately," she answered coolly. "I am Dr. Mellencourt of the University of Central London—I'm a specialist. ID's in my jacket pocket."

The leading officer considered and then nodded once. "Okay," he said, "*very* slowly produce your ID. *Do not* make any sudden moves."

Kara did exactly as instructed and presented her university identification with raised hands. He edged towards her and checked the badge. "Stay put. I'm going to take this to the inspector now."

Kara lowered her hands and tapped him lightly. "We've not time for this, surely? Listen, I know you lot are having trouble getting in there, which is why I'm here. I need to try something."

"Like what?" he asked, aggravated. "If you know what's causing us trouble, you'll know it's possible there are people inside injured, maybe even dead. You're not going in on your own."

"No. I'm not. I'm taking my *research assistant,* here, with me." She pointed to Jennifer, who shot him a feral glare. The policeman looked confused, but returned Kara's credentials. He backed up a step.

"I can handle myself as well as anyone here," Jennifer said with an unflinching gaze. The officer nodded and stepped aside.

"All right. Go on through. These two are cleared!" he told the others. The two moved quickly through the cordon. Kara gave Jennifer a knowing glance. Just metres away from the front entrance, they felt a familiar cold but also a powerful sense of dread. Suddenly, they could understand the trouble everyone else had.

From the moment they stepped through the entrance, the air shifted. At first, there was silence. Wrong, taking into account the commotion outside. Both shivered before agreeing to press on, whatever they faced. "It can't be any worse than back at the house, can it?" Kara asked, forcing a smile. Jennifer nodded nervously.

After a few more steps, they could hear the distant howling of wind. As expected, it was similar to previous experiences with Mary.

At the box office, the light breeze flared in intensity, contorting their faces with its force. Kara was blasted back several paces, but clung grimly to the box office desk. She hauled herself steady, crouched to lower her centre of gravity, but it was not enough. She slid backwards. Jennifer caught her, threw her over her right shoulder and stayed low.

"We've made it farther than anyone else, I imagine," Jennifer yelled over the wind.

"Reckon so! Keep going if you can!"

Jennifer pressed on slowly, her face reshaping, every working muscle bulging. Her left hand became talon-like again and she dug into the wall, anchoring herself as she moved. She forced her way through what seemed to be a barrier of air, only to stop dead.

They could both hear it on the wind. A hundred whispers grew to howls. A few seconds' listening distinguished voices amidst the cacophony.

"Turn back, if you want to leave alive."

"Please! Make it stop!"

"Feel as I feel. Feel as she MADE us feel! Come closer."

"Your time draws nigh, girl!"

"Cease your quest—she is already doomed!"

"Dead! Like us!"

"What will you do? What use can you serve here?"

Hundreds more shrieks and howls tormented. The pair covered their ears as banshee-like wails threatened to deafen them.

Kara's hands were red with blood from the aural assault. She squirmed out of Jennifer's grip and pressed into a doorway, leaning back on the wall. Whatever Jennifer called out was lost in the noise. Jennifer got a few more paces ahead before stopping dead. She screamed in utter terror. Kara had never seen Jennifer so undone.

She felt a wave of fright wash over her. Instinctively, she swamped her mind with complex mathematical equations, ten-second histories of every country in Western Europe, and everything she had ever read from the Bronte sisters—anything to block out the panic.

Whilst she wouldn't allow anything to penetrate her thoughts or throw her off-course, her otherwise-tough friend fell to pieces—trembling, ruddy from sobbing, scrabbling in an effort to return to her feet.

Kara lowered herself to the ground and crawled from the alcove to drag her friend—mostly quivering dead weight—back into it.

"Come on Jen," she said, "You're through all that now. There's someone else we need to help now—both of us." She slapped Jennifer on both cheeks to snap her out of it.

"Jennifer? Jennifer, listen to me." She turned her friend around to look at the screen entrance ahead of them. "Rose is in there. And I'll bet whatever she is dealing with—*alone*—is ten times worse than anything we're facing out here. I need you to get a grip. Fast."

Groggy mumbling followed; Jennifer looked to be miles away. *"Alice . . . don't go. I'm not losing you, too."*

"Jen, with or without you, I'm going in there on the count of three."

Still no response. Shrugging, she leaned Jennifer against the wall and sat her upright. "Fine!" She clenched her fists tightly and crawled to the door. In the thick of the howling she could again hear the warnings, the threats, visions of her own death in a violent and sickening manner.

"Tricks o' the mind, Kara," she told herself. "Tricks o' the mind."

But they were so vivid; it was as if it all happened in front of her. Barber was there, pulling her apart from the arms like a wishbone—but that was of course impossible; hallucination, chicanery.

She continued her battle against the unnatural force, and was now just feet away from reaching Rose and whatever evil she battled.

Kara would help her succeed—or die trying.

CHAPTER FIFTEEN

Mary's journey disorientated her. The turbulence forced her to rely on instinct more than sight. It was like the escape from the hospital all over again—though slower. She still had no idea how time and speed worked in this place, relative to her own. That was one for Kara to theorise about.

For her, the difference came down to motive. This journey was urgent, but not governed by blind fear for her life. She still needed to figure out where she was going. Travelling through the mezzanine area of the theatre, she returned her vision to that of the living world. Her mastery had improved: her focus allowed her to retain a ghost-like presence across both worlds.

Through the wall, as expected, she found nothing but a large and silent expanse. Another fundamental difference: she could feel the cold lash at her from *both* worlds. Just to confirm everything was exactly as her first impression had given, she forced herself back into her world in full. She stood still, careful not to exercise a single power. The winds did not recede. Swirling waste blowing all over the box office battered her enough to hasten her return to her discorporate form.

The sight was unexpected. A box office was present, but looked nothing like the one she had previously seen—not even standing in the exact place. The two bright lights she saw must have been Jennifer and Kara, but why had they stopped there? She resisted the temptation to phase back to check—there wasn't time.

A strange radiated energy around her like a greyscale *Aurora Borealis*. The winds blew with ferocity, and created a spectacular effect as they cracked the rippling light.

From the ripples, bumpy shapes appeared. They grew even as she watched, taking humanoid shapes, appearing all around her. The shadowy figures came in all shapes and sizes, and with every blink, their features became clearer. Male, female, young, old, bony, rotund, tall, short, happy, sad and despairing, each wore attire from a considerably earlier period.

Some stylish individuals reminded her of Tally and her Victorian ways. But there were people from more recent times. A 1980s feast of hair gel and eyeliner walked beside an 1880s gentleman who chose not to see them. 1940s servicemen made their way past 1920s high society.

It appeared they only interacted with their contemporaries. But as she became transfixed by the sight, watching as the opacity of each of the figures increased, one gentlemanly shape from Tally's era doffed his hat at her as he glided past.

The wind noise was gradually drowned out by chatter from a hundred voices, each talking loudly to each other, to themselves. Some of the closer ones even talked to her. Most offered a polite greeting, but the occasional man or woman would attempt to initiate more detailed conversation about the weather, a recent increase in prices, the divine performance they had seen for two straight evenings and wanted to catch for a third, or to offer her refreshments.

Mary took several slow blinks to see if it would all go away. It didn't.

Confused as she was, she tried to remember her objective, to close that portal as quickly as possible. But then she remembered her fundamental problem with doing so. "How?"

"How what, sweetheart?" asked a passing American serviceman. She glared at him, to his surprise. He gave her a wide berth as he passed.

"Jeez! Was only tryin' to help!"

"I know you were," she muttered under her breath. "Sorry." The concentration of bodies grew to a crowd.

She battled through them to a small clearing in the masses. Her ears tuned in to a brisk rendition of *"Mad Dogs and Englishmen"* being hammered out on a pipe organ. She smiled, remembering the tune from a time back in her care home, when she studiously watched a television documentary for an upcoming exam, her true ticket out of there.

Yeah, stick at it, Mary. Ignore those prats playing football around you, because if you don't pass this, you'll be stuck here another year.

Wait a second—more memories? Now?

She was eighteen, and though she couldn't recall exactly what that documentary was for, it had everything to do with a tough exam: an A-level, crucial to university acceptance. She'd passed her degree in Art with flying colours, remembering what she had said to herself on the day she got her results: *"If you set your mind to it, Mary Hall, nothing will ever stand in your way."*

She opened the door to the theatre hall; another assault of waste paper and empty cups from the savage hurricane, which had no right to be. The people she had seen just moments ago vanished, but the storm had not. Looking through the door, she could see exactly why nobody else could even entertain the idea of coming near this room.

The dim house lights, coupled with flickering shadows and illumination from the still-running film, blazed onto the huge vacuum in the centre of the room. It was about the size of a small car, churning everything of a light weight within the room. Even the light streaked toward it. It was beautiful, fascinating—*terrifying*—and very, very wrong.

It pulsated like a giant, dark heart. Crackling, tenebrous bolts of void lashed out from it like a corrupted form of lightning. Her heart raced, but she stood her ground. She reminded herself that in being there, she had progressed further than many people professionally trained for a crisis or even a war.

As she looked at it, her eyes ran black—she could *feel* it happening this time, as if a cold liquid slowly poured into her eyes. The action was involuntary, which set her on edge more than anything to that point. The darkness was reaching out; it could *sense* her.

After a short moment, the probing ceased. It let her be. The power was there to tear another being apart, or suck it dry of life—just as she could to some extent, if she applied herself.

But it knows *me. I smell of the dead. I've got nothing it wants.*

It wouldn't dare.

That was it, that same source she had tapped into, to terrify, to take life. It was the route through which she could travel faster than any other human. It was the very essence of that other world, one which should never have come into contact with her own, let alone impose itself upon it.

She stood staring at it, contemplating. She could feel the raw power behind it, a clarion call which drowned out any other noise. She could have it *all;* she just had to ask for it.

This. Is. WRONG.

But the power! Think of the power!

A lot here. Maybe too much. Could I control it?

If you set your mind to it . . .

"Tally?"

She hadn't even realised she had called the name.

A small cyclone emerged a few feet in front of her. From it, the grey storm she had seen became visible in her very own world.

Particles of light swirled and spun, faster and faster, joining together and forming a familiar shape. Tally manifested, this time dressed for a social function rather than peril. More to the point, she appeared entirely solid, in no way transparent.

"*Rose.*" Tally looked perplexed, sounded as if she had been disturbed from something important. But she soon shifted her lips into her more regular, almost arrogant smile. "What can I do for you?"

"*Mary,* actually." She pointed at the vortex and watched as bolts from the void crackled at her like a plasma ball. "I need some help sorting *this.*"

"I thought you might." Tally straightened her hat and surveyed the scene around her.

Mary switched her sight, following suit. No light, no life, came from any of the bodies on the floor. Swirls of light circled above, loudly howling as they passed her. She realised that they were *actual* screams she heard.

"Well? How may I assist?"

"How do I close this thing?"

Tally met her with a dull look. "You already *know* how to do it, my dear."

"What, just absorb the bloody lot?"

"Until you use it all, yes. It surprises me that you have delayed this long in doing so. No doubt it has already called to you?"

"Well, *yeah*, but something's very *wrong* with that."

"Something worse than cheating certain death and walking around as if nothing has happened, perhaps?"

Mary glanced at the dead on the floor. "It's straight from *them*, isn't it?" She looked up to see Tally nod. "Yeah, that's not right. *Not at all.*"

"You appear to have made up your mind." Tally straightened out the kinks in her dress. "In which case, you shall need an alternative."

"Which is?"

"*You* already know," Tally said, looking irritated. "But I cannot help you with that. Think: what have you accomplished thus far?"

She thought of putting Serge to rest and her restoration of Kara. "Yeah," she said, "I remember that." She narrowed her eyes at the dead bodies. "Took an awful lot out of me. I don't know if I can."

With sudden intensity, Tally took Mary's face in her hands and drew her close. "Did you know if you could do *any* of what you have thus far? And has this ever stopped you before?"

Her earnest manner caught Mary off-guard. "Well, no, but—"

"There are no 'buts' to be had, Rose. Your choices are before you, both with their own consequences. There is of course a third option, the one you are taking now, which is to do *nothing*, and that brings its own consequences. Those, you will find, are the worst. So for heaven's sake do *something*—and do it *now*!"

Mary looked around. She could not save the lives of the poor wretches before her, but she could save their souls. The focal point—the all-consuming vortex—rumbled directly opposite of where she stood. She closed her eyes and made one last calculation as to the best decision before finally taking the plunge. She summoned up every ounce of will she could to impose upon the situation.

Comparing the power surging through the room to what she had done to Kara with a mere fraction of it sealed the deal. She knelt down, focused her sight on the dead world, and stretched out her arms. She took deep, meditative breaths.

Casting her mind to the peace and serenity felt upon helping Serge came easily, even under the stress of the current situation. The tangible darkness, despair, and dread around her felt like sticky smoke in the air, stifling everything it touched.

Her very presence seemed like throwing a lantern into the room. Acute awareness of every one of the fallen victims filled her being. She could count every one of them. The bodies around her lacked life, but more than that, they lacked the energies of their very souls.

No faces this time; just lines and shapes floated around in the storm. It was nothing like it had been with Serge in the *Half Moon*—his was most definitely there in its entirety. These were vacuums, holes where real beings should have been. And it made her physically sick, more with every passing second.

As she focused her mind on the void, weaker shades drew themselves back into the hole, offering little resistance. They seemed older than the others, somehow. The void shrank by the tiniest amount, and as it did, the force of her will strengthened.

Tally returned from the shadows to offer a slow round of applause. "Incredible." she said, that satisfied smile on her face again.

"What is?" Mary asked, indulging her monitor.

"This is nothing short of a *miracle*. Anyone else in your position would have just drained the room dry and sealed the breach."

"I know." Mary's concentration faltered at the distraction. "Are you *trying* to put me off or something?"

"Stop being foolish! It is highly impressive that you have managed to be so adept so soon. It normally takes *years* to reach your advanced level. And *this* has never been done before."

More of the smaller shapes disappeared, but those more conjoined struggled as far away from the void as they could manage. They were gathering together, communicating with a sound similar to bats screeching and forming beautiful patterns in the air. Other remaining shapes darkened from warm white to a baleful red. Mary had seen that before somewhere.

The icy, alien winds angered again and forced her to raise her voice. "Do you know what these things are?"

Tally, who appeared brighter than Mary had ever seen her, answered her question. "You *know* what they are!"

"Stop being fucking cryptic!" Mary snarled. Her hold on the void wavered.

Tally tapped her foot against the floor with impatience. "Very well—what you see here are mere shades of souls, torn from living bodies. You know how it happened—and as you have probably sensed, there is a lot of anger and torment, which tends to be infectious. I wonder if *Kara* can feel it."

"Kara?" Mary asked, looking around.

A light slowly enter the room. Bright, like herself.

Another living being.

Kara pulled herself to her feet and stared open-mouthed at the scene. Shaking and oblivious to anyone else, the parapsychologist took a step back towards the door, but then suddenly stopped. "You were saying something about shades and torment?" she asked.

Mary's concentration crumbled. She turned to gape at the pair of them.

"Kara?" she repeated.

"You can *hear* me?" Tally asked with wonder.

"Never mind that," Mary said, shaking her head. "She can *see* you as well!"

"Finish what you're doing, Mary," Kara commanded, not once

taking her eyes off Tally. "I can't see this portal thing, but it's still there, isn't it?"

Mary nodded and returned to her meditative position, her concentration centred on her original task. The winds lashed at her as she drew more of the fragmented souls into the void, reducing it a fraction. The red apparitions swirled around each other more rapidly, lashing around like spinning whips before closing in on her.

Though focused, she noticed Tally stagger back a step.

Mary watched ripples from the black winds turn inward at the pulsing hole. As with every other spectral force in the vicinity, it pulled Tally toward it. The red forms took shape, cloud-like entities with nasty barbed, vine-like growths functioning as arms. In the centre, demonic glowing eyes sizing her up.

Tally continued her lecture over the howl of the winds. "At some stage, most human beings contemplate death and, of course, whatever might come next. In turn most experience a stage of fear as they work out the uncertainties.

"Their collective fear fuels this place—a crowded mass of restless souls. This shadow world, responsible for many of the 'ghosts' the living see, gathers those of us with unfinished business for whatever reason. However, some simply find themselves stuck here. They find nowhere better to go, unable to attain true rest."

"And what is *your* unfinished business?" Kara asked.

"To see Rose through this successfully."

"You can't tell me you've been waiting around for well over a hundred years for Mary?"

"As it happens, I can." Tally's eyes darted around once again, her balance precarious. "But now, I must go. It is unsafe for me here. You seem to be doing a fine job helping her."

"Wait!" Kara cried. "I have loads more I need to ask!"

Tally fled before she could finish, vanishing from sight.

"Bugger."

Mary had shrunk the hole to half its previous size. She drove back the storm, most of it returned to the original source. She was so close—but weakened with every moment.

Just one last effort . . .

"MARY! WATCH OUT!"

She had not heard Kara's cry until too late. Pain seared her left arm, like someone had slashed at it with a hot blade. She screamed, but remained at her task.

"What the hell *is* that, Kara?"

"I can't *see* anything," her friend replied. "I can only *feel* it."

"Feel *what*?"

"Rage. Pure, unadulterated rage."

She winced as a second and third slash hit her. A fourth proved too much. She screamed out and was bundled to the ground. Her efforts ruined, she looked up to find Kara had tackled her down. "What the *hell* are you doing?"

"Saving you, I think," Kara answered.

Mary looked around to identify the threat. "Oh, yeah," she said, frowning hard, "*those*." The red clouds she had seen before, each the embodiment of torment and fury, had focused upon her.

She threw Kara off and rolled in the opposite direction as a thick, glowing, red appendage with dagger-like barbs lashed down between them, slicing through the air with a wail.

"Get out of here, Kara!"

"Hey, I came here to rescue *you*! I can't just *leave* you here!"

"I don't know what these things are, and you can't even see them! How can you help me?"

"Working on it!" Kara looked around nervously. "I can sense it, though—every time it goes for you—wait a minute, did you say, '*them*'?"

Mary leapt over a section of chairs, another attack just missing. All three entities came for her as she examined her injuries. A glancing slash tore a long gash in her arm, light but extremely painful. She cradled her arm whilst dodging several more strikes.

"Yes," she hissed angrily. "Three of the bastards."

"That's it!" Kara stood and smiled triumphantly.

"What?" The barbs coiled and lashed. Each missed strike destroyed theatre seating as the attacks intensified.

"Like evil spirits, you know? It would make sense with all Tally said. What do they look like to you?"

"Big, red clouds with huge whips for arms!" Mary threw herself to the floor.

"Hang in there—I'm thinking!"

"Think *faster*!"

"Right." Kara started to pace up and down, well away from Mary. "Hmm . . . evil things—no. *Angry* things—furious entities—drawn to extremely violent deaths. No. *Made* by the violent deaths. Supernatural and unnatural causes. Now, where did I read up on this?"

"Kara, if you've got a bright idea, I *really* need you to hurry the fuck up with it!"

Mary was tired. The relentless assaults mostly missed, but sapped her strength with every whip. A blow glanced her left leg, hobbling her. The three spirits closed in to encircle her, jab at her, taunt, mock and take their time rather than move in for the kill.

"Ah, yes, that journal: December 10, 1943 entry." She closed her eyes as she recited. "*'Whilst spirits are not my area of expertise, it has been my experience that they manage to be the embodiment of one or a small set of emotions, unlike other 'ghosts,' which have as broad a range as a human being.'*"

"Kara! Shut up and help me, will you?"

"Shush! I'm trying to remember something! Where was I? *'Spirits are, therefore, less likely to rest of their own accord unless'*—that's right—if they crave death, destruction, and the like, they shouldn't be made to feel their own pain or anger as it just feeds them. One must destroy them utterly, the method being the exact opposite of the cause of their creation."

"You mean, bring life to the same number of people?" Mary said, exhausted now, each attack getting closer. "Yeah, can't do that."

"Bring calm to their anger, perhaps?"

"Tried that, remember? Just seems to have made them worse."

Kara returned to her trance-like recitation. "*'By allowing the spirit temporary possession, there is a chance it can be controlled or contained. However, be warned that to absorb one is to take in all of that spirit's driving emotion. Do not allow the emotion to overwhelm you, lest the spirit will do likewise.'*"

"We are so screwed."

Mary shifted her footing and charged headlong at the nearest red cloud, leaping directly into it. A flood of fury instantly welled up inside her. All strength returned in full force.

She clenched her fists and roared, "YOU'RE NOT WELCOME HERE!" She cast devil's glares at the other clouds. "PISS OFF!"

She felt it again, that commanding echo in her voice. The nebulous body began to dissipate, splitting into the original smaller, grey, more human shapes. She easily latched on to one of them as it attempted to escape. "BACK IN YOUR HOLE, YOU LITTLE SHIT."

The shape faded into the darkness. The other shapes comprising it fled through the hole at great speed, sealing more of the void behind them.

"*The other method is to defeat the entity in a battle of wills, but take great care in adopting this approach as failure almost inevitably leads to possession.*" Kara grinned. "Ah," she said, "you're ahead of me, I see."

Before Mary could answer, she was struck hard in the back and sent flying across the room. Though winded, she picked herself up, still empowered, returning her focus to the entity closing in on her.

A door flew open with a sudden crash. Mary turned to see Jennifer standing on the threshold, stumbling, out-of-sorts, but as determined as ever.

"Hurry up, will you?" she croaked. Kara dashed over to catch her, easing her to a seat.

With fresh resolve, Mary looked around just as the second spirit's tentacle-like arms bore down on her. Her eyes burned with malice. The curtain of darkness in the room rippled around her as she surrendered to malicious, destructive thoughts. Light-absorbing crackles of other-worldly energy manifest from her hands. She yanked the being towards her, too fast for it to respond.

"I. AM. NOT. FUCKING. DYING. HERE."

Both Jennifer and Kara covered their ears at the tortured roars of the spirit as it shred into pieces.

All at once, Mary expelled that same force at the onrushing third spirit with the sound of a thunder crack and such force; it looked like a motorcycle being hit head-on by a train. Mary's will overwhelmed all. She sealed the remaining nothingness with a wave of her hands.

The house lights flooded the room as Mary collapsed onto a nearby chair with a sigh. After a few moments, Jennifer, supported by Kara, headed over to her.

"That was the most amazing thing I have ever seen!" Jennifer wheezed.

With the reminder, Mary allowed the darkness to dissipate from her eyes and returned to more mundane vision. She took a moment to examine the cost of her success: the nasty, bloody welts all over her arms and legs, and a friend still returning to her senses. More than that, she stared in horror at the floor, strewn with soulless bodies. Kara gagged; Jennifer bowed her head.

"I'm not sure they thought the same," Mary said, mournful. "Well, one down—only two more to go."

Jennifer snapped out of her dazed state, looking flabbergasted. "What do you mean, *only two more?*"

"That's what I said," Mary answered, pulling herself to her feet. "We've no time to waste."

"What use are we going to be in *this* state?" Kara asked. "We had enough hassle with that one." She paused, sticking her head forward and cupping her ear. "Actually, let's have this conversation later. Looks like everyone's on their way in now, so we should probably be on our way *out.*"

"They'll have all the exits covered—except maybe *yours*, Mary," Jennifer stated. "Kara and I at least are going to have to face them."

"I'll stick around," Mary replied. "I'm in no state to risk anything flashy. I'll take the old-fashioned way there."

"Where is *there*, incidentally?" Kara asked.

"Where this all started for me," Mary answered. "I think another one of these opened during my 'incident' back at the station."

"Well, that *would* explain why they haven't reopened it yet," Jennifer chipped in.

Kara gave a nod. "Okay," she said, "you two go on ahead. I'll catch you up."

"What?" Mary asked.

"Trust me." Kara wandered ahead just as a team of armed police rushed through the entrance and barked orders for them to drop to the floor. Kara directed a nod at her companions before doing as instructed. She spotted the constable from outside and met his gaze.

"Dr. Kara Mellencourt—you sent me in a while ago, remember?"

He nodded.

"That's her, sir," he said, addressing the inspector.

The inspector dismissed the constable and gave Kara a cursory glance as he examined his surroundings. "Strange," he said. "I hadn't sent for anyone from UCL or any other university. Never thought of it, to be honest."

She slowly reached into her jacket pocket for her university identification. "Came over straightaway when I heard there were problems accessing the building, Inspector . . .?"

"Inspector Hammond," he replied curtly. "Now, exactly how did you—"

"Get around it? I'll tell you. But the situation isn't resolved. There are other forces at work, and we need to hurry."

"I can't let you do that, Dr. Mellencourt," Hammond responded. "I need you all for questioning."

"I'm the only one who can give you sensible answers, Inspector Hammond. But believe me—you need to let these two get on, or we'll have worse trouble than you see here." She pointed to the bodies. "Time *is* of the essence."

Hammond considered the situation. He stood his unit down and beckoned the three back to their feet. "Okay. But you need to tell me *everything*. This is related to the hospital situation, isn't it?" Kara nodded. "I thought as much. And *she*," he pointed to Jennifer, "was there, wasn't she?"

"Yes, she was. Now can we stop wasting time on this please?"

Hammond frowned. "Fine, but I'd feel better if these two were accompanied. Where are you going?"

"Bond Street Station." Mary answered, feeling no compulsion to lie.

"Ah, another restricted area. You'll definitely need us. Wilson, Rogers—take these two over, straight away."

"*Sir*!" The stocky officer who had spoken to Kara, along with a tall, wiry-looking black constable, broke from their formation and moved to escort the two women. They all shuffled toward the exit.

"I presume this is some government exercise, then, Dr. Mellencourt?" Hammond asked Kara.

"Yes," she said with a smile, "you could say that."

CHAPTER SIXTEEN

After half an hour of singing some less-crude versions of the pub songs in which she was well-versed, Tally had finally managed to get Violet to sleep, and little wonder. The girl suffered far less fear than previous nights. The tot of brandy Tally slipped her contributed, in part.

Once she ensured the girl was settled, she took a large snifter for herself. She changed for bed and prepared for the early start in the morning.

She placed her glass down after one last sip and wandered over to the lamp. She inhaled, ready to blow it out. It flickered without her aid when a sudden breeze took the room. She shivered in her nightclothes.

Her breath released with a whoosh as, silently, a ghostly figure drifted through the wall next to the door. Tally stifled her scream. Once through the wall, the figure became clearer.

She jumped backward but armed herself with a lamp, waiting. The tall figure solidified in the room, appearing *through* the wall and slowly looming toward her. She retreated from him slowly, one eye on the girl she had sworn to protect. Still he advanced.

"Very well, fool!" she blustered. "If you have come for the girl, you have to come through me first. And I shall not fall easily!"

The cloaked figure did not move. She knew that through the darkness of the cloak, whoever was in there stared intently at her, sizing her up as she had him.

"If you have come to kill me, get it done with, damn you!" However, she fought to maintain her bravado; her true emotions grew impossible to keep to herself. Tears of rage surfaced in her eyes, and she bared teeth in an unbreakable clench. "But I will *not* let you harm her, mark this now; not a hair on her head! Do you hear me?"

The figure finally spoke. "Yes." The male voice reverberated deep into the pit of her stomach, and yet was soft, calm, and, to her surprise, in no way unpleasant. It sounded like any other young man she had encountered—with a greater bearing than most. "I hear your words."

His short engagement in dialogue threw her off her stride, but not from the duty undertaken. Her legs wobbled. She held firm. The lamp remained within reach if needed. "Then you will cease your torment of Violet and allow the girl to live a proper life?"

The figure paused just long enough to ruffle Tally before eventually speaking once more. "I am not here for the daughter of Aurelia Raine. I have come for *you*."

Shaking now, Tally moved away from the lamp but still allowed no space between herself and Violet. "Then do what you must, but for the sake of all that is good, ensure she gets a better home than with those depraved parents of hers!"

"I cannot interfere with that business," the figure said solemnly.

"Then I am sorry, I will not leave."

"I can *make* you, you know . . ." The words were more matter-of-fact than they were forceful. Tally did not doubt that he spoke the truth.

"I say again—do what you must, but do not expect me to freely leave Violet."

"The girl means much to you." His hands lifted to the top of his cloak of shadow. Black leather gauntlets covered them, adding to his unnerving nature. Tally stepped once forward, closing the gap between her and her adversary.

"She does," she said. "Are you willing to discover just how much, *intruder*?"

Another pause. "Then it is clear that you are the one I have been looking for."

"What are you—?"

Before she could finish her question, he pulled back the hood to reveal his face.

He was an extraordinarily handsome man, swarthy, with a full-bodied head of golden hair running down just past his shoulders. Everything about his face seemed sculpted.

Tally took a deep breath and then shook herself thoroughly. "Very well," she said. "What *exactly* do you want of me?" Unnerved as she was, an air of mischief remained in her voice.

"*Actually,*" he began in a voice of clear purpose, "I was thinking you might be strong enough to deal with Lady Raine."

"What game are you playing with me, trickster?"

"No games. Lady Aurelia Raine is an uncontrollable menace, and if not soon brought to heel, she will be *unstoppable*. She is an agent of pure evil, a threat to the city of London and before long, the country, as well as a traitor and an enemy to the very order which took her in from nothing."

"*Order*? Are you to say there are a number of people running around, looking to bring this woman to book?"

He nodded.

"Then *why* has she been allowed to run free, terrorising the poor girl—?"

She turned to check that Violet still slept. Fortunately, she slumbered soundly despite the raised voices in the room.

". . . and my mother and father, and likely myself? Also, what of her servants?"

The man sighed. "The servants you speak of are all dead. Thus their rather . . . off-colour appearance."

"Dead? How was one of them able to fight with the strength of ten men earlier today?"

"Indeed, this was precisely *how* the manservant did what he did. He quite literally possessed the strength of ten men. You have witnessed the woman calling upon the power of the sapphire pendant she wears around her neck."

"As you say."

"Then you know precisely how much of a threat it poses. She has power to manipulate the very souls within the stone—lost, trapped and tormented as they are—into doing her bidding to the last."

Tally gaped in horror and fascination. "Why do you allow it to continue while you do nothing?"

"I have no choice."

Tally drew herself to her greatest height. "Permit me to be entirely clear here," she replied. "You are able to somehow pass freely through walls, are a trusted confidante of the family, turn up to her shows and to act independently in her presence, and yet you have '*no choice*' but to allow her to commit such horrific acts?

"Well, I do not believe you, sir. Clearly you are a fraud to one or both of us. I would thank you to go back from whence you came. If you intend to alert Lady Raine to my whereabouts, do so and dispense with the affronts to my intelligence."

"No walls can hold me, Iris Grenshall. I am certain this statement is also true of you in many ways. But other things certainly can. Believe me when I say that nothing would bring me greater satisfaction than to see this . . . *witch* stopped in her tracks.

"However, you should be aware that your other statements are in error. Why would I intentionally turn over my freedom to the one person who would see me indentured for the rest of my existence?"

"*Indentured*?"

"Yes! You have no idea how much it sickens me to see her turn souls for her own ends, to deny rest to those who seek it, to tear asunder the very fabric of both worlds she touches."

"Both worlds?" His words seemed more addled with every sentence. "What are you talking about, man?"

"You know something of the nature of Raine's power, which is more than most who do not fall victim to it. It takes the most ironclad of wills to learn, the most indomitable to master. Should one attempt to gain mastery of such darkness, unready for what it has to give, then the practitioner becomes the servant. Are you prepared for such a challenge?"

"You have said much, sir, and yet you have told me nothing. Pray, what precisely are you asking me to master?"

"The very arts which are being used against your family, the sleeping girl, and likely against *you*. Surely, Lady Raine has discovered you have taken Violet from her."

"She cares nothing for little Vi!"

"You are in part correct. She cares nothing for the welfare of Violet Raine, her own progeny. But she cares greatly about the slight inflicted upon her by the servant she interrogated and is likely still torturing him for his part in all which has taken place. Even now those who serve her scour the streets of London for your whereabouts, and I hazard will not go lightly upon you when you are found."

"So she will send horror my way as soon as she locates me, no doubt. Am I to assume you are not here to delay my escape?"

"If I was intent upon preventing your escape, you would not escape."

"Very well." She sat back on the bed, shaking her head in resignation. "Tell me all you know against her. And tell me Mama and Papa are not in immediate peril!"

"If you wish to hear the truth on both matters, one will take more time than you have just now, and the other may be a falsehood."

"Then let us at least make a start."

"As you wish. Come with me." He offered a gauntleted hand to her. Her thoughts turned quickly back to Violet, still torn between her need for information and the safety of her new ward. They could be separated so many ways, but Tally had never anticipated doing so voluntarily.

"Promise me she will be safe while we are gone."

His expression did not change, but he nodded and stretched his hand out further. "This is the best hope for both of you."

"If you insist." She took his hand as requested and waited to be dragged out of the room. No such thing happened. Instead, he stood and muttered one word that she could neither hear nor understand. His hood went back on, obscuring any trace of his face once more. A shiver ran down her spine as the temperature dropped. She saw Violet turn once in her sleep and pull the bedclothes firmly over her head.

The room faded from view, replaced with darkness and shadow. The only beacon of light she could see emanated from beneath the grey mound of the coverlet. Whereas the cloaked figure appeared as a solid lump of darkness, Tally's hand looked as bright as a star.

"Where are we?" She attempted to pull her bright hands toward her eyes for closer examination but was met with firm resistance on her held arm. "Under no circumstances are you to let go of my hands whilst we are here, is that clear?"

She felt a child being chastised so, but the unfamiliar and disquieting surroundings told her that disobedience was a fool's option. "Perfectly." She brought her other hand upward in front of her face and stared with fascination as her exposed flesh shone like moonlight in a clear sky. It was a thing of beauty in a desolate environment.

Her accomplice showed no such reflections. In fact, his cloak looked as if it attempted to absorb every ray of light it could catch. Within it, he formed the darkest shadow around her. She felt no horror, however, only intrigue.

The cold bit hard. She shivered.

She turned towards him. "Where are we?"

He peered down at her. "Good. The environment has not caused you excessive terror. That is what it does foremost for outsiders such as you or me."

"Outsiders?"

"The living. Those who draw mortal breath as normal. Where we stand, in this darkness—this void—is not natural to us."

"Well, that is all well and good, but can you explain this place? Is it some form of Purgatory?"

"I imagine a similar name has been used in the past, but that is not for this place. I fancy that, should such a place exist, it lies far beyond this path for most souls. This is almost next to the world of the living."

"It is darker here than a night in the woods, and a realm of naught but shadow and silhouettes. I shall have it as the *Shadow of London,* I think."

"Interesting."

"What could possibly be so interesting about that?"

"My Order's records tell the tale of several previous Guardians and travellers who have called this world a very similar thing. Perhaps there is the blood of a Guardian in you yet."

"*Guardian*? What are you talking about? No, wait—I would know more of this world you speak of. And why I am bound to your hand!"

"This world, in its way, like some of the others, is a creation of the mortal world. Since the very existence of mankind, their instincts have often been expanded into thought, and into reality. Imagine in the dawn of humanity, millions of separate wills unknowingly focused on a single concept. This gives the merest glimmer of the sheer power of mortal thought!

"The knowledge of one's mortality has played upon every mind capable of comprehending life and death. Consider—every tribe that has ever walked and communed with their ancestors. Every ritual burial whereby those present wish for the return of their lost loved ones. Every child who has ever wanted to have one last conversation with his grandmother. Every individual struck down in battle. Frightened, fallen people who have met their end, thinking of nothing other than their homes, family or friends.

"Perhaps in every hundred of these wills, one consciousness dominates the others and binds others to it. On such rare occasions, the power of a single entity controls the whole. Multiplied over the millennia, these combined forces have constructed, piece by piece, a shadow of our own world: hungry, cold, dark, in which legions of restless souls wander in an attempt to resolve their imperatives.

"Some remain for revenge. Some for love. Some for duty. Whatever the reason, it shackles them to the mortal world. Yet, despite this cumulative power, few are strong enough to walk amongst it—and fewer mortals still see the weak imprint they create upon it.

"Even less are willing to see even what they do. You see, this, here . . ."—his free hand swept from left to right—"To most, this is the unknown. And regardless of whatever anyone you speak to mentions, herein lies their greatest fear. After all, who truly can speak in authority on life after death? Even you cannot—now that you have been here—for you still do not have all of the answers.

"Not all are as intrepid as yourself. Know this: the living fear the dead, in any form that they manifest, for they have little interest in contemplating it themselves.

"However, those 'unresting' are drawn to the living like moths to flame. They suffer for it, too; even those who successfully manifest go ignored, to their great frustration, rage, and eventual madness. In the mortal world, some can help them. In this place—heat, light, as you see radiating so strong from you, is something they can feed from—they crave the very warmth and life they do not possess."

If everything he said were true, then, unlike him, she was an exposed target for any trapped and desperate dead. "I feel you may be hinting as to some imminent trouble I may be in?"

The shadowy head shook. "I took care to scout the area before moving here, and am reassured it is safe. My skills are far too limited to risk being somewhere hostile."

"How very reassuring."

She looked around to get a proper measure of her surroundings. She saw an environment in comfortable order. Gas lamps made pockets of darkness, even there. A version of the bed existed. Soot and dust, or whatever it was there, caked the covers. Everywhere else, an exodus of dust whipped around and past her. Tangible walls stood more like frames to a window than impassable obstacles.

The only other light in this place lay between the sooty covers which moved gently up and down. Still, the cold affected her. She shivered as wind hammered her incessantly.

As she listened to him explain the differences in time and space, she looked at her hand, glowing with life, watching as every wave of breeze wafted around it, rather than at it. The same was true of the nearest winds circulating around both the guide and herself, doing its very best to avoid the pair of them, it seemed.

She reached for the evading dust and could see that the scattered soot swirling around her slowed, eventually stopping completely before moving toward the outstretched flaring hand and wrapping around it in layers like a silk cloth. Opening her hand on a whim, the black winds returned to their erratic business as if nothing had happened.

"What—what are you doing?"

Tally did not hear him. She was both surprised and pleased that it took no more than the force of her own will to manipulate her environment, watching as the very world around her obeyed. She was quite confident she no longer required the guide—other than to discover how to travel freely between the worlds.

That same heady desire to stay and control this force flowed through her. It echoed of her first sight of that stunning sapphire necklace around the neck of her adversary. She could manipulate this . . . *art*—far more gracefully than that dull, brutish woman.

"Would you say that this world is somewhat more malleable than our own, then?" she asked, barely containing her self-satisfaction. Still his face could not be seen, but his silence spoke volumes. "You know much of this world," she said, reverting to humility of a sort, "and yet you say your skills are limited? How so?"

"My skills are limited to abilities which the cloak confers upon me."

With this, she examined his attire in more detail and realised that it was the first point at which the breeze was deflecting; anything nearby was affected by association. Watching carefully, she saw the winds repelled from the cloak but danced closer to her. It fascinated her that just a piece of material made such a difference between life and death.

"And what have you managed to gain from the cloak?" she asked.

"I have been able to survive the rather nature of this place," he stated, "and can traverse it as freely as most entities here. Once one becomes accustomed to the ways of travelling, the ability to pass back into the living world becomes second nature."

Tally looked at her hand once more, and closed her mind to anything but the world around her, as she had before. In this way, she could reach out and feel the world immediately present, and could see strands of it acting as routes to places worthy of exploration and places to avoid. She could see familiar destinations and some unknown to her.

Tally focused on reaching the end of that which felt the most familiar and strongest route, took a single step forward, then watched as everything which had surrounded her disappeared in an instant, replaced by stronger winds and blurred, ghostly faces.

She travelled much faster than her feet would allow, and much beyond the comfort of her guide, who clung to her more grimly than ever before. She felt no fear; indeed, she felt an unexpected affinity with her surroundings. It was amplified once they reached the end of the route: a poorly illuminated Grenshall Manor.

Staring in some astonishment, she looked closely at the place she had been drawn to. She felt a connection to every part of that mansion. She intuited that she was in the North Wing, an area no one frequented—even her parents. And yet here she stood, *inside* the North Wing chamber!

An obsidian stone gathered everything around it—the darkness, the ashy surroundings—a dark cyclone drawing it all in. Tally stared wide-eyed at the monolith. She heard it calling her to come and touch it. The guide raised his hand and walked towards it slowly, as if compelled.

Tally forced herself to look away from the stone and to her surroundings. Writings in numerous languages decorated the skirting both high and low around the vast room which comprised the entire wing.

The end of the chamber and thus the wing itself appeared a considerable distance from where she stood. The vortex obscured everything, yet she sensed that there was more to it than met the eye.

Tally still in tow, the guide slowly walked closer to the stone. She sensed danger. "Excuse me?"

"Hullo?"

"*Guide*?"

He continued his relentless march toward the stone. She felt strained, as if her insides wanted to escape her body. Light flowed from her in hundreds of small grains, pulled outward and towards the stone.

Once free, each faded to darkness—dragged into the hurricane that they were heading straight for. Tally wrenched herself free from his grip. She felt every ounce of air being drawn from her lungs and clawed urgently for air. As she drowned in this black, dusty void, the guide turned to her and flailed for her hand. But she was drawn away from him, quickly, and closer to the stone!

She felt the darkness lunge for her. Her bright light started to fade.

Darkness began to consume her. The cold became unbearable. The obsidian slab laid bare every fear her safety, for Violet's and Lord and Lady Grenshall's. Soon, she would be one with it, where she could join the never-ending hunger which beckoned her.

"*NO!*"

The devouring darkness slowed but did not desist its attempts. She forced herself back into a steady breathing pattern through the deadly dust. Not enough for any concerted action, but enough to keep her from being lost entirely.

Consumed by my own HOUSE! This is ridiculous! I must compose myself!

The Guide, in his protective cloak, waded through the dust storm and seized her hand. At his touch, the room disintegrated until all that was left was darkness and void. A harrowing sound of distant moans and screams echoed in the distance.

The sound ceased; the light returned for the most part. The room seemed clearer, less dust-plagued—still dark but purely the state of an unlit room. Her first massive inhalation proved unnecessary, as there was plenty of air in the world of the living. Tally was as relieved to hear her own footsteps as anything else.

They could see a black stone in the centre of the room, taller than either of them and wide enough to cover both if they stood by it. The strange markings skirting the walls remained visible even in this low level of light, clearly visible, if not quite illuminated, in a dark room.

"We are in Grenshall Manor," she said to the Guide. "No one could know we are here."

The Guide removed his hood before looking around, fascinated by the markings.

In the silence, scarcely audible whispers drew her to the centre of the room—to the stone, an unpleasant discovery she wanted to be away from. She searched and found only one clear way out: a visible door to the south. She found it locked.

"No windows, no light, no entry, no comfort," she said. She turned to each corner as she spoke. "What *is* the purpose of this room?"

"To contain the stone." The Guide slowly wandered the room, examining the writings. "It serves no other function."

"The North Wing *was* the original Grenshall Manor around a century ago."

"Absolutely. Lord Alphonse built it around this stone—this *gate*. I do not know its origins, however long your family has had possession." He continued to walk around, intent on the markings. "I cannot understand these writings, though it appears there are a good seventeen distinct languages written across here."

This inscription—from one Lord Alphonse—says simply: '*This House, And Those Who Hold It, Guard The Gate.*' I believe that to be true. A novice would find the Gate's fearful effects impossible to overcome."

"What about someone like Lady Raine?" Tally asked.

"Even one who has acquired gifts or artefacts as Lady Raine has could find themselves confounded for days, weeks, perhaps even months as they attempted to clear the wards and seals here." The guide swept an arm toward the inscriptions as he spoke.

"You say this despite us getting here as simply as we did. How exactly *did* we get here?"

His response came after some considerable pause. "Actually, I am uncertain. I know how to travel the Shadow World, within the limits of what I can see, but I did not know how to enter your mansion safely—I have never dared try, the danger far more clear than the path.

"Yet, *you* knew how to call upon the place, and *you* survived the greatest test of the Gate with little difficulty." He looked upon her in awe. "I have received some limited training, and I have the aid of this cloak, and yet I have never seen a true Guardian in action—up until now!"

"Then why do my mother and father know nothing of what they have?"

"That is not for me to say. Perhaps you should ask them?"

Tally wandered the room herself, examining for herself the differences in language and lettering. She picked out French, German, and Spanish easily enough, Arabic she guessed at, and others she did not recognise. It seemed each language contained unique wordings.

Tally had seen enough to reach her own inference. "The necklace. Nothing about it would match, to my mind, the motives of one of these 'Guardians,' Grenshall or otherwise. Unless they are created with the purpose of harvesting these lost souls, that is."

"They most certainly are not. At least I do not believe so."

He turned to face her, appearing crestfallen, weary. "Lady Raine wields the Teardrop. Despite the dangers she poses to me, I must complete my task. I require your help."

"And how exactly am I supposed to assist you?"

"I have managed to limit her destruction in a small way, but I cannot stop her. The key to her downfall lies in Grenshall Manor—and you. She knows both obstacles well."

"What does she have planned?"

"Who can say?"

"I was rather hoping you could. Give me something of use."

"I have convinced her of my usefulness. It is entirely due to the cloak's abilities."

"Is that so? Given how she treats the majority of her associates, I might reasonably expect your usefulness to stretch beyond possession of a cloak."

"I am the only living being capable of operating it."

"Or so you have told her."

"Precisely."

His reasoning wavered as he spoke, and his actions spoke far louder than his words. She considered all he gained providing her naught but dubious assistance, and her doubts welled into certainty.

"You *knew* that the only place I could even attempt to go to would be Grenshall Manor, the only place I call 'home.' I guaranteed your own safety! And you *knew* I was your only chance of getting in here!" Tally glared at him. "You have been working for the Raines all along!"

He pulled his hood over his head as Tally leapt at him. A fraction too late. He vanished, leaving her sprawled on the floor.

As she turned and picked herself up, a ghostly cloaked figure floated ahead of her.

Tally exploded into sobbing. "You . . . you *bloody liar*! You dragged me away from Violet, my parents, all so that you could get to our house!"

"I am genuinely sorry it has come to this, Iris." His sincerity mocked all reason. "You provide a real challenge to the Lady Aurelia—more than we believed. However, this domain is my lady's to claim."

"*We?*"

"Without your continued compassion toward young Violet, none of this would have been possible. Your little escapade even provided us a means of getting you out of the way for good. Now it just remains to deal with Lord and Lady Grenshall and then my lady will be free to conduct her business."

My lady. His lady. The Guide's chosen allegiance throbbed in her mind. Tally remembered the great stone behind her. It was a deadly risk, but there was much at stake. As it had called out to her before, Tally attempted to call out to it, one powerfully focused thought to do something about him. But she did need to keep him there.

"You do keep saying that, as if you were Lord Raine himself!"

He snorted. "You misunderstand. I shall *be* Lord Raine in all but name in a matter of months, and have no use for a worthless peerage. Already he is beyond any use to her other than in name. Once she is rid of him, I shall be free to care for my daughter the way I see fit."

The small whistling breeze gathering within the room dissipated as her concentration broke.

Violet.

"The lying, scheming, evil—"

She lost control. Forgetting that he was nothing more than a shadow to her, she lunged for him again, screaming with rage. Striking at his hood with a clawed hand, she surprised even herself when she struck true, her fingernails bloodied as she knocked him off his feet.

"I will *not* let you anywhere near her! Do you hear me? *You will not harm a hair on her head!*"

He stood. "I have no wish to harm her." His words were high-pitched and shocked. "Why do you think I would?"

"What kind of fool *are* you?" Tally accused. "Violet has been plagued quite literally by monsters of late."

"Do not worry about the girl. I have been assured that her *visitors* will leave her alone for good once her mother is successful in her endeavours."

The spirit drained from Tally's face. "*The girl?*" she echoed, sounding defeated. "She has a name. And as for her mother—" She shook her head. "Someone such as Lady Raine is never satisfied. She will demand more and more, until there is nothing left to take."

He was silent for a moment. "We shall see," he answered, before vanishing from her sight. Alone, the door locked, effectively a prisoner in that vast expanse of a room, no one would hear her. He gained the information he sought, her plight likely his intention all along.

She thought of each critical moment she was trapped there, powerless to aid Violet and her own family—there was nothing she could do about it. She dropped her to her knees, sobbing in despair.

No one heard her cries.

CHAPTER SEVENTEEN

No walls can hold me . . ."

Tally felt a brief moment of despair, but such despondency would help nobody she held dear. She was a *Grenshall,* damn it. *"A Grenshall does not despair—a Grenshall masters, and a Grenshall triumphs."* That alone gave her hope.

She reasoned through her situation. If Mama and Papa complied with the woman's demands, Aurelia Raine would still come back for her, no doubt seeing her to a grisly fate. If they did not, she remained trapped with little chance of rescue. She could be there for days.

She found no gap around the door's edges, suggesting it had been tightly sealed. Another push proved her weight useless against its mass.

Tally dropped back to her knees—voluntarily this time—to get to eye level with the large, brass doorknob on this unique construction. There was no lock anywhere she could see.

Next, she tapped firmly, first high up the door to get the sound of its full thickness, then again around the door handle at each of the logical spots that a lock would have been. The sound did not change.

Tally shrugged, and then tried tapping around the door, trying to find a lock in a less logical place. But there was no success. The rather thorough assessment led her to conclude that even with a full running charge, she would inflict damage only to herself. Defeated, she stumbled to the stone.

"Oh, this is *no use at all*!" she shouted, bashing hard at its centre with clenched fists. "LET ME OUT OF HERE! LET. ME. OUT!"

After her final punch to the stone, she collapsed forward on to it and sobbed gently. After a short time, she stopped. She heard a low rumble, a howling wind, a brief whisper, and for the first time since she had been here, a certain feeling of familiarity.

The noise died, leaving her alone again in the room.

"No, no, NO!!" she cried, again bashing the stone. This time her attack on the Gate was deliberate, a controlled attempt to recreate the effects. Which failed.

She sat and tried to piece together anything which might have helped her figure out what had happened, how to do it again. It was the best plan she had right now. Before long, tiredness from the rigours of an unusually difficult day got the better of her, and she closed her eyes, sleeping the sleep of the brave.

~*~

It was a scorching summer day, and Tally had worn as bright blue a dress as she dared, standing at Paddington Station with a parasol in her hand. It was somewhat soothing to be in one of the few places she ever felt relaxed—waiting to travel the *Hammersmith and City Railway* for simple pleasure.

Other travellers passed by, each doffing a hat or presenting a pleasant smile and a wave to her. The sound she could barely catch in the distance was her train approaching. It would be here in relatively short order. She considered whether or not there might be time to quickly purchase some light refreshment. After all, there had been plenty of time to pick one up while she waited for the train to arrive.

Exactly how long HAVE I been waiting for this train?

The thought felt irrelevant as she dug into her purse to pay for a cake. She raised a finger to the baker to indicate she only needed one, because Violet was not there to join her on her travels.

Come to think of it, where is *Violet?*

She wandered out of the baker's shop before collecting her bun, completely preoccupied as to the whereabouts of the girl. This in itself was strange; she had not seen her since she had arrived.

But there was no time to think about that now; the train was here, and everybody boarded in good order. She embarked, in synchronisation with the others, and the milling crowd soon sat down in unison with her. The doors were closed, and the train started to move, just as Tally realised she had not been her usual organised self. She should have bought her ticket by now . . .

. . . but she *never* bought a ticket. Something was amiss. How had she escaped the room?

"I must be dreaming."

"You are!" came a voice from the passenger seat immediately to her right.

"Wha—?"

She turned to see an elegantly dressed man in his early forties smiling at her as the other passengers had. Something was far more genuine about his expression than the others, though.

"I am most pleased to see you in person, Iris Grenshall."

She looked at him, and something immediately reminded her of her father: the mannerisms, the movement, even his face. He offered his hand, and she shook it, uncertain of any other recourse to take. His grip was firm and unrelenting, and never once did he break eye contact. It was just like her father had taught her to shake a hand, should the need arise.

"I feel the need to ask who you are," she said, the left corner of her mouth upturned. "But I believe it an educated guess that we are related?"

His smile remained warm even as he formally broke the handshake. "Related by blood, no. But stronger related than most who claim the name by marriage. In duty, I would say, stronger than the most recent crop of those claiming to be here by birthright!

"Why young Iris, it heartens me to see you in person for the first time—even if that is not the case, strictly speaking. And as a reward for your tenacity, insight, and perception, I shall introduce myself. I am Lord Alphonse Grenshall the Second."

"The *Second*?"

"And we were doing so well up to then. Yes, you know—succeeding *The First*?"

Back at ease in her company, if not her surroundings, she did laugh at his retort. It was the answer she would have given.

"I must say, Iris, you look quite the princess. It is a rare given thing that a man gets to see his great-granddaughter, especially one he never knew. But my, I am not disappointed. She is the very image of radiance!"

Tally blushed, though was aware things were just a little *too* ideal at the moment, nothing like they had been before she had closed her eyes, in the dark room she could not escape.

"Listen, I have to go. Whilst this is quite pleasant, it is also strange, and I am, it must be said, pressed for time."

"By all means." He nodded, still looking pleased. "Disembarking at the next stop will take you back where you started—however, I am quite certain that you not long ago requested my aid? It was a *most* particular set of circumstances which brought us together in the first place and I am loathe for us to be parted so soon after we have met."

"Brought us together?" Tally asked, confused. "As I understand it, I am dreaming of an entirely idealised situation whilst my true predicament is dire."

"It is one of the great advantages of dreams," Lord Alphonse said, nodding at her words. "You can idealise almost anything, anywhere. I had rather hoped you would be more comfortable this way and as such accommodating. But I understand your concerns entirely. Indulge me at least the attire though, would you?"

The second he stopped speaking, he snapped his fingers and the bright summer was replaced with darkness. The train and the crowd had gone, leaving the two of them back in the more familiar dark room. She was still wearing the bright summer dress, though, and closed the parasol she was carrying out of habit. "Now," he said, looking around, still jovial. "Is this more to your taste?"

"Taste? Goodness, no. However, you are correct; this is where I find myself stuck. Would you, perchance, know the way out?"

"I would." There was a mischievous grin about him. "Why, you can walk straight out that door!"

"Well, therein lays my problem," she said. "I cannot. I have tried everything, turning the door, looking for a lock to pick, forcing my way through, and trying to find an alternative exit. But I have been unsuccessful, sir."

"You have most certainly made good efforts to leave." He ran his hand backward through his dark hair, smoothing it down. "Tell me, what is so pressing that you must leave so soon?"

She explained the multitude of threats to herself, her family, and to young Violet.

"Hmm," he said, rubbing his chin. "I am beginning to understand your urgency. The *Teardrop* is the ruin of those who possess it, one way or other. And though you have covered most of the worst eventualities, you have missed one which might not have been obvious to you from the start."

"Oh?"

"Yes. I am afraid the room is sealed, and I expect shall run out of air before one has to worry oneself about concerns of the stomach. You see, I never intended this room to be visited; just to contain the Gate.

Though Grenshall Manor was created purely for that purpose initially, the architects I commissioned graciously reminded me that constructing a building structure of any kind is subject to certain physical rules. Four walls, then, effectively sealed the thing off from being carried out by more enterprising thieves."

"That, and the sheer weight of it, I should fancy."

"Quite. That was enough for me. But then I had a timely reminder one night with a rather shady attempt on my life that normal walls just would not serve. Hence, I built myself a bit of a fortress as well.

"Now, the casual observer would see none of this, because of its seeming as a residence and nothing more. But by building an extra floor and with a careful expertise, I was able to have the Gate release just enough force from the Shadow world that people would, for the most part, stay away from here. Now this did lead to further difficulties, but in essence, this was the start of Grenshall Manor."

"Of course." Tally said, nodding. "You will not have been around when any of the rest was constructed. That was down to Sirian and Papa."

"It was." Lord Alphonse sighed, a look of disappointment replacing his smile. "Neither showed an aptitude for Guardianship, and only knew half of what I tried to instil in them about what it meant to be a Grenshall.

"Certain values of nobility and maintaining the estate came easy to them, but alas, nothing more. It was both pleasing and fortunate then to discover that the Hall of Containment did its job far better than I could possibly hope. Nobody has been here since my son's final visit—until you and the invader."

"Then you do not consider me to have invaded here?" The pang of guilt she had felt at allowing herself to be fooled into coming here resurfaced briefly.

"*Invaded?*" He laughed heartily and almost squeezed the life out of her with an embrace. "Goodness no, Iris! I have been watching and waiting for years for a Grenshall finally worthy of our true birthright! I will credit your father where it is due for finding you.

"From that first night that you entered the family, I have watched you grow and live in this house as if you were born to it. And I left you a small knowledge as you slept over the years, wondering if you would ever call upon it. To travel even the most rigid paths in the Shadow is not a thing to be undertaken lightly, so the one thing I could usefully give you, even if you never used it in your life, was your way home."

"So *that's* how I knew how to get back here!"

He gave a satisfied smile.

"It is good to know, though, that even as there lacks a suitable Guardian, there too lacks a fully knowledgeable foe! For if he, or the ever-charming Lady Raine was, they would know that dreams are as much part of the great mortal consciousness as much as life after death—more so in fact.

"Hence, with just a little preparation, dreams are as easy to traverse as shadow—though are altogether more flexible in the hands of those suitably imaginative. They confer another particularly relevant advantage, in that time is less of an issue."

Tally considered his words. "What would you have me do?" she asked.

"Well," he replied, "seeing as I vowed to ensure the Gate does not fall into the hands of the tyrannous and the wicked, I am honour-bound to aid you, regardless of family status. The Gate is plainly under threat. So, as you have charged yourself with the task of preventing this foe, I shall ensure you have the tools necessary to do so."

For that one moment, Tally felt the full weight of pride and responsibility that had simultaneously and collectively been thrust upon her. She solemnly acknowledged her agreement to his wishes and offered her hand, which he accepted.

"I shall do everything within my power to protect this place from them, and any others who would cause harm. But please—help me save little Violet as well."

"Hmm," he said, making his way to the corner of the room left of the door and turning around. He started to count under his breath in time with very slow and measured steps directly to the other end of the room. "Well, the first thing you will need to do is to escape alive." He went back to his muttering. "The second is to learn how to get back *in* here."

"I shall likely have to steal the cloak from that Guide. Would you happen, by the way, to know anything of this Order he spoke of?"

By no means," he answered, still keeping his count. "The cloak, like the *Teardrop,* is a nasty little bauble created for use by those who take the lazy path to power they cannot comprehend. Never leads to good practise, that. Fifty-five, fifty-six, fifty-seven, fifty-eight—there!"

"What are you doing?" she asked, as he stopped his slow march and rotated in a militaristic turn on his heels to face her.

"Your search was very thorough indeed," he said, chuckling quietly, "but you looked everywhere apart from one direction—straight *down*. You would not have known this of course, but precisely fifty eight steps from the left hand corner nearest the door, there is one loose stone in the room, and one alone, which one simply lifts . . ." He did so.

". . .and then turns the little dial fifty-eight degrees as marked. See?"

There was a click and he lifted open a small metal safe door in the new gap.

"Finally, one pushes the button *there*, and your airtight seal is broken as the metal entrance unlocks for opening. It is of course prudent to place everything here the way it was found, and then closing the door fully after you. This way, you reset the trap."

"So, this is what I have to do when I wake?"

"Just so. But do me one small favour. Alter one of the inscriptions as soon as you can, would you? There should be some appropriate materials in the South Wing study. Doing so will scupper any unpermitted visitors who do not come through the main door."

"Gladly."

"And if you want to learn how to become a proper Guardian, which I am sure you do if you truly want to take care of those brigands, come back into this room as soon as you can once your outside business is concluded."

"As you wish."

"Excellent," he said, grinning. "But before you leave, allow me to ensure you have your first lesson. Remember: time operates differently here, so there is no real rush."

CHAPTER EIGHTEEN

Mary watched Jennifer as they sped from the cinema in the back of a police vehicle, the best way to get through the chaos gripping London. It afforded both her and her friend a moment of recuperation. She wondered what exactly Kara was telling Inspector Hammond about their cinema ordeal.

Jennifer's strong inward focus, coupled with a swig of water, appeared to rejuvenate her lingering injuries inflicted by Thomas Barber. However, Mary recognised the traumatised look in her eyes. The horrors of exposure to the influence of the unresting spirits would require a longer recovery time.

Mary felt exhausted after expelling the energies she had absorbed from the spirits in the cinema. As a consequence, the pair sat quietly on their drive, ignoring the interrogation from the two policemen escorting them.

"If you don't know," Jennifer muttered, "it's probably best things stay that way."

They clearly wanted to question further, but Mary emitted enough supernatural threat to silence them both. Barely above a whisper and just below the engine and siren noise, Jennifer addressed her.

"He was *much* stronger this time—even quicker. What the hell is he, and how does he fuel that strength?"

The question conjured images of the monster's otherworldly tethers in Mary's mind. "Violet's slave," she answered. "Nothing more. I don't know exactly how, but chains from the ground pull him every direction. It's some kind of spiritual torture."

Jennifer stared at her. "Did you say *from the ground*?"

"Yeah. With chains. At least, from what I could see with my shadow sight."

"*Draw your strength from the earth . . .*" Jennifer said, eyes closed, as if reciting something.

"*What?*"

"Before Kara, someone showed me how to control the basics of my abilities. One thing she told me was how to draw the raw physical strength I needed. '*Draw your strength from the earth,*' she'd say, '*your whims from the air; flow through the water as it would flow around you, and control the flames, or burn with them.*'"

"Which means what, exactly?"

Jennifer retreated from her question. Mary patted her shoulder in reassurance, offering whatever support she could. It seemed to help. Jennifer managed to re-establish eye contact. "I never found out properly," Jennifer replied solemnly. "She died before I could get an explanation."

"Who?"

"Her name was Alice Winter. She saved my life."

"You never mentioned her before."

"She helped me a lot. It's always painful to bring up. Kara knows I was adopted—briefly." The car pulled around to the station entrance. "She'd probably have taught me everything I needed to know—if she'd had the chance."

"What ha—"

A cold, horrific feeling pitted in Mary's stomach, demanding her undivided attention. It was that same terror she had felt on reliving her sole memory of waking in the hospital. And it was all coming back to her. Hard.

"Let us out. *Now*."

The constables looked around frantically, flight or fight responses kicking in. The malevolence—the evil that had been so prohibitive back at the cinema—felt less engulfing, but more intense, more personal. That which shouted previously now whispered in their ears.

PC Rogers, the driver, did exactly as he was told and released them. Wilson moved to a cover position behind the car, drew his firearm, and pointed towards the unmanned, cordoned doors of the Underground entrance. "What's going on? There should be guards there, on the door."

"Right. There *are* now," Jennifer said. She shivered but presented a commanding presence. "You two need to stop anyone going in or out."

"But we're meant to keep an eye on you," Wilson replied. He never took his eyes from the entrance.

"Best way to do that is to watch those doors," Jennifer responded. Mary, drained, scarcely heard her friend answer.

A memory flashed before her eyes of friends hugging as the Three Musketeers parted ways.

At least this time she had Jen with her as she stepped into the station. She took her by the hand and pulled her through the entrance. "Can't believe this place has actually been closed since I was last here," Mary sneered. "Ongoing maintenance, my arse!"

"Well, technically it's true," Jennifer answered, chuckling, shaken as she was. "The last thing you want from this are a load of terrified drivers accelerating through the stop. That could go very wrong in a lot of ways. Personally, I'm grateful that they . . . hey, are you even listening to me?"

There was far too much going on for that.

Mary looked up. The lighting was on but appeared weak, dim. The temperature was cold—odd with a summer's day outside. She stopped in her tracks and pulled on Jennifer's hand.

"We had proper light that night," she said, looking around slowly. It all came flooding back to her. "Not like this. There were no staff about, which I thought was weird." She walked over to the ticket machine. "I'd lost my Travelcard, so I went to sort out a single ticket back to Finchley Road; I don't live far from there. Couple of minutes' walk at most. The girls had taken me out to celebrate my graduation.

"Vicky and Jess. Two of my best friends. I was just happy to take the degree and get on with it, but no—Jess insists on a bloody party, doesn't she? So, I agreed, as long as they made it fairly low-key. I'm perfectly happy for a slap-up meal and a few at the Intrepid Fox back in Soho.

"The first part of the night went fine. Then they carted me a few doors down, we started on the shots and the karaoke, and it all got a little blurry. Anyway, we eventually decided to stagger on home."

They moved away from the ticket machine. Jennifer's eyes darted around. "Something else happened which I couldn't remember to tell you in the hospital," Mary continued.

They made their way to the ticket barrier. Both bypassed it in their own unique ways; Jennifer vaulted over and Mary faded out of her current world, reappearing on the other side of the barrier. "There you go again, upstaging me as usual," Mary said with a wink. Jennifer just glared at her.

"It was about here things got *really* odd. I worried about the fact that there was nobody else down here. But the station was open, nobody was throwing me out or anything, and I had no reason to think the trains weren't running."

They got on the escalator, and a number of familiar theatre advertisements scrolled past as they descended. "I got down to the platform. Staggered over in *the* most uncomfortable fucking heels ever, and sat down, mumbling and singing, as you do, while I waited for this sodding train.

"I got bored after a while—then some nasty, pissy smell I caught a whiff of nearly made me puke. I'd had enough about then, so was going to check what was going on, and then . . . then I bumped into him."

They had reached the bottom of the escalator and were about to turn onto the platform when Mary stopped Jennifer.

"He's here. Again. I can feel it. He's down there and he's got that dead girl with him."

Jennifer gave a sideways glance. "I *thought* I felt a little rough. Still, it's not as bad as it was back at the house. Must be getting used to it. Fine. Let's get him out of the way, get the portal closed, and get out of here."

Mary gave a weak nod. "This was the point at which I sobered up really quick." Her voice had lowered to barely a whisper. "Fucker grabbed me right about . . . *here*." The illumination dropped to levels Mary had become accustomed to on her realm shifts. She saw Jennifer twitch and examine her surroundings with predatory alertness.

"Mary—you're right, they're here! I can sense them now."

Mary froze, though her every instinct told her to flee. It was all happening again. Her breathing constricted; she could feel the veins in her face fill with blood. She choked until she fell to her knees.

"*Mary!*"

Jennifer ran toward her. Before she could reach her, the monstrous Thomas Barber stepped out from around a corner. He stuck out an arm and sent her careering into a nearby wall. After impact, she slumped to the ground.

"You see, Natalie? I *told* you this would be an effective plan!" His guttural voice scraped against Mary's nerves.

She watched the giant look around, smile at Jennifer's unmoving form, but then shake his head at his companion, who stared blankly. The fresh blood splattered all over her stolen flak vest from another unfortunate armed response officer made Mary gag.

"Why do I bother talking to you?" Thomas asked the freakish woman. "Even if you understand me, it's not like I get a sensible answer."

He sighed and turned back to face Mary, who still fought for breath against an invisible force. "Oh well. At least I get to finish the job this time."

CHAPTER NINETEEN

She lived it all over again: the choking, the fight for her life, the despair. Only it was much more powerful this time. Barber hadn't attacked directly. He hadn't needed to. The darkness overwhelmed her. The terror petrified her.

She heard the screams and echoes of the dead from decades past. The winds of the Underground, normally so warm from the tunnels of arriving trains, blew bitterly cold. The hole had grown; she could sense its touch from where she stood.

'Looks like your train was on time after all!' Thomas's last words echoed through her mind.

He had thrown her into the tunnel, and while flying through the air, she had heard a sound like rolling thunder. An engulfing blackness had opened just above her. The heavy, dull thud and shattering of bone had preceded that horrific landing.

Just before she had faded out of consciousness, a feeling of sorrow and disappointment had overcome her. Not hers; someone else's.

It should have taken her.

He had stepped towards the track to try and throw her into the void as he had intended—as was meant to have happened. But her sheer will to survive had prevailed. It had been too late. The train came.

Get on your feet.

Stay alive.

That's it! Mary thought as Barber aimed a kick at her ribs. She drew herself from the Bond Street Station world into its shadowy echo, watching as the heavily chained foot swung straight through her and into a wall. *I remember now—this opened just before I hit the tunnel wall.*

She stood up and watched the soul-shackled slave become confused, then enraged. She examined his spiritual tethers carefully, only the face of the man visible under the thick chains.

They stretched hard in opposing directions, like a torture rack. The chains extended from the ground—*from the earth*—stretching him into that impossibly muscular form, warping him in every way.

His accomplice moved towards the blinding, bright light from Mary's friend.

"Jen!"

Wrapping the chilled winds of the void around her, she moved to stand between them. Focusing her will, she reached across the veil to bop Jennifer firmly on her forehead. *"Wake up,"* she commanded with the irresistible grim echo. "She's trying to kill you!"

Jennifer gave a startled shiver, then rolled out of the way of a pulverising blow. Using the wall for support, she pulled herself back to her feet and spun away from a second charge. Still dazed, she launched into a rote-like sequence of kung-fu manoeuvres, sending the possessed girl crashing to the floor.

"Good girl!" Mary grinned.

Natalie's restrictive barbs constricted to push her back on her feet.

From this world, Mary heard the girl screaming, the barbs tearing through her flesh. Carried by the wind, she stood above Natalie in an instant.

Behind her to the left, she could see ripples of light from the floor heading toward the main illumination—Jennifer—causing her to glow brighter still. She was fascinated; the dazzling, white light against the baleful red. She could have watched it all day—except for the horrible ripping sound as Natalie stood.

There was an ear-shredding shriek from the undead. Instinctively, Mary drew her hands upward and caused the winds around her to double their intensity. Flowing straight into her hands, she blasted the gathered force at Natalie, knocking her back to the ground.

The barbaric coils around Natalie had eyes of their own—yellow, ferocious, and trained on her. Through the vines, Mary saw an excruciated face, a plight no more wanted than Serge's had been. She leaned down, slapping away the snake-like vines despite the sharp barbs tearing at the sleeves of her arms.

Mary saw them for what they were: tortured souls who did not belong there, retained and ordered against their will, guiding, bullying, and cajoling Natalie's soul. None of it belonged—none of *them* belonged.

They murdered Natalie, her soul torn away while she still lived—and should have lived far longer. But instead of a release to peace and rest, the sapphire enslaved her, forced her to reanimate her lifeless corpse. Only the most callous mind—or the mindless—would ever consider inflicting such torture.

"You're not here by choice, are you?"

". . . No . . ." came a faint whimper from Natalie's contorted face. Immediately, the coils stopped lunging at Mary and slid downwards and outwards, stretching Natalie in each direction until she screamed so loudly Mary recoiled, deafened. Angered, Mary seized one of the vines with both hands. "STOP!"

With the echoed command, the coils released the girl immediately and within seconds let out one final, collective chorus of shrieks before sinking into the ground and vanishing. Sudden movement of bright light behind her, pursued by a second red light and the jangle of chains, distracted her from her friend's peril. However, she stooped down to Natalie, flat on her back, who whimpered.

"Nobody should have had to have gone through the shit you have," Mary said. She held Natalie by the back of the head and grimaced. "I'll sort everything out for you, Natalie." The terrified woman began to cry uncontrollably. Mary squeezed her hand hard.

Clear your mind of all pain, rage and suffering.

Be calm.

"You should rest now." She released her hand and moved to gently close Natalie's eyes for her. She could see her hands glow with increasing intensity as Natalie turned pale, then faded away. Soon, a dark shadow in her shape was all that remained.

That's the body back in proper London—not this shadow place.

"Mary! If you can hear me, hurry up and get that hole closed!" The tired, echoed shout came over the sound of Violet's lackey smashing tiles. Mary turned to see red and white light blur as they clashed.

Mary shifted back to the living world, yet retained her shadow sight. Much more refined than at first, it no longer blinded her with the severe contrasts in darkness and light. A distance away, Jennifer struggled to contain Barber as he came at her more ferociously than before. There were holes in the wall where Jennifer had narrowly evaded his blows.

"About time!" she cried. "I can't hold him much longer!"

"On it!"

Her words seemed to rejuvenate her friend, who launched a salvo of kicks at Barber, staggering him with each blow. He remained on his feet, though, and lunged at her. Jennifer extricated herself from his grasp and vaulted over his shoulder, hoofing at his hamstring. He remained standing, oak-like.

Mary knew she had to find the spot where Barber had originally thrown her. It was the only way.

It did not take her long to find it. Different from the rift at the Odeon, she saw no swirling vortex sucking in pieces of the world and blasting souls around. About the size of a person, it appeared pinned to the wall. Although it was of the same darkness as the last, there was something altogether more surgical, more deliberate about that rift.

Before she had time to consider why, she saw Jennifer fly uncontrollably in her direction and ducked. Turning, she watched as her friend rolled and then staggered back to standing, but Barber regained her attention with a deafening roar.

Angered, Mary reached toward the hole on the tunnel wall with remarkable strength and gathered a gust of the dark winds, clenching her hand into a fist aimed at him. That silenced him, but still she opened her hand, and a focused blast hit him with the force of a fast-moving car. *That* took him off his feet. Mary stood aghast, realising what she had just achieved.

She called upon the darkness again—all too easily—and pointed at Barber as she attempted to scrabble backwards. "*What* makes this hole different?" she asked him in a guttural voice.

"What hole?" he asked, confused. "How should *I* know?"

She hit him with a second blast, knocking him flat on his back. "Don't lie to me! Start talking, or I throw you through it."

"Don't know what you're talking about!" He had to shout now, being halfway along the platform. The arrogant smile had gone as he tried to stand again. Mary's heels echoed off the tiles as she strode purposefully toward her floored opponent, raising both hands up to the height of her face as she gathered another attack.

"Don't you lie to me or I'll tear your fucking limbs off. TELL ME!"

"Mary!" Jennifer shouted from behind her, sounding edgy. "The hole, remember? Close it!"

"DON'T TELL ME WHAT TO DO!" She spun round and blew two holes in the wall near Jennifer's head and reached out, ready to draw the immense power out of her useless companion.

What am I doing?

The darkness drained out of her eyes as her sight shifted back to that of the living. Stunned, she staggered back to the void, her hands trailing behind her as she willed all of the cold, dead wind to follow, ready to be placed back where it belonged. Barber, lacking his usual swagger, got up and glared at her, ready to attack, but held off. Jennifer did not hesitate and walked purposefully towards him. His teeth shaped into a smile once more.

Jennifer slowed to a stop, arms down, flicking her fingers frantically, but that was it.

"What are you doing?" Mary asked as Barber exploded into laughter.

"This place—" Jennifer replied, "it's weakening me somehow."

With the new knowledge, Barber lunged at her. She evaded him with a matador's sidestep. She danced quickly around him; hit and run, hit and run. She landed several blows and kept him well occupied.

Mary concentrated for all she was worth on closing the portal. With no malevolent spirits distracting her, no bolts of dark light lashing around for a victim, and the entire area much more under her control, it proved a significantly simpler task. She brought the full force of her will to bear on the void. She imposed calm on the area and launched the winds back through the closing hole, sealing it once and for all.

Although it was easier, it was not *easy*. The experience once more took a physical toll on her. She staggered in search of the nearest bench to recover. Though weakened, her alternative sight no longer required major exertion.

As she slumped back, Mary could see Jennifer's frustration that Barber healed despite everything she threw at him.

He's as cocky as ever. Even with the chains.

That's it—the chains!

"Jen!" she rasped loudly. "What you were telling me earlier about the earth? He's chained to it. He can't draw that strength on his own. He doesn't know how!"

Jennifer nodded and launched a series of punishing strikes, enough to occupy him, but not close to stopping him.

"Now what?" Jennifer asked, catching breath as Thomas's wounds disappeared yet again.

"I can probably break them when I recover." She forced herself back to her feet and began to stagger towards the fight. "Just put him down hard so I can."

Jennifer smiled, hope restored, and took three quick steps back. "Done." Her left foot hovered just over the electrical track, and she winced. "*Draw your strength from the earth, your whims from the air, flow through the water as it would flow around you, and control the flames . . .*"

She slowly lowered her foot. Even in combat she reached an almost trance-like concentration.

"Wait," Mary called out suddenly, "have you recov–"

"... *or burn with them.*'"

Jennifer's foot went down on the live rail. Mary watched a mighty surge of power rush toward Jennifer's luminous presence. A sudden flash blinded her. An itchy tingle ran down every inch of her spine as a high-pitched buzz scraped past her ears.

"Jen?!"

She blinked several times. Enough vision returned for her to see Jennifer surrounded by lightning—all of it pouring from the track into her. She did not judder in the same way a shocked victim might, though. She held it, channelled it—but just barely.

Jennifer stepped forward and slammed her fist into Barber's chest with all the unearthed energy. A deafening boom, the volume of a cannon, followed, his wail fading into the darkness.

Jennifer panted, exhausted, and stuck two thumbs up at Mary. "He'll be somewhere down the tunnel," she said. "Sorry about that."

"Okay," Mary said, blinking rapidly. "But it'll take me a while to get there—I'm still not at full speed, you know!"

"Says you," Jennifer replied, smoke floating upwards from her.

"And I can barely see!"

"Obviously; the power's gone—all the lights are out!"

"I can spot you anywhere, though, even with my eyes closed!"

"Uh-huh. Hang on. I'm coming over."

Jennifer lifted Mary's eyelids with her fingers for examination. "They look fine!" she said, blowing into the first, and then the second. "Now, hop to it!"

Mary's eyes watered; a tingling sensation hit them, prompting blinks and a light shiver. It was far from unpleasant—invigorating actually, and after the third blink she could clearly see her friend smiling at her and returned the sentiment. She started to ask a question, but instead shrugged and walked across to the other end of the platform, ready to locate the downed Barber and deal with him.

She had almost reached the other end when she heard footsteps coming from the stairs. She spun to see two flashlight beams dancing around at high speed. Jennifer, too, had noticed and moved with feline grace to intercept. Two pairs of boots could be heard running down the stairs, and her guard lowered a little.

"PC Wilson? PC Rogers?"

"You all right?" Wilson shouted back, the movement doubling in speed.

"Yeah, think so! You?"

They reached the platform and shone the lights on the end of their weapons around until they had found Mary and Jennifer on either side of it. "The power went and we heard an explosion. What happened down here?"

"Well, we—"

Jennifer stopped talking suddenly and lurched forward, clutching her stomach. Before the others could ask what was going on, her knees buckled and she turned to vomit on the track.

"Bloody hell, what's going on?" asked Rogers.

Before Mary could answer, a whiny, child-like voice echoed around them. *"Go away!* This was *our* place! You're breaking EVERYTHING!"

A savage, freezing gust whistled across the station and knocked them all to the ground. Holding her hands out to catch herself against the wall, Mary saw a shadow form behind the two constables, a chilling, blue light growing ever brighter.

Wilson and Rogers dropped their guns as they were lifted off their feet. They clawed at their necks, fighting for breath. Mary tried to summon the shadow winds as she had before, but none responded to her call.

She could see the veins of the constables blackening, ready to burst out of their skin, silent agony on their faces.

"*Violet!*" she cried, still not able to see her clearly through the blue light. "Leave them alone!"

Two crunches sounded, and the officers crumpled onto the track. Their killer solidified in full and stared at Mary, letting out a playful giggle.

Her hair was a dishevelled mess, sticking out at all angles. Her clothes looked expensive, designer even, yet torn and filthy. Violet's laughter switched to pitiful sobbing in an instant. Black mascara streaked down her face. She took a couple of drunken steps toward Mary.

"*You ruined it!*" she said in a discordant tone. "*I hate you!*"

Tiles ripped from the walls as she walked by, spinning around her as if caught in a tornado. Without needing to switch her sight, Mary could see black clouds form at the top of the tunnel, swirling around them all.

The same terror she fought when first in the station intensified, and a sharp pain suddenly hit her left arm to such an extent that it gave out completely. She screamed and felt a crushing blow to her face, as if she had run into a wall.

Just like the first time I was here.

"Stop it, Violet." She mumbled the words through what felt like a broken jaw. Reaching up with her right hand, she felt around and identified that it was not.

All in the mind.

Violet laughed playfully in response and took more clumsy steps in her direction. The pain of Mary's relived injuries increased. The more she laughed, the more agony Mary felt.

"*In the way, in the way, no one wants you, GO AWAY!*" The laughter stopped. Spinning tiles flew towards Mary at great speed. Mary managed to roll and shield herself with her right arm as they shattered on impact with the wall.

She tried again to summon the shadow world, but once more failed. Violet was closer now, and her darkened eyes were like an abyss. Her face twitched, almost as if something was trying to get out. Mary could hear dozens, if not hundreds, of voices whispering and muttering.

Switching to her shadow sight, her immediate attention fell on the jewel around Violet's neck. It bathed the darkness in eerie blue light. The voices clearly came from the jewel and not from Violet, whose face contorted every other second to a different expression.

The deathly storm, which had served Mary's every whim until now, rallied like a hellish cyclone around Violet. But it was nothing compared to the next thing Mary saw. In the storm, she saw her left arm detach and blow away like ash in the wind.

More ash blew from her, and everything she had healed from the Underground station relapsed—she found nothing more than a mess of tendons and blood everywhere she examined. She screamed and stopped in her tracks, shaking.

"*Hate you!*" Violet shrieked with an echo which rattled Mary's very soul. She raised her hands into the air. At her silent summons, some of the black ceiling clouds pulled towards her. "*Shall tear you into tiny pieces!*"

Mary put all of her weight onto her good arm and tried to get to her feet. It was all too late. Violet's hands came down, and the cloud tore jagged forks into the darkness. Harpoons of death slammed into Mary.

The anticipated agony failed to materialise. Mary felt uncomfortable, dull thuds, but these were a mild inconvenience compared to the trauma from the illusory open wounds. If anything, the attack made her feel a little stronger.

She used her newfound strength of will to pull herself back to her feet. Her arm returned; her jaw felt just fine. Lifting both arms in front of her, she decided to try another trick—her best so far.

Calm your mind.

Peaceful thoughts.

Let her rest.

Relief flooded her as her hands grew bright once more. "Sarah Bliss?" she said, casting the name hopefully. "I know you're in there, and I know you don't mean any of this. Come on out. *Talk to me.*"

With greater ease than she had ever managed to exhibit, Violet stopped dead, clawing at her ears. A transparent, light copy of her leapt clear of the sapphire and sailed at speed towards Mary.

"Thank you!" a voice echoed delicately from the light source. "They almost—"

"AAAGGH!"

The strength of Violet's shriek yanked Mary's sight back to normal. Violet closed in at an impossible speed to punch Mary hard in the face. It hurt, but again she sensed it could have—*should* have—been a lot worse.

Violet's hand closed around Mary's throat and lifted her from the floor with ease. Her sharp, cold fingertips dug into the skin and muscles of her neck, attempting to sap the life from her. Despite a numbing sensation, it still inflicted a fraction of what might have been. "*You ruin everything! EVERYTHING! Why won't you just* die *and join us like you were meant to*?"

Mary's insides felt as if they were about to be crushed.

She reached for the necklace, but Violet fought off the attempt and stretched out of reach. Mary remained in the grapple as Violet increased the pressure to a deadly level.

"VIOLET!" yelled a voice behind them. Jennifer staggered over. She looked sick, weak, but broke into a charge just as Violet brought her other arm to bear on Mary's neck. Jennifer's brutal contact made all three of them collapse to the floor. Violet's grip was broken.

Violet turned slowly to Jennifer, a drooling grin washing over her face.

"You! *So much power! So strong!*"

"No!" Mary spluttered. "Leave her alone!"

"Yeah, that's right," Jennifer said, crawling away and, though she coughed unpleasantly, she wore a triumphant smile. "And you don't know the half of it yet."

She leapt at Violet, who effortlessly swatted her onto the track. Somehow she landed on her feet, but Violet stood, pointing at her. Mary could see Jennifer struggle for balance—similar to the way Tally had back at the cinema.

She fought with all of her strength back to the platform. But Violet waited to launch a vicious kick to her face. Unusually slow to react, Jennifer failed to evade it and staggered back.

Instead of pressing her advantage, Violet dropped to her knees and started sobbing. *"Why won't you all just LEAVE ME ALONE?"*

Her words empowered the storm, but Mary had recovered and returned to her feet, making another lunge for the necklace. This time though, Violet sent a bone-crushing blast of the dark winds straight at her. Mary heard a deafening rip behind her and knew immediately what had happened—another hole had been created. She was hit by a second blast, which knocked her straight through it, and into . . .

Nothing.

~✳~

Mary had been stuck in a gut-churning spin for some time—she didn't know for how long, but she had to regain control and quickly. Shades, objects, *places*—flew around her, nausea destroying her concentration. She was nowhere, drifting wildly.

She had to latch onto somewhere, *something* familiar before she was lost entirely. A friend in trouble; a brilliance in the darkness: Jennifer. It had to be worth a try.

But she could not sense her. Dizzy now, desperate, there was one last chance before she blacked out.

The cacophony of loud voices, the foul beacon of blue in a land of light and darkness—they stood out in her current state. With a concerted effort, she latched her focus onto it hard.

She was spewed out of the very same portal she fell into, landing on the station platform and rolling several times before coming to a stop.

The dramatic entrance caught Violet's attention. She rose from her stooped position, raised a hand, and tore at the air in Mary's direction. Cracks in the world itself smashed into Mary's stomach and knocked her back further. Other than being winded, Mary was unharmed.

It was only then that Mary realised she could not say the same for her friend. Jennifer lay motionless, hair sprawled, porcelain-skinned, and body covered in bulging black veins.

Mary screamed in horror. Violet broke into inane giggles again, poking the body with the heel of her boot.

"Don't touch her! Don't touch her!"

Mary struggled to remain calm, forcing slow, deep breaths as she stretched a hand at the open portal. But it was no use. She wanted to tear the creature limb-from-limb. The entire station shuddered with her fury, dust and debris breaking and falling from the ceiling.

Becoming the very cyclone upon which she travelled, she flew at the static Violet and seized her firmly, carrying them both straight through the portal, with no care for where they came out—if they did at all.

CHAPTER TWENTY

Tally and Lord Alphonse sat by the Gate as he spoke of adventures of the past.

"It concerns me that the *Teardrop* was created in the first place," he said to her as he considered what she was up against. "Originally crafted into a blade, it speaks volumes of the creator. However, its re-housing has actually made it worse. The knife would have been focused—one target at a time—on the direct intention of expediting death for its victim. This is far more insidious.

"In your generation, there are those who would freely dabble in unknown arts and aesthetics for the sport of it. Such carelessness would create opportunities for destruction with a *necklace,* even amongst those who mean no harm.

"What then, when one comes to possess this with naught but evil intentions? A troubled soul interacting with a great number more likeminded or even more twisted still? They'd conjoin their blasphemies and corruption with the gem's living controller. It would destroy everything it came into contact with. It knows no better."

"To hold it and this gate would undoubtedly unleash a terrible darkness," Tally asserted. He agreed with her entirely, as much sadness as the truth brought him.

"The Guide mentioned that the trapped souls eliminate any owners they believe . . . *unresponsive* to their persuasions—*killing* them, to be precise. Which raises the question: with one such as Aurelia Raine, who is in command? The wearer or the *Teardrop*?"

"Aurelia Raine has proven she possesses a powerful will." Both sighed. Lord Alphonse continued, "I have never heard of the Raines as one of the more traditional families of power—and I knew a good few in my day.

"What I *do* know is her sort. I would not believe her born into privilege. Rather, she has proven opportunistic, uncaring for any she destroys along her way. We, the Grenshalls, are just the next obstacle for her, with you, her one true barrier, earning her most fervent enmity."

"Even disregarding what we know of her true intentions," Tally posited, "Mama and Papa know full well that she holds us all in the highest contempt. And from what I have seen of her attempts to disgrace us all, I wonder what prevents them from moving against her."

"I find that question more difficult to answer," Lord Alphonse said more quietly than his previous words. "I do not dare get close enough to Lady Raine to find out for myself. For, knowing what I am now—little more than a being with a sole remaining purpose—were she to discover my presence, I would seal a fate one hundred times worse for myself.

"Her hold over your father, is, as you have discovered, unfounded. But he does not know this, and some transgression must have taken place, or he would have no such concerns. She can still cause irreparable damage with the right words to the right people."

"She has played her hand very well," Tally observed. "But to what end? Surely even for her, there is only so much purpose to such mindless destruction?"

Lord Alphonse responded gravely. "Think of it this way. The

Gate we sit by is just that—a doorway between ourselves and a great quantity of the dead who cannot rest free, each one remaining with an unachievable purpose. This leaves them ripe for further torment or insanities—and with free rein to walk amongst us.

"She believes the Gate would allow her, with the aid of the *Teardrop*, to draw upon power without limit. But that power would ultimately be beyond her. A gate permanently open would do nothing other than drain the living surrounding it!"

Mary shuddered at the thought of all manner of unimaginable horrors unleashed upon the world.

"An experienced traveller is perfectly capable of creating his own gates," he continued, "powerful enough for even the most ignorant to walk through, were they so inclined. I learned that opening and closing such a portal on the exact same point hundreds of times, or just leaving one open for long enough—months, years—creates such a gate.

"It may feel like onyx to you, but in truth, it is a vast concentration of the dust and debris you experienced when you found yourself in the shadow world. And yes, it is made of exactly the same material.

"Thus, what you are looking at here is nothing less than a vast concentration of souls lacking the will to find purpose. Such entities adhere to an open door, and over time as they straddle both worlds, they bind together and form a solid object perhaps a hundred times the size and power of *Death's Teardrop*, perhaps more.

"I will tell you this, though: the blade originally holding the stone cuts as sharp as anything I have seen. Dab a bit of melted gold on it and it will carve warding inscriptions like a dream."

Tally laughed. "Sounds like a vain use of precious materials to me."

Lord Alphonse smirked. "Yes, it is, rather. Now, before you depart, I have one last word of advice."

"Oh?" She had only met Lord Alphonse in dreams, but knew in the short time they had spoken that she adored him. His aura of pride and self-assurance seemed an even more self-assured version of Papa.

"The Raines have mastered the art of forcing some of these weaker-willed yet single-minded souls into doing their bidding. However, they are entirely reliant on the *Teardrop* to do it. Know that they are following a recipe as dangerous as the conjurations of an expert, although bearing none of the understanding. Use this knowledge against them. Use it wisely."

Tally considered all of the many terrible ways direct confrontation could go wrong—not least of which, some dreadful wrenching of her own soul. "How do I even begin to contend with this?"

"Remember the first thing I told you to do," he said with a smile, standing up. "You may always call for me in this room—the Gate Chamber." He then lifted her off the ground by the waist as if she were a doll and threw her away from him, into the air. "I shall see you soon!"

Tally was left with nothing but darkness, the Gate, and a renewed sense of urgency when she awoke—after all, she knew nothing of how long she had actually been asleep. Nonetheless, she remembered the exact way she had been instructed to leave the room, and thought it was as worthwhile an attempt as any she had tried.

CHAPTER TWENTY-ONE

Urrrrrgh."

Mary Hall woke up on her own bed, still fully clothed, the room spinning. This was how it should have been the morning after the graduation party. But there had been other days since that. *Plenty* more.

10:30 am, according to her bedside clock. She'd been out for a long time. Unable to blame a night's drinking, she tried to remember the last thing she'd done before getting here. She'd thrown herself and Violet through a dark portal and shunted herself with the one thought she could muster: *home*. When the spinning in her head slowed, she noticed a shaft of sunlight forcing its way through the curtains and shining bright on her face.

What she had called 'home' before her recent overnight stops at the hospital and Kara's place was this bedroom in a small flat. She'd have to be out of in a couple of weeks, now that she'd finished her course.

That was her collection of movies and movie posters on the wall. Those were her beaded necklaces on the dresser. Perhaps she *had* just been out drinking the night before. Perhaps it was all just a bad dream.

Nope.

What she was feeling was no hangover. It was the combination of a million memories flooding at her all at once. Not all of them were hers.

The memories ordered themselves, took shape. She took a moment to settle her mind, let the room stop spinning. Her attempts to relax were disrupted by a squeal from the bottom of the bed.

"Where am I? Where am I? *What did you do??*" the voice cried. She whirled around to see a faint, translucent version of the gangling blonde woman she had battled last night—or was it? There were no traces of straggling hair and her makeup was professionally neat, but that was not the most noticeable difference. This woman facing her was looking straight *at* her rather than straight *through* her. As a result, she appeared considerably more . . . *human.*

"*Violet?*"

"Why does everyone keep calling me that? Or are they talking about the necklace? Though it seems a strange name, it being *blue* and all—"

"*Necklace?*" Mary suddenly connected what she remembered. "You genuinely have no idea what's going on, do you?"

Poor cow.

Mary *did* know, including this woman's last moments. It was impossible to save her now. The necklace—so much more than a necklace—had seen to that.

"*Sarah*, isn't it? Oh, God, I'm sorry, I really am! I was—"

"Sorry?" Sarah looked confused. "Why are you apologising to me?"

"I—" There really wasn't any easy way to say what she had to say. "I think I may have killed you."

"What?"

"Look, I'm new to all this stuff, really new. And I didn't mean to—well, I was hoping you'd get back in control and stop all the killing, only it wasn't you and—oh bloody hell, this has all gone to shit, hasn't it?"

"Oh, no doubt," Sarah agreed. She actually looked somewhat amused. "But it wasn't you. It was that Thomas Barber creep. He started all this."

"So it was all true—the news speculation?"

"Unfortunately, news headlines have been lost to me for some time."

Mary grimaced. "Actually, it turns out you made the front pages. And not in a good way. They reckoned you and Barber worked together to steal the *Teardrop*."

"God, no! He forced the necklace on me. There was a bit of a struggle. Think that's what finished me off in the end. Then . . . well, I have no idea what came next. But it was you who got me out, I know that much. You saved me."

"*Saved* you?"

"Saved me. I was kind of stuck. In that necklace. Not long after he put it on." She rubbed her forehead, looking agitated. "There must have been hundreds of us in there. I wish I knew how we all got in. It was horrible—they're all just so *angry*. I don't get it. As crowded as it was, they constantly complained about how lonely they were.

"It was awful in there. We all knew that; everyone just hated everyone. I was actually angry enough to want to *kill* people. Can you believe that? Didn't help that I kept thinking of what Thomas did to me."

"You still haven't told me how I saved you."

"I kept my wits about me. I only managed that because I kept thinking of something to cling onto apart from this weird mob mentality. It felt really obvious at the time, instinctive. I was lucky, in that the body they were using was mine. It wasn't much, but it gave me something to fight for—the chance to hold onto my own *self*.

"And also, because that bastard broke in and tried to force the thing on to me, I was fighting from the start. I've been doing a lot of that."

"I can fully sympathise."

"He might've killed me, but I never stopped fighting. Never stopped hearing voices. They just called and called at me. Felt like I was dragged in with them. I was lost. Like them. Don't think I'd have had much long—hey! You got me out just in time!"

"Well, that was lucky, then. As I said, I can sympathise. I've been fighting, too. Since day one of this whole thing. But never for control of my—"

As Mary spoke, she came to a sudden realisation. The return of her suppressed memories of that night burst upon her and illuminated the possibilities. Barber's attack in the Underground. The void. The failed attempt. What if someone *had* been attempting to steal her body?

Her thoughts turned to poor Natalie. She shuddered. There were so many ways this could have been worse for her.

Sarah looked solid now—human. Normal. Mary felt the apparition returning her own close evaluation. Looking at the idealised version of this ghost, she felt her own fatigue. Confidence and self-assurance shone through the spectral image, a hearkening back to her living, breathing days.

"You most definitely *are* a fighter," the ghost observed. "You've made their life, if you'll pardon the pun—a living hell. Whatever they're planning, you've probably held them right up."

"What *were* they planning, Sarah?"

"Sorry. Too busy not getting eaten to be in the loop, really. I know it was something to do with one of those holes. The huge one we always had thrumming in the background."

"What huge one?"

"You can't miss it."

Mary concentrated, let the inky darkness wash over her eyes. She stretched her senses, reaching for the loudest noise, the greatest disruption. Sarah was right; she couldn't miss it.

That did not mean she could zero in accurately on it, either. The chaos was nauseating to detect, especially in her already-exhausted state. Mary had just wished to go home, the last place she remembered being before all this started.

Perhaps she had complicated her own command. All Mary knew was that Violet had ended up elsewhere. Probably just as well, given how long she had been out cold on the bed.

"Do you know any more about who this 'Violet' is?" she asked. "I've heard one or two things but not the full story. Maybe you know something?"

Vexation appeared to age the ghost several years, but she answered after a short pause. "I don't know exactly *who* she is, but hers was the only voice I could always hear over the others. She was like a megaphone or something. She sounded really young—a child. But she seemed to be holding the whole thing together, running things."

"You've been missing for months. How come this has all only happened in the last few days, and not sooner?"

There was a strained look on Sarah's face. She concentrated very hard, but with no success. "Not sure. I don't even think I was part of the plan."

"There's a *plan*?"

"Yes." Sarah replied sternly. "I don't know what it is because it got lost in the noise, but it's something to do with that third . . . hole . . . portal . . . whatever. Everything going on revolves around that, somehow."

Mary took a moment to digest the information. "This may come as an insensitive question," she asked, "but now that you're out of there, how come you're still around?"

"I've thought about that," Sarah said, an out-of-place grin on her face. "I've had no chance to go anywhere else. I got roped into this and have only been out since you helped me escape. I could just go home to Robert, couldn't I?" The confidence drained from her face, the apparition greying and fading in front of Mary's eyes. Sarah was shaking. "Oh, no."

"Try not to think—"

"Nobody will have told him, will they? They never found me! He'll think I'm—"

"I know it's hard, but calm down."

"I-I'm just not sure what I'm going to do now."

"I am."

Mary rubbed a hand over her face, got to her feet, and moved to Sarah, who watched her curiously. She then cleared her mind of the chaos of new possibilities and focused only on the lost soul in front of her. The room cooled slightly and she could feel her own soul lock with Sarah's. This time there were no outside disruptions, just the two of them.

"Like you say, it was me who left you in this state, so it's me who needs to sort it out."

Sarah's face was now awash with fear and uncertainty.

"It's okay," Mary offered, understanding precisely how she was feeling—living the emotion, in fact. "You've helped me—so now I'm going to help *you*. I've done this before a few times."

The ghost pondered her words for a moment, and then settled a little.

"Listen," Sarah grabbed Mary firmly by the wrist—though what Mary felt was concentrated pressure from cold, moist air. "I can't say I know exactly what you're going through, but I've got a better idea than most. You've got another—whatever I am—like me, hanging around, haven't you? Not here right now, but close to you, somehow."

"Tally?"

"If that's her name, yes. Has she been good to you so far?"

Mary nodded. "Without her guidance, I'd have been clueless—probably dead."

"Well, it was brief, but when you freed me, I felt like I was in your head for a while, could see a few of your memories."

"I've got some of yours, too. And I'll probably see more if you let me help you rest."

"That's what I was getting to. You must have this to some extent with Tally."

"What makes you say that?"

"When you reached out for me—that's what it felt like you were doing, anyway—I found myself holding on, like I was anchored to you. I think she's tethered to you, as well. More solidly, though."

"You reckon?"

"When I got free, you pulled me towards you, and if you'd stopped, or failed in some way, I don't know what would have happened to me, but I doubt it would've been pleasant. And every time one of those portals appears, it draws me towards it, too, but nowhere near as powerful as the necklace—or *you*."

"But I don't have anything like—"

"I *know*. That's one of the reasons Violet hates you so much. You *terrify* her. You're a serious threat!"

"Someone needs to be. She's killing people indiscriminately."

"I know. Which is why I can't hold you up any longer. Do whatever it is you have to be free of me so you can get on with it."

Mary frowned. "Don't say it like that. That makes it sound like I'm desperate to get rid of you. I'm not."

"Well, you should be. I know hindsight's a wonderful thing, but I wonder if I might have done more to prevent this from happening?"

"Don't be silly—you fought as hard as you could against that thing."

"I wasn't talking about that."

"From what I saw, you fought hard against Barber, as well."

"I know. That's sort of what I mean."

"Hang on—are you saying you shouldn't have tried to fight him off?"

"No, I'm saying he deserved better than I gave him. Before the changes. Before the necklace—all this. I was never going to get his number or anything like that, but I was a real bitch to him."

"*Hey!*" Mary responded angrily. "Don't you *dare* blame yourself for any of this. I remember when you saw him. He could have moved on, got over you. But he didn't. *He* chose this path for himself, to become what he is now. Not you—*him*. So leave the guilt for someone who deserves it and get back to the fact that the selfish bastard denied you a damn good life."

Sarah thought about Mary's words, saddened at first, but finally perked up. "You're right," she said, nodding. "Sort him out for me, won't you?"

"Don't worry," Mary said, determined, "I will."

Mary adjusted her breathing to a state of calm control, the light lowering in the room as her concentration increased. She merged the two worlds she walked, and the palms of her hands gained a lambent glow. She exhaled slowly but paused halfway through her rite.

"Problem?" asked Sarah, at last looking calm and relaxed.

"Yeah." She sighed. The light from her hands faded and wrinkles formed on her brow. "When I've done this before, it's felt right—a lot better than when I've just forced the life out of people—but after that, peaceful as they look, I've no idea where everyone goes. How do I *know* it's better for them? How do I know I'm not condemning them to another form of torment? Something worse?"

"I think you've managed to answer your own question, Mary."

"What? As in, I *don't*?"

"You could look at it that way. Or you could trust your own instinct that you know right from wrong. It's clear to me that your morality is in the right place. How about when you sent Serge on his way? That's what you were thinking when you first offered to help me; what changed your mind? Did you actually take time to think more clearly about what Barber and Violet have done?"

"That's nothing I can ignore, is it?"

"Nobody's asking you to. But you know full well you're against whatever they're doing. That tells me a lot. Not everyone with that choice took the one you did—and that looks good on you, speaking as an opinionated dead person. Now, pep talk over—save some lives!"

Mary's hands illuminated with renewed intensity. She could feel herself freeing the tentative hold the world of the restless dead had on Sarah, and felt an air of peace. She watched the ghost nod in encouragement as she raised her hands and drew the essence to her. "You seem to know so much."

You could have done great things—it feels like such a waste.

Sarah chuckled. "I wasn't just a pretty face, you know, whatever anyone might have thought."

"Of course not," Mary replied, real lament in her voice, "you were the head girl at your school, one of the highest achievers on your degree course in your year, and never failed an exam in your life!"

More memories. Sarah's, not Mary's.

"I'd forgotten about that actually," Sarah said, beaming.

"You shouldn't have."

Mary's strength had left her. She had given so much of herself of late, but this last push had her sitting back on the bed. Sarah was now barely visible—a faint pale beacon against the gathering dark clouds that remained.

But a brief, happy life flashed in snapshots before her eyes: success, the promise of more, an impending marriage to someone perfect for her, and a brilliant future. She smiled with hope through the tears for what might have been.

"You know, we could have easily been doing this the other way round? I'm never going to be as sharp as you were."

Just a voice now, whispering in the air. "Don't sell yourself short, Mary. You did really well. Before you go off, take a look around. Put all your own memories together, and above all, listen to your own advice more often. It's not who you *were* that matters . . ."

With that, Sarah had gone completely. All that remained of her rested firmly in Mary's mind. Tired, drained, and aggrieved over Sarah's tragic end, she collapsed sideways onto the mattress and sobbed for a moment, considering whether she could even get off the bed for the rest of the day or not. But ultimately, people were depending on her—Jennifer, Kara—who knew how many others as long as Violet was still on the loose.

That thought alone was enough to have her spring from the bed, lunging for the bedside table where she always left her mobile phone— wrecked in Bond Street. However, as soon as she plucked the cordless landline from its housing, she heard a dial tone which beeped intermittently, indicating waiting messages. Though it was hardly the time and incredibly unlikely, she keyed in the numbers required to listen to any messages in the slim hope that one of them might have been Kara.

"You have four messages."

One of them had to be Kara, surely?

"Mary, it's Vicky. Just so you know, we're back home okay—you

can go to bed now! Oh—looks like you already have. No worries. Speak tomorrow, yeah?"

"Not so much . . ."

"Mary, it's Jess! Your mobile's going straight to voicemail and you're not picking up here—you all right? Is he drop-dead gorgeous, you dirty dog? Give us a buzz when you get this!"

"Yeah, I wish . . ."

"Mary. Seriously, getting worried now—the news is going mad, you're not answering your phone. Just let me know you're all right, okay?"

"Haven't really got time, but I'd be a crap friend if I didn't at least get in touch."

"Mary, we called round today, but no answer. Thought we'd better let the police know. PLEASE tell us you're well—worried sick!"

"Okay, okay! Jesus!" She deleted the messages and then slammed down the phone. This was completely side-tracking her, but it couldn't be left unresolved. She had enough business with the police as it was.

Mary never knew for certain why Vicky and Jess were her best friends. They had next to nothing in common, other than being on the same course, but they'd put up with her regular foul-mouthed rants. She'd even put up with Vicky's chain smoking in return, and Jess's tendency to get so sozzled that she'd need to be carried home every time they went out.

Looking around the room, there was a pile of brightly coloured clothing on the floor next to a sewing machine and an open wardrobe. If she didn't know better, it would have been a reasonable guess that someone had broken in and ransacked the place. But she *did* know better.

The thought occurred to her that getting in last night should have presented the small problem of her keys being in the same handbag she lost on the night of the initial attack. But, then again, not having house keys was never a problem when you could walk through walls like they weren't there. And thinking about it, that must have been exactly what she had done.

"No walls can hold me."

She froze for a few seconds and frowned hard. "*Where* have I heard that before?"

She looked down, pensive. Drop cloths covered her entire lounge floor—protection from paint. Several canvas blocks lay there, in various stages of completion. Each one was a part of her final-year project. It occurred to her, for some time before the Underground incident, many of her paintings proved to be a soul-searching exercise. A search for a past she never had, and never truly knew.

The first was a self-portrait: her in an elegant navy blue velvet dress against a stately backdrop. Bolsover Castle, Derbyshire. Something about the place felt comfortable, a sense of home. She could never place why.

The next was called '*Tooth.*' The tooth in question was in a box under the bed, a reminder of the bullying she received at school. Specifically, a reminder of the day it stopped. It wasn't *her* tooth. She knocked it out of the mouth of the chief instigator. She got suspended for her troubles, but kept the tooth as a souvenir. She had no regrets but a reminder of the dangers of losing control. *People got hurt.*

Mary shuddered at the next painting. '*The Family Curse.*' She had no pictures of Mum and Dad. When she asked for them, people didn't know where to look. When she asked about records, no one had answers. Nobody wanted to know.

So she remembered as best she could. The dozens of shadowy

people in the background represented the family she never knew anything about. The two at the front: her parents as she imagined them.

Funny. Looking at it now, 'Mum' looks like Tally. I still think she may be a figment of my imagination.

Her 'father' was easy. She took direct inspiration from Walter Stark, the father of rock sensations Katt and Leile Stark. Their poster hung on her bedroom wall.

I used Walter because he had a tragic end. Car went off a high road and flipped all the way down—never had a chance. Could have been a musical legend himself. I never knew Dad, but I like to think he could have been a legend, too, if given the chance.

As for the last image—more detailed than the rest—the scythe said it all. He came for them. Her head hung as she examined the painting and remembered why she had done it. Nobody had ever got to the bottom of what had *truly* happened to the Hall family. And she still desperately wanted to know. She wondered if that was the reason she had clung to life so grimly. It seemed she had unfinished business long before Violet and the *Teardrop.*

In an almost trance-like state, she returned to the open wardrobe full of clean clothing. Concerned as she was for the well-being of her friends, she wasn't any good to anyone running around in shredded clothes.

Her collection seriously lacked dark clothing, apart from a few rags she used for painting. She retained one suit for interviews, a dark blue, similar to the colour of the velvet dress that she had on the painting, with a loose, comfortable fit. Dark enough, and easy to move around in. Perfect.

She grabbed the phone and dialled Vicky's mobile number. They'd called each other so often that the numbers had been keyed in before she had given it thought. It rang out, connecting to voicemail. That actually suited her just fine.

"Vicky, I was just ringing you to let you know I'm—" She wanted to say 'fine', but that would have been a lie too far.

"... I'm still alive." She hung up, her hand over her face after the call.

The second call was a much trickier task as she didn't have the telephone number. She tried the most obvious thing and checked the phonebook for *Dr. Mellencourt*. The number to a Covent Garden address which corresponded to Kara's house rang out and moved on to a non-personalised voicemail.

Drawing on information gleaned from healing Kara, a few harmless prevarications at the university switchboard connected her to the professor. After a shorter time, an agitated Kara picked up. "Mum?" she asked, her accent broader than at any time previously. "What's up?"

"Kara, it's Mary."

"How did you know my mum's name? Oh yeah, of course! Never mind that—thank God you're alive. Where did you go? What happened? Hang on, *is* Mum safe?"

Mary winced. "As far as I know, yeah, your mother's fine. I just couldn't think of any other way to get hold of you. Where's Jennifer?"

The line went silent.

"Kara?"

Mary knew the answer, but when Kara uttered the words, they still hit her hard. "She's gone, Mary. There was nothing anyone could do."

It was Mary's turn to be silent now.

"Kara," she said at last, drumming her fingers on the table, "I need to see her."

"Yeah," Kara mumbled, "we probably should identify her with whoever has her—"

"That's not what I meant." She considered her next words carefully. "She's *not* dead. I would have known."

"Mary," Kara squeaked, "are you *insane*? I was first on the scene. She had no pulse, her heart had stopped, she wasn't breathing at all, and she had black veins all over her just like the other people that *thing* murdered lately. How in God's name can you even *think* she could still be alive?"

"Look, I don't know." Mary winced, realising how absurd she must sound. "But trust me on this. Where is she?"

"Well, the morgue, I imagine."

"Okay. Get 'em to call off any autopsy—whatever it takes—and then come and pick me up. I need to see her. Then I have to do something about Violet before she kills any more people."

"Where is she now?"

"A third portal. Reckon I can find it, but we haven't got long on it. But then, we haven't on Jen, either. Meet you at Finchley Road Station."

CHAPTER TWENTY-TWO

Kara's Mini screeched to a halt in front of Mary and the deserted station. In the distance, the shouts and screams of fear and violence.

"What kept you?" Mary asked. "You normally drive like Gene Hunt."

"Got here as fast as I could. Have you seen it out there?"

"I can *hear* plenty. But I haven't seen that much from here."

"Lucky you. I asked Inspector Hammond which mortuary they took Jennifer to. Had to look it up; damn navigation system's on the blink."

The academic shoved the car into gear and set off, spinning the steering wheel left. "There's about two radio stations that *aren't* on emergency broadcast just now. Traffic's just hell, even for London, and pedestrians are herding like wildebeests at a safari park. Wherever they're going, they have no care about oncoming cars. There are abandoned, crashed vehicles and injured walkers everywhere."

Mary peered out of the window as they weaved through the chaotic streets, down the back of alleyways, and across pavements. She was growing accustomed to Kara's remarkably skilful driving.

Tension prevailed in the air. Several arguments and fights had broken out along the way from no visible cause. The absence of emergency services boded ill.

Once she thought to look for it, Mary noticed the subtle taint of the death winds. With the benefit of her shadow sight, the turbulence levels appeared higher than ever. In the shadow London, there was a storm so volatile that it echoed even in the mundane world. She relayed this to Kara.

"Well, that explains everything," Kara said, deeply concerned. "But driving's becoming almost impossible, and we're still about ten minutes out, even on a clear day."

Mary mulled the issue over. "I've got a plan. These people seem to be moving around in some sort of order. It's to do with the shadow place."

"You're thinking it's more widespread than the stations?"

"I'm thinking it's all over bloody London!" Mary's eyes glazed over with liquid darkness. She could see some of the pavements and roadways appeared darker than others, almost pitch. There were obvious pathways around the large crowds of people from which they did not dare stray. "Time to clear a path."

Holding her hands as if in prayer, she summoned the nearby dark winds, bending them around her. She extended her elbows and pointed forwards, forcing her hands wide apart, nearly clobbering Kara in the process. The nearby crowds moved rapidly out of the way of the vehicle, a channel of subtle terror created in front of them.

"Bloody hell, Mary! I don't know whether to be delighted or terrified."

"Decide when we get there," Mary snarled. "Mush!"

Kara jammed her foot all the way down on the accelerator, the tyres smoking as she got the car rapidly moving.

The wandering crowds parted ways as soon as it moved their way. Kara grinned, although the inside of the car acted as a small wind tunnel. "*Amazing*!" she hollered. "They appear to be *migrating,* like birds flying south for the winter. Entire mobs of them, all changing direction at once. It's *surreal*."

"Yeah," Mary answered, a smile now on her face making her look no less sinister. "*I'd* dive out of the way of the crazy bitch rally driving around London, too."

Ten minutes later, driving at that breakneck pace, Kara handbrake-turned into a space outside the morgue. Smoke poured from the tyres as a lone member of staff stood outside in a filthy lab coat, enjoying a cigarette. Kara shrugged, and the two women stormed into the building. At the empty reception desk, Kara examined the computer and rotated the monitor their way.

The man from outside ambled past them. He reached a door on their right and started opening it, but turned around.

"Those five minutes I get every other hour for my cig break?" he said, shaking his head. "Quite precious to me, as it happens."

"Sorry," Mary mumbled. He gave a half-baked nod, just enough to confirm he heard.

"So then,"—he established eye contact—"how come you haven't buggered off with everyone else?"

"Was going to ask you the same question, actually."

"I *work* here."

Mary gave a dismissive grin. "Not what I meant, but point taken. We need to see someone you've got in here."

"Unless you two are coppers, you'll have to wait 'til the funeral, like everyone else."

Mary shook her head. "You've got someone in here who may not be dead."

The man gave a small chuckle. "They've been trying to work that out about me for years!"

"We haven't time for stand-up comedy, mate."

He muttered something under his breath before answering, "Someone in *there*, you mean?"

Both of the women nodded in unison. With that, he took on a sour expression. "So you're doctors, are you?" he asked.

Mary tilted her head in Kara's direction. "Well, *she* is . . ."

He gave Kara a sceptical glare. "Listen, nobody in there ever gets up and walks out, let me tell you!"

"Seriously," Kara interjected, stepping forward, "I *am* a doctor. Do you have an untagged young blonde girl in here? Came in from the incident at Bond Street Station?"

He scratched his stubble for a while. "Oh, yeah, *her!* Police said to steer well clear for the foreseeable and left a guard on, but then—well, they all just buggered off, like everyone else."

"When did that happen?" Kara asked, pensive.

"About two hours ago. I remember exactly. That was my last cig break. I missed one a bit earlier 'cos I wanted to know what was going on with her. Pale, like she'd been dead for a while, but they only brought her in yesterday. From the station."

Mary rolled her eyes. "*Please* tell me they haven't started work on her yet?"

"That's the thing." He threw his hands into the air, looking confused. "They were about to, once they got everyone out of the way for long enough, but then . . . just—"

"Yeah, yeah," Mary said, grinding her teeth. "We get it: *they just buggered off.*"

"Yeah, just like that. Bloody weird, even for here."

"So where can we find her then?" Mary asked, agitated.

"I may as well take you over there. Might get into trouble for it, but—"

"—but there's nobody here going to drop you in it, is there?" Mary snapped. "Get on with it!"

The staff member did exactly as he was told, provoking a smirk from Kara. As soon as they arrived, Mary could hear a number of voices, none she recognised, attempting to communicate with her. She made a conscious effort to close them out.

~ * ~

Jennifer had been laid out on one of the open slabs with dissection tools scattered on the table in a haphazard fashion. The white cloth protecting her modesty had been pulled back, revealing the afflicted body, porcelain-skinned, with blackened veins. Even her normally golden hair looked a drained grey.

Mary caught Kara as she broke down in front of the motionless body. "See?" Kara said, barely able to speak. "She's just like the others we saw."

Mary examined the body, picking Kara up and comforting her a little. Mary shook her head, determination set on her face. "*No*, she's not," she answered. "Through my eyes, she always shone much brighter than most. You weren't wrong when you called her a force of nature." She reached out and touched Jennifer's arm. There was no pulse. She leaned in close to her face, a hand on her chest. No breath. The signs were not encouraging.

"Thought *she* was the doctor?" the man accused.

"I look at things *differently*," Mary answered. Her eyes darkened as he watched, giving him pause.

"Here—you're *not* medical staff, are you? You *know* her—"

Mary's concentration had been totally disrupted. "Listen, mate, appreciate your help here and everything, but for your own good, you should probably walk away. Now."

"Don't be stupid!" he said, looking at them both suspiciously. "What are you *really* up to?"

"You don't want to know." Mary stared coldly at him. Twice now he had resisted her coercive efforts.

Kara cleared her throat. "Actually, we were hoping to pick up our friend here and walk out. So, as she said, you're probably best leaving us to it. It's probably not worth the hassle to you."

He looked baffled. "You do know that's illegal, right?"

"This is potentially the *least* of our worries with the law," Kara replied. "According to the news, two of the three of us are wanted for questioning on suspicion of terrorist acts. But I wouldn't panic; you're not getting in our way—*yet*."

He paused to ponder his options. His eye gravitated to the surgical tools tray, but Kara watched him like a hawk. She had already spirited a scalpel into her hands; nobody else noticed she had slipped it under her sleeve. Through a combination of indecision and defiance, he started to shake and went red.

"Listen—I-I don't know who you are, or what you're up to, but I can't just let you up and leave with a body. I might not be up to much, but there's no way in hell that I'm going to let you do anything sick here. I mean, frigging hell, have you *no* respect for the dead?"

Mary sprang forward until directly in front of him. She glowered at him and spoke coldly, this time with no unnatural influence. "More than anyone you have ever met, or ever *will*."

She turned back to the lifeless Jennifer, directing Kara to move out of her way, who duly obliged. With renewed focus, she examined the body, perfectly filtering light and shadow until she could see only the pale grey shadows of the dead around her.

The slabs to her left and right were the grey she expected, but as hoped, the central slab holding Jennifer was slightly different— *slightly* brighter than the other two. There was hope; the faintest spark of life remained.

"She's not dead," Mary said to the others. "*She's not dead!*"

"Oh, now you *are* mad!" the man said, throwing his arms into the air. "That same thing that killed those people at the cinema got her, I'm telling you."

"You don't know as much as you think," Mary said to him. She called on her own life energies, willing them to transfer over to her downed friend. Kara and the staff member both gasped loudly as with Mary's touch, the blackened veins receded, and Jennifer took several slow, deep breaths. It came at a price. Severely weakened, Mary collapsed to the floor, dragging the surgical tools with her.

"*Mary!*" Kara cried. Mary clawed at the table in an attempt to support herself. Kara grabbed her and helped her back to her feet. "What did you *do*?"

The mortician backed into a corner, wide-eyed and silent as he watched the perceptible rise and fall of Jennifer's breathing. Kara checked for a pulse. She weakly nodded at Mary.

Mary turned to the man, who was looking straight over at the table, shaking his head and muttering. "Can't believe it . . . not possible . . ." over and over again. Her patience gone, she gave him a slap across the face, and rediscovered her strength in doing so. From the corner of her eye, she saw Kara grimace at the impact.

"*Hey!*" She grabbed the lapels of his lab coat. His babbling stopped. "She can't leave here like that!"

With one last glance at Jennifer, he ran off. Still hobbled, Mary returned to her friends, employing her conventional vision. Kara looked at the grey, marble-like appearance of her friend on the table and gave a small scowl as she looked back at Mary.

"One thing," she said, "*tell me* you didn't just bring her back to life *that* way? You know, like Violet or whatever it calls itself has been? Because you know, if you did, I'd never forgive you."

"I'd never forgive myself, either." Mary shuddered as she finished her answer, but her resolve returned quickly.

"She looks rough," Kara said, still concerned. *"Really* rough."

"She is." Mary stretched her arms and shook out her legs, as if she had sat awkwardly for a prolonged period. "It's a miracle she held out this long. I tried to help her back, with a little bit of my own life force. Maybe some help from Serge and Sarah, too. But it took everything I had just to get her breathing. It wasn't mine to give."

"What do you mean by that?"

"When I accidentally attacked you, I could get you back to your feet properly because what was missing, I'd stolen from you in the first place. But it was Violet taking this time—she took almost everything from Jen. As I say—tough, tough girl.

"By some miracle, her soul never detached from her body, and though she faded a little, she clung on. All I did was give her a little push. I can't say whether it saved her. But I'm sure she's got half a chance if *we* look after her."

Kara looked pensive. "Would the hospital be able to do anything?" she asked.

"She's already been pronounced dead. Apart from anything, we'd need to sort that one out. Even then, they wouldn't have a clue what to do with this. We should just take her home."

"Time to check the staff locker room methinks." Kara left the room briefly, returning with a mishmash of abandoned clothing, and the pair dressed their friend as quickly as they could manage. The task complete, they each lifted an arm over their own shoulders and dragged her out of the room.

They stopped near reception, just short of the trembling man. They looked at each other first, before turning back to him.

"Right," Mary barked. "Either you piss off home now without breathing a word of this to anyone, or you can make yourself useful. Your choice."

He nodded, immediately attempting to replace Mary as Jennifer's support. He was pushed away when he tried.

"No, not that. I need you to keep an eye on her once we drop her home until we get back. Where are we going, Kara?"

Kara frowned. By the time they had made their way back to reception, she had come to her decision. "I would have suggested my place, but seeing as it's a little worse for wear just now, maybe we should just go to yours?"

Mary nodded. "I do have a few issues with the place, but in the grand scheme of things, they'll keep." Their guide forced the double entrance doors apart for them all to make their way back to the car.

Seconds after they headed outside, the man shivered uncontrollably and pulled his lab coat tightly over himself, moaning in discomfort. They, too, felt it momentarily: a bitter, sharp cold had descended upon the city during their time in the building.

"What the—?" Kara exclaimed and shivered.

"It's the middle of *summer*!" said their guide. He looked up to the sky as if to confirm his apparent betrayal by Nature. "It was warm when I went in this morning—this ain't proper."

Unlike the others, her recent exposure had given Mary a certain amount of immunity to the worst effects of the sinister cold. She shivered with the chill just the same.

"Keys!" she barked at Kara. "*Now!*" Kara pushed the button on her key fob and all but Mary piled in. Kara started the engine and turned the heating to its highest. Mary looked up to the sky and called upon her extra sight.

She rued her decision. The view from the other side revealed a far more sinister London stricken by a dark blizzard. The sky itself, whilst black as night, was torn asunder by an awesome display of malevolent red lightning.

She turned away, fishing her sunglasses from her inside jacket pocket before continuing her search. Before long, she spotted a distinct pattern that the bolts followed, chains of red which on her line of sight flashed to a particular point.

In this world, pieces of building flew everywhere. Dark vapours floated away like smoke in a hurricane—but not of buildings—of *people!* Those people wandering the city, walking in rows and columns around the streets, each had the tiniest essences of . . . something . . . blowing off them and into the distance.

"Jesus!" Mary had seen enough.

She ditched the glasses and her mystic sight, just in time. Kara banged on a steamed window, winding it down. "I thought we were in a hurry!"

Mary slowly nodded, staggered around to the passenger door, and opened it. She practically collapsed into the empty seat, then slammed the door shut behind her. Despite the sweltering heat, she pulled at Kara's shoulder and gestured violently past her.

"Window. Close it. Quick!"

Without understanding why, Kara pressed the button and sealed the window. Mary, breaking into a nasty sweat, shut off the heating. "What did you see?" Kara demanded, turning the car right back in the direction they had come. "What did you see?!"

Mary took the time to pull herself together and to wipe sweat from her brow. The longer she delayed, the more anxious her friend became.

"Third portal." Her response was barely above a mumble. "Whatever's going down there is going down *now*. Drop these two off, quick as you can, and just pray we're not too late."

"But what did you—?"

"Just fucking *go*, will you?"

The blackened eyes had returned involuntarily, cowing Mary's companions into silence. Considering the company, she kept what she knew to herself. She would fill Kara in on the details once they headed to their final destination.

CHAPTER TWENTY-THREE

The proper instruction made leaving the Gate Chamber a simple matter. Tally hummed quietly and followed Lord Alphonse's instructions to close the door behind her. She stood in another previously unexplored part of the mansion.

The corridor, more of a sloped tunnel, led her back to the rest of the house. She felt she had changed floors, but could see nothing beyond the surrounding walls. From a door hidden within a tapestried wall, she eventually emerged into familiarity. With her newfound understanding of the manse, its peculiar architecture became more evident.

She stood on the upper floor, on the landing where dual staircases met and connected the distinct sections of the place. She gazed down upon the main entrance hall, or South Wing. The East and West Wings housed two main residential areas, each capped with the manor's famous towers.

Directly beneath the landing of the split staircase, after a brief search, she located a hinged wooden panel. Behind it, a miniature brass door the size of a mouse hole. After a little fumbling, she found the tiny catch and flicked it loose. The door opened. As Lord Alphonse had instructed, a ring of keys sat inside, all there was space for in this hole. She snatched them and crept back to her own quarters.

Tally changed from her nightclothes, slipped out of her bedroom window, and saddled a horse from Lady Grenshall's stables. She rode hard until she returned to the Baileys Hotel. Although she knew the likely outcome before setting out, she needed to see with her own eyes the empty, undisturbed room.

Tally fumed all the way back to Grenshall Manor, furious that Lady Raine stayed a step ahead, furious with herself for abandoning Violet. But she remained determined. She remained a Grenshall—and was not beaten yet.

She headed to the unused East Wing study as Lord and Lady Grenshall slumbered. She found a drawer containing items of unique construction: an ornate paintbrush, a chisel with a diamond tip, and a grey, metal half-sphere on a small detachable stand. The inner surface of the vessel appeared gilded. In a small drawer underneath the stand was a black candle.

Recognizing their special purpose, she gathered each item and dashed back to the Gate Chamber, lamp in hand. Scanning the room, she discovered Lord Alphonse's own inscriptions occupied every inch of wall space. Was there room for another stone slab? What if it needed a precise type of stone? How could she manage it?

She cried out in frustration, bashing the wall as she did so. The temperature in the room dropped sharply.

"You really are going to have to mind that temper of yours if you want to protect this place." Lord Alphonse's voice broke into quiet chuckling behind her. The sound travelled on the sudden gust as his ghostly form manifested between her and the Gate. "But I should not be so jovial—there is little time. I see you have the materials required to reconstruct the seal."

"So it seems," she started, anger resolved in shame. "More or less. It appears I lack something to write upon."

Chortling more to himself, Lord Alphonse shook his head. "Not so, young Lady of the House; not so. Look again where you are standing."

She did so. "What has this—?"

"The one in front of the tile which activates the exit mechanism. Lift it up."

A secondary tile lay beneath that, which Tally lifted from the floor. When she flipped it over, she discovered a stone surface, perfectly prepared for an inscription. .

"This was every bit the awkward construction it appears," Lord Alphonse said whilst she set up for her work. "I anticipated a number of contingencies and prepared the room as it neared completion."

After half an hour of meticulous chiselling on her part and unbroken lecture by the apparition, Tally turned to the Grenshall patriarch. "I believe the longest Lady Raine will delay is one full week," she told Lord Alphonse. "However, she appears to lack the patience to wait for me to die. She will be here soon."

"I agree," he said. "Hopefully, that fine perception will remain with you for a long time. Now, there is a very clear space in here for your little masterpiece. I should like to see you work it out without my help."

With that, Lord Alphonse left her alone in the chamber. Tally carved without break until the inscription was complete: *'Death Awaits the Uninvited.'* Fired by the black candle, the crucible heated beyond what she believed possible. The gold melted with ease to use for the lettering. She held the slab aloft as she searched for somewhere to place it. She found clear space right on the entrance door.

Now, how to secure it?

She found the means of adhesive in the black candle wax. She burned her fingertips applying the wax to the tile but managed to secure it in place. With the pride of having completed a masterpiece to grace the South Wing hall itself, she departed.

That evening, she returned to the Gate Chamber in search of her ghostly tutor.

"Lord Alphonse?"

"Grandpapa?"

"Iris! Having trouble keeping oneself away, are we?"

"Well, yes," she chuckled. "You did pledge to teach me *everything*."

"Indeed, I did." He vanished but reappeared in front of the most recent addition to the room. "It would appear you at least have the basics—resourcefulness, resilience, and an eye for the obvious. Do you remember what I said to you last time you were here?"

She remembered only one part. "Something about watching my temper?"

"Exactly!" He vanished again, this time reappearing directly in front of her. "Because this particular art is dangerous enough in the hands of practised individuals, let alone the uninitiated."

"I will do whatever is required to stop her menace," Tally swore solemnly.

Lord Alphonse did not look entirely convinced. "Is that so?" he challenged. "Tell me: would you be willing to let the girl go?"

She froze, knowing her answer. "I cannot," she replied, her head bowed low, "any more than I can let Mama and Papa go."

She felt a cold, gentle weight on her shoulder, and another chill touch that lifted her gaze. Lord Alphonse smiled and nodded just once before giving her a swift hug.

"I am grateful to hear that your mind is not governed by vindictiveness," he said. "You place a higher value on a human life than gratifying the need for vengeance. This is pleasing. However, consider this: the path you have taken may pose more challenges yet. Would you be willing to let the girl go if thousands of lives depended upon it?"

Tally gasped. "I remain fortunate in the knowledge this is not the case."

Lord Alphonse grunted. "*Knowledge?* Your situation may alter in a heartbeat; remember this. And if it should, you may find the question asked of you again. Only it will not be me asking. Be wary of such tests catching you unawares, Iris. The consequences will be dire."

Lord Alphonse's lessons to Tally commenced forthwith. First, he taught her how to see within the dead world. Over the course of the next five nights, he tested her by remaining in his world, each night hiding somewhere in the shadow mansion for her to find him.

"Bravo!" he said when she succeeded. "Tally-ho!"

"Not you, too."

She next learned to safely shift between the worlds. However, one evening just before they started a practice session, the chamber shuddered heavily, knocking her off her feet.

"An attempted breach of the Gate Chamber walls," Lord Alphonse explained.

"Lady Raine," Tally added, "and that horrid guide of hers."

Lord Alphonse nodded. "Well, there is no danger of them getting in here any time soon. Take his cloak, and see how well he 'guides.' Take her necklace and see what she knows of moving a soul. Take both, and see for yourself two sorry little meddlers who are as much a danger to themselves as they are to others."

"This is the first time they have been back since he left me here to die," Tally mused. "They return with the reasonable expectation of finding a corpse. It also means they have had no contact with Mama or Papa, for if they had, they would know I was alive and well. Even though they believed my escape impossible, and their journey here being routine enough, can they not simply surface somewhere else on the estate?"

"They *could,*"—he rubbed his chin and tweaked his moustache—"if they took the time to recite every part of that wording to bypass the protections—for which I spent twenty-four years of my life researching and applying with meticulous care.

"It is designed to prevent unwanted intrusions from the other world—though the living may wander freely, of course. The ward's defences have earned us a few more nights. They will need to recover from this day's misadventure—assuming Lady Raine *survived*, of course."

Tally considered Violet's plight—imprisoned in her room, with only Lady Raine's undead minions for company. "What about poor Violet? I need to get her out of there."

"And how will you do that?" His eyes narrowed in disappointment. "You will have as much trouble getting in there as you had before. Perhaps more so."

"I need to go whilst I know it will be safe from that monster!"

"At least be certain that she will not return first!" he demanded. "There are so many unforeseen possibilities. Why, you could find yourself walking into some kind of trap. And where would we be then, young lady?"

Tally had no answer and almost burst trying to come up with one. Eventually, she let out a frustrated shriek before calming herself. "Very well. Perhaps we had best continue."

Within three nights of the attempted invasion, Tally had learned how to make use of all her senses on either side of the veil. She could feel every part of the otherworldly winds when she attempted it and grinned triumphantly as she felt every last wisp pass her by. As they touched her, she almost felt like she could move them or control them, manipulate them as she pleased. But she had not yet learned safe travel in that place. That would take longer.

"Just remember, girl: be sure to master it, that it does not master *you*. Your prowess is quite remarkable, but mind yourself on matters unexplored!"

She took a deep breath and let go. "I shall, Grandpapa."

A sheepish look washed over him. "I need to let you into a little secret, young Iris."

"I feel as if you have let me into a number of secrets already."

"This one is different in nature." He paused for a long time, gulping. "I feel I owe it to you to confess that I deliberately condemned myself to this fate in order to fulfil my duty to its fullest. The moment my mortal health began to deteriorate, I secretly took my own life in this house, an act of servitude, waiting as an unresting guardian of this place. It was the only way I could be absolutely certain I would remain to instruct my successor."

"Would it not have been better that you simply survived?" she asked, confused.

"Better to remain in control of my fate in this instance than to have died and left nothing." He shook his head, disappointed. "Sadly, I could not rely on either your mother or father for this. I am just *so* grateful you came into their lives—*our* lives."

He smiled. "Now. Back to the matter at hand. That fool guide scouted here earlier today, trying his best to discover a way in unnoticed. He did not think to look for ghosts travelling around as he does, and had I felt I would get away with it, I would have given him what for, myself!

"But I think they shall return this night, Iris, and not in a manner I can protect against. Do your duty as best you can, for it would be folly for me to linger whilst Lady Raine wields that dread necklace, crudely as she does. I have done all I can to thwart her efforts, but I serve no one consumed as fuel by the wretched thing."

Her heart thumped as the apparition started to fade. "What can I do?" she pleaded.

"It is not always the most powerful aspects of your gift that bring success," he said. "Sometimes it has nothing to do with the gift at all. *Outsmart* her, Iris. You have done so before."

With that, he vanished entirely, beyond even her extended senses.

~ ✻ ~

That evening, Tally crept out of her bedchamber window and made her way to an old, familiar tree, one she had not climbed for years. Even after all this time, it felt strange watching for external invaders to her home. Her enemy had come. Not a small, loosely organised mob this time, but a necromancer and her entourage.

She withdrew swiftly, back the way she came, and ran to the entrance hall landing. Before she could raise the alarm, Lord Grenshall gave a knowing nod, all hands in the house called to arms.

Within moments, the main door burst open. Two of Lady Raine's undead servants strode forth, hurling the Grenshall footman aside. Soon followed Aurelia Raine herself, a murderous look in her eyes. Tally crawled underneath the table upon which a small onyx bust of Lady Grenshall rested.

Lord and Lady Grenshall moved quickly to confront the woman, but Tally resisted the urge to join them. Rather, she waited to assess the true strength of her enemy.

Lady Raine's eyes settled upon Lord Grenshall. She glided toward him. "I shall offer you one final opportunity to do the honourable thing," she said with venom.

Lord Grenshall towered over her. "You enter our house uninvited, you threaten our lives, and you speak to *me* of honour? I shall give *you* one opportunity to leave of your own volition, or I shall have you thrown out."

Lady Raine waved away her advancing servants. She revealed *Death's Teardrop* from underneath her cloak and held the silver gauze cage in both hands. She opened the small door retaining the jewel.

Lady Grenshall scowled and moved alongside her husband. "I have a good mind to remove you from this house myself."

The Guide's apparent absence spurred Tally to shift her sight to view the shadow world.

It proved prudent. The sooty winds still settling after sudden movement professed *something* had been prowling about the mansion. Tally saw the trail clearly despite the target's swift movements. If it was the Guide, he must have known that the Gate Chamber itself would have been impenetrable to him.

Was he was looking for her?

Tally returned her attention to the scene below her, unprepared for the three blazing lights of the living in that dead world. She turned away, dazzled. Further movement close by drew her eye. Suddenly, shadow, dark enough to look like a hole even in there, obscured her view. *The Guide.* He flowed and moved around the table, exposing her once more to the glare of the living. Between the bright lights, eerie red forms glowed—which could only have been Lady Raine's servants.

Tally dashed out of her hiding place, but fast-moving hands from the black shroud grabbed her. However, the Guide had seriously underestimated her. She spun out of his grasp, seized the bust on the table, and swung it hard into the side of his head. The man bounced from the wall and dropped to the ground like a stone. Tally appropriated the cloak and wrapped it around herself.

She instantly felt displaced between two worlds. She felt lighter on her feet. Power rose up within her to move *fast*.

As two of the undead grabbed her parents, Tally raised her hood and summoned otherworldly sight. She shielded her eyes and took one step forward—into the centre of the group of life lights below. She whipped the hood from her head and her sight reverted once more to reveal her parents' terror.

"I shall not tell you again, *Augustine*," Raine threatened. "Give me the mansion and leave, or this will end as badly for you as it has your daughter."

"Our daughter?" Lord Grenshall asked, bewildered. "What about her?"

"Her meddling in my affairs has cost her dearly," she said. She jerked her chin at her rival. "*Kill that one.*"

"Step away from my mother," Tally growled fiercely. Lady Raine looked around frantically, blind to Tally, who stood right next to her.

"WHERE ARE YOU?" Lady Raine roared. Her fury bled into the sapphire, which flashed blue. The entire mansion shook from the storm summoned in the dead world. However, only Tally knew it. She clutched at the cloak as a sudden gust of shadow wind attempted to rip it away. The dead servants each gave a bloodcurdling howl.

Tally adjusted her sight to the dark vision. Caught in the tempest, she wrapped herself tighter in the cloak and crouched against the wind. From the corner of her eye, she caught Lord Alphonse's head peering out of the central entrance to the North Wing, beckoning desperately.

She acknowledged him and cleared her line of sight to move to him, partially distracted by shouts behind her. She turned back to the intruder and her captured parents.

"Did you hear me?" Lady Raine yelled. "Come out, or I shall kill them both!"

The woman demanded Tally's original intent, so she ceded to it. She dropped her death sight and turned to face her enemy. She meant to either pluck her parents to safety or to defend them against Lady Raine before she caused further harm. She could focus fully upon neither, and felt all the more powerless as a result.

Lady Raine gestured to her servants with a roll of her eyes. Without hesitation, Lady Grenshall summoned a number of her own staff to arms and advanced on her adversary. The undead servants quickly overpowered the living.

"So be it," Lady Grenshall said. "I shall deal with you my—" Lady Raine seized her throat in her iron grip.

With a roar, Lord Grenshall evaded the undead attempting to hold him and charged at his enemy. A blow to the back of the head dropped him to the floor, face-first. He brought himself up to his knees, clearing the blood from his mouth.

Tally swung a fist at Lady Raine, but it went straight through her. "Leave them be!" she cried in horror.

Her words fell upon deaf ears, carried away with the deadly winds. Lady Raine looked upon the jewel in her hand and harnessed its power. It glowed as shards of darkness crackled forth. They slammed inside Lord Grenshall's gaping mouth and latched inside him. He howled in agony.

"Stop it!" Tally cried, sobbing. "Leave them alone!"

"That will do no good. I am the only person who can hear you!"

The croak came from a fading Lord Alphonse. Powerless to affect anything around her, she willed a path to him, her only hope.

"Help me!" she begged, grabbing him by his spectral ruffles.

He took one last look at the events unfolding on the floor below before turning back to Tally. He shuddered, blinking in and out of sight.

"You could simply remove the cloak," he said. She instantly reached for it, but he grabbed her hand. "But if you do so, it may well disorientate you long enough for you to be imperilled— unless you calm yourself and focus your mind."

"This is not the best time for that," she retorted.

"Precisely," he said, embodying control, "but you already know what you want to do and know how to do it. It is simply a matter of extending what you have already achieved with your sight. Only fear prevents you—fear of failing them, failing me, and failing *yourself*. Remember: master your art. *Do not* allow it to master you."

"Last chance, girl," Lady Raine gloated. "Come out, or they die."

Lord Alphonse gave her a reassuring look and patted her on the shoulder. "I have every confidence you can do it. Go on!"

She nodded and lifted the hood on her head. Her vision unimpeded, she selected her return position—directly in front of Lady Raine—and moved with unstoppable determination toward her target.

Tally reached out with her hand to the living world and clutched the necklace by the chain. Lady Raine reacted quickly, thwarting the raid. She called upon the power of the *Teardrop*. Suddenly dizzy, Tally lurched forward. She felt light—a flying sensation. Towards the sapphire. To her doom.

She knew if she did *not* stop, all would be lost. She would lose that battle of wills with Lady Raine.

Thoughts of everything she held dear surged through her.

"*Violet!*" she cried. Her adversary roared with laughter at the utterance, breaking Tally's concentration. She muttered something inaudible, and jagged crackles of black light flew from the sapphire into Tally. The fiend released her grip on the talisman and her eyes blackened.

A cobra-like strike forced Tally into the mortal world. A hand with the strength of ten gripped her under the chin and hurled her down the length of the hall. She landed awkwardly and whimpered in pain.

The Guide, stunned and groggy, stumbled down the sweep toward his mistress.

"The Grenshall girl yet lives!" Lady Raine accused, murderous eyes boring into him.

"I-I . . ." he stammered.

"You are of no further use to me." She lifted him by the hair with one hand and slashed him across the throat with the *Teardrop's* fanged cage. Splattered with blood, she dropped him to the ground. The sapphire flashed in her hand as she snorted and turned away. "Now. Do you suppose I toy with you, girl?"

Tally struggled to lift herself from the floor. A stake of wood skewered her right leg. A gout of blood spewed from her mouth as she forced herself to her knees, supported by the nearest table.

"I shall rip out every soul here until you grant me access to that chamber."

"Some . . . some servants have run for the police," Tally coughed, blood trickling from her lip. "You shall never get away with this!"

Lady Raine sneered. "Even had they made it clear of your front gate, what do you suppose anyone would do when they got here, other than serve me? Now hear me girl: I might allow your extraction to be . . . *relatively* painless if you obey. This is your last chance."

Whatever transpires here, she shall not enter the Gate Chamber.

Tally struggled to her feet, coughing more blood. Crimson drizzled her grin as she looked up at her enemy. She winced as her injured leg bruised and swelled.

"As you know," she coughed, "the Gate Chamber is shielded against unwelcome intrusion. That most *certainly* includes you. That poor wretch you just murdered knew most of it, apart from one key alteration I made. The ward now specifically instructs that *you* go to Hell."

Lady Raine lost any semblance of composure. Blackened eyes practically burned out of her fury-contorted face. The sapphire's glow faded as she drew the strength of every soul trapped within. With outstretched arms, she clenched her fists and called on the full might of the shadow world. For a fleeting moment, the dimensions appeared to merge. Tally struggled for air. A tidal wave of malignant, dead-world energy hit the mansion.

Tally shivered as the unnatural deluge washed over her body and soul. With nothing left to animate them, the dead servants fell to the floor. Lord and Lady Grenshall dropped to their knees, choking and spluttering, but spared from the wave of death. Tally's scramble toward them drew Lady Raine's attention.

Enveloped in shadow, Lady Raine, gave a laugh which echoed with a thousand malevolent voices. She cast a withering glare at Tally's parents, crumpled on the floor. "I was saving those two for something special, but you have forced my hand."

The shadow carried her to Lady Grenshall, whom she lifted to her feet by her nostrils. Tally's icon of ladylike grandeur and maternal devotion beat at the villain in futile resistance. Veins blackened and swelled on her mother's head, her skin shrivelled and turned ashen. The demon snapped her neck with a flick of her wrist.

The crack echoed through Tally's soul.

The pretender tossed aside the empty shell of a truly great lady and turned her attention to Lord Grenshall.

Agog, he attempted to scramble away. She shattered his ankle with a single stamp. With tenebrous hands, Lady Raine pressed onto his shoulders and his writhing ceased. Tally could not believe her eyes as her beloved father, friend, and benefactor appeared to drown, despite the clear air. He collapsed to the ground, grey and covered in black veins, just like his wife.

As Lady Raine turned to face her adversary, drunk with unassailable power, Tally trembled with equal parts terror and rage. Her soul wailed for vengeance but was powerless against such an enemy. She possessed one thing Lady Raine did not, though—something that explained why she yet drew breath. Knowledge.

"I would have given them simpler deaths, had you done as you were asked," Lady Raine crowed. "But you *insisted* on defying me."

She reached out into the darkness, pointing at Tally and concentrating her will. Howling wind whipped around both of them as Tally felt every muscle in her body tense and lurch, as if fighting against being dragged forward. At last, she understood the drain of her life essence to the insatiable appetite of the jewel.

She was not prepared to die so *cheaply*. Weeping uncontrollably, she pulled the hood back over her head and desired escape. Her sight shifted to the dark place. There, a tempest of chaotic destruction blew about every shadow that was not a fixed point. Lady Raine dominated her view, an all-consuming vortex in human form.

As Tally grasped for a path through the darkness, a series of small, dull dots appeared in front of her, all moving, appearing briefly and then disappearing. She could not settle on a direction. Amid the chaotic combination of injury, grief, and uncertainty assaulting her, she felt even more lost and disorientated than ever before.

With a herculean effort, she gathered enough will to transport herself as far as the door to the North Wing, bashing at it hard with both fists. "Lord Alphonse!" she wailed. "Grandfather!"

The phantom stuck his head through the door once more, looking confused. "Please!" she begged, barely uttering the words through her sobs. "Help me!"

Lord Alphonse, terror-stricken, faded and contorted with every second he spent exposed to the apocalyptic storm. He reached for her and pulled her straight through the door, not stopping until they were halfway down the Forbidden Corridor. There, the shadowed turbulence subsided to familiar levels.

"What in *God's* name has she called down?" Lord Alphonse blustered.

"She killed *everyone,* Grandpapa!" Tally sobbed. Her violent trembling forced him to support her. "I . . . I tried as hard as I could, but she just—"

"I am so, so sorry," he soothed. He offered a feeble attempt at comfort. "She has allowed it to consume her utterly—to the point you are no longer fighting a mortal being. I was foolish to set an inexperienced girl against such evil! She could *destroy* this place."

"She could," Tally said. She gained a little self-control as she considered the possibility. "Yet, she almost drained that sapphire of its power when she attacked me . . . and . . . and . . ."

Lord Alphonse already knew what she was going to say. "I should have never allowed this to happen."

"*Allowed* this to happen?" Tally asked, pushing herself clear of him as she flooded with anger. "It was *I* who could not save them—she came after *me*! But everyone else died. And you—why, you're merely a ghost! What could be expected of you? You would have been *devoured*!"

Tally fell to her knees and pounded the floor with her fists, grief consuming her. Lord Alphonse stood over her, mumbling. "Ghost, yes . . . suppose there was little I could do . . . no match for . . ."

Then, with all of the force he could summon, he pulled her to her feet and slapped her about the face. "Iris Grenshall, pull yourself together or we are *all* lost! You are the *last* of us now—ensure those who died did so for *something*."

"I have no chance of fighting against that!" she squealed, beating at his chest.

"Yes, you do—even if not today. Remember, she cannot breach these walls. These walls will hold even if she leaves an army in the rest of the mansion. You can happily tread where she cannot! Remember that her trinket has mastered *her*, and not her it. Here I shall wait for you when you are ready to learn more—and I will teach you everything at my disposal for you to defeat this fiend!"

"I . . . I cannot."

"Yes. You can. You must." He brooked no refusal. He looked at her, calm and assured. "Remember, you are the only hope for her daughter."

Tally thought of nothing else once he reminded her. And in doing so, one of the dots fleeting in the shadowy distance held fast as all of the others vanished. It grew in size, becoming a line. Thus, as the path to Violet became clear, Tally discovered how to reach a destination or person dear to her. She managed a smile and pulled Lord Alphonse close to kiss him on the cheek.

"Thank you!" she cried, gathering her will once more.

"Never mind thanking me," he answered. "Just make sure you do not forget about me. Come back regularly and *learn* what you need. You know the way."

"I shall *never* forget," she vowed. She took a step forward with both mind and body. Tearful, she left Grenshall Manor at the mercy of Lady Aurelia Raine—and under the protection of the deceased Lord Alphonse Grenshall.

CHAPTER TWENTY-FOUR

Mary navigated through the pedestrians, guiding Kara as she drove toward the eye of the storm. As they raced across town, Mary told more of Tally's story.

She could see the marks in the blood-red sky converging—a series of clouds between the explosive, destructive lightning: as far as the eye could see, celestial arteries pulsating with the malignant energy of countless unresting, desperate for escape from decades, centuries of detention. They were tangibly close, perhaps two or three miles from the source.

They came off the main road onto a poorly maintained track just wide enough for the Mini. Kara slowed the car down in increments until she stopped completely.

"I really don't think there's anything up here," she complained. She looked blankly at the cobbled road ahead of them. The overgrown hedges encroached heavily on either side.

Mary knew that the shadow world again weighed down on Kara, the power of the Gate at its greatest at such a short distance. "Keep going," she demanded, nudging Kara hard. "Let's see this through."

Kara took several deep breaths and nodded, mumbling a raft of trivia, clearing her mind by the same method she had at the cinema.

"Nothing's been down here for years," she observed. "That's why this is so overgrown. Lucky we can get through here at all."

"Oh, we're getting through, one way or other."

They both noticed the nature of the vegetation, abnormal at best, unnatural at worst. No occasional shafts of light, wood warped into vine-like shapes, with no leaves on the trees despite it being the middle of summer. They saw a real lack of the fauna one might have expected in a hedgerow: no wildlife anywhere to be seen or heard. Nothing around there at all, apart from them.

Mary's mind began to swim with more memories. Tally's memories. She wrestled to make sense of them, which made them feel far more suppressed than the others for whatever reason. Her head throbbed dully as the recollections started to come into focus. She felt something important lurking in there, perhaps key to their next task.

Holding her head, unable to speak, she yanked Kara's sleeve to grab her attention.

"For the love of—are you *trying* to kill us both, Mary? This road is tricky, you know—"

"Slow the car down." Mary made a concentrated effort to speak.

Kara complied but turned toward her, confused.

"I think I know what happened," Mary said, quiet with certainty. "With Tally and Violet, I mean."

"Well that's great, but how's that going to help us with *this*?"

Mary rubbed at her temples and blinked a few times, but with her improved clarity, her malaise faded considerably. "This power. I think I know how it all works now."

"Looked to me like you have done for a while."

"No." Mary shook her head. "Most of what I've been doing has just kind of happened. Now I think I know *how it actually works*."

Kara looked baffled as she negotiated some particularly tough, dense hedges which soon obscured the road. She examined the terrain for a moment and then put her foot down hard, carving her way through the overgrowth. "You know, they sell the Mini on personalisation. Well, nothing says 'unique' like paintwork scratches from surprise off-roading."

Mary felt the strength of the shadow world's influence there dwarfing any she had encountered previously. Its effect stretched for miles, an insidious, crushing pressure that thickened the air for those with her sensory gift. Others felt it as oppressive revulsion—an unconquerable murk that blinded, paralysed, and suffocated the soul.

Mary could always feel the effects, but she knew, unlike herself, most people could not conquer the subconscious repulsion. Even so, while the portal in the centre of London held Britain's most intrepid at bay, Kara managed to shrug off her urge to flee simply by hearing a few simple words. That was extraordinary in itself. "Any powers of your own you're not telling us about?" she asked.

Kara burst into surprised laughter. "Of course not!" she snorted. "Don't you think I might have done more one way or other up to now if I did?"

"Well, I suppose, but—"

"So, go on, then. What brought that on?"

"Well, the fact you're here, not clawing my eyes out to make us go the other way."

Kara chuckled. "Now, why would I do that?"

"Same reason as why you stopped the first time. This stuff doesn't seem to bother you as much as it does anyone else."

"Illusions at whatever scale are still just that—illusions."

"But nobody else has been able to do that."

"Not many people believe in ghosts either, do they? They fear what they fail to understand. You've given me solid proof they're out there. It's just a matter of knowing what to expect."

"That isn't enough for everyone," Mary protested. She thought back to the only other people she met who remained functional somehow. Jennifer's resistance came as no great surprise, given she had some quite extraordinary abilities of her own. However, the mortuary assistant was another. She'd have to quiz him about that sometime, if she got out of that mishap in one piece.

She knew Kara lived for this kind of thing. The woman wandered headlong into every peril she faced with a grin and a notebook. Maybe that was more than enough for her.

CHAPTER TWENTY-FIVE

Although the journey was almost instantaneous, it was by far the roughest Tally had taken. Even when she stopped, it felt as if she was still flying uncontrollably. Nausea washed over her, but she composed herself and looked around.

In the centre of the room, she found Violet's bed, a bright glow muffled by bedclothes. The girl was awake even at that late hour, undoubtedly terrified at sleeping in a room containing living nightmares.

They were clear for Tally to see: four twisted, ghostly shapes surrounding the bed, far more terrifying than any she had encountered before. They stood about eight feet in height, shadows cast in baleful light—winged, horned, taloned creatures of demonic appearance.

All four creatures rounded on Tally, and the temperature plunged in the already icy room. Violet's warm glow shivered beneath her coverlet. The girl was in grave peril.

"Violet?" Tally called, drawing their attention. A winged, barely humanoid creature with two rows of uneven canines turned to face her. Its eyes burned pure fire. Confronting her, it opened its massive mouth in a silent roar.

What little control Tally retained withered under the assault. The physical effects of the travel flooded her. She shuddered uncontrollably, her equilibrium destroyed. The world whirled around her. She collapsed to one knee and emptied the contents of her stomach. Her sight lurched back to sense only the living, although she knew the four creatures remained.

Violet sat up suddenly, pulling in her knees, shaking. She opened her mouth wide in a hysterical wail, yet Tally heard nothing. Violet beat and tore at her sheets. She threw numerous bedside objects. Still, silence reigned.

"There, there," Tally soothed. Violet ignored her completely. "Come on. We must leave."

However, when Tally reached out, her hand struck an invisible wall. It felt like a pane of glass between them. She shouted and beat the barricade, but her injuries soon caused her to stagger back, wheezing.

Tally felt the malignant power of the unseen fiends. They would soon finish her, feeding off her vibrancy, her very life. She barely had the strength to stand . . .

. . . but she had one job to do—to get Violet out of there. She told herself this once . . . twice . . . three times . . . mumbling at first, but her volume increased as did her resolve. Back on her feet, she shuddered for a moment but remained focused. She shifted her body completely to the living world and collapsed onto the floor. Her presence began to settle Violet's hysteria.

"Tally?" Violet called tentatively. "Is . . . is that you?"

Tally scrambled to the bed, relieved to discover the otherworldly wall had no effect there. The feel of soft, smooth bedclothes provided unexpected solace. She reached for Violet and smoothed the bedraggled straw-coloured strands of hair from her face, and a real sense of relief hit her.

She offered the child a nod and a reassuring smile when words would not leave her parched mouth. She gathered her little friend into her arms, sobbing. "Yes, Violet." Tally pushed past the taste of stale vomit on her tongue. "Yes, it is."

The foul presences remained as strong as ever. "Come on," she instructed as she lifted Violet to her feet. Tally did not have the strength to call upon her gift, but the resolve to keep them both alive gave her enough to run. They heard ponderous footsteps nearby. More of Lady Raine's abominable creations— the remainder of the Raine house staff.

"Follow me," Tally ordered. "Do not stop for *anything*, do you understand?"

Violet nodded, but looked dazed and confused.

"Good—*go!*" The pair ran to the staircase as rapidly as they could manage. The girl's feet were fleet indeed for one of her size, and Tally had to work hard to keep up. Violet froze at the top of the stairs. An undead, formerly young woman, climbed the sweep. She looked intently at the child.

Tally caught up and positioned herself ahead of the child, even as a male servant at the far corridor strode swiftly toward them. She attempted to push past, but it was like hitting a wall. He shoved her backward and moved toward Violet. Desperate, she leapt at the girl, threw the flowing cloak around both of them, and covered her own head with the hood. "Close your eyes," she said to the petrified girl, "and hold your breath until I say!"

As the dead servants closed in, Tally grabbed Violet and looked down at the bottom of the stairs, past the automaton reaching for them. She shifted to the shadow world with Violet in tow.

Quick as a blink, they were at the bottom of the stairs. They were thrown back into their own world with a jolt.

Violet clung on with an unbreakable grip. A door opened and two more of the fiendish house staff joined the pursuit.

Tally scooped the coughing and spluttering girl into her arms and staggered as quickly as she could to the front door. She barely managed to get the door open and the two of them through it before the servants caught up with them.

"*Help!*" Tally cried, hoping that someone would hear. "Help us! *Please!*" Sooner than she could have hoped, several gentlemen on the street rushed to their aid. She pointed to the door. "They . . . they tried to—*Please* . . . do not let them harm us."

Injured, bedraggled, with the feverish-looking girl in her arms, she knew no further explanation was required. Despite the likely outcome, if it allowed her and Violet time to escape, she would have plenty of time to feel guilty about it later.

The onset of a hard rain and the encumbrance of a young girl slowed her considerably, but Tally spotted a hansom cab slowly making its way down the street. Everything around Tally became a blur as she rode the very edge of despair, but she managed to flag down the cab.

Barely on her own feet, Tally sought the help of the driver to seat the girl. The moment she had, the horses gave a disturbed whinny and lurched against the reins. Tally seized the edge of the cab and leapt on.

As her foot hit the step, the horses burst free of the driver's restraints. Careering wildly, they gathered pace and showed no signs of stopping. The driver, no longer in control, clung on. Anyone in their path dove out of the way, other than a small mob of Lady Raine's servants, who attempted to obstruct their escape. The driver leapt clear.

As Tally glanced down at the still-motionless Violet, she felt her terror turn to imperious rage. The girl had blackened eyes and veins, her skin an unpleasant blue tinge. Violet lay motionless, her eyes were wide open—and blank.

Tally's heart pounded, her lungs tight. Was that what happened to weak, living souls in the unresting world? Why had they not warned her? Surely, Lord Alphonse . . .

She had done all she could to protect sweet Violet against the ravenous dead, but her mentor failed her.

She smelled the terror on the horses, though, and knew the true reason why. A howling wind from the dark place surrounded them, softening and splitting into many whispering voices. Each called her name as if they knew her.

They had *always* known her, *Iris Grenshall*. And they were more than willing to help with anything. She need but ask . . . if only she would channel that delicious rage of hers and call out to them, show them how much she needed them.

"DON'T YOU DARE STOP, ANY OF YOU!"

Tally watched the horses when she made her demand, but, unmistakably, she whispered to the voices. They were willing to assist, of course. Nothing drove harder than that most base of instincts: fear.

"TO STOP IS TO DIE," Tally's echoed voice called. "RUN, AND WE MAY SUFFER YOU TO LIVE."

The horses heard. They galloped hard, mowing down the obstructing servitors, not daring to stop; not daring to infuriate Death itself. Tally gave a satisfied smile. They could go *anywhere*.

The shadow wind whistled around the beasts with an unforgiving scream, clearing the way and answering Tally's every call. The winds were her reins, the shadow shifted at her whim, and the horses obeyed. Her instincts led her flight to just one place: home.

But in one horrific moment, Grenshall Manor had ceased to be her home. To return there now would be an act of suicide. However, *Iris Brown's* place would *not* be known to her enemies. And she would never forget the way back there, try as she might.

~ ✶ ~

Despite their speed, the journey back to Iris Brown's old tenement felt like mere minutes. The horses stopped; they fought to draw breath as if they stood in the dead world. Utterly spent, they gave one final wheeze before they collapsed as one, dead. Tally gasped as she realised they had indeed travelled beyond mortal speed.

Long-since abandoned, the building endured, ramshackle as ever—a broken hovel if she had ever seen one. Tally marvelled that it yet stood, one in a row of teetering houses, rotten and decrepit, fit for rats alone. She hoisted Violet in her arms and staggered as she carried the child across the derelict threshold of her old place. Through the front door, carelessly boarded, down the narrow passage to the stairs at the back of the house.

She never thought to seek a more convenient place to rest. Rather, her instincts propelled her up flight upon flight to the tiny garret in which she and her mother once dwelled.

She paid no heed to the darkness. Awash in her recollections of the past, she saw only the perpetual twilight of a house forever overshadowed by the other tenements propping one another up, battling for a sliver of sun. She saw only that which once pervaded the place: the filth and squalor of the destitute, the desperate—until she stumbled onto the bed she and her birth parent had once shared.

She blinked and came 'round to herself, aware of Violet yet in her arms. She never questioned from whence came the strength to carry the child so far, but wrapped her tightly in her cloak—so cold to the touch, too long in the night air. Tally trembled, her breathing heavy and quick. She checked Violet for any signs of breath, heartbeat—*anything*. She found none.

"No, Vi," she muttered as she slipped to the floor, a quiet corner of the room. She rocked back and forth, keening. She scrubbed at the tears obscuring her sight of her charge. "We succeeded. We escaped. We should be safe here. A good night's rest and we can go anywhere, you and I. America, India–where would you like to go?"

Violet did not answer.

Tally shrieked repeatedly. "Violet! Stay with me. They left me. Please stay. You—you are all that I—" She broke down, tearing at the floorboards with her fingers. "GIVE HER BACK TO ME! WHATEVER YOU WANT, GIVE HER BACK TO ME! I have lost more than enough this day. DO YOU HEAR ME?"

"There, there, Iris . . ."

The night closed in on her, heavy and oppressive. She did not know whether she had crossed worlds or whether she was just crying in the dark. But that was *certainly* Clara Brown's voice behind her, that woman who had never truly been her mother . . .

It sounded nowhere near as soothing as it should have, but that was nothing new from that woman. That shrill squawk had never comforted. Tally turned toward the sound, and the spectre from her past dropped to the floor beside her.

The gesture struck cords in Tally long-since suppressed. A fresh wave of desolation washed over her. She clutched Violet's motionless body to her breast as she sobbed with abandon. In turn, Clara eased Tally's head to rest on her shoulder. The action brought Tally an ounce of solace, even though they had not seen each other for years.

For a moment, it felt as if she had never run away. For perhaps the first time, her *mother* acted in a manner worthy of the name. It took a moment before she realised that the person who supported her felt as cold as death.

Tally pulled away and looked directly at Clara. Her hair looked greyer than she remembered, but it seemed she had barely aged a day since she departed. She had not deteriorated with age, at least. If anything, she had improved. Perhaps she had finally defeated the demon drink. Of course, it was difficult to tell in the dark.

Although she did not see the rigours of time in her mother's eyes, she saw something *worse*: a distant stare she had seen before. The distance of another world.

"*No*," she rasped. "Not you, too . . ."

The manifestation of shadow fed upon terror as daily bread. Tally reeked of it. The spectral charlatan smiled and summoned a gust of wind with a sweep of its hand. The door slammed shut. Terror bubbled in the pit of Tally's stomach. This thing was *not* her mother, nor any creation of Lady Raine's—rather, a malevolence of its own creation.

Iris Brown's worst nightmare stood manifest in the malignant form of Clara Brown. The false mother gave a self-satisfied smile before slowly and deliberately peering at the motionless Violet. It reached toward the girl's head and whispered something incomprehensible in the wind. The wind itself echoed its murmurs.

Tally watched the outstretched hand drag what little light there was in the room into itself. Her soul screamed. She had set a terrible thing into motion, but the very air in her lungs dried and burned her protest into silence.

Just short of placing the shadowy hand on Violet's forehead, the idol paused to savour the despair which seared through Tally. It met her gaze with eyes as lightless as the hand which it withdrew and spoke.

"You can save her, y' know," it mocked in the voice of Clara Brown. "I . . . we . . . they . . . can save her, but you must hurry, before it is too late."

Tally shivered from its hollow musical tone. "How?"

"You can help us greatly."

"What do you want from me?"

"Set us free from this endless nothing. Give us more time to walk the earth. Your strength brought us here. By your strength we can remain."

"My strength? How?"

"Allow us to become part of you."

"Why would I do that?"

"You are no match for her mother." The impostor stroked Tally's head. She twitched and drew away. "We can help you—make you *more* than a match for her. Surely the murder of Lord and Lady Grenshall meant *something* to you?"

She shuddered.

"The bearer of the jewel has caused enough harm. Who else will deal with her, if not you?"

"Who else . . .?" she echoed. The deaths of Lord and Lady Grenshall possessed her mind in vivid detail. And yet . . .

"And what of young Rose?" it questioned.

"*Rose?*"

"Deary me." The mocking Clara Brown voice again. "All this time lording it over everyone in your new life, and not once did you think to look into your old one. Fighting to save this little one while your sister Rose could starve, for all you cared. Good thing someone took her in when I finally popped my clogs, eh?"

"*What?* You could never have birthed another child. You could barely stand!"

"And you left us both anyway. Poor thing never stood a chance. Another one you failed to save. Abandoned, I tell you."

"I was *nine years old*!" Tally snarled. "How would I have helped?"

"You would have *been* there. You run away from *everything*. The only reason you came back *here* was because you *ran away*. Again."

"I was trying to save the girl!"

"And fine work of that you have done."

Tally shook uncontrollably and bawled with rage. "Enough! Just help her, will you? Help *me*."

It looked at her, amused, before nodding. "It will be done."

With that, the apparition vanished and the light in the room altered subtly, still dark but naturally so. The deadly chill dissipated.

Feeble spluttering drew Tally's attention. The child in her arms breathed again.

Tally searched Violet's face, tense, afraid of what she might see. But Violet looked normal, more so than she had in some time, with only one difference: her eyes.

Rather than a glazed look of possession, they hinted of distance, dread. Through her carelessness, Tally had sent Violet, an innocent, helpless child, into the shadow world. Tally's mistake had nearly killed her. Both had paid a high price.

Devoured by guilt, Tally released Violet and scrambled backward into a corner, hyperventilating. The weight of her deeds crashed down upon her, and she cowered beneath the burden. Unable to meet the child's gaze, she abandoned all control and wailed.

A light, warm body wrapped its arms about her and whispered softly, "Thank you."

Tally looked up, hiccupping as she fought to calm herself. "Wh-what for?"

"Coming back for me."

Tally gulped down control as she gathered Violet up in her arms. The girl looked at her, exhausted. Tally managed an anaemic smile. "Just you and me now, my girl."

Violet nodded. Her eyes closed and she snuggled into her protector.

"Just you and me." She had fought so hard for this. She had endured so much. She had earned some time to rest.

~ ✳ ~

Cracks of sunlight lanced through boarded windows and doors, and Tally woke from her slumber feeling completely rejuvenated. All the fatigue from her previous ordeal ceased to be. But it was more than that. She felt power coursing through her.

She stretched out, examining her injuries from the previous night. They had vanished. Not a mark or bruise blemished her. If not for damaged clothing, there would have been no evidence of her adventure.

Suddenly, Tally realised she had not heard anything at all from the child since waking up. Her own return to rude health no longer mattered.

"*Violet*?"

The girl was nowhere in sight. Tally turned the place on its head searching for her, slamming doors and overturning furniture, but to no avail. Faint with fright, her knees buckled.

"*Violet*?"

Silence greeted her call. She roared in wild abandon, splintering the remaining planks boarding up the door with a single strike. She took deep breaths, attempting to calm herself—only for her mind to return over and over again to *yet another* failure.

You promised *to take care of her. You just had to watch her this one night. But you fell asleep. Fool!*

This place had been the bane of her existence since her first night in it. She had but one purpose for returning, and once again, it had let her down. Worse, it drove home even more proof of her ineptitude.

She *knew* what had happened to Violet. They had found her—Raine's minions, even here—and returned her to Grenshall Manor, its walls now breached, the house—the family—fallen to that servant of evil.

Apart from the impenetrable fortress of the Gate Chamber.

Tally still had much to fight for, and now she had the tools to do so. Her wrath vented against the tenement produced not even the smallest bruise on her hand despite the force of her blows. What had she done? What had she *become*?

She remembered her grandfather's words: *If you cannot control yourself, it will end up controlling you.*

She had willingly invited this minion of shadow into her mind—her body. Her soul. Tally clenched her fists. She would control that rage, the power which flowed from it—all of it.

"Lady Aurelia Raine, abomination, murderer of Lord and Lady Grenshall and tormentor of young Violet—*your own daughter*—I am coming for you. I am coming for her. You will not stop me this time."

Only the sound of her breathing broke the deathly silence. She thought only of the missing young girl and her own culpability as she forced her way into the light of day. With unswerving determination, she abandoned her childhood home for the second time in her life. This time she ensured she had no excuse to return. She clenched her fists and tested the integrity of the bargain struck in the depths of her despair.

She brought the power of the shadow world to bear and shook the tottering tenement to rubble.

CHAPTER TWENTY-SIX

Kara's Mini Cooper continued down the lengthy path. "So, Tally's given me everything she knows," Mary explained. "Which is how I happen to know any of this."

"Apart from what I found out for you, of course," Kara said, looking morbidly happy at the situation. "Sounds like a heck of a job she took on."

One hand on the steering wheel, she mopped her brow of sweat. "Impressed you managed to cram it like that, too. Once we're done here, though, I'm getting the full story off you. I'll have my own TV show if you keep this up!"

"That's what I'm afraid of," Mary muttered. Her temples throbbed, threatening to explode. "Just up the top of this stretch and we're pretty much there."

"Nice one! Still want to know what happened to Violet, though. How does an adorable nine-year-old end up as Jacqui the Ripper?"

"I'm not sure—aagh!" A sharp pain stabbed Mary's forehead, blurring her sight. She clamped her eyes shut against the light. Perhaps another of Tally's memories caused it. She clung to it grimly, determined to extract them all. When she regained her sight, she spotted a large shadow, an outline of a human, cast just before the bend ahead, its source out of sight. She turned to Kara "You see that?"

"Yeah. If it's a person, it'll be the only one we've seen for several miles. A bit suspicious." She slowed the vehicle to a stop. Mary cleared her mind, took calming breaths, and shifted her sight. She detected a combination of death tied to life, which she had seen several times before—and all on the same person.

"*Oh*. It's *him*. Do us both a favour and step on it, will you?"

"I can't just. . . Barber?"

"Yep."

Without further hesitation, Kara dropped a gear and shoved the accelerator to the floor. Mary's eyes narrowed. Nothing, nobody, was going to stand in her way.

As they hit the corner, they caught a glimpse of Barber, more monstrous than ever. He loomed larger, a dark, shambling mound cast with the harsh light of the storm upon him. He gave a guttural roar before charging straight at them.

"Have some o' this, you bastard!" Kara yelled. Mary braced for the collision.

The engine whined with the sudden jolt of impact, but they fell forward against the torsion of their seatbelts. Barber held each side of the bonnet in a monstrous grip.

He held both women transfixed as he held the car several feet off the ground. Muscles rippling, he lifted the car into the air and turned them around.

Like a diabolical shot putter, Barber launched the car with all his might. The car smashed hard into the courtyard's centrepiece fountain, which was twice the size of the car. A marble arm shattered the centre of the windscreen and snapped off, missing Kara's left shoulder by inches.

Heads still spinning, the two heard familiar raucous laughter sounded, advancing on them from behind.

"We need to get out of here," Kara pronounced. She reached for her door handle and leaned hard against it. She fumed in rhythm to her bashing at the door. "He's wrecked my house and my car trying to get to you. And because of him my best friend is all but dead. I am *not* happy."

Mary saw Barber ponderously pacing towards the fountain and snarled. "Yep," she spat, turning back to Kara with a determined scowl. "Time to take care of that self-loathing prick once and for all."

She bridged across her shadow connection and passed through the passenger door—and stepped right into the turbid muck. The basin appeared eerily the same in both worlds. Through the dead sight, the shadow weeds eyed hungrily the first signs of life to enter the water in years. Mary found it unpleasant, but not enough to throw her off stride.

She trudged through the giant stone dish, slimy and sodden to her knees, and motioned toward the slavering giant. She shifted back into the living world but retained the dead sight to identify the chains around him, aware of the excruciating pain he endured with every step.

The chains had consumed all but his face, but showed enough for her to recognise the man who had surrendered his soul to shadow, only to suffer perpetual torture. Mary fully understood his growl: one of his many efforts to alleviate his torment. Another would have been to ensure her own.

She heard the other door forced open—followed by a splash and a squeal. Mary chuckled at Kara's mishap even as her attacker charged, which served to enrage Barber further. He opened his arms, ready to crush her. She stood waiting, laughing harder, as he threw his full weight into taking her head off . . .

"You probably didn't know this," Mary said from behind him as he stumbled past where she stood an instant previously, "but I'm about to do you the biggest favour anyone's ever done you. You can thank me for it later."

Another enraged roar. He spun around to face her. Mary gave a satisfied grin. "Why are you smiling?!" he growled with ground teeth. "You should be screaming, like a tragic little victim! Why do you look so fucking *calm?!* What good is that to me?"

He charged again, out of control. As he closed in on her, he clubbed at her ethereal form over and over again with enough force to put her into the ground—had he hit anything but thin air.

She was *right in front of him*, but he could not lay a hand on her, which angered him further. Tears of frustration streamed down his face as he continued his attacks. Each swing pulled him in twenty different directions. The monster attacked nothing more than a ghost.

And this ghost was *laughing* at him.

"Not so fucking funny now, is it?" Mary gloated, watching as he eventually tired and fell to his knees. "I can't begin to imagine how many people you laughed at as you murdered them. Maybe they'll be able to rest when I've dealt with you."

The dead winds carried Mary closer to him before she again became fully corporeal. Barber hurled himself at her. She waited until the last possible moment before dematerialising once more, rotating to watch him fall face-first into the ground.

She extended her arm and made a lifting gesture. The chains attached to him stretched upward, taut at her whim, forcing his body to stand straight. He levitated a foot off the ground. She rotated her wrist in a circular movement, turning him to face her. He gave an anguished bawl as the chains manipulated him against his will, Mary his puppeteer.

"Mary," Kara shouted from behind her. "You mind you don't lose your head! You might not be able to come back from it if you do!"

"Don't worry, Kara,"—she released him with a thud—"I'm in total control here." She solidified again and watched Barber desperately scramble away from her. He charged toward Kara with a demented howl.

"You sure, love?" his new target shouted. The beast closed on her with great speed, but just as he reached the fountain, his legs buckled. He fell and cracked his jaw on the concrete bowl.

"Absolutely."

Mary pointed straight at the big man, prone and coughing blood. She drew him closer, dragging him backward with a gesture of her upturned hand. He clawed the ground in a futile attempt to resist. With him just feet away, Mary turned him upwards and glared down into his terrified eyes. He struggled for a moment, but she dropped her hand to her side and he stopped all movement, pinned at her command.

"Over the last few days, I might have forgotten *who* I was for a while," she said to him, "but never did I forget *what* I was. That—and some bloody good friends—saw me through this *shit* you put me through.

"I met Sarah, you know. Seems there was nothing to stop you from having a good, happy life—not a thing. But you made one *fucking awful* decision, and it led to you becoming nothing more than some *corpse*'s bitch. Now, I appreciate your position before you made that choice, I really do. People can be bloody hard work sometimes. But what you've done since? No excuse."

She made fists and his back arched in agony. His screams echoed across the courtyard. Kara ran towards them, shouting her name, but stopped several feet away.

"AAAAAAGGGH!!" Barber cried desperately, suddenly sounding *human* as he degenerated into whimpers. "I'm sorry, I'm sorry, I'm sorry, I'm sorry . . ."

"I'm sure you are."

Mary lifted her arms from the elbow upward as if pulling a dumbbell and watched him almost snap himself in two trying to escape obviously excruciating pain. He no longer had the strength to scream.

"It's not me you need forgiveness from," Mary told him. "But you'd do well to look for it every day from here on out. I told you I was going to do you a favour, and here it is: REST. ALL OF YOU."

She opened both fists and lowered her hands, watching as he let out one more stifled roar, biting down on the agony. Each of the chains forced her to stretch them taut before they would surrender their hold. However, the links, once severed, vanished. At the end of her gesture, he fell back to the ground. His muscular body atrophied at an alarming rate.

Mary pointed to the front entrance of Grenshall Manor. "If and when I step out of that door, should I *ever* see you again, I'm not going to be as friendly. Now, turn yourself in to the police, if you know what's good for you and get out of my sight, you wretched piece of shit."

He crawled away. Mary turned back to the mansion. Kara put an arm on her shoulder. "I ever tell you that you can be a proper scary bitch when you want?"

"I get that a lot," Mary answered. "I don't imagine Jen's opinion would have changed much on that."

After a moment's consideration, Kara responded. "You know, she never made friends easily. But you were definitely on her list. And there was nothing she wouldn't do for a friend."

"You're talking about her like she's already dead," Mary said quietly.

"There's no guarantee she'll make it, is there?"

"There's no guarantee *we'll* make it, Kara." Mary stared at the mansion before her. "You know what we're up against."

Silence.

"We'll just have to do what we can," Kara finally replied. "All of us." She glanced at the fountain. Even with a Mini mangled against it and surrounded by grubby water, the statue of a nameless male stood with regal elegance in smooth black marble. "You know, I'm never going to be able to get insurance for anything again." She flung a hand in the direction of the car in the fountain. "How do I explain that?"

The winds returned, lashing the two women hard as they edged closer to the house; huge drops of rain hammered down upon them. Even the heavy downpour did nothing to dispel the taint in the filthy pool, almost as dark as the statue itself.

Standing there, they finally got an idea of the abnormally large size of Grenshall Manor. It was no country club; instead, the four sharp towers anchoring the two opposing wings threatened to pierce the impenetrable clouds directly above it. East and west, they provided the only break from the ominous, red sky surrounding them.

Dark grey clouds belched upward like steam from a cooling tower, from somewhere beyond the front facade.

The savage howl of the storm almost deafened them as they crossed the pebbled approach and reached the elaborate semi-circular stairway. Its concave sweep created a ripple effect away from the circular fountain.

As they approached the top of the stairs, dead-world energy overwhelmed Mary. She stopped and oriented herself to it. It felt nothing like the portals she had dealt with up to that point; she felt an epicentre of utter, unstoppable rage, destruction, and hatred.

As she locked onto it, she felt a certain kinship with it, a desire to tear apart everything in sight, to punish it for her suffering. She turned to Kara and snarled, baring her canines like fangs. She felt like *tearing her fucking head off* simply for daring to stand so close, for taking her there, for exposing her to it.

Kara's will to be anywhere near the building wavered as she gaped in terror at her companion. She turned away from Mary and fled down the stairs but stopped. She stood to fight the compulsions which had overtaken her.

Mary followed her friend. A supersonic shriek burst her ears. The air blackened around her hands at her behest as she heard the banshee wail and joined in the cacophonous chorus. She prepared to summon something truly dreadful from *that* place.

But that was not her. This was Violet talking, her echo of hatred amplified by the Gate's sheer power.

Kara, too, appeared to sense the aural battering. "That's Violet, isn't it?"

Mary did not answer. Rather, she fought the dark influences blasting through her mind. The surrounding rage threatened to crush her will, her spirit.

Kill the bitch. She got you into all this. Tear out her spinal cord. You'll feel much better.

No. No you won't.

She's right.

"Yyyyeeaaah . . ." She wound down the howl she was about to unleash, forcing every bit of effort into piecing a half-coherent word together. She took several deep breaths, then blinked to steer her thoughts away from slaughtering her friend out of turn. "It's her, all right—don't know what she's doing in there, but she's really, really pissed off. Totally lost it. I can feel it from here."

"You told me on the way over you'd managed to free the Bliss girl from her back at the station," Kara answered. "I wouldn't be surprised if that was all that kept her *that* together up to now."

"Agreed," Mary said. "And what she's feeling is infectious, so I'm not sure it's a good idea you follow me in there."

She turned around and went back up the stairs to face the massive iron double doors. She spotted a weathered, faded square in the centre of the door, pointed at a long-faded coat of arms. Ornate, carved letter 'Gs' adorned the corners. "'*G' is for Grenshall*," she muttered, grinning.

At the top step, she turned the handle on the doors almost twice her height. The turn stopped well short of opening. Mary had no chance of doing anything other than bouncing off it up to that point.

"Worth a try," Kara called out with a chuckle. "That door and the attempt to get rid of me. I told you, I'm here to the end. And if that recent stunt of yours was anything to go by, you're going to need me."

"I just don't want anything happening to you," Mary answered, frowning. "And I especially don't want it on my conscience if it does."

Kara rolled her eyes. "It's only been a few days, Mary. You really don't know me at all, do you?" She took a look the entrance, impressed. "I'm a nosy, stubborn cow who *always* sticks her head down the rabbit hole when the chance arises. Anything I *ever* do, I put on my own head. Got it?"

"Can't argue with that," Mary snorted.

"Damn right! Now how about you stop trying to get rid of me, ghost through that door, and let me in, eh? Oh, and don't bother ditching me outside here, 'cos if that door's not opened in the next minute, I'll figure out a way to bash it down!"

Mary nodded and focused on the door. "No walls can hold me . . ."

CHAPTER TWENTY-SEVEN

Once through the door, tempestuous winds deafened and disorientated Mary. She had long-since accustomed herself to the near total darkness in the dead world. However, within the manor, it seemed thick, black smoke obscured her view of the physical world.

Only a small radius of clarity remained around her and a veiled figure in the distance. Down what seemed an endless, arched esplanade of immaculate gold, Tally stood at the end of the North Wing farthest from the main entrance.

Mary returned herself to the living world as she reached for the door handle and grabbed it. Ordinary darkness once more became an issue.

Somewhere out of sight, sporadic clattering superseded a rumble and howling reminiscent of an old, industrial engine. A familiar, cut-glass voice sounded; the ghost's rather hassled protests resonated through the space.

"No, dear . . . now you *mustn't* touch that," she heard Tally scold. "It really will help nothing. Oh, Vi, *no*! That has been in the family for years! Please—oh, too late . . . again. Look, it shall do you no good to object, I shall *not* allow you in there. You have no idea what you're doing. Yes, I am sure that is what you think you want, but it will help nothing. Oh, *sweet girl.*"

Mary removed a large wooden wedge from the centre of the outside door, but the obstacle remained locked and unmoved.

"AAARGH!"

"Oh, Rose, would you *please* control your temper!" Tally's voice immediately behind her made Mary jump. "Set an example to the young girl!"

Mary turned to the censuring apparition. "Tally, impressionable as she is, I think the necklace whispering evils at her might be a bigger worry."

"I suppose so, yes." Tally looked back and listened as extremely loud, slow, and rhythmic pounding started.

"Poor girl is so lost to the thing that there is not a rational thought left. Her rage alone was enough to open the Gate! But she is now trying to batter her way into the chamber with her bare hands as well. Simply shifting worlds is too much for her now. And although her strength is quite staggering, she could assault the chamber entrance for fifty years and never so much as crack the walls.

"Hence, she has vented her wrath upon the softer parts of the mansion. She bashed part of the West Wing to rubble the moment she arrived. Had she materialised in the Gate Chamber, the day would have been lost."

"Are there any keys around for the front door?" Mary asked.

"There are," said Tally, sounding puzzled, "but what would you want them for? I mean, you are already here and what you want is that way . . ." She pointed ahead.

"I need to let Kara in."

"Are you out of your mind, Rose? This is a terribly dangerous place to be for someone so . . . fragile. Violet would kill her out of turn. Leave her out there. Give her half a chance at survival."

She's right. The decision weighed heavily on Mary's mind, knowing that Kara would indeed be in grave danger if she set foot through the door, but would never forgive her if she didn't. *People have died over this—over me—already in the last few days. I really don't want another person dead thanks to me.*

As she froze, weighing up her choice, the pounding stopped, replaced by an echoing whisper coming from all directions of the mansion.

"Destruction . . . let them ALL join us . . . open the worlds . . . kill them . . . she's here . . . will try and stop us . . . not let us live . . . kill her . . . tear her apart . . . hates us . . . hate her . . ."

"Tally." Mary spoke barely above a whisper, low and gruff. "Keys for the front door—where?"

"Rose—Violet and the necklace are up there. I really would recommend . . ."

"Tally, stop pissing about and tell me where the keys are!"

Tally did not respond immediately, a hissing in the distance the only sound. As it grew louder, the voices localised, low and incomprehensible. Mary's head throbbed as if it was going to explode as pure embodied fury centred upon that spot. Tally's continued stalling shortened her temper; violent thoughts filled her mind again.

"Tally!" Mary battled to suppress the urge to destroy everything in sight. A rolling black cloud closed on their position, much like the one she had seen with her death sight, but there with the living. It sheltered someone or *something* within it, but Mary found it impossible to discern any clear shape.

Sticky air suddenly circulated around her clenched fists as she instinctively summoned the void's most pulverising energies, ready to blast the thing from whence it came.

She heard a weak wheezing next to her as Tally started to fade from sight, distorting like a poor television image. Seeing this, Mary realised what she was calling on would have destroyed any entity in her presence *except* the one she intended to. Releasing her grip, she took a deep breath. Tally wheezed louder, sounding as if a living being gasping for air.

"*East Wing* . . ." Tally spluttered, holding her throat. "Kensington Room—hanging on a peg, left-hand side as you go in. First room on the left." She vanished.

Mary decided to take a chance by shifting herself to the dead world. She marked the exact place Tally mentioned and willed herself outside the Kensington Room in a blink.

An ear-splitting squawk from the North Wing brought her to her knees. The powerful, rhythmic bashing continued.

That girl has rage in a way I can't even imagine.

The door opened with little resistance. Mary sneezed uncontrollably from the sudden cloud of dust and scrambled through a host of cobwebs to retrieve the keys, exactly where Tally described.

The distant bashing continued for a few more seconds before ceasing with an anguished shriek. A loud tearing sound. A heavy crash and splintering. The thunderous assaults recommenced.

The second it did, Mary returned to the entrance door and tried the first key she came to. It rattled, but did not turn.

The second key gave a satisfying click in the lock. Upon opening the door, Kara dashed in, glaring at her. "Took your time, didn't you, girl?" she accused.

"Look, I was as quick as I—"

She stopped herself. The noise behind her had stopped once more. She beckoned Kara inside but stopped her when she tried to shut the door behind them.

The dusky red light streamed through and created a clear run on the chequered floor. A sweep of stairs on either side met in the centre at a tattered and crumbling balcony.

Scattered around the floor, large chunks of stone and a couple of broken doors lay, testament to the cloud creature's rampage.

"Right, smartarse. I stuck my neck out getting you here. Make yourself useful, eh?"

Kara grinned. "You were talking to someone."

"Tally." Mary glanced around. "Dunno where she went, though."

"Not your problem right now. *Violet* is. You need to find her."

"Won't be as hard as you think."

She pointed at the wreckage. Kara gulped. "Not sure what *I'll* be able to do about that," Kara said. "But now that you mention it, I *do* wonder where Tally went."

"Probably staying well away from me, I imagine."

"Huh?"

"Never mind."

The banging had stopped for long enough to become a worry.

Mary looked up to the centre of the balcony where stood the entrance to the North Wing corridor. After taking a step forward, she turned sternly back to Kara. "I'm going up there. I might at least be able to shut the Gate before it does—"

"*Look out!*"

Mary stumbled as Kara pushed her out of the way. The storm of destruction steamrollered by and caught Kara with a glancing blow. Kara spun back into the entrance door head-first. She fell flat on to the floor. The cloud hurtled back, and blade-like talons splintered the nearby door.

A humanoid shadow lurked within the cloud. Massive bat-like wings, retracted and mottled, reached from it to the top of the cloud.

It bared two rows of bestial canines through which black, tar-like drool oozed. Mary recognised the creature: an amalgamation of the nightmarish beasts which plagued the child all those years ago.

With a shriek, it turned to shred prone and helpless Kara into gobbets.

"Hey! Violet!" Mary strode toward the creature with all the menace she could muster.

This has to be the worst idea I've ever had.

The mansion shook to its very foundations with Violet's deafening roar. The creature faced her, its bright yellow eyes burning translucent through the obscuring haze. A dazzling blue light, pulsating and otherwise shrouded in darkness, created the illusion of a heartbeat at the beast's throat.

A confusing rumble of a train came from behind the beast, growing louder and louder.

Distracted, Mary hesitated, but the creature barrelled toward her. Mary reflexively shifted to the dead world. The creature's crunching impact knocked the wind out of her lungs.

Stupid! OF COURSE she can hit you! She's from here!

Mary dropped to the floor, narrowly ducking a pair of rending talons. She scrambled under the beast to avoid its scything claws, then rolled back to her feet. A simple gesture called on the death winds to force open the door as she dashed for it.

A brilliant human-shaped light lay flat on the floor. Next to her, Tally would have been impossible to see if not for Kara's borrowed light. "Tally!" Mary called out, still on the move. "Make sure she's okay."

The shadow before her became distinctly clearer, and Tally pointed to her left, back to the staircase leading to the North Wing passage. "It's where she wants to go, dear!" Her voice came faintly over the storm.

"Take her that way; it should keep her occupied. And if you go in, use the power of the Gate to help you!"

The beating of wings, an industrial wail mocking the terrible dirge, the screeching brakes of an oncoming train. Mary narrowly evaded a slashing attack. Off-balance, she fell sideways but quickly regained her footing. Violet turned to charge again. However, Mary strained her sight through the storm and could see the target door, illuminated by bright gold markings. She hurled herself forward with the shadow winds a split second before Violet could get hold of her.

There, she read the bold writing which covered the entire door:

IF YOU CAN READ THIS, YOU ARE ON
THE OTHER SIDE OF THE LIVING.
KNOW THIS CORRIDOR FORBIDDEN
TO YOUR CROSSING.
NONE BELONG AT THE GATE WHO
KNOW NOT THE FULL EXTENT OF ITS PURPOSE
AND MEANING OR CARE NOT FOR
PERVERSIONS OF THE SOUL OR
THE SUFFERING OF OTHERS.
HENCE, UNLESS YOUR PURPOSES FOR
BREACHING THIS DOOR ARE TRUE,
TURN BACK NOW OR FACE THE FATE
OF THOSE YOU WOULD DISRUPT.

As Mary fumbled for the keys, Violet flew toward her again. Mary summoned the dead winds and trapped the creature in a cyclone. Concentrating hard, she redirected the flailing beast into the floor with a heavy thud.

The first key proved ineffectual. "Second one *will* work!" she told herself.

Lumps of freshly destroyed marble flooring shattered into dust above her head. Shielding herself with her hands, another roar pierced her eardrums. The creature's full shadow wings kept it hovering near the damaged balcony as it held another lump of broken rock in its grasp. She launched it with tremendous force. Mary threw herself to one side as the rock exploded just feet behind her. The debris cut into her arms and legs.

Yellow eyes burned with maddening fury. From the tips of the wings, two spear-like coils hurtled toward her. Mary leapt to her left and evaded the rightmost spear. The second plunged hard through her right shoulder. She cried in agony as it pinned her to the door suspended from the floor. The missed coil retracted several metres to aim squarely for Mary's forehead.

Mary assumed incorporeal form, but the door remained a solid obstacle, a ghostly echo of the barb still stuck in her shoulder.

Hand trembling, she reached down and yelped as she turned the key. The lock clicked. She gritted her teeth whilst pulling the coil out of her shoulder. She dropped to the floor as the second barbed coil lanced viciously just over her head. She turned and fell through over the threshold.

The creature contracted its wings and retracted the deadly coils until they floated probingly in front of it. It stared intently at her, preparing another attack. Pressing against her shoulder with her left hand, she winced at the debilitating pain, but stood.

Concentrating hard through the distraction, she vanished into the echoing winds and reappeared instantaneously in front of the door at the opposite end of the passage. Violet charged straight through the space she had previously occupied, slashing and stabbing with each of her weapon-like appendages in a mindless frenzy. It howled again murderously. Several seconds elapsed before it regained enough control to locate Mary once more.

Mary shifted back to her own world. The agonising shoulder injury damaged her ability to concentrate. She would be fine to go in, after a short break . . . but with Violet stalking her, that would be impossible. Burning eyes and the fierce glow of the *Teardrop* were the only light sources in that confined space, but that was little use to Mary where she stood. She found no lock nor door handle. Try as she might to push, the door was going nowhere.

Come on . . .

She examined everywhere, padding with her hands for a method of entrance, but there was nothing there. Violet charged down the passage with a bloodcurdling battle cry, claws poised to gut her where she stood. Mary had no real room to manoeuvre in the tight, dark corridor.

CHAPTER TWENTY-EIGHT

Without time to evade, and injured to distraction, Mary crouched forward and prepared to receive the attack.

One chance to grab that necklace.

"HEY!"

A voice called out from behind Violet. The creature shrieked and stumbled, its two frenzied talons missing Mary by inches. Violet turned to address the interference, and Mary seized the opportunity to step straight into the cloud. She dodged the swirling barbed coils and squinted as she reached straight for the blinding blue light directly in front of her.

The creature's massive jaws snapped at Mary's head, forcing her back. She ducked and broke off her attack. A powerful kick smashed into Mary's stomach. She skidded several feet away on her back, winded. Violet closed in, lifting a mutated stiletto high in the air, ready to bring it down on Mary's head.

"*Oh, Violet . . .*"

The creature turned again. *Kara.* Her friend stood behind Violet, crouched and armed with a broken banister, a concerned Tally just behind. Violet moved toward the new threat. Mary screamed out in pain as she pressed both hands against the floor and swept a leg at the creature.

Violet stumbled. Kara charged at her with a tremendous battle cry and swung the banister cleanly between the yellow eyes with a satisfying clunk.

The monster staggered, but did not fall. She unleashed a ferocious counter which Kara barely parried, her weapon obliterated as she was sent flying through the air. Two coils prepared to tear Mary's companion apart.

Mary seized a shard of wood and jabbed at Violet's left leg, plunging the splinter as hard as she could. The shadow howled. The monster launched both coiled spears in retaliation.

With more reflex than focus, Mary blinked away, reappearing back at the closed door. Still in serious pain, she slowly stood, waiting for Violet to turn around.

The rage of the beast radiated so strongly that Mary's temples pulsed. She could see that Kara experienced this too; veins bulged on her forehead.

Mary seized the initiative. With a stubborn exertion of will, she vanished and reappeared just in front of Violet. She reached into the cloud and snatched at the sapphire. She caught her wrist with the metal fang on the cage, which drew blood and agony.

But she would not be denied. She grasped for the chain. As she touched it, her entire body convulsed as if electrocuted, the cloud compressing into a mighty bolt of void lightning. The bolt reached critical mass and exploded. Mary hurtled backwards into the door, Violet the opposite direction.

Mary took several quick breaths. The blast had floored Kara as the out-of-control Violet slammed past, but Mary's stalwart friend staggered closer. All was dark, blurry. The next thing she knew, Kara slapped her around the face. It kept her conscious.

"Think . . . think you slowed her a bit there, Mary," she said. Her shredded right sleeve exposed a bleeding arm with three slashes across it.

"I couldn't get the necklace off," Mary mumbled, "but that hurt her, too. It must have."

"It most certainly did." Tally appeared at her side, the only unruffled entity in sight. "I am quite surprised that you can draw breath after that, but take the chance whilst you have it. The Gate Chamber awaits."

"That's great," said Mary, turning to face the impenetrable door, "but how do I get through it?"

"The same way you get through most locked doors, Rose dear." She smiled sweetly. "Simply walk *through*!"

"It felt like it wouldn't let me before," Mary answered, nursing her injuries. "Not impossible, but . . ."

"Well of course it did, dear. It would be a very poor ward that could be ignored, would it not? That is the point of it, you know. It helps to keep the bad people out."

"Like Lady Raine, you mean?"

The ghost shuddered, briefly flashing out of sight and back again. She removed her hat and smoothed her curly hair with trembling hands before replacing it. "Yes, Rose. Exactly. Hurry, do! Violet will recover, you know!"

"I'll see if she's out of it," Kara said, moving back up the corridor. "Might be able to get the *Teardrop* off her if she is!"

Tally gave a tentative nod, but Mary cut her dead. "No." That forceful authority resurfaced. "Don't even think about touching it. It may well kill you."

Kara considered defiance, but heeded her friend's instruction. "You're the expert . . ."

"Hardly."

Mary turned back to the door, and she closed her mind off from the wounds, from Violet, from everything else. She drew all her will together and straddled both worlds, clenching her fists as she went for the door.

Mary closed her mind to everything other than accessing the Chamber. Within a matter of seconds, she felt weightless, heard no sound at all, and levitated slowly, precisely, forward through the door. She felt as if she passed through jelly. It tickled every nerve, but she remained fixed on her task, aware that every part of the ward tested her worthiness to enter.

The seductive oblivion offered by the storm of the dead lulled her with its siren song. She longed to submit. Echoes whispered in her ears as she floated in timelessness.

Her sense of being ceased to matter. It was a beautiful thought, a wonderful feeling of relaxation, of peace. All she had to do was close her eyes and let go, and she could have it forever.

Mere seconds passed. Everything fell silent. *She* had done this. But the brief respite ended in a disorientating cacophony of cyclonic wind rattling everywhere. And Mary found herself in . . .

. . .nothing.

There was no room ahead, no sigils, no obsidian stone in the centre of her vision, no walls that she could see. She thought she had turned around, but found it impossible to tell without the feeling of a body at the moment.

Even the door she had come through—how long ago was that, again? That, too, had disappeared into the darkness that surrounded her. It would have been easy to have become lost.

Focus.

Mary concentrated hard to filter the noise more accurately. Within the winds, she heard hundreds upon hundreds of voices, all speaking at once, all at different volumes. It was like listening to a radio tune itself, with incomplete clips of speech everywhere. With a little more concentration, one voice stood out from the others, a low but powerful call, like a deep male voice singing to her, a chanting she could not understand, either an indeterminate language or words not properly heard.

She turned again in the opposite direction, but this time she could feel the motion more strongly, could identify the movement of her arms, legs, and head. Still, it felt more like swimming than normal movement.

The previously unclear voice whispered in soothing English, hypnotic in its tones, calling her to drift peacefully through.

She pulled her thoughts together, closed her mind to the whispers and promises, and battled the gentle tugs against her soul. She tried to coax it free from the discorporate body that she still occupied. With every determined mental lunge she used to resist this call, she felt less like floating, less like swimming, and more like walking. Sigils appeared around her, clear as day, marking out a room. She concentrated her mind and flitted to the floor.

Mary Hall's will grew to its full strength as she pulled both hands into fists to harness the spiritual storm. Opening her hands, she pulled back the dozen or so dots of brilliant light that had floated in front of her, taking on the brightest light she had ever radiated. She singlehandedly illuminated the entire chamber.

She saw hundreds of souls in as humanoid a form as their mindless selves could take, flying around the room along with the black wisps of sandy wind, dominating her vision. But now there was a clear focal point, the one she had come for: the Gate itself.

A vast and pulsing black heart, it pumped its alien cold and darkness not only around the room, but also upwards, straight out through space, blasted through the roof. Up, up into the furthest visible point in this dark sky. It was like a malevolent reactor, sending power outward and away . . . on to the focal points in London she had seen earlier.

"This is *bad*." She sensed no pain; the chamber had healed her, somehow. Grim, resolute, she strode towards the Gate, feet now on a semblance of ground. It felt like walking underwater during a heavy tide, but she would reach it no matter what.

Reaching out to the portal, its endless power attempted to rip her soul from her body. It wanted to consume her whole.

She pulled her clenched fists backward, and with it, yanked her core essence hard and returned it to exactly where it belonged. She reclaimed complete control of herself once more.

Mary had mastered her power, and, though screaming through the spiritual assault, knew full well that if she failed, the consumption of London would follow swiftly on her heels. She resisted with a mighty mental shrug.

The Gate played its final and most potent card yet. Instead of resisting her connection to it, it gave her *everything*.

It started with the decades of murderous rage from which Violet drew to throw open the Gate from beyond the chamber wards—the force that prevented her from wresting the *Teardrop* from Violet's neck. Pure, unadulterated rage, hatred, and a burning desire for all to suffer as the trapped entities had.

The full power of the Gate was at the whim of the necklace's wielder. It would pull London apart with nothing more than fury. But Violet could not get close enough to the Gate to give the command. Mary would not allow it.

Far less painful, the Gate connected Mary directly to each and every one of these unresting souls at its command, and with them every reason they would not—*could* not rest. Their overwhelming sensibilities flooded her mind, which nearly collapsed under the strain of all that anger, hatred, and despair.

It got worse. She could see small dots of energy in her mind and pushed her consciousness around each of them at light speed. Of thousands of people—living people—sleeping in London, she could access every single one of them. She could visit each of them in their dreams, if she wanted. She could feel it!

Mark Lucas from Bow, she could have fulfilled every one of his desires. Charlie Blake from West Norwood needed to know there *was* life after his wife, Theresa; he just needed someone to tell him. Mary could do that. The dead and the living were all hers to speak to, to influence, to command. It was just a simple matter of her asking the Gate to allow her to do so. She wielded immense, irresistible power; hers if she just *said the word.*

Mary focused her concentration to stem the flood of information. She could see three nearby minds, all of them so very different. The first was chaotic, with many others tied to it. Focusing on this tested her self-control. The sudden urge to destroy everything proved infectious.

For her own sanity, she switched her attention to the second: a soul not at peace, feeling the need to do something vital before it could even consider resting. It could not do it alone. The final soul was still living, still conscious, and barely visible.

She forced her mind far away from the lure of the Gate. Her efforts threw her backward into the warded door and into the living world.

Shaking it off, she sprinted to the corner, making a visual estimate on where to make fifty eight exact steps, drawing a line in her mind.

The room was in total darkness, the Gate still strangely visible in the all-consuming black light. The sight was unnerving. The Gate weakened her in its continued attempts to consume her, but she steadied herself. A quick but gruelling blast of will freed her from the Gate's pursuit, and it resumed its terrible mission.

The muted black became a dull red and drew Mary's eyes to the scattered rubble around the stone and the precise hole it blasted in the ceiling above.

A psychic command hissed past her, many voices in chorus. She heard a sudden buzz, then an explosion of blinding red light seared a crimson image of the stone and a column of light into her sight. She fumbled for the nearby wall, using it as a support. The power of the Gate prepared to tear every soul in London asunder and leave the place a literal ghost town.

Mary closed her eyes, the image still branded onto her retinas, and staggered forth. She knelt, regaining her balance from the strange inertia in the room.

She fumbled for the Gate, swearing in pain from extending her right arm forward. The shoulder hadn't have recovered as much as she'd hoped.

Eventually, she reached her objective. She touched it. It felt soft and jelly-like. Immediately, every ounce of her fatigue overwhelmed her.

Another trick. But Mary was in no mood. She imagined herself in front of a blank canvas, painting the mansion with as much detail as she could, changing the red sky to a bright sun, imposing an image of Tally and Violet playing a forbidden game of skittles on the massive lawn.

The image brought her inner peace, control of her emotions. But the unstoppable fury which powered Violet continued to batter her anima.

Calm would prevail. She willed a wash of peace over the relentless wave of destruction gathered around her. Her art, always an outlet for peace in the past, gave her an anchor of control.

Violet's rage fell silent. Cold terror, the urge to flee, to never stop until safe, crawled into her brain.

Mary's will would not be denied.

The mindless rage subsided. Mary wrested control of the Gate from Violet. Now, at her command, it was ready to open or close like a well-oiled door.

YOU WILL CLOSE.

The mystic gate snapped shut. The room fell silent. The blinding light faded. Dazed, and totally exhausted, she collapsed to the floor, not an ounce of strength left.

CHAPTER TWENTY-NINE

Rose. Get up!"

Unsure as to how long she had been lying there, Mary blinked a few times. The negative image of the Gate had finally resolved—her natural sight returned. The night sky was visible. Rain from the outside subsided but still trickled into the hole in the centre of the chamber, dripping on the stone. Tally stood above her, looking shaken.

"It's closed, right?" Mary asked, dozily.

"Yes, dear, it is now closed. Now you only have to part Violet from her necklace, and it is done."

Mary groaned as she took three attempts to get even to her knees. On the third, she crawled to the closed gate, now just an obelisk in the centre of the room, and leaned up against it, facing the entrance. Sweating and pale, she looked up at Tally, deeply concerned. "Kara . . . is she—?"

"Kara is fine. She may not be in a moment, though. Quickly! Seize your advantage and deal with Violet!"

Mary struggled through every step of escaping from the shielded room.

She pulled at the loose stone. She turned the small dial with a shaky hand. She found the switch and pressed it. The solid old mechanism clicked and the door shifted ajar.

Mary hobbled to the door and then into the corridor tunnel. Tally followed, issuing instructions, but she said nothing Mary heard.

Mary went through the second door and propped herself up on the unstable railings of the staircase. She looked down at a surprisingly slow-moving and subdued Violet, perhaps crying, standing in the centre of the hall. The cloud had dissipated to reveal an unpleasantly stretched, corpse-like female, with giant bat-shaped wings. It stopped and looked up at Mary, then around at Kara as she advanced, though wounded.

"Kara?" Mary called. "What the hell are you doing? Get away from her!"

Kara walked slowly toward Violet without fear.

"It's okay, Mary," Kara said calmly. "Violet, you're okay, too. You'll be all right. There's nobody around to hurt you anymore."

Violet gave a loud shriek, her face contorted into destructive intent as she charged toward Kara. Finding strength she was unaware she still had, Mary pulled another loose banister and threw it as hard as she could at one of the wings. It bounced off harmlessly, but, as hoped, claimed Violet's attention.

"Come and get me, *bitch*," Mary snarled. She stood and beckoned the creature. Extending its wings to full span, Violet flew at the dangerous precipice. Mary rolled out of the way as Violet shattered the staircase. A support crumbled as the creature flew up through the floor. Despite the destruction, Mary dived free of the impact. Half of the landing collapsed—the half opposite Mary. She caught herself as a section slid downward and crawled up to a flatter part of the floor.

Mary ran to the edge of the staircase and turned to meet Violet's inevitable attack. As soon as it came, she shifted worlds.

"My dear, she can still injure you from . . ." Tally started, but combat was never Mary's intention. She had already plotted another rapid movement, no more than a sidestep away. Within reach of the deadly claws, she snatched upward for the glowing blue necklace, plucking it clean from Violet's neck.

Suddenly, the remaining landing gave way. She flung out and seized a bent railing. The necklace dropped to the floor as she dangled from the precipice. "Smash it!" she called to Kara. "Break it, now!"

"Do as she says, Kara!" Tally called, watching intently. Kara hesitated. She fixed her eyes on Mary. Violet crashed head-first into a wall. When Kara looked down at the glowing necklace before her, she fell transfixed.

Mary identified the needless delay, had an educated guess as to why. "*Hey!* That really won't go with what you're wearing. You're meant to be trashing it, not bloody accessorising!"

Kara shook her head, looking dazed. "Ah—the damn thing would kill me one way or other." She opened the silver gauzed cage which held the sapphire. But she soon froze again at its touch, staring at it longingly.

"Get it *done*, Kara!" Mary called, still clinging on. She knew it wasn't as simple as that. The jewel would lure far more powerfully, whispering promises of power, beauty, immortality . . .

Kara shuddered. She fumbled as she attempted to reach the jewel. She shook her head. "Get away from me, you evil, little thing!"

She turned away as she reached down with a shaky hand, eventually gaining a solid enough grip on the sapphire to tear it clear of the cage and the chain. Throwing both components down in disgust and shaking her arm as if it was covered in acid, she moved to lug a large piece of crumbled stone.

"Oh, do hurry!" Tally called out as Kara strained to lift the rock.

"It's *heavy,*" Kara protested.

Mary's single-handed grip slipped. With her injured arm, she reached for the protruding piece of rail. Wailing, she pulled herself up on to flat, stable floor before dragging herself to her knees. Kara had lifted the rock and staggered back to the sapphire.

Violet sprang to her feet. With a shriek, she hurled herself at Kara. Mary called to the dead world, to the dark winds. She blasted Violet with all the strength she could muster. Violet's trajectory veered, but she still knocked Kara away from her target.

Furious, Mary roared. She seized a nearby piece of the broken landing and lifted it with her remaining strength. She hefted the rock over the edge, as far as she could manage. The lump bounced awkwardly on the way down but fell directly on to the glowing jewel. The *Teardrop* shattered into a million pieces.

From under the rock, a multitude of bright lights in many colours swirled, and Violet crumpled to the floor. In front of her, Tally looked delighted. She shifted into a two-dimensional version of herself, shrinking into nothing more than a glowing yellow wisp and vanishing into the other lights.

"Did we do it?" asked Kara, looking awestruck.

"I think so." Mary watched the flowing lights curiously. They each converged on what had been Violet's body, which took on a dazzling glow. The wings contracted and vanished. The body knitted itself back to its original form—but the transformation was not complete.

Barbed hair smoothened, straightened, and for a second, the pretty face of Sarah Bliss lay peaceful, a contented smile looking up. The lights glimmered around her, creating a beautiful spectrum in an arc around it. The surrounding light gave the corpse an angelic image, a more fitting end for Sarah.

The lights converged upon the body, now itself luminescent. It grew too bright to comfortably observe.

Kara looked less jubilant now, more suspicious. "Why is all that light still travelling *there*?"

"I wish I knew." Mary got to her feet and hobbled down to join her friend. "I would've expected that to have all just vanished, all things considered."

Once Mary arrived, she could see that the hair was darkening, curling, the face pinching slightly, looking more . . . haughty.

"Oh, no." Kara shook her head in disbelief. "She wouldn't have—would she?"

"Have what?"

The lights stopped. The body on the floor was a perfect likeness of Tally. It moved, rolling over to stand upright. It stretched and yawned, and all at once, every single gaslight in the house illuminated as it smiled.

"Thank you!" Tally said, looking around at her damaged mansion. She looked down at her hands as black crackles grew around them, dozens of bright sparkles glinting through. Suddenly, she pointed both at Mary, and two thick cable-like strands flew from her hands, blasting Mary backwards into the collapsed staircase.

"But now your task is over!

Mary struggled weakly out of the rubble. She laboured up on to her hands and knees, barely aware of the chaos around her. Her mind filled with the carnage Tally was about to wreak upon Lady Raine and her servants.

Had wrought upon Lady Raine and her servants.

Deathly cold surrounded Mary, but the air grew stifling, dry, and she felt it being pulled out of her lungs with an unbearable heat, greater with every passing second.

From the corner of her eye, Mary saw Tally summoning other-worldly power, similar to that which had knocked the wind out of her only a moment ago. Too many more such blows would prove fatal.

But to stop Tally, she had to know *why*.

Despite the crushing blow Tally had just delivered to her, strangely, a sudden weight had been lifted from her. The one memory that Tally had exerted herself so hard to hold back had been freed, and came to her in a flood.

She now understood why it had been so firmly withheld.

She now understood *everything*.

CHAPTER THIRTY

Her bargain with the shadow entity, sealed with Violet's life's breath, drowned Tally in echoes of long-dead evil. It gave her strength, indomitability, fire and force from the furthest corners of unresting darkness. However, she did not feel entirely in control. Her power over the shadow art might have been unlimited—but perhaps uncontrollable.

During the day, a brief scouting task ensued. She stretched her senses to spy on her own mansion. Rowdy wails came from the corridor to the Gate Chamber, flooded with invading spectres. Each employed by Lady Raine in her attempts to breach the sealed room. Even from several miles away, Tally established communication with their miniscule minds and ordered them back to the depths of their world.

However, her partner from the shadow offered a more effective trick.

Send them back to her, and they will soon return . . . it said to her. *Take their strength for your own and they will be gone once and for all.*

The suggestion had seemed entirely reasonable. *If I can deal permanently with one or two of these, it will keep opposition down when*

I liberate Grenshall Manor. With their aid, the usurper murdered my family. Stole my mansion. They shall serve me as I reclaim it.

Besides, they are creatures of minimal sentience. It could do no real harm . . .

That same night, she navigated her way into the Gate Chamber, and into the besieged corridor.

She could feel the phantoms before she saw them, the dozen or so beings bearing down upon her. Amongst them, presences who inflamed the dangerous fury struggling to escape her—the fear that had been pushed beyond simple concern. A crushing sadness threatened to bring her to a standstill.

But she could not afford to fail. The price was too great.

Steadying herself both in posture and nerve, she called upon her knowledge of the other world and drew forth its bitter winds. Her controlled gust halted the advancing spirits in their tracks.

At her behest, the breeze gathered and ensnared each of the shadowy creatures. She drew the squall of imprisoned souls toward her, one by one.

The gale fell silent. Tally sank to her knees. At once, she felt every one of their emotions in raw form. *Envy. Terror. Rage. Despair. Bitterness. Loathing.*

But with all that came something new—the exhilaration of total and utter indomitability. She was ready to deal with Lady Raine, who had doubtless sensed the activity from within the mansion.

Oh, how Tally had yearned for this moment, one in which she would finally see herself and her family avenged for the transgressions of the terrible beast-of-a-woman.

She strode forward, ready to unlock the outer doors and reclaim that which was rightfully hers. Nothing would stand in her way. Not even her greatest enemy.

Lord Alphonse emerged from his impregnable lair to confront what Tally had become. He stood before her as she prepared to turn the handle on the outer chamber doors, to step outside and mete just punishment on the invader.

"Iris Grenshall, do *not* do this!"

Not even he would stop her.

She leered at him as one intoxicated by the invigorating strength she possessed, well past caring who or what had fuelled it. The power was as uncontrolled as it was unstoppable. The mourning cries from an imperceptible distance simply reinforced her capacity for destruction.

Even Lord Alphonse was not safe from her. She ruthlessly and relentlessly dragged his soul towards her, condemning it to the furthest reaches of the other world, devouring his strength and echoes of his knowledge for her own.

Tally stood alone in the chamber corridor. Only then did she take stock of what she had done. She felt the merest sliver of guilt at destroying her dead mentor, but it was fleeting. The cold touch of fear clung to her spine, but it was as nothing compared to the sheer terror she intended to call down upon her greatest enemy. The imperious, unrestrained power coursed through her and muted every other feeling, any other care.

She now held Lord Alphonse's potency at her command. Together, he and Tally proved more than a match for the shadow entity, a gestalt of five. As a whole, they created a force to be reckoned with. Apart, their divided talents faltered. She had no further use for those weak beings that relied on others to focus their will.

With but a thought, she expelled the entity riding her soul. With another, she wrenched them apart. Her third command sent them reeling toward the Gate, back to their eternal imprisonment.

Each may have screamed, but she did not hear.

Iris Grenshall would share this battle with no other being. It was between her and Aurelia Raine.

With slow, purposeful strides, Tally made her way down the corridor and with minimal effort battered the first door open. She strode to the balustrade and looked down at the alerted Aurelia Raine and a cohort of unresting guards. The gauntlet had been dropped.

As she retreated back down the passage, she smiled, thinking of the destruction she was about to wreak—the terrible revenge she was to reap. *Death's Teardrop* would be worthy of the name. It would be Lady Raine's noose.

~*~

Tally's open invitation into the previously impregnable corridor drew Lady Raine's minions like moths to a flame. Crowding into the enclosed space, followed by the encroacher herself, they put themselves at Tally's mercy.

Tally easily identified the eerie, blue glow of the *Teardrop* with her death sight.

With a cry of rage, Tally outstretched her arms. The howling tempest drove back the underlings. A low moan amplified into a bellow. It soon became deafening. It expanded outward, scooping the minions from their feet and sending them whirling.

The cyclone spun faster and faster. Tally opened her mouth and roared again. Her command tore open a vortex between the worlds—a manifestation of all-consuming darkness.

Dozens of screams rang through the mansion. The assault died out as quickly as it came. After they had gone, only the mansion, Tally, and the wretched bearer of *Death's Teardrop* remained.

Somehow Lady Raine had survived the Gate's onslaught. But she lay sprawled on the floor, dazed and badly wounded. Despite the *Teardrop's* protection, Tally believed Lady Raine no match for her. She advanced, confident and determined.

But her power suddenly failed her. Drained, she collapsed at the base of the stairs, sobbing uncontrollably, overcome by the forces she meant to harness. Try as she might, she could not stop herself, wracked to the point of debilitation, forced to watch as her enemy slowly returned to her feet, dusting herself down from the blood and the shower of broken glass, flung as she had been by the winds from the mouth of the passage to the hard stone below.

Lady Raine lifted the sapphire and muttered something beyond Tally's hearing. She laughed with ever-increasing vigour as it shone gradually brighter and bathed its owner in bright blue light. The injuries she had just sustained diminished, then vanished with incredible speed.

"Within the secrets of the dead, and that which makes them rise again, lies the greater secret of immortality, Iris Grenshall," Lady Raine instructed. "I could not allow your foolish adopted family to continue to neglect the incredible mysteries which lay under their nose any longer."

Tally wanted to say so much then.

Yet she could not move for crying—and could not stop herself, try as she might.

"You seem exhausted after such an *impressive* display," Lady Raine gloated, closing in on her fallen opponent. "Perhaps you should furnish yourself with one of *these*." She lifted the *Teardrop* in front of her, and the deathly whistling increased in volume, joining the discordant percussion of Tally's whimpers.

Despite Tally's easy dispatch of the hordes opposing her, she could do nothing but cower from her nemesis.

The image of her noble mother and father came to mind—her *real* mother. Even the ghost of Lord Alphonse. She had abused her gift, her legacy, and now they each held her accountable for it. Including the loss of Grenshall Manor. And for allowing this . . . *monster* to defeat her, as she inevitably would. That focused fury was all gone, and had left her vulnerable against such a relentless foe.

Helpless, despairing, she curled into a smaller ball and waited for her inevitable fate.

She was better than that, surely?

Am I not Lady Iris Grenshall, mistress of this place, and Guardian of the Gate?

No. I am none of these things. I am a charlatan, and a liar, and a fraud, and a coward. I am not fit to claim any of those titles.

Tally felt dwarfed by the menace that radiated from Lady Raine as she loomed over her, smiling triumphantly. Tally's body felt no more than dead weight. However, as her foe called upon the power of the *Teardrop*, Tally met her gaze, fists clenched. The litany of wrongs against her and her loved ones chanted in her ears. The demon would pay—dearly.

"I . . . I will not allow you to continue this . . . this . . . desecration of my family name any longer."

"*Your* family?" Raine cackled. "You have no more right to call yourself a Grenshall than I!"

"The Lord and Lady Grenshall you murdered saw fit to call me 'daughter,'" she spat in a venom-laced tone. "The last true *Guardian of the Gate* told me I was suitable to the blood for his purposes. Those closest to me loved me."

"Those 'close' to me serve me just fine."

"Yes, without ownership of their own souls." Conviction once again built within the young Grenshall. The monster stood before her as a reminder of everything she stood for, everything she stood against. That gloating face gave her the strength to escape the prison of her own terror. "What has beautiful Violet done to you to condemn her to such a tormented death as you offered?"

"*Death*?" Lady Raine looked genuinely surprised. She shook her head and laughed as an adult responding to the foolish question of a child. "Dear Lord, girl. I have no intention of seeing the girl dead. Not yet, anyway. With such prodigious mastery of the dark mysteries as you have shown, I assumed you understood as much."

"*What*?" Tally returned to her feet. Lady Raine stepped back.

"I thought you would have been delighted at this news. After all, you mean *so much* to one another . . ."

"What have you done to her?" Tally made a clumsy lunge for Lady Raine and was sidestepped with embarrassing ease. Lady Raine laughed again, triggering a spark of rage in Tally—but only a spark. She would do nothing until she knew the whole truth.

"I can assure you," Lady Raine answered, unaffected, "that no harm has come to her. Come see for yourself! Speak with her."

Lady Raine led her straight into the mansion's East Wing. The woman beckoned Tally through a familiar door.

"Oh my . . . what have you done here?"

What had been a drawing room the previous day contained a small lectern, an unlit lamp adorning it. The stone floor gleamed, freshly polished. A small shelf, a new addition to the room, held sealed glass jars, each labelled in writings of unfamiliar languages.

In the very centre of the large room, passive and unresisting, Violet lay chained on a solid, flat-carved slab of rock. She wore a grey dress far too large for her of similar design to Tally's cloak, although Tally saw no signs of physical harm.

Tally ran to the plinth, grabbed the girl, and kissed her several times on the forehead. "Oh, *Vi*! Thank God you are well!"

"Why?" Tally spun 'round to face Lady Raine, now the very picture of rage. "Why are you doing this to her?"

Lady Raine gave the most menial effort at a smile. "You honestly have no *idea*, do you?" She shook her head. "You have been greatly privileged. Not only are you touched with the talent for the oldest magical arts in existence, but you also control access to the most powerful known conduit of it *in the living world*. Yet you sit here claiming to be *'protecting'* it, rather than using such a resource? Truly, that sanctimonious attitude disgusts me.

"I see so much more in you—if we could just bypass that terrible predictability which afflicts you. I wonder if you would fight me with such vindictiveness if you were privy to one of the Chamber's greatest mysteries?"

"Free her from there," Tally demanded. "*Now.*"

Lady Raine shrugged. "That would be foolish. It would ruin *everything*."

Tally lashed out at Lady Raine with a punch to the mouth. It drew blood, but did not floor her opponent or even remove the smug grin from her face. Tally watched as the *Teardrop* flashed once and the wounds of its wearer faded away.

"Wonderful healing properties, the essence of the dead. Which is what I am trying to communicate with you. Think on it, girl: immortality! No need to ever concern yourself with losing those beautiful looks of yours. The ability to *truly* master the secrets of the world. And I believe you more than capable of unearthing many of them, too. Imagine it: you and I, with nothing to oppose either of us."

"Give me the keys to those manacles, get out of my mansion, and do not darken my presence ever again. That way, you may live to see *one* more day."

Lady Raine nodded with approval. "*Good*," she responded. "Conviction and strength to see through the objective, no matter what. A willingness to take a life. The *true* legacy of the Grenshalls is yours for the taking—if you want it."

"All I want," Tally said, "is for you to give me the key and leave."

"You would refuse one of the most jealously guarded secrets in the history of mankind, for the time it would take me to impart it upon you? Think more carefully, Iris."

"The keys." Tally's face stretched into a snarl, anger stirring in her heart. "*This instant.*"

Lady Raine extended her hand toward Tally, the key in her palm. As Tally snatched at it, she pulled it back at the last second. "Would you like to speak to her first?"

Tally seized the key. "Wake her up from whatever it was you did to her," she demanded.

The sapphire glowed in perfect synchronisation with a wave of Lady Raine's hand. Violet stirred and looked at Tally with wide eyes.

"Tally?" Violet called faintly. Tally responded by getting to work on the shackles. She rushed to hug the newly freed girl. Violet responded in kind.

"Violet! Dearest, dearest Violet! Please, tell me you are safe?"

The answer did not come from Violet, but from Lady Raine. "You can see for yourself she has come to no harm. No thanks to you, of course. *Fancy* leaving her like that! After all, you *promised* you would never do so."

Tally turned around and glared at her foe, who smiled at her triumphantly.

Lady Raine advanced on the plinth, Tally unable to intercede. Violet sat, paralysed with fear. The woman reached out and stroked the silky locks that tumbled over the child's shoulders.

"Such pretty little bait, is she not?" she cooed with all the pride of maternal affection. "And so to the purpose."

Tally meant to utter a protest, but a look from Lady Raine forestalled her. She flicked away the curls in her hand and turned from her daughter to face her nemesis.

"Here you are, Tally, *home* again—outside the protections of the Gate Chamber. Did Lord Alphonse ever trust you with that knowledge—to create such a ward? No? I thought not. Just like him to keep the secret for himself. As with the immortality rites, which *of course* he will not have mentioned!

Lord Alphonse.

Tally's conscience surfaced, however momentarily. He had done nothing to deserve it. He had only tried to help. Done his duty. But she had definitively destroyed any chance she had of gaining his help now. She was on her own—the last Grenshall.

"Lord Alphonse would never have kept anything from me!" she blurted.

"Is that so?" Lady Raine sneered. "I would wager he agonised over whether to entrust you with the secrets to come in here and confront me. Did he try to convince you that you were not ready? Did he try and talk you out of your birthright?"

"He tried to *protect* me. I have seen first-hand what this kind of power does if one allows it."

"You mean as you did to your *loyal, dedicated* servants? It felt *good* though, I shall wager?"

"Illusory satisfaction."

"But satisfaction no less. *Immortality*, Iris! Let me just tell you how!"

The words strengthened Tally's resolve. She would allow no harm come to Violet. The girl was hers to protect—acquired at great cost.

"You *need* Violet." Tally hesitated as she worked it out in her head. "She is a tool . . . a necessity."

"Go on . . ."

"Her life holds the key to your immortality. But you must have need of the Gate or else you would have done it by now." Lady Raine gave a slow clap.

Lady Raine grinned. "I knew you were an intelligent sort, Iris Grenshall. Violet is safe from me. As are you. You should be at my side, not at my throat. I *do* wish you would understand that."

"Your interest in me lies only in my knowledge of the Gate Chamber."

"And there was me hoping that I would have appealed to your . . . better nature. Still, no matter. After all, you left the doors open when you came to confront me. That should serve."

As she spoke, one of the ornate jars launched and shattered around the back of Tally's head, knocking her to the ground. A second jar smashed into her as she attempted to stand.

"Have it your way." Lady Raine moved quickly toward her and lifted her by the throat. "I offered you apprenticeship, but you insist upon antagonising me."

Violet rushed at her mother, screaming and weakly beating her leg. The *Teardrop* glowed brightly. With one arm, the fiend lifted Violet and slung her back at the makeshift altar. The girl slowed in mid-air, floating unnaturally. She landed gently on the stone as the shackles animated themselves and closed once more over Violet's limbs.

"No!" Tally wiped the blood from her face. She tried to crawl to the girl but quickly collapsed. Through hazy vision, she saw Lady Raine take the *Teardrop* into her hands. A faint blue light floated around Tally. She felt a sudden pull towards Lady Raine—no, the sapphire. The light around her . . . it *was* her! Her spirit had left her body, a ghostly echo extracted, inching further away from her living self.

"I will *not* allow this!" Tally hissed. She focused her will, railing with all of her strength against the artefact's deadly attack. However, her injuries decisively weakened her defence, and she slipped away.

"You will not *stop* me . . ." Lady Raine said wilfully. She kicked Tally back to the ground. "That is something I have been trying to get through to you since you first confronted me. Violet *must* die as part of the rite. You, I shall destroy for sport. I shall enjoy having you as my first maid when I rebuild my house staff." She drew an ornate curved knife, concealed within the folds of her dress.

Distract her. Think of something. Quickly.

"So- so why not use me *instead* of her?" Tally could not focus her sight.

"You will not do. You are not of my blood."

"Wh-why do you believe this will succeed?"

"Because none other has even *dared* try."

"I suspect they have—and failed."

"No matter."

With Lady Raine distracted, Tally used every last ounce of strength she had left to cover herself with the cloak. She shifted worlds, her spirit form crashing back into her body. She travelled where Lady Raine could not follow. It would provide only a temporary advantage.

Tally heard a piercing scream behind her and could feel Lady Raine's rage as a searing ripple of heat against the chill winds surrounded her. The *Teardrop's* baleful light in the shadow world slowed her, drowning out everything within its shimmers. The echo of her own soul against her shaded body added to the disconcerting sights.

She burst past the blinding light and the searing glare emanating from her adversary, over to the other source of light within the room. Violet struggled against her shackles. Without thought, Tally grabbed the girl and attempted to wrest her clear of the slab. All the while, she felt herself being sucked backwards, and the longer she remained static the stronger the effect. It was clear that the *Teardrop* was still working on her, even there.

There was no time to use the key now, but if she could walk through walls, chains would pose no obstacle.

With a mental command to the dead world, she was able to get Violet free of the slab and she ran again, away from Lady Raine and her deadly jewel, toward the back wall of the shadowed echo of the room.

The pull of Lady Raine's fury intensified, but Tally dug in, stubbornly holding her position. Her sight clarified a little in the disorientating mix of light and void, and she was again able to pick out distinct shapes. Lady Raine's vehemence created distorted, rippling turbulence against the jewel's blast. The attack was wild, clumsy.

But the jewel's assault latched on to Violet as well. Tally struggled for both of them.

As she fought on, her vision turned to something else: another shape, small, human, lying motionless on the slab.

The shape was in dark shadow—just like everything else she could see which was inanimate . . . and crucially, not living.

No . . .

She looked down at her hands, where millions of specks of light outlined the young girl. The specks fragmented, slowly disintegrating the form of light. She looked back up again, across to the shape on the slab, and realised what had happened.

There should not have been a body back there. Tally had not rescued Violet at all—in fact, she had done the reverse. She had pulled a spiritual Violet clear of her body just as if it had been done through the sapphire. And now there was no protection between her soul and its engulfing power, leaving her very little time to repair what she had done and save the two of them.

Violet's spirit and Tally's fully incorporeal form were both dragged towards the frenzied *Teardrop*. Lady Raine channelled so much power that they began to hurtle towards the baleful oblivion.

But she could feel one other force around her. The bitter winds whipped up all around them, keeping a distance from the other forces, but present in a manner impossible to ignore.

With the help of the cloak, she stirred the death winds and carried herself and her spiritual passenger straight to the Gate Chamber.

A deafening howl filled the entire room. The obsidian stone rippled intensely, multiple tones of shadow growing darker and darker as if Tally stared straight into the abyss. She would be safe there for now, but could not mount an assault outside the Chamber's walls. They were trapped.

The weight in her arms had almost disappeared as Violet's glow faded against the heavy darkness. She could see the young girl mouthing something at her, but was unable to make out what it was, and could not hear her speak.

Tally felt weak again; not just a result of the recent conflict, but at every little thing Violet had endured since her clashes with Lady Raine. She wondered if she could save her, put her soul back where it truly belonged, but another thought filled her mind.

She cannot sacrifice something which is unavailable to her. If I take that from her, and the Gate Chamber, she is lost. And I cannot allow her to continue with what she is doing. It is not just Violet and me at stake here.

She shook from her lament, but even through the storm she could hear shouts from Lady Raine—sounding like whispers from where she stood, threatening all manner of torturous existences for the pair or them.

Violet, I am so, so sorry.

She kissed Violet's fading forehead, sobbing. She took a step forward and nudged the child into contact with the black gate, then turned her head away. She felt the remaining weight drawn away. She tried to close the Gate with all of her training, all of her will, all of her strength—but she had nothing further to give. The Gate would not seal.

Promised I would never leave you . . .

She brought herself back out of the shadowed world. That much cost her nothing. And still the Gate could be heard, a terrible, low, machine-like rumble coming from behind her.

With all the cursing she could hear from the lower level of the mansion, closing the chamber door became an urgent task. She cleared the room and pulled the door closed, walking down the corridor still crying, without any signs of stopping.

Whether it was the Gate listening to her, *Death's Teardrop* living up to its name, or something else entirely, the lighting dimmed throughout the mansion. A chilling storm followed her, so cold that it frosted over every piece of furniture she passed. Even with the winds around her, silence reigned. Silence other than the echo of her crying.

She descended the stairs slowly, barely balanced. Lady Raine waited for her at the bottom of them. With one look at Tally, even her murderous anger gave way to whatever she saw in Tally's eyes.

Tally watched the noble woman as she stood, silent and staring as her adversary descended every single step, glowering and raising her blade.

"I shall take my time with you, girl."

"Do as you will."

Tally's words were as frozen as the surface on which Lady Raine trod. The intense crackle of ice turned her on her heel as she reached the foot of the stairs. She shivered, dropping her frosted blade in front of Tally.

"I shall find another way." She blew a heavy cloud of icy breath in her retreat.

Tally did not pursue her. She turned left at the foot of the stairs and returned to the room she had fled, heading straight for the table upon which lay Violet's pale, motionless body. She took her by the hand and sank down to her side, with nothing but a glazed stare and an endless flow of tears.

"Forgive me," she said. The stone and the body upon it were cold to the touch.

"Please, forgive me."

It was the last thing Tally remembered.

It was the last thing Mary had seen.

CHAPTER THIRTY-ONE

Tally launched a bolt of darkness at Mary, blasting the breath from her. She could feel her bones rattle as if they might shake her apart. She took stock of the situation. Fresh memories of Tally's emerged.

Memories previously withheld from her.

Tally appeared a cool, calculating individual. However, Mary knew her greatest secret, the spiritual scar which allowed her no rest.

"What the *hell* are you doing?!" Kara screamed at Tally as Mary recovered from the blast. "And how did you do *that*?"

An object glistened near the rubble. Mary edged towards it as Tally replied to Kara. A curved knife, once belonging to Lady Raine. She snaffled it into her hands.

"*I* have had over a century to perfect my art," Tally said, effortlessly calling more of the dark energy to her fingertips, "and unlike Violet, the capacity for rational thought."

"Could have fooled me!" Mary wheezed. She pulled herself upright and forced a defiant smile.

Tally looked at Mary, half with surprise and half approval. "As I was saying, over a century has been devoted to honing my talents."

Tally rolled her eyes, and with every bit of the mastery she boasted, effortlessly engulfed herself in otherworldly shadow for a moment. She dropped out of this shadow form, save her hands manifesting with the light-consuming abyss Mary had witnessed before, in dream if not in reality.

Mary fought for breath.

"With sufficient mastery, one can wrap a single layer of shadow on top of another—and so forth—with each layer serving to amplify the force considerably. Not for the uninitiated, that one."

Keep talking, bitch.

Mary edged to the East Wing entrance, praying she did not have to withstand any more bolts. Unfortunately for her, Tally raised both hands and launched a set at her, too quickly and accurately to evade. She caught both square in the stomach and slammed into the wall behind her. She coughed blood and clawed for breath. She could not hold her head straight, but saw Tally draw upon another set and aim her hands again.

Mary flinched at a sound of an exploding floor tile, loud as a gun-shot. Somehow, Tally had missed. Getting onto all fours, she peered around the chair that provided her a semblance of cover and saw Kara had tackled Tally, forcing her tenebrous missile wide. Tally sent Kara sprawling with barely a flick.

"Hmm . . . you may have reminded me of something important," Tally said, staring at Mary and ignoring Kara. "Your shadow world prowess has given you a measure of resistance against even the heavier assaults. One of these bolts should have snapped you in twain. However, I wonder if your friend is as resilient?"

"Leave her alone!"

"Had I meant her dead, I have had ample opportunity. *You,* on the other hand, require more focus." A flaming shadow engulfed Tally's form for the briefest moment. When it settled, only her hands burned. The dark flame stole the light from the room rather than provided it.

Raising her shrouded hands high, she swiftly brought them down, producing two bursts of black fire in front of Mary. She kicked the chair out in front of her, hoping to block the onslaught. The assault cracked down on the chair with a supersonic howl, instantly disintegrating it from existence.

Despite the chair taking the brunt of the attack, Mary's left arm and leg seared with pain. She felt intense heat, yet deathly cold where her clothing had been shredded by the blast. She cried out with anguished rage.

Kara, though dazed, scrambled back to her feet. "Yeah, about that," she said, advancing a couple of steps. "Why do you want her dead, but not me? What's so special about *me*?"

Tally smirked. "Are you not grateful for my forbearance?"

"Oh, don't get me wrong, I am. It's just, well, why me? Why not Mary?"

"*Mary*?" Tally looked confused, as if Kara had mentioned someone completely unknown to her. She shook her head, turning in time to see Mary attempting to sneak out of sight. Tally snapped another gout of shadow flame at her, shouting in annoyance as Mary flung herself forward to evade it. She was not far away, and a smoky-looking trail lingered in the air over her line of attack. Tally flicked her hands downward and prepared another salvo.

"*Hey!*" Kara said, expressing great umbrage at being ignored. Any further protest was interrupted as she suddenly choked and gasped for air. The fire in the air became suffocating, even from there. "You . . . haven't . . . answered my . . . question!"

"You live because I find you intriguing," Tally retorted, sounding irritated. "I plan to keep you around when I have dealt with Rose here."

"And *why* do you keep calling her that?" Kara pressed, throwing her arms into the air. She cast a discreet glance at Mary to check her condition. "Why do you want Mary dead so badly when you've gone through so much trouble to keep her alive up to now?"

Mary pulled herself back to her feet, wincing. Tally looked back at her, unable to focus her divided attention.

"I think I can answer that one, Kara," Mary said. Tally flushed herself in the darkness for another half second and settled once more with burning hands. Kara jumped back from the strange conflagration.

"You see, Tally never *wanted* me to live through Mr Barber's first attack. I get killed right there, Tally steps in, heals the lump of meat that was once me—like she just did with poor Sarah—and then walks away. Simple."

Mary and Kara patiently awaited an answer, while Tally twitched her way back into composure. She nodded reluctantly.

Kara's frown grew, and she eyed both of them curiously. "So, why Mary?" she demanded. The flame in Tally's hands faded a little. "What made her special over all the other accidents within the Tube stations over the years? It's not like you haven't had the time."

"Because—" Tally started.

"Again, if you'll allow me . . ." Mary interrupted. She subtly positioned herself by the East Wing corridor entrance.

"As one Aurelia Raine explained to Tally, the greatest power within this horrible . . . *gift*,"—she spoke with utter revulsion—"comes only from the greatest sacrifice. Now your choices: go on a massive killing spree—which really is not practical for even the hardiest ghost to pull off—*or, you do for your own blood. By which, of course, we mean *family*."

The baleful flame in Tally's hands dissipated entirely. She looked at Mary, stunned.

"You mean to say you and Tally are *related* somehow?" Kara asked.

Mary nodded. "Stick a lot of 'greats' on the front, an 'auntie' at the end, and there you have it. But I'm all she's got now and well she knows it. The trouble with insanely hard rites is that there's never anyone to tell you whether you've done right or wrong. You get one chance at it and one chance only. And Tally, here, *blew it*."

"But she's standing here now!" Kara protested. "Surely she's just achieved what she was trying."

"*She* is standing in front of you," Tally said, incensed, "and would appreciate if you spoke to her directly." The flaming hands rekindled, one pointing at Kara, the other at Mary.

"Sorry, Tally," Kara said, as trivially as if she had accidentally nudged her whilst walking through a crowd.

Mary perceived it far more seriously however. "Do *not* apologise to her! Not for what she was trying to do. *Is* trying to do. She still needs a family member to get the job done, doesn't she?"

Tally trained both hands on Mary and attacked again with the deadly black fire, but Mary flung herself clear in good time.

"Well, if *you* won't answer Kara's questions, *I* will!" she called from underneath a Grenshall-inscribed table. Tally switched to the more focused lightning-like bolts and unleashed a volley at her with meticulous aim, mindful not to hit the table. Mary dodged. Tally advanced a few steps, herding Mary away from her target corridor.

Think, Mary, think!

Tally's attacks reverted to less discriminate and far deadlier fire. Mary focused on escaping the hits. A route to the other world failed to materialise, whether from lack of concentration or severe exhaustion. Hounded by Tally's relentless attacks, she had finally run out of ideas.

"Tally! Mary!" Kara demanded. "Don't care which of you tells me, but who the bloody hell's Rose?"

Tally turned to Kara for a second—which was just enough. Mary crawled back towards the East Wing entrance. She called out an answer once she had enough breath.

"Young Iris Brown had a kid sister," she wheezed. Tally looked confused. "Rose was Tally's last living relative back then. She wasn't born until after *Iris* left Bethnal Green and became Tally Grenshall, so Tally didn't find this out until after she died. She knew I was family, but never knew my name. Rose was one of a few things Tally had left to cling to.

"Trouble is, a hundred years is a long time to rely on anything. She held on to Rose—only the memory that her baby sister existed—a pretty flimsy tie to reality; bugger-all by now. So she used me to keep that one going."

Tally's arms lowered slowly, her conviction wavering under Mary's relentless verbal barrage.

"She remembered she loved the London Underground, different as it was back then. Which is why she was able to get there. And she remembered the rite. *Lady Raine's* rite, mind you, not hers. But it had all kind of blurred in together, by then, hadn't it, T?"

"I-I . . ." An array of conflicting emotions warred on Tally's face.

"See, you *do* remember all of this, but not properly. And only the bits you want to. How would I know any of this if you didn't?"

Tally's twitching became even more pronounced, underscoring her apparent indecision.

Mary stood tall, strengthened by her increasing confidence. It mounted with every sentence she uttered. "You don't even *know* why you wanted to kill me, do you?" she pressed. "There's no reason for it at all. I took care of the threat to the mansion, the Gate's closed, only you and I know how to get in there safely, and Violet won't be bothering anyone ever again."

Mary realised her mistake as the words fell from her lips, and not only from Tally's looks. The body formed into sustained fiery shadow, engulfed in unmatched rage.

"Violet *never* bothered me!!"

Tally fired a concentrated burst of heat and cold duality, black flame, of incredible intensity, directly at Mary. She rolled into a protective ball, but it instead impacted behind her. The blast threw her backwards into a wall. She landed awkwardly on her right side and screamed, dropping the knife as she nursed both her arm and leg. She scrabbled for her dropped weapon, pocketing it with her good hand.

Tally spelled out her second error. "I know *exactly* why I need to kill you. I alone am charged with protecting this gate, and I cannot do so if I am no longer around!"

Kara again provided timely intervention. "You look perfectly present to me, love," she said. "Tell you what, how about we get out of here and leave you to guard the place like you have been all this time, and we say no more about it, eh?"

Tally dropped out of her shadowed countenance and turned, raising a hand toward Kara. As she held it, a focal point of low moans and howls emerged behind Kara. Tally closed her hand into a fist, and another portal appeared. Kara eyed the obvious threat from over her shoulder.

"Just because you intrigue me, Kara, does not place me above destroying you."

"Rose Brown." Mary disregarded her peril as she spoke. "Married to Jonathan Merritt. One son, Marcus Merritt. Marries Angel Slater at age twenty."

Tally pivoted an abrupt about-face. "What are you doing?" she demanded, paralysed by the drone of Mary's litany.

"Has two sons, Daniel and Robert Merritt. Marcus, Daniel, and Robert all killed in action during the Great War. Angel returns her widowed name to Slater. After the war, discovers Daniel has a daughter called Maisie by one Beatrice Penrice. They never marry. Nobody learns the identity of Maisie Penrice's father, other than yourself."

"Stop it!"

"Maisie Penrice marries James Hall in 1936. Becomes Maisie Hall. Over the next four years, Maisie has two sons—Daniel, named by suggestion of her grandmother, and Richard. She also has a daughter, Lucy. During the Blitz, Lucy and Daniel both die, leaving only Richard."

Tally retreated a step or two from Mary, looking utterly stunned and increasingly unstable. "Mary . . ." Kara said cautiously. "What are you doing?"

"I'm just filling in the gaps that Tally can't remember for herself." Mary climbed back on her feet despite the pain. "Memory's a really useful thing sometimes. Especially when someone tries to possess you after they fail to kill you the first time."

Stunned speechless, Tally twitched more and wrenched her hair as her fury mounted.

Kara kept one eye on the portal looming behind her. "Is this a good idea?"

"It's a bloody great idea!"

And it's the only one I've got!

Tally finally responded, her words quiet, forceful. "I admit it. I never expected to become desperate. Everything a Guardian does is *so* much more difficult when one is a ghost, it seems . . . It took such a very long time to amass enough power to do this. All that planning. All that *effort*! And after all that time, the one family member—the only *possibility*—an obstinate, recalcitrant girl!"

Mary seethed with contempt. "Oh, *boo bloody hoo,* Tally! What does one expect when one is going about their life without causing trouble and some bastard comes along and tries to kill them, eh? And you want my sympathy? Did you bump off half of my other ancestors too?

"Like Kara said, what's wrong with just taking the body you're in—which, by the way, now looks *just like* you—and pissing off?"

"Why is it that you never manage to mind your language?"

Tally launched a salvo at Mary, who kicked over the Grenshall table for cover until the attacks disintegrated it. She broke into a sprint and burst to the East Wing entrance.

"*BUUUUURRRNN!!*" Tally screamed. Her black flame charred the air as it passed through the corridor. Mary sped on toward her ultimate goal. To stop would be to die.

All too late, Tally realised where she was going. "*No!*"

She stopped short at the threshold of the chamber she dared not enter. But Mary had already leapt through the doorway. She dragged herself again to her feet using the slab for support. Her hand tapped against a light object, which scuttled on to the floor. A small human bone. The ritual components were still in place over a hundred years later. It remained horrific after all this time.

Especially to her pursuer. As soon as she entered, Tally leapt backward, screeching repeatedly.

Kara lurked in the corridor, utterly disregarded.

Mary pulled out her blade. She hesitated; Tally's memories relevant once more. This foul thing, used to kill for centuries, was a component of a terrible ritual that thankfully never took place. Last intended for family blood, this time, there was no need for it to kill. Her target was already dead.

Tally's fire lacked the devastation of her most previous attacks, but Mary harboured a healthy respect for the layered, unfocused bolts hurled at her. Not until she flung herself over the table, knife in hand, did she feel reasonably secure.

She reached for one of the bones on the floor and lifted it above her head, waving it.

Not something I'm ever going to boast about doing, but given what I've just seen . . .

Tally whimpered from her place outside, and Mary felt brave enough to stick her head out. "Now, where was I?"

"Please!" Tally called, sobbing. "Stop that!"

Answers at least one of my questions, anyway.

She stood and continued with her recital. "Ah, that's right. We're on Richard Hall, aren't we? Yeah, well he lives a safe enough life— good to know—has a couple of sons, William and Derek Hall. Derek marries Lucy Graham, leading to another Lucy Hall. She fairs a bit better than the first Lucy Hall, but then surviving the 1970s was a different kind of challenge, I guess. But those two make it to what—1990? Then they divorce with no kids, and don't last five years without one another. Pretty sad, really."

Tally's anger shook loose her torpor. "Will you *shut up*?" However, her infernal ordnance dispersed as soon as Mary waved the bone defiantly.

"Make me," Mary said, leaning over the slab.

Tally summoned a bolt, but Mary rapped the bone against the stone. Tally broke off her attack.

"Oh, you *can't*, can you?" Mary's smug looks defied her trepidation.

Despite her edge, she didn't quite have the full measure of the situation. "Not unless you come in here and finish the job? Go on. I *dare* you."

Tally stayed exactly where she was.

"That's what I thought. So, that brings us nicely to William Hall, doesn't it? He marries a little later on than Derek, to a pretty young lady, Claire Baxter—now, of course, Claire Hall. They have just the one daughter, but never get to see her grow up because, of course, *something* happens to them. Not what you had planned for them at all, was it?

"Still, despite some complications, I can report that their little girl is alive and well. Never better in fact—apart from this small matter of having some insane ghost trying to kill her for no sensible reason. Her name is Mary Hall. Hi."

"The death of your parents was not my doing." Tally said, nervously. "There was an accident."

"It *wasn't* an accident," Mary denied gutturally. She threatened to shatter the bone. "Sorry, but, you screwed up. Yeah, I never got to know them, but I managed to keep it together. Now, I'm kind of over it. Which brings me to my next point."

I'm not really over it at all, am I?

"It really *was* an accident!" Tally protested. "I watched them the whole time!"

"Yes, you did. You tried to decide whether my mother's body would be any use to you. Only by then, you hadn't the first clue where the *Teardrop* had gone. She lost control of her body for a while, and you lost control of the car. You stupid cow! You can't drive! 'Course you can't. What were you thinking?! They never had a chance."

"I-I never meant to—"

"*My next point*," Mary insisted, low and still, "is that you never got over Violet's death—her *actual* death, not the thing you let loose on my city recently. Yeah, I know—her soul got trapped and you had this grand plan to get her out in one piece to let her rest properly. I appreciate that that went horribly wrong, but I told you, I'm hardly going to be giving you sympathy for what you did to me."

"What would you have done?" Tally asked tearfully.

"With Violet?" Mary asked, suddenly feeling world-weary. "*Exactly* the same thing as you did in your position. Way too much was asked of you. But you did it, and you prevented something so much worse from taking place."

Mary gave a small nod, knowing that at least during the last days of Tally's mortal life, the weight of the world had encumbered her shoulders. "I get it, Tally," she said gently. "I understand."

Appearing exhausted, Tally slumped to her knees.

Knife in hand, Mary placed the bone carefully back onto the slab and moved it. Tally seemed unaware of the movement.

The sound of shattering glass crashed in the corridor, accompanied by the slap of stumbling feet and a muttered curse from Kara.

The clatter sprang Tally back into action. A killer blast hurled Mary back over the plinth.

CHAPTER THIRTY-TWO

Come on girl, pull yourself together or everyone loses.

That last bolt hurt—a lot.

Mary shook. Her trembling bordered upon spasms. The room swam around her, churning her stomach. After one or two aborted starts, with support from the slab she gathered herself to her feet.

The room slowed and the shakes steadied as she moved around the lump of stone. Another hit like that would finish her. She shook her head to clear her sight: Tally, mutated, extra limbs protruding.

"Gkk . . . hrr . . . m . . . M . . . Mar . . ."

Fear and adrenaline flowed through Mary in equal measure. Her vision cleared a little. Tally held Kara in a death grip. Mary moved quickly towards the pair, hoping for a lucky blow.

She'd dropped the knife.

She turned to look for it quickly, but it was nowhere to be seen.

Mary saw the life being choked out of Kara and knew she had little time left. She reached for a nearby bone to her right, but her injuries got the better of her. She winced, dropping the weapon.

"Not so simple now that you are presented with the decisions yourself, is it?" asked Tally bitterly.

No. It's not.

Mary reluctantly accepted her only expedient. "All right. You win. Killing Kara is pointless, but that stopped mattering to you long since, didn't it? So just get it done with, will you?"

Tally allowed Kara to draw breath, but Mary could see that her life hung by a thread. Tally aimed a burst of shadow flame at Mary.

But Tally's own veins now matched those of Kara's—blackened and protruding. Her skin took on a mottled hue. Her face had shrivelled.

Mary jerked her chin towards the animate corpse. "Er, Tally . . . you're looking rough as. Something the matter?"

Tally's hand wavered. A look of horror flashed over her face, quickly suppressed and replaced with one of feigned ignorance. She increased her grip on Kara just a little but directed her words across the room.

"I am running short of time, you foolish girl!" she accused through gritted teeth. "You damn near ruined everything. You exhausted my reserves not once but twice, and both times thwarted my efforts to set things *right*. This body will not last me, because it is not of my blood."

"You set me up from the start! You set us *all* up! And now that you're done, you think you're just going to murder the hired help? You're sounding more like Lady Raine by the second."

"Why, you—"

Tally pulled her arm back and prepared to hurl another blast of death energies. Kara prodded Tally hard on her jaw. "And there I was, thinking you liked having me around," she wheezed, as Tally dropped her to the floor.

Tally looked at her with some surprise at first, but then sneered, even though her body started to wrinkle. "I said nothing about needing you *alive*, silly girl! That said, you *are* rather too entertaining to risk rendering you a mindless automaton. What do you think, Kara?"

"I think you need to hurry up and kill me if you're going to," Mary interrupted. She leapt back over the protective slab, sending bones scattering far and wide. She miscalculated and landed sprawled on the floor with a yelp.

Tally, however, shrieked in horror. "*Monster*!"

"I think you're going to have to come and get me if you want to. I'm not going out there."

"Then your friend dies!"

Mary leant against the altar. The bone she had dropped still lay out of reach—but the knife hilt protruded from under the bookshelf.

"Fine!" Mary called. "I'll cry my eyes out about it in here. But I ain't coming out!"

Tally raised two flaming palms in the air, ready to bring them down on Kara and wipe her from all existence. "You know that body's about to fall to bits, don't you?" Kara interjected. "Probably the minute you use up power killing me. How about you just possess *me* for a minute or five? That'll give you the time you need to get yourself sorted, right?"

"*Hey! Girls*!" Mary dived for the knife but failed to reach it. She straightened herself up and leaned against the slab as soon as she could see the pair again. "Will you stop carping and remember it's *me* who's important here? Tally's time's running out, and—*oh my God*. Tally, you look *terrible*!"

Tally reflexively hid her hands behind her back. "Yes," she said. She drew energy from the shadow once more. "Yes, I suppose so." Her weaker attack required conscious effort to call upon. "Now do me a favour and die, will you?" She took aim. Mary knew evasion was beyond her.

"Tally, I don't know why you won't go into that room . . ."—Kara shoved the door at the spectre— ". . . but I'm dying to find out!"

Tally stumbled two steps over the threshold of the room she hadn't dared enter for over a hundred years. One of Violet's bones shattered beneath her tread. Her screech reverberated through the mansion as she leapt backward and collapsed against the wall. She curled into a foetal position, whimpering.

Kara herself had fallen face-forward, a victim of Tally's life-draining attack.

Mary knew she had to finish the task she had started. With support from the bookshelf, she hauled herself up, knife in hand. She hobbled to Tally, incapacitated, nearly catatonic, and placed the knife on a mahogany sideboard. Battered, bruised, every move a torment, she crouched down and took Tally by the hand.

"Tally . . ." she murmured softly. "Tally. It's okay. Come on . . . Let me help you up." After a difficult struggle, she did just that—and took in the further decay of the body Tally had hijacked.

Mary knew Tally yet could deliver a fatal attack, but she feared the woman no longer. Instead, she lifted her sobbing face, shuddering and mumbling incoherently.

She heard no distinct words, but Mary knew her thoughts as Tally wept.

"It's all right, Tally," she soothed. "You don't have to worry about this anymore. Any of it. You've had more than enough grief for one lifetime. You don't need anyone else's."

"But I . . ." Tally looked Mary straight in the eye, her own wracked with torment. Mary placed her fingers gently over the woman's, pre-empting her protests.

"You've more than done your bit," she said, forcing a smile. "But you need to pass this on now. You're no longer fit for the purpose, I'm afraid. There's no way you can remain *Guardian of The Gate*."

"I know," Tally bleated. "It is no task for a ghost. Which is why I need a physical form."

"I understand that," Mary replied, sighing deeply. "But if that's all you think you need just now, you're very wrong. I'm sorry to say it, but you've lost your way with the world—*both* of them actually. You've become the very thing you were guarding against. I know there's been nobody else for all this time Tally, but now there is. *You* shouldn't be here."

"I know," the broken form answered. "But who else?"

Mary gave a reassuring smile. "Well, I'm the last surviving link to the Grenshall family line, and the only one who knows anything of what you and those who came before you have to do. So I'm claiming the job. I've already proven myself enough, I think."

Tally gaped at her as she attempted to assimilate the startling possibilities. At last, she offered a begrudging nod. "You have nothing left to prove to me, Rose. But I cannot leave here; I *cannot!*"

She started to sob once again. Kara's shivering, frosted breath demanded Mary's attention, as did a familiar silvery tinge crossing outwards from Tally and across the room. The brutal cold that emanated from the decaying woman had to stop.

Mary reached behind her for the knife, never taking her eyes from Tally. She ensured her grip on the weapon firm and solid. "I meant it when I said I would have done exactly the same as you did for Violet in your position. I forgive you for that—for *everything* that's happened— but it's not enough. You have to forgive *yourself.*"

Tally stared at her. "You would forgive me??" she asked. She sounded completely dumbfounded. "Even with everything you have witnessed?"

"*Especially* with what I've seen you put up with. I don't know many who could have come through it the way you did. So I'm asking you again to forgive yourself, to allow yourself some peace after all this time. *You deserve it.*"

Silence reigned as Tally pondered again, but the decision had already been made for her. With one swift stroke, Mary brought the knife in front of her and plunged it into Tally's heart, closing her eyes as soon as she connected. Despite the violence of the act, Mary remained calm, as if in prayer.

Her right hand slid to the very back of its hilt, and she moved her left to cradle Tally's head. Mary could see the sudden pang that Tally felt, although, as she focused her mind, she could *feel* far deeper than that. The blade, despite being detached from its host jewel for so long, remembered its purpose and found its *true* target just as easily.

"I know what this knife *was* made for, but now I'm changing the rules. It's a different rite—a better one. No more tears; no more *Teardrops*. It's time to bring you peace, Tally."

She pulled Tally forward and kissed her on the forehead, stroking her greying hair gently. She closed her eyes briefly and felt the edge of the hilt warming gradually. As she opened her eyes, the broken body was nowhere to be seen; instead a dark shadow, as Tally had appeared earlier, surfaced in its place.

Mary secured the knife with both hands and focused upon her own calm and restful state. She could feel within the body a lighter movement independent of it, and then a gentle pull as this made contact with the metal blade. Soon the shadow brightened, and then the brightness grew. Within seconds, the coarse construct had gone; in its place, a statuesque and opaque silver body bearing a great resemblance to a certain Iris Grenshall at her pomp.

She met Mary's gaze with tearful, crystalline eyes. Her lips very slowly pursed together and forced themselves into a smile. All visible signs of anxiety quickly dissipated. The glowing shape slumped slowly to a state of relaxation. She mouthed some inaudible something.

"*What?*" Mary took care not to break her own concentration too much. Wispy light travelled from the body into the weapon, causing both to burn with a fierce light and for Tally to take on an increasingly translucent appearance.

"I said you are a worthy Guardian! *A true Grenshall!*" She looked down at the protruding hilt and then back at Mary, no longer with murderous intent, but instead the look of a proud mother who had just watched her daughter come of age. "I-I . . ."

"Shhh," Mary said. She recognised on Tally's face acceptance of her fate, a satisfaction that everything was going to be fine, even without her. "I told you to rest." Tally leaned forward, toward Mary's ear and tried again.

"I just wanted to say, I never quite got the measure of that little trick. The one you are using now. Use it well. You—you will be the greatest of us . . ."

The hilt grew white-hot, and Tally more transparent. Even though holding it caused pain, Mary saw it through. The tinge of frost started to melt away, starting at Tally before rapidly spreading across the room. Kara closed her eyes as the cleansing warmth reached her. Her blackened veins receded with its touch before vanishing in short order.

Sudden pangs at every recent injury pained Mary but soon receded to almost no feeling at all. Tally waved and offered a grateful smile—an image that Mary would never forget—before the ghostly figure drowned the surrounding ruin with one last radiant flash of light.

A luminous string, the last vestige of the spirit, vanished into the tip of the knife, leaving nothing but thin air. Then everything dimmed to the natural darkness of the room. Her focus now spent, she crumpled against the mahogany sideboard, breathing the first true sigh of relief she had been able to for days. Her head swam, full of memories, but only those of a young girl who, a long time ago, had the audacity to force her way into a mansion, and most importantly the hearts of its owners.

Despite what came after, above all else, Mary chose to remember that about Tally Grenshall—and what allowed the true lady of breeding that forlorn little girl became to let go of all of the darkness which followed.

A dull groan reached Mary from beyond the door. She turned to witness Kara dragging herself over the threshold. She slumped at Mary's feet and looked up. "Everything okay?" Kara asked. Mary just about managed a nod. Kara continued her crawl all the way over to Mary. She propped herself up next to her.

They sat in silence for several minutes, taking in the first real peace and quiet they had experienced in days. Both hoped the calm carried to the outside world, but thoughts rapidly turned to the future: Jennifer, her fate uncertain; Grenshall Manor and how to claim the title of *Guardian of the Gate*.

And the future of Dr. Kara Mellencourt, who finally managed a smile. "Listen," she said to her newest friend. "I want the first interview with you when this all settles, okay?"

Mary sighed. There was a lot to talk about.

THE END

ACKNOWLEDGEMENTS

There are many to thank for finally getting this out.

Katy Turner, for helping lots with
helping me bring the Victorian era to life.

HW, for valuable support and advice.

Joy Phillips for unwavering patience and cheering me on.

Debbie Smith for years and years of faith in me,
and constant checking in on my progress!

Ninfa, Ed and David for Society membership.

My editorial team for being AWESOME!

And every other friend, old and new, and
family member who has had my back on this project.
Honestly, thank you. This is a dream of mine realised.

ABOUT XCHYLER PUBLISHING

Xchyler Publishing proudly presents its first full-length novel, Oblivion Storm. As another first, R.A. Smith anchors his series *The Grenshall Manor Chronicles* with this fast-paced, thrilling, and intensely gratifying work.

Xchyler will release several exciting titles in 2013, from such master storytellers as Kim Dahl, Caitlin McColl and Candace Thomas. Working with our progressive editorial staff, they will introduce their imaginations and the characters that populate them to the world.

In addition to Paranormal, Xchyler Publishing also plans releases in the Steampunk, Fantasy and Suspense/Thriller genres. Watch for the March 2013 release of *Vanguard Legacy* by Joanne Kershaw, the first installment of her paranormal series of the same name.

Held quarterly, our short-story competitions result in published anthologies from which the authors receive royalties. 2013 themes include: Classics Redux (Steampunk, spring release), Mind Games (psychological thrillers, summer), and Extreme Makeovers (paranormal, fall).

To learn more, visit www.xchylerpublishing.com.

Made in the USA
Charleston, SC
04 February 2014